SWEET REVENGE

Jill S. Flateland

ISBN 978-1-961227-97-2 (paperback)
ISBN 978-1-961227-98-9 (digital)

First printing - February 2015
Second version – June 2023

An original Publication of Mystery Book Nook Publishing, a division of Seneschal, Corp., Arvada, CO 80005.

Website: JillSFlateland.com

Cover illustration by Kendra Petersen.

Printed in the United States of America

10 9 8 7 6 5 4 3 2 1
First Edition

DEDICATION

I dedicate this book to my husband, Byron B. Flateland. I am grateful for his continued support. He is my greatest inspiration and the love of my life. I feel blessed knowing he loves me and will stand beside me always. For this I am truly grateful.

Special Tribute To Cindy Lea Williams

I am blessed with a fantastic family. They never let me down, especially during challenging times. I must say, if I had a twin, it would have been my youngest sister, Cindy. She is such a delight to have in my life, and my heart is filled with gratitude as she dropped everything at the last minute to extensively review this book. Cindy's editing expertise and feedback were Godsent as the final hours flew by before publication. Thanks. I'll love you forever.

ACKNOWLEDGMENTS

My true blessings are our daughters, Kirsten Sielaff and Crystal Fletcher, and their husbands, Tim Sielaff and Jason Fletcher. Kirsten set aside time to edit my novels, making many corrections and patiently reviewing my rewrites. Thanks to Crystal for her great sense of humor, honest appraisal, and for supplying me with updated criminal information I can use in many more novels.

Our greatest additions to the family are our granddaughter, Elsa Hana Sielaff, and our grandson, Wyatt Samuel Fletcher. I hope they'll enjoy reading these books in years to come.

I would also like to give special thanks to my illustrator, Kendra Petersen, who designed this creative cover. The little bird made my heart flutter. Her creativity amazes me every time I get my first peek at her work.

Special thanks to my dear friend and editor, Jeri Lou Maus. Her prompt and thorough feedback is greatly appreciated.

Last, but far from least, I give thanks to my writer's group colleagues, who I'm privileged to call my sounding board for creating this novel. They helped me refine the chapters and bring them to life.

***Introducing the Agent Joshtine Cordelia-
Hastings Crisis Series
By Jill S. Flateland***

<u>Sweet Revenge</u> is the first book in the series. Cordy is a peculiar breed. At twenty-three, she is adventurous, quick-witted, and energetic. She's any man's equal, although absolutely female. Her shoulder-length, strawberry-blonde hair is often pulled back in a professional French braid, which reveals a heart-shaped face, ivory skin, and alert eyes the color of a spring pond.

Her Irish-French heritage rings true when it comes to contrasts. Her father's Irish side makes her honest to her core, loyal, and unlike her father, slow to anger. However, once she hits that breaking point, watch out! It gives rise to a heart of a French lion. Just like her mother, she fights for what's right, refusing to admit defeat.

Cordy's world is a massive planet of asynchronous electronic puzzles to be analyzed, decrypted, and decoded. It's a perfect fit for a woman to have risen to lead the U.S. President's cyberspace crisis team. She has honed her skills through past experiences as a forensic scientist and an FBI Intelligence Analyst. Always plotting her next strategy like a three-dimensional Chess game, she figures out five moves ahead of every play.

Table of Contents

HER FATHER'S DAUGHTER

Thursday, June 5 – 0600, MDT Loveland, Colorado

Officer Joshtine Cordelia woke up early with an uneasy, gnawing feeling that refused to go away. *Something about Dad's old files, I'm sure, but what about them—and why today, of all days? One year after Dad's death.* Even a hot shower didn't calm her. That feeling plagued her, and it was determined to win. Past experience told her it would only go away once she came up with a solution.

Cordy walked into her dad's former bedroom and spied his beloved hand-crafted chessboard—a checkerboard made of alternating mahogany and rosewood squares. The black and white marble pieces were already laid out, waiting for a new game. *Yes, finding a solution would be like playing Chess.* Her father had taught her how to strategize the game at age four, demanding perfection until she excelled. He nearly popped his shirt buttons when she first checkmated him at age six. She had to plot and plan each move, staying two to three steps ahead of her opponent while making complicated calculations. *Every move has a consequence, so what's my next step? Chess might be a clue, but there's more.*

That inkling grew stronger. *Dad always told me, "Listen to your soul. It can save your life."* Cordy had to get into the right frame of mind, so she played her father's favorite classical music as she rummaged through his closet.

She had gone through several cardboard boxes, but nothing sparked her interest. *One more box.* After pulling it away from the wall, she spotted a piece of plywood in the far right corner. One side had hinges. This was the first time she had noticed the hidden door. Curious, she cleared a path and swung open the plywood. The opening revealed an antique wooden chest sitting on the floor—and that, too, she had never seen before. *Why did Dad hide this in his closet? I wonder what's inside.*

The soft scents of cedar and sandalwood rose to her nose and filled her senses when she lifted the lid. Like a time capsule, the aroma took her back to when her father was alive—when the world was full of comforting parental love. She stood with her eyes closed and inhaled deeply. She could breathe that scent forever but still had work to do.

Spying her dad's favorite ski sweater on top of the files, she gently clasped the soft dark green cashmere with reddish-brown reindeer and white snowflakes knit around the back and front. Her mother had given it to him that last Christmas before she was diagnosed with the big C. Pancreatic cancer took her life three months later.

Hard to believe that it was over ten years ago when Cordy had just turned thirteen. A prime time when a teenager needs her mother to guide her into womanhood, but her father did his best and stepped up to fill the void. It had been hard for both of them when he was away on all those special ops missions, but she dreamed of following in his footsteps to become an FBI agent.

Dad had enrolled her in the FBI Teen Academy in high school, and she went on to the FBI Honors Internship Program while in college. She took accelerated classes in Junior High School. At sixteen, she had enough credits to graduate—her GPA was 4.17, and she enrolled in MIT. Last fall, she earned dual PhDs in computer and forensic science. Her father hadn't lived long enough to see her graduate, but he would have been proud. As soon as she turned twenty-three, the required minimum age for an agent, she applied at the FBI. While waiting for approval, she worked with the local police force.

Cordy held the sweater close to her heart and knew this wasn't what she was looking for, but she took a moment to unzip the sweater and slipped into it, enjoying the feel as if her parents enveloped her in a warm hug. She couldn't put it back into storage. Even though the sleeves hung over her fingers, she would wear it on those cold blue days.

When her phone rang, she glanced at the caller ID, "Chief Jackson." *Why is he calling me?* "Hello, this is Officer Cordelia. How may I help you?"

"Hi Cordy, this is your father's oldest partner."

A thread of fear tugged at her core. "Chief, yes, you worked closely with Dad before you left the FBI, and I appreciate all your help getting my application in the proper channels."

"It's been an honor. Josh was a great mentor, and I promised him that I would do everything in my power to keep you safe. Now that I'm a private investigator, I'm worried I'm unable to keep my word."

"What do you mean?" Cordy felt a chill come over her, knowing what he had to say would not be good news.

"I just heard that Vinny Corenelli is being released from USP Beaumont later today. Your father and I were on the FBI team that led a sting operation that ended in his capture. Vinny will go after everyone involved in that raid, especially Fritz Von Schlegen. He was the lead agent on the case, and you were also involved in the death of his brother, Frank. Vinny will want revenge."

Cordy knew immediately what she had been searching for—*Dad's old records on the mafia.* That odd feeling of bells clanging was back. Shivering, she held her cell between her shoulder and ear and crossed her arms, wrapping each arm above the elbows of her Dad's sweater like a bear hug. *Thanks, Dad.* She knew what to do—and now she knew why. The records were sitting right in front of her, but the last thing she wanted to do was dig up old wounds. Frank had kidnapped her along with Fritz's sister, Frieda Von Schlegen. *Dad rescued me but lost his life last year, tracking down Poppy, the mob boss and Vinny's father. Those nightmares still haunt me.*

"Cordy, are you there?"

"Yes. Thanks for the warning, Chief Jackson. I appreciate you letting me know, and you stay safe, too." She disconnected the call.

My worst nightmare—the mafia's back on my turf.

VINNY

Thursday, June 5 – 1350 CDT,
Federal Penitentiary, Beaumont, TX

The warden's bushy eyebrows rose as he signed and stamped Vinny Corenelli's release papers from the Texas Federal Penitentiary. "Make good on the outside."

"I plan to." Vinny took the paper bus pass and a change of clothes handed to him. He couldn't wait to ditch the orange jumpsuit.

The warden reached under the counter and handed Vinny an envelope. "Compliments of the feds—your accumulated pay over the years."

Vinny slid his strong, calloused finger under the flap and pulled out several crisp bills.

"Don't worry. It's all there. Nearly $15,000. That's more than most get when they exit the system."

"I worked hard for it—cleaning nasty toilets, scrubbing pots and pans. I still have scars from the steaming laundry vats."

"Go on and change, then see the guard. Let's get you back into society." The warden turned to the next in line.

Vinny wasn't surprised to see the clothes from the feds didn't fit. The pant legs didn't reach his ankles, much less his shoes, and he needed to put an extra hole in the old belt he came in with, but it was better than the bloody, shot-up rags he wore when entering the PEN.

A grizzled guard waited to escort the soon-to-be ex-con through the gates to freedom. "Best of luck on the outside. I don't want to see your sorry ass again."

"Believe me. You won't." Vinny sucked in the humid, *free* air. The older cons had made him wiser. The fights made him stronger, and the connections made him more dangerous. Nothing would stop him this time.

The guard parted with one last gift of advice. "Stay away from the Aryan Brotherhood. You know who I mean—your frat brothers."

Stay away? Yeah, right. He hadn't spent the past twenty-five years organizing his boys for nothing. Vinny had led a cellblock of the oldest, toughest, and most unrepentant felons. He nodded in mutual respect. Inmates learned early on not to touch a guard. Cons were killed for less, especially his gang.

Being inside the slammer had its challenges, and it was easier when Poppy had been the boss until his death a year ago. The plan had always been to turn over control when Vinny got out. It would still happen, but not without a fight.

The steel gate groaned as it slowly closed, separating the two men. The guard walked inside without looking back.

Vinny stepped into the sunshine, double-timed it to the main road, and waited for the bus into town. The break from his routine unnerved him. Stillness filled the air. A rush of heat radiated from the asphalt and hit his bare ankles. Prison was never this quiet.

Vinny knew how built-up tension, sparked by a rude word or simply cutting in line, could cause a fight. Payback often grew into an open assault when the guards weren't looking. A con couldn't just dial 911 during an emergency. The result was utter chaos.

Life had been rough, but Vinny set the tough guys straight, earned respect, and made the right choices during turf wars. Vinny's first cellmate was a punk who attempted rape, but only once. Someone shanked him in the shower. The guards never found the culprit, but the prisoners knew who to watch out for, and Vinny never worried about rape again.

Free at last, it was time to get his house in order—and that meant more challenges with no phone, no gun, and only these clothes on his back. His only possession was the money stuffed in his front shirt pocket. However, Vinny had a plan. He always had a plan.

Vinny had friends, and he had enemies—especially one, perilous Joey A, the most powerful crime boss, who took over Poppy's old position. Joey wanted Vinny dead and in as painful a method as possible. Vinny would avoid him for the moment. That left the schmuck FBI agent who put Vinny in prison. Fritz the Kraut moved to the top of his hit list—Fritz Von Schlegen. *Payback's a bitch, or you die. I'm never going back to the PEN.*

"Pfft." Air brakes disrupted his silence. The hydraulic doors hissed open. Cold, air-conditioned ventilation embraced him. Lost in thought, Vinny couldn't recall how long he'd been waiting for the bus. He shivered in his plain cotton shirt and wished he had a jacket. He'd remedy that soon.

At the top of the steps, he gave a quick nod to the bus driver, handed him the paper pass, and scanned the other riders, looking for an open seat. He spied one halfway down the aisle and focused on the passengers as he walked past. Some glanced his way with accusing eyes. Others ignored him as they chatted with their neighbors. Vinny lifted his head higher.

The doors closed, and the bus bounced as the driver released the handbrake. Vinny lurched forward and braced himself. He quickly moved to the empty seat and sat down as the driver shifted again. It caused another jolt. *Where did this guy learn to drive?* That reminded him he'd have to get a car, but first, he needed a current driver's license—one more item for his to-do list.

He must gain access to his hidden bank account, contact the old gang, and reestablish his authority without bashing too many heads. However, after buying a used car and checking into a motel, his first agenda was to dine at a fine restaurant. Steak and beer would be on the menu, something real to eat. He'd have a thick, creamy chocolate sundae loaded with whipped cream for dessert. His mouth watered at the thought. Then he'd track down his baby brother, Jules. *It's time to teach him the family business.*

BEACON OF HOPE

Monday, June 9 – 0855 CDT, Beaumont, Texas

It had taken Vinny four days to get his affairs in order, get a driver's license, buy a van, and access additional funds. He'd bought some fine clothes, a warm jacket, a pair of comfortable soft leather shoes, and other necessities. They all fit nicely in his new duffle. One more stop, and he'd set off for Colorado.

An hour later, Vinny checked his watch and paced outside a dilapidated wooden structure known as Beacon of Hope. Scaffolding surrounded the steeple. *What kind of orphanage is this?*

A chipped flagstone walkway led to a small chapel. Rows of roof tile lay scattered on the ground. Many old stained-glass windows, now lined with cardboard, had shattered into tiny shards during a fire and lay mixed in the rubble. *This can't be the place.* Vinny walked around the building and through a wrought-iron gate that swung in the breeze. At the rear of the property sat a smaller building, undamaged by the fire, with walls of flint rubble and chipped bricks. It resembled an old farmhouse rather than a converted monastery.

Vinny's wrist alarm sounded as he trudged through the long grass to a narrow doorway below a hand-painted sign marked 'Residential Treatment Center.' His broad shoulders squeezed through the constricted opening. He kept to the shadows until he reached a large winged statue and hid behind it as a group of people entered the room.

A slender priest came through the door, adjusted his windblown robes, tugged on the knotted rope, and rang the bells. Ten young men in long, tattered, faded brown choir robes filed through the door. One of them was Vinny's long-abandoned brother, Jules.

Vinny only had an old photo of his brother, but he recognized Jules immediately. Jules' black hair, long, aristocratic nose with the familiar bump at the bridge, and wide, dark brown eyes seemed a perfect reflection of a younger Vinny.

The boys knelt in the first two pews and followed the priest's lead. Jules fingered red rosary beads as he prayed. Unlike the other boys, who closed their eyes and bowed their heads, Jules' eyes gazed around the incense-filled room.

How could Poppy leave an infant son to be raised in such a dreary place? No wonder the lad ran away a year ago and stole a car. Since Jules had never developed any street smarts, it took the police less than a day to capture him. Every time Vinny thought about it, he snorted. If Jules had learned the family business, as he should have, he'd still be free. Instead, the law returned Jules to the treatment center because he was a minor then. Now he was of age—way *beyond time to learn the family business. I was five when Poppy set me up with my first job.*

Vinny's watch alarm vibrated again. He must have hit the snooze button. It was getting late—he had to leave Texas today. His gang waited for his arrival in Colorado—and waited none too patiently.

Vinny glanced around the room, and when he was sure no one else saw him, he gave Jules the pre-arranged whistle imitating a bird. The young man returned a cautious wave.

When the priest finished his prayer, Jules excused himself, "Father Wallace, call of nature. I'll be right back."

The priest nodded at Jules, then turned back to the others. "Let's turn to page 288 in the hymnal."

Jules went out a side door, paused, and scanned the area.

Vinny slid back through the shadows the way he had come and met Jules outside the chapel. He scrutinized his brother. "Did you bring the gun?"

The lad returned a glare. "You know you'll go back to prison to finish the rest of your sentence if they catch you with a gun."

"You better have it on you," Vinny warned. With hands on his hips, his bulky body rose to full height and towered over Jules.

The lad stood firm, facing Vinny. "Father won't be pleased when he finds out I went to a pawnshop to buy one."

Vinny clenched his fists. "I told you what would happen if you didn't come through."

Jules gasped and backed away. "I'm only looking out for you." He lowered his head.

Vinny stepped closer. "You either stand with the family or against it."

Jules lowered his arm, and a Ruger slid from the baggy sleeve of the robe into his hand. He held it out to Vinny with his fingertips. "Okay. I did as you asked, but you'll be in trouble for taking that gun."

"Who's gonna tell?" Vinny picked up the pistol and hefted it in his hand. His fingers ran along the barrel. He ejected the magazine, counted the bullets, reloaded, spun around, and aimed it at an imaginary target.

Jules backed toward the door. His eyes bounced from the chapel to Vinny, debating his next move.

"Where do you think you're going?" Vinny clicked on the safety and tucked the gun into his waistband. "You're coming with me."

"I can't do that," Jules said. "I have choir—"

"Get in." Vinny darted forward and grabbed Jules by the arm, shoving him toward the van. "I won't take no for an answer."

Jules shuffled his feet, eyes on the ground, and walked to the passenger's door. His head shot up. "Vinny, someone sliced your tire."

Vinny scanned the area once more, then darted around the van. He knelt to check the rear wheel. "Shit! I don't have time for this. Gotta get another vehicle."

Father Wallace poked his head out the center's door. "Jules, where are you?"

"Over here, Father." Jules waved.

"Son of a!" Seeing Father Wallace approaching, Vinny held his tongue, darted around the fender, knelt, and whispered, "Get the center's car."

"What?" Jules backed away. "I can't."

Father Wallace paused and glanced around. Curiosity etched his face. "What are you doing out here?"

Jules moved around the van's rear while Vinny remained crouched behind it.

The priest pointed his index finger at Jules and swung it toward the treatment center. "Get inside right now!"

"I'll be there in a minute." Jules nearly tripped when Vinny seized his ankle. His eyes darted from the priest to his brother, then back again.

"You know the rules," the priest insisted. Gravel crunched as he walked toward the front of the van.

Vinny rose with one arm over his face and a gun in the other. "He's coming with me."

Father Wallace paled. "I'm responsible for his care."

"Not anymore. A car or your life."

Father Wallace's hands flew up in surrender. "Take the car, but leave Jules with me."

Vinny came closer, and after a swift kick behind the priest's knees, Father Wallace stumbled and hit his head against the van. He didn't move. Vinny leaned over the priest and checked for a pulse before searching his pockets and retrieving the key. "Let's go."

"What about Father?" Jules leaned over the priest and blotted away blood from his head wound. "I'm no doc, but I want to be someday, and I think he has a head injury." He turned to Vinny. "You can't just leave him." Vinny's glare must have convinced Jules, who turned back to the priest. "I'm sorry. Forgive me."

"He's safer here than with us. Don't worry. He'll wake up soon, and we'll be miles from here." Vinny motioned for Jules to move. "I don't want to pull the gun on you, too. Where's the car?"

"I want to stay here with Father Wallace," Jules said. "I'll take care of him and make sure he's okay. I won't tell anyone about you or the gun."

Vinny yanked Jules' arm and pulled him to his feet. "Let's go, or else."

The lad glanced back at Father Wallace and then headed to the garage. "Follow me. If that key doesn't work, you can hotwire it. I know you've done that before."

Vinny didn't deny it. "It was many years ago, and cars these days are harder to wire." They found a 1988 black Ford Falcon. "Don't they have anything newer?" Empty grocery bags sprawled across the back seat. A starched priest's collar lay on the floor. "What a pigsty. This won't take us very far. No more stalling. Get into the car."

Jules climbed into the passenger seat and slammed the door. Showing his defiance, he fished the collar from the trash, ran his fingers along the edge, and put it on under his choir gown. "I hope Father will be all right."

Vinny snorted a chuckle at the lad's insolence. It would serve the boy well in the future if he didn't go overboard with his attitude. Vinny inserted the key, started the ignition, backed out of the garage, and drove across the churchyard.

Jules kept his eyes on Father Wallace until they turned down a gravel alleyway.

A navy blue sedan turned into the path behind them.

Vinny watched his rearview mirror as he sped up and turned onto the main road. The vehicle also turned and stayed behind by two car lengths. "I think we're being followed."

Jules spun around and gasped when Vinny swatted his arm. "Don't look. Let them think I don't know." He made a sharp right and took the nearest exit.

"Okay, but why are we getting off the freeway?" Jules asked.

The sedan also exited.

"Just checking." Vinny crossed over the exit road and went back onto the freeway.

The navy blue sedan crossed over and followed but stayed behind by two car lengths.

Jules leaned forward. "Checking for what?"

Vinny peered into the rearview mirror once more. "We're definitely being followed."

Jules pointed to a navy blue vehicle as it swung into the left lane and whizzed past Vinny. "Is that the car?"

"Yeah." Vinny blew out a breath. "Gettin' spooked by everything is no way to live." He turned on the radio and drove the speed limit. An hour later, Vinny glanced up and was surprised to see the same navy blue sedan. Without warning, it swerved in front of him.

Vinny hit his brakes. "Rotten bastards." The tires screamed in protest. He swerved into the left lane on a curve and barely missed another vehicle heading straight for him. It pulled into the right lane to avoid Vinny's Ford, and "bang!" It slammed into the navy blue one.

The car's horn blasted along with crunching metal and shattering glass.

Vinny didn't stop to help the victims. He moved back into the right lane and drove away as if he hadn't been the cause of the accident. No worries. There was no damage to the Ford he was driving. No way to tie him to the crash.

Vinny picked up speed and kept checking over his shoulder. He hit a bump and fishtailed. Glancing at his watch, he realized he was behind schedule.

Jules braced his hands on the dash. "Slow down! You're going to get us killed."

Vinny looked at the speedometer. The needle had crept near 80 mph. A swirl of red and blue lights in the rearview mirror caught his attention. "Damn! Where'd he come from? Wasn't there a minute ago!" Vinny knew he was speeding, and he had a gun in his possession. He refused to go back to prison. "Hide this."

"Are you crazy?" Jules' voice cracked.

"I can't believe you're my brother," Vinny said. "You're a coward."

"No, I'm not. You'll see. I can get us out of here without pulling a gun. Stop the car, hide that thing, and play along with me." As Vinny pulled over, Jules shouted, "Quick, switch sides." Jules climbed over the gearshift, opened the driver's door, and slowly climbed out while Vinny scooted into the passenger's seat and hid the gun in the side panel.

Vinny took a deep breath and waited for the patrol cruiser to pull up behind them and the officers to get out. Nothing happened for a few minutes. *Must be running a check on the license plate.*

Then, a tall, freckle-faced cop stepped up to Jules. Burly and all Irish, he said, "I clocked you at seventy-nine in a sixty mph zone. May I see your license and registration?"

"Yes, officer." Jules held out his license.

The Irish officer nodded. "Where's the registration?"

Jules pointed to the passenger's side. "It's in the glove compartment."

"I'll get it." The other officer marched past Jules and opened Vinny's door. "Step out of the car, please."

"Wait." Jules moved toward Vinny. "Let me help the old man."

Vinny caught the panicked look in his brother's eye. "Relax." He straightened Jules' crisp, white clerical collar and moved it higher on Jules' neck. "I may be old, but I'm not helpless." He pushed Jules away and made his hand tremor as he lifted one foot to the ground. "I'm obeying, officer, but it takes a while. These old bones don't bend like they used to—arthritis." He wrapped his hand under his knee and hoisted his other leg over the car's ledge. His hand continued to tremble as he reached for the door handle and rocked a few times before pulling himself out of the vehicle. "My boy is a fine man, tending to his flock in need. Aren't you, Father Jules? Have some respect."

When the cop turned to face Jules, he backed off. "You're a priest?"

"I'm on my way to the hospital to give last rights," Jules said. "I wanted to get there in time. You know death awaits no one. Sorry, it won't happen again."

"This vehicle was reported missing and presumed stolen," the officer said.

"No. There must be some misunderstanding, officer." Jules stepped away from the door. "It belongs to the church. Check the registration."

The Irish officer opened the cubbyhole and pulled out a slip of paper. He squinted for several seconds.

Vinny leaned against the Ford as if his legs would give out. *Dumb cop can't even read.* Jules raced to his side to prop him up.

The officer frowned, peered at Jules, then shoved the paper back into the compartment and slammed the door. "Registration checks out. Sorry, you can get back into the car." He moved toward his partner, and after a short conversation, the Irish officer turned to Jules. "I'm letting you off with a verbal warning. Watch the speeding."

"Thank you, officer. We do appreciate your service." "God bless you." Jules made the sign of a cross.

The officers piled back into the patrol cruiser and drove away.

"That was close." Vinny made sure to hobble to the passenger's side of the Ford in case the officers were still watching.

Jules said, "I told you this collar would be useful—"

"Not now." Vinny moved back into the driver's side. "Get in! We'll need to ditch this one soon. I'm running late. We need a faster one."

Jules said a short prayer and climbed back into the Ford. "You can drop me off, and I'll find my own way back to the center."

Vinny turned in his seat. "Forget it. You're my brother, and you're not ever going back there. Do I make myself clear? Fish that gun from the side panel."

Jules cringed but did as he said. "What do you plan to use as wheels if you get rid of this one?"

"It depends." Vinny drove into town, spied a bus stop, and pulled into an elementary school parking lot filled with cars. He snatched the gun and pocketed it.

Jules got out of the Ford and paused, waiting for instructions.

Vinny joined him on the curb. "See any wheels here worth taking?"

"You can't make me steal another car," Jules said. "I don't want to end up in jail."

"Everything will be fine. You'll see."

Jules crossed his arms. "No, it won't! I'm not an idiot."

"Wait, I have an idea. There's a bus." Vinny watched Jules closely as they caught a ride and headed for the terminal building. When Vinny reached the ticket window, a Greyhound for Huntsville was about to pull out. "Two tickets, please, and hurry." Vinny laid cash on the counter, grabbed the stubs, and they climbed aboard.

The bus was nearly empty. Vinny took the back seat, at least four rows from anyone else. Jules hesitated but finally followed. "How long is the ride?"

Vinny checked his watch. "We should be there in two hours."

Jules folded his arms across his lap. "What do we do next?"

"We get a faster car." Vinny beamed a smile. "That'll be your first task in the business."

Jules whispered, "You want me to steal another car? No way! Been there—already accused of doing that. I'm not ever going to do it again."

"Shh," Vinny warned and glanced around the bus. "I'm not talking about stealing one." Vinny patted his pocket. "Tell you what. It'll be a little gift, your first car, and in your name only. We'll buy a used one. It'll be legit."

"You're buying me wheels of my own?" Jules paused. "What's the catch? I can't pay you back."

"No catch," Vinny promised.

"Can you afford it?" Jules asked.

Vinny laughed. "Don't worry about the money. I have plenty. Plus, I have a stash hidden away for better days. We'll pay in cash. Most dealers cut the price when they see a wad of bills. Have you ever bought a car before?"

"No," Jules admitted. "What do I have to do?"

"I'll teach you a few tricks," Vinny said. "Ones you can use for the rest of your life. Pick out a dark-colored SUV, an American-made model that won't stand out. I'm sure you'll get a good deal in Huntsville."

"What if I can't find anything?" Jules asked.

Vinny pointed to Jules' neck. "Make sure the dealer sees your collar."

"But it's a lie," Jules argued.

"You're the one who wanted the collar." Vinny chuckled at Jules' scowl. "Okay. You don't have to tell them. Let them assume."

Jules snapped his head up, his frown deeper than ever, but he sat quietly, moping for most of the trip.

Two hours and ten minutes passed before the Greyhound pulled into Huntsville. As luck would have it, Vinny spotted a Chevy dealership as the bus drove past. Two blocks later, the bus pulled into the station.

Jules must have dozed off because Vinny had to nudge the boy. "This is our stop."

The lad stretched and waited until the rest of the passengers filed up the aisle.

Vinny gently prodded his brother off the bus. "We're in luck. I saw a used car lot. We can walk from here."

It took an hour to acquire a dark gray 2020 Chevy Tahoe, and Jules seemed pleased with the purchase. The salesman offered free drinks, so Jules took an extra soda as they left the dealership.

Vinny took the keys. "I'll drive."

"I thought this was my car," Jules protested.

"It is, but I know the way to Colorado. Do you?"

Jules thought a moment. "I'll get a map."

Vinny laughed. "Okay, we'll get a map, but I'll drive in the meantime."

Jules opened the can of soda. "How far is it to Colorado?"

"We'll be on Fritz's trail by morning." Vinny merged into the right lane.

"I thought Fritz died in the robbery that put you in prison."

"Yeah. So did I, but he recovered." Vinny slowed as he took the north exit to Highway 287. "He was an undercover FBI agent. After they patched him up, he went into the Witness Protection Program. Now he's in some Podunk town—Loveland, Colorado."

"How do you know that?" Jules asked.

Vinny set the cruise control to 65 mph. "The son of a U.S. Marshal, Gene Islet, was in prison. The cons planned to rape him. I saved his sorry ass. In return, I asked for a little favor, and he promptly delivered. I passed the info on to my boys but told them not to do anything until I got there. One of them thought he'd impress me. He botched the attempt to take out Fritz and got his daughter instead. Of course, he made it look like an accident."

"He killed an innocent girl?" Jules asked, astounded. "Are you sure the daughter is dead?"

Vinny nodded. "Yeah, but I didn't order the hit. I've learned over the years that if I want a job done right, I gotta do it myself."

"You wouldn't kill someone who didn't deserve to die, would you?" Jules asked.

"Never have and never will," Vinny answered. "By the way, Fritz doesn't go by that name anymore. His name is Lars Konig. You know he set me up, right?"

Jules leaned forward and stared at his brother. "Yeah, I heard that, but it all happened before I was even born." Vinny nodded. "So, if you're dealing with Fritz, you know Braun is close by." Jules seemed to be fishing for more information.

"How do you know that?" Vinny asked.

"Midget told me the two went after him a few years ago," Jules said.

Vinny asked, "You know Midget?"

Jules cringed. "He's our long, lost brother, but back to Lars. How do you know where he will be?"

"I have my boys tracking his every move," Vinny said.

"Aren't they expensive?" Jules took another sip of soda. "And they better be top-notch. Braun shot Midget. He'll never be the same—locked up in that loony bin in Colorado all these years. I don't want to join him."

Vinny nodded and patted Jules' knee. "Don't you worry. I have enough money hidden away to buy the best and another stash in process. My boys are waiting for me. You'll meet them and the rest of your brothers soon."

"I still don't want any part of this," Jules said. "And I'm not looking forward to meeting Midget."

"Speaking of Midget, he died last night." Vinny crossed himself. "Heart attack, or so Doc says."

"Midget never had a heart," Jules said. "I wrote to him a few times. We talked over the phone weekly for a while, and he informed me about the family. He wanted me to see him at the nuthouse—even told me how to borrow a car. When I tried, the police caught me. They said I stole the car even though I planned to return it. I knew it didn't seem right in my gut, but I was so naïve back then. Midget didn't lift a finger to bail me out of jail. He abandoned me."

"No heart? That's a good one." Vinny chuckled. "Guess that explains everything, cuz he's alive 'n' well today."

Jules frowned. "Huh? I don't get it."

Vinny was enjoying this kid. Jules made him laugh more in the last few hours than he'd laughed in 25 years. "It's a secret, but I guess I can trust you." He leaned closer. "I learned about a drug from Doc while he was in prison. It's a neurotoxin like you find in pufferfish. If the dose isn't just right, it'll kill you. It slows the heart rate and breathing to almost nothing. The body's temperature drops below normal. Doc developed an antidote and then used the drug to fake his own death to get out of jail. One of my men gave Doc the antidote, and he's a free man now. You'll meet him soon."

"You sure made a lot of friends in prison."

"Yeah, they're the best." In typical Italian fashion, Vinny's hands flew as he spoke. "They have contacts all over the world."

"Look out!" Jules shouted when they got too close to the shoulder.

"Oh, yeah. Sorry about that." Vinny straightened the wheel and swerved back into its proper lane.

Jules leaned forward, engrossed in the story. "So why'd you say Midget died?"

"Cuz Doc gave him the drug after he 'died.'" Vinny raised and flexed his two index fingers, indicating quotation marks. "My men retrieved his body from the morgue. Doc gave Midget the antidote, and today, he's our number-one hitman." Vinny let out a low, rumbling laugh.

"Guess you have enough help. You don't need me." Jules shuddered. "Lars already lost a daughter. Does he have other family?"

"A wife and a granddaughter," Vinny said, "and I heard Braun had a girlfriend who's a cop, but they're on the outs at the moment."

Jules crossed his arms in his lap and gave that famous scowl again. "I refuse to take any part in this."

"I'm not asking anything of you. Just come home. You're family."

"Family? Right. Like anyone cares about what happens to me. I've asked questions about my family ever since I could talk. The priests refused to give me answers. Father Wallace finally told me the truth when Poppy died last year. That's how I tracked down Midget. Did you know we've lost four brothers while you were in prison?"

"Yeah, I suppose that's why after Momma died, Poppy had you raised in an orphanage—

"They're no longer called orphanages. I live in a residential treatment center," Jules corrected him.

"Whatever! Poppy wanted to keep you safe. Out of his ten sons, you're the youngest. Not many of us left."

"Being a priest might be a better payoff. If you screw up, remember, vengeance is mine. I will repay, saith the Lord."

"Take off that clerical collar. It's cutting off the blood supply to your head. Before we know it, you'll claim you're an honest-to-god priest like your uncle, Father Murdock."

Jules' eyes lit up. "I have an uncle who's a priest? Maybe I can live with him. I need somewhere to live while going to medical school."

Vinny rolled his eyes and shook his head. "Medical school. Where would you get the money? Anyway, it's not likely you'll ever meet him. He's broken all ties with the family."

Jules tugged at the collar, but he left it in place. "What if you're wrong about Lars? You could burn in hell for eternity if you harm someone innocent."

"Knock off that crap. I'm not wrong." Vinny tapped the steering wheel to the beat of the Rolling Stones blasting from the radio. He beamed a wide smile. "I can't wait to see the surprise on Fritz's face."

BRAUN'S BACK

Monday, June 9 – 1630 MDT, Loveland, Colorado

The closing whistle blew at Schaum's Candy Factory, yet Lars Konig wandered into the quiet company's warehouse, staring at the dog-eared wedding photo of his daughter that he always kept in his leather wallet. *When had she grown up?* In a blink of an eye, she went from being a tomboy in pigtails to a blushing bride in long blonde curls.

Diane was twenty-four years old, a gifted artist, a wife, and a mother. Lars paused his pacing. This is where he stood, only last week, when he last saw his little girl alive. She had run into the room, giggling, and blurted, "Dad, guess what? Steve got off work early and made dinner reservations to celebrate our fifth wedding anniversary. Can you and Mom watch Marta? Maybe she can spend the night."

Those snappy brown eyes didn't have to beg. "Sure, honey. We'd love to." She threw her arms around him in her usual bear hug he'd always loved.

"Thanks, Dad. Oh, wait." Diane turned, panic written all over her face. "I just remembered, our car is in the shop."

Without thinking, Lars had said, "No problem. Take my car and have fun."

She stood right here and gave him another kiss on the cheek before dashing off. "You're the greatest. Bye, Dad. Love you. See you later."

Her words still echoed. How he wished he could see her again, but two hours after she hugged him, Diane was dead, along with her husband. They died in a car accident. Steve was driving, and according to the police officer, he swerved to miss a cat in the road and slammed into a tree, totaling the Honda. When the cops arrived, they found Diane's body thrown clear of the vehicle. *Why? She always wore a seatbelt.* The ME determined their deaths as an accident. Lars wasn't so sure.

Tears flooded his eyes and dribbled down his cheeks. *Their deaths are my fault. I should never have lent her my car. The mechanic said the brake line had worn thin and must have ruptured. I don't care what he says, someone tampered with my car.* Fortunately, Shep, their manager, had agreed to drive the family to and from home until he could replace it.

His daughter and her husband's blurred image cleared as he blinked back tears and wiped a sleeve across his face. *Even from prison, Vinny murdered Diane, or it was one of his brothers. I'd bet on it—they probably meant to kill me, not Diane, but they'll be on my doorstep before I know it. Even a name change won't stop Vinny from getting his revenge. My time is running out. I have to tell Laura my true identity soon.*

Caught up in the moment, he was startled when the front door pinged the arrival of another customer. Lars sighed and walked from the warehouse. He'd lock up for the night as soon as this person left the showroom. The rich aroma of chocolate and caramel grew more intense as he entered the candy shop.

"How's the king of chocolates?" Braun Hastings' familiar baritone voice echoed off the highly polished, vintage wood paneling. The man's head brushed against a wooden sign advertising candy that hung from the eye-catching tin ceiling. Braun shrugged off his rain-soaked overcoat and strolled closer to peruse the glassed-in candies stacked beneath the bright red-tiled counter. Water dripped from his dark hair that fell limp across his creased brow. "I'll take a pound of my favorite buttercream toffees."

Lars' jaw dropped and closed with a snap. "I don't think so." Anger flared at the sight of his ex-FBI partner, who he had trained as a rookie while working special ops missions. "I told you never to come here again."

"That's no way to treat a customer." Braun laid his coat on the candy counter. He didn't look as if he planned to leave anytime soon.

Lars glanced over both shoulders. No one else was in the room. "Every time I see you, we end up on some assignment no one else will touch—breaking every rule of the Witness Security Program. My dream of working for the FBI became a nightmare. Remember that jewel heist sting operation to capture Vinny? Look how well that turned out. It got me into the State Witness Protection Program until Vinny's trial."

"I know, Fritz—"

"Lars! Not Fritz. My name is now Lars."

"Whatever." Braun eyed the candy. "The FBI didn't abandon you when Poppy swore he'd skin you alive. Remember, you didn't only put Vinny in the slammer. He also lost two brothers, Alessandro and Leo."

Lars' temper flared. "But we didn't stop there. A couple of years later, even after I went into the Federal Witness Security Program, you begged me to go after the next in line and one every few years after that."

"That was Chief Jackson," Braun moved down the counter, nearly drooling over the chocolates. "I didn't join your team until six years ago. Poppy's boys had moved on from jewel heists to illegal arms deals."

Fritz ignored his comment. "You knew that I had a wife and daughter to protect by then. I caved. I'd have done anything to keep them out of harm's way. Laura would have killed me herself if she knew what I really did on those 'fishing trips.'"

Braun pointed his finger at Fritz. "Hang on there. You don't have your facts straight. I told you that wasn't me. I was only four years old when you took down Vinny. That was Chief Jackson."

"Yeah, Jackson, and I know you were involved…" Lars stopped his pacing, thinking back. "Am I that much older than you? Really, that's not how I remember it."

Braun poked at a chocolate. "Yes, really. I didn't join your team until we went after Lorenzo six years ago. And remember Midget? He's still in the loony farm."

"And I got shot. What a tall tale I had to dream up to tell Laura. No, I'm done."

"I was such a rookie back then. If you hadn't taught me the ropes, I would have died in that op." Braun popped a sample of candy into his mouth as if in defiance.

Lars peered up at Braun. "Don't try to butter me up. You had your sample chocolate. It's time to leave."

Braun held up his hand. "Don't forget, four years ago, it was **you** who called **me** when Frank kidnapped your sister. Remember? Who dropped everything and came to your rescue? I ended up behind a desk for six months with a busted ankle."

"Yeah, and I already thanked you for that. After my sister's rescue, I told you there were no more special assignments, but do you respect that? No. Here you are again. I'm not helping you this time."

Braun swallowed. "I'm not leaving."

Lars clenched his fists. "I can't keep doing this—living a lie, keeping secrets from my wife and family, and putting everyone at risk again. No. Go away. My FBI days are over."

"Okay, we'll put the past behind us."

Lars couldn't stand the furious look reflecting at him from his ex-partner's mirrored glasses. "Take off those shades. There's no sun out today."

Braun lowered his voice. "You know why I'm here. I promised to leave you alone until—"

"Until what?" Awareness flew through him like a rock skipping water as the ripples widened straight to the PEN. "Vinny's been released?" Lars's icy fingers brushed away the beaded sweat on his forehead. Weakness tugged at his knees. He held himself upright by leaning on the counter. "I wondered why the U.S. Marshal called and left a message. I didn't take the time to call back. It just slipped my mind with Diane's death and the funeral." Lars swallowed the lump in his throat. "When did he get out, and how did Vinny manage to serve only twenty-five out of his forty-year sentence?"

"Four days ago, he got out for good behavior—can you believe it?" Braun eyed the store as if someone lurked in the shadows lying in ambush. "News among the inmates, he's heading your way. The chief put a trail on the bastard, but we lost him somewhere in northwest Texas."

Lars frowned. "The chief? Our old boss? I thought he retired two years ago."

"Not for long. Action is in his blood. It didn't sit well with him when the FBI moved on from the Corenelli family. He swore they were doing a half-assed job and started his own detective agency to get the job done right. I left the FBI to join him." Braun helped himself to another chocolate from the countertop samples, pulled out a chair next to a small round serving table, and sat down.

"Don't get comfortable. You won't be here for long," Lars stood straighter. "Don't worry, I won't ask for help this time, so you can leave now."

Braun leaned back and crossed his legs. "Well, that's not happening."

"The old man's addicted to the adrenalin rush, but what's that got to do with me?"

"Plenty. The chief wants to end this for good and wants you in on the play. It's a good thing you've stayed fit over the years."

"Play? No way." Lars frowned.

"Gramps…" Marta dashed from the back office with her latest masterpiece in hand.

Braun rose from the chair. At 6'4", he stood a head taller than Lars.

Marta stopped short. "Who are you?" *She was bold, curious, and imaginative like her mother at that age—already a budding artist.*

Braun removed his glasses and knelt beside the little girl. "Who is this adorable child?"

"I'm no child! I'm nearly four years old, and you didn't answer me. Who are you?"

Braun flashed a smile. It sparkled to his clear gray eyes. "Well, now, sweetie, I need to ask you the same question."

"Uh-uh. I asked first, didn't I, Gramps?" She brushed a lock of curly blonde hair from her face and gave a sly smile. Her dimples deepened as she scrutinized the tall stranger.

"What did you draw?" Braun studied her artwork, ignoring Lars' comments. "Why is the man inside the birdcage and the little red bird flying outside it?"

Marta pulled the paper away. "That's for Gramma Laura! She told me to draw a picture while she's adding more caramel to her candy. Her work is going slow, but she says that's okay cuz she's making turtles."

That brought out a chuckle from the men.

"It's a nice picture no matter what Braun thinks, and as I mentioned, he's leaving, aren't you?" Lars suggested with a scowl on his face.

"Brown?" Marta asked. "That's a funny name."

"No, it's Braun, but you can call me whatever you like." He patted her shoulder. "Okay? Your gramps and I have to talk."

"Not yet." Marta's caramel-brown eyes peered up at Gramps. "You promised me a story. Tell me the one where you used to be a lion tamer. I like that one."

Braun smiled. "I'd like to hear that one myself. Taming big game, are we? Sounds appropriate."

Lars knelt and hugged Marta. "Run along now. Tell Gramma I'll see her at home for dinner."

Marta stood with her feet apart, hands on her hips. "You have some 'splaining to do."

Lars gave her his warning glare. "Marta?"

She sulked and then turned. Her cowgirl boots clattered across the tiled floor as she ran out of the candy shop door. "Gramma," echoed down the kitchen hallway.

Braun laughed. "Yeah, Gramps, we have some 'splaining to do. Let's talk somewhere safe—away from prying ears. Your secret life is over. By the way, there's an extra guard on duty outside and another at the gate. They're compliments of the agency. Vinny will attack where it'll hurt the most, your family. We need to move your wife and granddaughter tonight."

"Tonight? We can't. I haven't told Laura…" Lars choked on his words.

"It's been over twenty-five years, Fritz. I mean Lars."

Lars shook his head. "Maybe if I had, Diane would still be alive. She borrowed my car to pick up her husband at work. Both died in the accident." He gnawed on his lip. "What will Laura do when she hears that I'm ex-FBI?"

"Tell her the truth. I bet she'll do anything to protect Marta."

"Braun, think about what you're asking. Laura's father died last year and left her his business. I can't ask her to leave the factory."

Braun picked up his coat. "But you will. We both know Vinny. He strikes like a cobra. They have to disappear."

Lars straightened to his full height. "Not without me to protect them."

"You can't be with them. Vinny's hunting you! Look, Fritz, ah Lars, we will fight him together."

Lars wasn't too sure about that and pulled a handkerchief from his pocket to dab his forehead. "Let me talk to Laura first."

Braun headed for the door. "Later. I have a car outside. The chief is waiting, and I'm not leaving without you."

Lars crossed his arms and stood his ground. "Get this through your thick skull. We just lost Diane. It's too much to ask."

"All the more reason to see the chief. We need to develop a plan of action to protect Laura and Marta." Braun grabbed Lars' arm and nudged him to the door. "And you, too—the sooner, the better. The chief won't let this drop. He says it's urgent."

Lars took a deep breath. "Okay, but only as a favor to you, and I'm not joining the team again. Be sure to make it quick. I have to talk to Laura."

MARTA'S VISION

Monday, June 9 – 1840 MDT, Loveland, Colorado

Laura stood in the doorway of Marta's room. "Time for dinner, sweetheart. You can feed your children after we eat."

Marta sat at a small red tea table, pouring fake drinks for her dollies. The chair opposite hers was empty, yet she studied the space. She placed her hand over the chair and moved her fingers as if she were patting something. "I'll get you a tissue, Momma, and you'll feel better.

Laura gasped and clutched the doorjamb. *Something is going on—Lars snuck off without a word, there are new armed guards at the candy factory, and more here at home. Now Marta is acting strange.*

Marta took a tissue from her bedside stand and returned to the table. She wiped the air above the vacant seat. "There now, put on your glasses. Then you can see me better."

"Marta, it's time to eat," Laura gently prodded. "I made your favorite: Pepperoni and mushroom pizza with extra cheese."

"Okay, Gramma. I'll be down in a minute. Momma has something 'portant to tell me."

Laura walked into the room and knelt beside Marta. "Now, honey, having imaginary friends is okay, but your mother is in heaven."

Marta stomped her foot, shaking her head, and making her curls bounce. "No! She's right here."

"Okay." Laura patted her shoulder. "What did she say?"

A quizzical frown crossed Marta's face. "She's here to warm us. Huh? No, that's not right." She leaned closer to the chair. "Oh, to warn us. A bad man is coming. We must hide, and I better pack."

"Nonsense, child. Come and eat." Laura took the girl's hand and led her from the room.

"Momma, come downstairs with me." Marta held out her other hand and clasped the air. "She'll sit by me."

Exasperated, Laura said, "Okay, whatever." They entered the dining room. Laura obliged Marta and placed an extra chair beside her.

The girl sat down and patted her hand on the seat next to her. "Momma, you sit here."

Laura brought out three plates and sat across the table from Marta. "I wonder what's taking your Gramps so long. You said he'd be home for dinner. He's late, and the pizza is getting cold, so let's say grace and hope he gets here soon."

Marta folded her hands and ended the prayer with, "God bless Momma and Daddy. Oh, and keep us safe. Amen."

Something nudged Laura's elbow. Glancing to her right, nothing was there. A shiver of fear raced up her spine. Pizza no longer sounded appetizing. "I'm going to call Gramps."

"Don't worry. Momma says he's on his way."

A moment later, the door opened, and Lars entered the dining room. "Laura, we need to talk."

She stood. "What's going on? Did you know we have a new guard at the gate and another on the grounds?"

"They're with me." A tall, muscular man ducked through the door and entered the room.

Marta leaned over the empty chair and whispered to her imaginary friend, "It's Mr. Brown. Do you know him?" Marta paused as if to hear an answer, then added, "Gramma, we'll need another plate for dinner."

"He can have mine. Welcome to our home, Mr. Brown." Laura nodded politely. "Please join us for dinner. We have plenty of pizza."

"This is Braun," Lars corrected.

"Thank you." Braun stepped up to the girl. "Hello, Marta. May I sit by you?" He pulled out the chair next to her.

"No!" Marta hopped up and pushed him aside. "That's Momma's chair. Sit over there."

"Sorry," Braun said. "I didn't see her."

"It's a new imaginary friend," Laura explained.

Marta stared at her Gramma. "No. This is Momma. She's sitting right here at the table. Can't you see her?"

Laura shook her head, but Lars interrupted, "We don't have much time. Something's come up, and we have to talk."

Lars turned toward Marta. "Please stay here with Braun. We'll be right back. Help yourself to pizza, Braun." Lars picked up a slice and motioned for Laura to follow him while he munched his pizza. "We need to pack. The two of you are going on a short vacation. You'll leave tonight."

"See, I told you, Gramma," Marta called after them. "We're hiding from a bad man."

TRUTH REVEALED

Monday, June 9 – 1900 MST, Loveland, Colorado

Secluded in their bedroom, Laura listened to Lars' story about his days in the FBI, the special ops missions that nearly killed him, and how he was now in the Witness Security Program. "We zeroed in on this crime family—the Corenelli's. Poppy headed the gang, but he no longer got his hands dirty, so we targeted his next in line, Vinny, who we feared would soon become boss."

"Twenty-four years! I've been with you for twenty-four years, and you never once said anything. Who have I been married to all this time?"

Lars stiffened. "You married me, your husband."

Laura shouted. "You aren't my husband. You kept secrets from me. I'll never trust you again."

"I didn't have a choice," Lars' voice shook. "I had to change my name. Vinny's family swore they'd spend the rest of their days hunting me down for my betrayal. They even threatened you, Diane, and everything belonging to us."

Laura wasn't impressed with his story. "So you bravely fought the mafia and nearly got yourself killed, but you…you couldn't find the courage to tell me the truth? What kind of fool do you take me for?"

Lars wrapped an arm around her shoulder and planned to sit on the edge of the bed. "I know this comes as a shock."

"A shock?" Laura jerked away. Her fists clenched as she paced the room. Pain wrenched her gut as she rehashed his lies. She wanted to slug him. "Talk about a sting operation! My God, Lars. You betrayed me! You lied to me! How could you do that? I thought we had an honest marriage. It cuts deep."

"I know you're angry, so I better get everything out in the open before we settle this."

"What do you mean? There's more?"

Lars backed away and tried to look into her eyes but failed. "Yes, there's more. I'm sure they murdered Diane. If not Vinny, it was one of his brothers."

Laura nearly lost her balance and landed on the bed. "Oh my God! How could they? If I had known, I would have protected her."

Honey, don't go there. All my life, I've been trained, and even I couldn't save her."

"All your life?" Laura questioned. "What?"

He stared at his watch and then wiped his eyes. "I have to make this quick, and you have to understand why. At times, I've been called in for special missions even while in the witness program—"

She watched Lars' Adam's apple bob as he swallowed. His ear tips turned bright red. She knew he was stressed, frustrated, and holding in his anger. Or was it fear?

Laura exploded. "While we were married? Behind my back? This is worse than I thought."

There was a knock on the door. "Choppers due in fifty minutes," Braun shouted. "Make it short and get packing."

Seeing Lars in a new light, she felt like a stranger had replaced her husband. "What is he talking about, a chopper? Why didn't you tell me sooner? Why don't you trust me?"

Lars stood ramrod straight. "Yes, I trust you."

"I don't believe it! You've lived a lie for the last twenty-five years. Lies about all those fishing trips. They were really FBI missions. I wondered why I never saw any fish. That stinks, Lars! How could you?"

"I know, honey, but—"

Laura stepped closer and glared. "Then today, you tell me our lives are in danger because of some job gone south that happened a year before we got married."

"Yes, I wanted to tell you sooner. I, I…" Lars stuttered.

"If you trusted me, why keep it a secret?"

Lars reached for her hand. "I was afraid you'd refuse to marry me if you knew the truth."

Laura shook her head and slapped away his hand.

"No, hear me out," Lars begged. "Then, you got pregnant with Diane. It didn't seem to matter after that."

"What? Were you just living your own adventures, and you thought that would be okay? Honestly?" Laura said. "No. Not telling me the truth is more than a lie, and I can't live with a man who doesn't trust me. You downright lied to me." She squinted up at him, her eyes burned with anger. "I bet Lars Konig isn't even your name."

Lars' lips tightened, and his head barely nodded.

"What does that mean?" She took a moment to think. So, Diane and I don't even have the right last name?" She was getting angrier with each revelation.

"No, they aren't lies." Lars lowered his voice. "Not really."

Laura stepped closer, fists clenched, and glared. "Yes, lies. You changed your name and career and left everything behind you. Then today, you tell me our lives are in danger because of some mafia sting operation that happened a year before we married. Now you're demanding that I leave, too?"

Lars gritted his teeth. "I'm *trying* to keep you and Marta safe!"

"And that's another thing," Laura shouted. "Poor Marta believes there's a bad man after us. Did you talk about Vinny in front of her?"

"No, I didn't—"

"You must have said something," Laura ranted, "Marta has gotten it into her head that it's her mother that's warning us of danger. She's mentioned it several times, and won't be persuaded otherwise. So don't tell me you trying to keep us safe—because, you're not. It's because of him." Laura pointed toward the door and stared at Lars' flushed face.

Lars exclaimed, "I'd set myself on fire, before I let anything happen to you. I've already failed Diane. I refuse to let them harm any more of my family."

Laura jumped up, "So, some old partner comes along not even two weeks after Diane's death. Someone I've never met before making these ridiculous demands." She placed her hands on her hips. "Then you say, I must leave and abandon my father's house. Run away with Marta. Leave everyone I know and love behind, even you." She spat out and stepped closer, "I'm not going." Her finger poked his chest. "And *you* can't make me."

"Please, Laura." His voice shook. It became a whisper. "We're a family. I love you. I want to protect you and Marta." His eyes brimmed with tears.

Laura stiffened. "How would you feel if I told you that I'm really a hooker from New York? That I screwed a drug lord, discovered he was a murderer, and that my testimony sent him to prison? A year later, I married you. What would you say and do if you found out the truth today—twenty-four years later?"

"Honey, look at me. I'm the same person you married." Lars brushed a curl behind her ear. "I love you. I don't care if you were a hooker, a mass murderer, or a cop. You're my wife. My lover. I want to spend the rest of my life with you, the only person in this world, now and forever."

"Please, don't ask me to go away without you."

Lars lowered his head. "We don't have a choice."

She leaned against the dresser with wobbly knees. "Who will run the candy store?"

"Shep managed it before we came," Lars said. "He'll do a fine job until we get back. It will only be for a few months."

"Won't the employees be in danger?" Laura asked. "This guy might attack them."

"Vinny," Lars said. "His name is Vinny, and I want you to remember that name. It could save your life."

"Okay, worse yet, Vinny might bomb the factory. I'd never forgive myself if he harmed anyone, and I'd never forgive you."

"The factory is the least of your worries, but there is some concern. Braun will try to cover the factory with his men. He promised to plant key patrols in the area. Two highly trained armed guards are at the front gates, and two more are on the grounds. With all this security, Vinny will pick another place to strike."

"Then why can't Marta and I stay here? We won't leave the building. I swear. You know I'll protect Marta with my life."

Lars squeezed her shoulders. "I know you will, but you don't know these guys, honey—they are vicious, and while they are out in the world, you and Marta will never be safe. I admit I don't know where they'll send you, but it's safe and well-guarded. The apartment is already furnished. All you need are a few clothes. We'll be together again after this is over. I'll never help the FBI again. I promise."

"When will I see you again?" Laura asked. "Can't we spend the night together?"

"The sooner you leave here, the safer you'll be. I'll help you pack. Braun's already in Marta's room, picking out her favorite toys. You can pack her clothes when we're done here."

"Can you believe Marta? She insists there's a bad man. Could it be Vinny?" Laura moved toward the closet. "Marta talks to Diane like she actually sees her. Is it possible our daughter came back as an angel?" Laura sobbed.

"We can surely use help from the other side." Lars lifted the suitcase from the top shelf. "I hope Diane can comfort both of you." He set the bag by the bed and then clasped her hands. "Come here." He pulled her into an embrace. "I can't stand to see you cry."

Fear that this might be the last time she would see Lars tugged at her heart. He was her anchor, and right now, her anchor was raking the bottom of the sea.

Lars wiped her warm tears away. "Please, let me hold you."

She desperately wanted his strength and his arms around her in solace. He was her best friend and confidante, even if he'd hidden the truth all these years. He reassured her during times of doubt and comforted her after Diane's death. He inspired her to run her father's business when he died, and with Lars' help, she'd made it a profitable quarter.

He hovered inches from her lips. The warmth of his breath feathered across her face. The presence of danger sharpened all her senses as she leaned into him. The musky odor of anxiety came from his pores. His heart beat rapidly. A small pulse throbbed quickly over his temples—probably faster than was good for him.

Taking his face between her shaking hands, she pushed aside the suitcase that lay in the way. It skidded into the wall with a small thud. Laura lowered her body to the bed, pulled him onto her, and watched his face flush, showing his vulnerability and exposing his desire for her.

Yes, she felt his readiness against her thigh and knew he had a sense of urgency, too. She adjusted to his larger, heavier torso. Lightly at first, their lips glided together as if questioning their action, then firmly sought an answer in response. His kiss deepened, seeking reassurance, comfort, and promise.

Yet, he was hers, the man she knew and loved, with all his history and needs. A flutter ran through her belly. A sensation she'd never tire of. She traced a scar along his neck. "Did you really get this during the war?"

Lars muttered a reply. "It was a battle, but not the war."

"Vinny?" A flood of anger burst forth as she felt the threat to their lives.

"Uh-huh," Lars said.

Like a new bride bedding her husband for the first time, she wondered what else she didn't know about the man she married. Familiarity battled with disorientation. It had a fresh meaning to her as she unbuttoned his shirt and lay in his comforting arms. How many times had she lain beside him, seeking to blend her body with his?

"Laura, you're beautiful." Cupping her breast, he rolled her over and moved his thumb along her cheek. Small nibbles teased her mouth, parting her lips with his tongue.

She savored the taste of him and captured his tongue with her own. A smile curved her lips at his groan. He always made her feel young, alive, and sexy. Over the years, she'd taken him for granted, but not tonight. She'd give him all of her. It might be their last time together.

Lars skimmed his fingers under her blouse and lifted it over her head. He buried his face and nuzzled tender kisses down her neck.

She needed to touch all of him, study his body, feel his strength, and memorize his touch. She unhooked her bra and let it slide to the floor. His tongue flicked against a nipple, driving her wild. Wanting skin against skin, she peeled off his shirt and grabbed his belt. Moments later, they lay together naked.

Lars planted kisses along her abdomen and then back up to her breasts.

She noticed his arm had a slight muscular tic. Although he didn't seem nervous, his body felt tense, eager, and ready.

Laura responded to his need with her own body's throbbing ache. Her physical hunger grew ravenous even after all these years of marriage. Making love tonight would only wet her desire for him. She'd always want more.

A new wave pulsed to her loins while butterflies danced in her belly. Her heart raced as she held him tight. Some part of her noted with surprise the intensity of passion and pain behind the years of not knowing the truth. Feeling her skin burn beneath his touch, she wanted to claim this man and renew the old love before they parted. "Take me now and forever."

He needed no encouragement.

Enveloped in his spicy aroma, she felt heat rush to her core. Her hips rose to meet him. All thoughts drifted away. Flooded with passion, they melded as one, climaxed, and collapsed.

A small knock on the door roused her. Laura bounced from the bed. "It's Marta." She ran to the master bath, turned on the shower, and then poked her head around the door. "Tell her we'll be right out."

Lars chuckled. "She knows it'll be a while when the shower turns on." Lars threw on a robe and opened the door. It wasn't Marta. "Oh, it's you, Braun."

"I thought it got awful quiet in here." Braun laughed." Tell Laura she has twenty minutes. Her ride is on its way."

"I heard you," Laura called from the bathroom. "I'll be ready."

Braun lowered his voice. "I packed Marta's things. She insisted on taking her colored pencils and sketchbook. I drew the line when she tried to pack all that acrylic paint. It could get messy if they leaked."

"Don't worry about it. She can pick up more supplies when they land." Lars closed the door.

Minutes later, Laura appeared with a towel wrapped around her head. Glancing at the bag opened on the bed, she saw Lars had packed their wedding photo among several sweaters. He threw some of her favorite clothes from her closet into the suitcase. She smiled. "That's not how I pack."

"Well, buy whatever you need when you get there." He gave her a peck on the cheek and headed for the shower.

Fifteen minutes later, Lars gave Marta and Laura one last hug and kiss. "Remember, I love you."

It felt like her soul had left her body as she climbed into the helicopter. Wrenched in sorrow, afraid she'd never see him again. Laura blew him a kiss. "I'll love you forever." She mouthed it over the roar of the engine.

He nodded. *Probably too choked up to reply.*

Marta waved from the chopper as it took off for the airport. From there, they would board a private jet to take them to make a new life. Where to? Laura didn't know. Lars and Braun were also in the dark.

Marta snuggled into Laura's lap and fell asleep.

Laura's mind raced. *How long before I will see him again? If I ever see him again—this pain is too real. It feels like my heart has fractured into a million pieces.*

RETURN TO FRITZ

Bone-weary, Lars watched the helicopter disappear into the night. He shivered as a sharp wind sliced through his jacket and whipped his hair. He hoped it didn't foretell of a bitter night ahead. Or maybe he trembled at the thought that this might be the last time he'd see Laura. Her love filled him with joy and light as bright as the glittering stars on a moonless night.

Braun stood on the bottom porch step and motioned Lars inside. "Okay, now that the hard part is over, we can get to work. You're going on TV in the morning."

"What?" Lars swiped the dampness away to clear his vision. "You're putting me out in the open? That's a great way to get shot."

"The chief pulled strings and has that covered. Remember Officer Russ Bracken?" Braun asked. "The ex-Navy Seal Explosive Breacher I met in Afghanistan. He's also a good friend of Chief Jackson and is now a veteran SWAT commander."

Lars thought back to his last Special Ops mission four years ago. "Yeah, he saved my life."

"Right," Braun said.

"What risks are we planning this time that we'll need SWAT?" Lars glared.

"Like I said, Chief Jackson is pulling out all stops. We may not need SWAT, but we have a whole team built around you." Braun moved to the veranda. He paused and turned. "By the way, you'll take back your old name, Fritz. There's no reason to hide."

"Fritz? It seems odd after so many years. Should I take back my last name, too?"

"Sure. You don't have a problem returning to Von Schlegen, do you? I'm sure you told your wife your real name, didn't you? Let's lure this jackass into our net and end it once and for all." Braun stood by the front door. "Are you coming?"

"Fritz Von Schlegen. It has a ring to it." *Did I tell Laura my real name? Everything happened so fast. She's going to hate the news when she finds out if I didn't. She'll call it another lie.* Deep in thought, he didn't budge from the spot where the chopper had lifted off with his family.

"Get a move on. You need to pack." Braun's voice clipped with impatience.

The night flooded with tension. It felt like the total weight of the world lay on his shoulders. Fritz's steps faltered as he headed toward the house. Pain gripped his chest. Unable to catch his breath, he stopped abruptly on the top stair of the veranda and leaned against the railing.

Braun lurched forward and grabbed his arm. "You, all right? You're pale as toothpaste."

Fritz took a few deep breaths and then straightened. "Vinny isn't the only one who wants a piece of my hide. What about Midget?"

"The more, the merrier." Braun patted him on the back. "It's how I justified bringing in the big boys. The government owes us, and we have two guards stationed on this property. More are at the candy factory. No one will penetrate the area, but you won't be here even if they do."

"That makes me feel a whole lot better," Fritz lied. "Who else is on Vinny's team?"

"Good question. We can talk more in the office in the morning," Braun opened the front door. "For now, pack a bag. We're going to a hotel."

Fritz went inside, climbed the steps to his bedroom, threw a few clothes and his travel kit in a duffle, and took one last look at the room. His thoughts drifted back to Laura.

"Are you done packing?" Braun called up the stairs. "We need to go. Chief Jackson is waiting."

"Coming." Lars closed the door as if leaving a large piece of his life behind, then met Braun downstairs.

"Shut off the house lights and lock up. We'll take my car." Braun went outside, turned on his flashlight, and his footsteps crunched as he headed down the driveway.

Fritz raced to the door and shouted, "Wait a moment. I'll get my Glock." He threw off his coat and rummaged through the closet for his holster. It was hanging from a peg on the right. He checked that his semi-automatic was loaded, slipped into the shoulder harness, quickly attached it to his belt, and grabbed his coat. It felt unusually bulky over the gun, but it gave him comfort as he stepped into his former life. *Probably overkill, but it won't hurt to be prepared. It sounds like tomorrow could be rough.*

Headlights approached as he walked back onto the veranda of his father-in-law's old Victorian house with duffle in hand. A dark SUV pulled slowly up to the house. "Hey, Braun, that was quick. I'll be there in a sec." Fritz set down his duffle, locked the front door, and walked to the railing.

The car's headlights turned bright, blinding him. Fritz ducked behind a post to shield his eyes. "Tone it down, Braun." A wood splinter flew at his face as a sharp pop sounded like a car backfired. "What the hell?" The roar of an engine grew louder. He grabbed his gun and hit the deck.

"Go back inside," Braun shouted from somewhere in the yard.

A sound like fireworks split the night. Bullets zipped overhead. One hit a shutter, ricocheted, and went through the living room picture window. Glass shards and wood splinters flew in all directions, covering the deck. Fritz's heart raced. *Thank God Laura and Marta got away when they did.*

Braun must have gotten off a shot. Loud blasts came from his right, followed by a blowout of the car's rear tire. Gravel spun beneath the wheels. The vehicle slid sideways and screeched to a halt.

Fritz shifted behind a wooden support beam, braced his weapon against the railing, and held fire until he could determine the location of the threat.

"Midget, get down," someone from the car yelled.

Midget's distinctive graveled voice shouted, "Hell no." A gun barrel appeared through the driver's open window.

Fritz took a nosedive, rolled, and fired through a slot in the banister. Glass shattered, and in the moonlight, he saw the SUV's windshield turn into a spider's web.

Another bullet whizzed past his ear and slammed into the front doorjamb. Unable to hear clearly, Fritz emptied the magazine in the car's direction. One man ran from the vehicle, yelped, and fell sprawled on the gravel driveway—he didn't move. The headlights went out. Fritz lay in the dark, checked his holster for another clip, and swore, "Out of bullets." Although his ears buzzed, it seemed too quiet. He couldn't see anyone. *Wonder if Braun's hit?* Snaking his way to the front door, Fritz managed to unlock it.

Another round of gunfire toward the car let him know Braun was still alive.

Fritz slipped inside the house as a car door creaked open. He kept to the shadows away from the windows and made it to the entry closet. His hand felt across the top shelf and snagged the ammo. Fritz reloaded his clip, jammed the magazine in place, and scooped up the remaining cartridges.

A few more shots rang out. Fritz found a black stocking cap in an old ski jacket and pulled it over his blond hair. Then he grabbed Laura's SIG Sauer from the gun safe, which she had inherited from her father. Fritz checked the chamber, found it was loaded, and flipped up the safety. Thrusting the gun into his waistband, he raced out the back door in search of Braun.

Gravel crunched near the car.

A dark shadow ducked behind a lilac bush along the driveway. The man steadied his gun on a limb, fired, and a flash of light erupted from the muzzle. The shot blew out another car tire. *It must be Braun.* Fritz dropped on all fours and crawled closer as clouds rolled over the moon.

"Cover me," Midget yelled. Shots came from behind the car.

The lilac bush absorbed most of the blasts and a clump of grass flew into the air, just missing Braun.

The driver's door flew open, and a short, dark shadow dropped to the ground, rolled onto the gravel, and under the SUV to the other side.

Fritz exchanged fire with the attackers while Braun zigzagged to the house. He made it to the chimney, where Fritz crouched behind the rocks.

Braun whispered, "Where are the guards? They must hear us shooting."

"Bet they're dead. How else did Midget get onto the property?" Sirens sounded in the distance as Fritz edged his way along the side of the building.

Braun followed close behind. "Sounds like help is on the way."

The cloud covering the moon moved enough to light the driveway. Fritz scooted forward and knelt near the front corner of the house. The driver's and rear SUV doors were wide open. He didn't see any movement in the car.

Braun crept up behind Fritz, tapped him on the shoulder, and pointed toward the woods. "I'll cover you."

A rustling sound came from the grass along the outer fence, and shadows of two men kneeling by the garden fountain caught Fritz's eye as he dashed into the driveway and rolled under the abandoned SUV.

"Let's get outta here," a thug said to Midget. He crawled under the fence.

"No," Midget said. "I gotta do this for Vinny." He ducked behind the fountain and opened fire. The railing of the veranda splintered. Windows shattered.

Fritz ducked when Midget riddled the car. Bullets pinged off the metal and hit the dirt. He wedged his Glock along the front wheel and pulled the trigger. There was a click but no bullets—*chambers empty and no more ammo.*

Red and blue lights flashed as the sirens grew louder. Fritz drew Laura's SIG and fired again. Midget screamed and grabbed his arm.

"You can stay and fight, but I'm leaving." The thug who came with Midget ran for the woods.

"Stinkin' coward." Midget raised his good arm and shot the thug in the back. A long, shrill scream ended in a horrible gurgle. As the rack of lights on the cruiser grew brighter, Midget ducked low and darted into the woods, zigzagging through the trees.

Braun crouched behind the abandoned car, raised his Glock, and pulled the trigger, but it only clicked, so he lowered his pistol. "Empty!"

Fritz flinched at Braun's voice, concentrating on the retreating figure, and his gun fired. Midget cried out again but kept running.

OFFICER CORDELIA

Monday, June 9 – 2038 MDT, Loveland, Colorado

An ear-splitting siren came to an abrupt halt as a squad car pulled in front of Fritz. A woman stepped from the car and knelt behind the cruiser's door. "Drop the gun and hands up. My partner has you covered."

Fritz threw the SIG to the ground and lifted his hands. The gun landed not far from the cruiser. "I'm the victim. This is my house."

Braun moved to his side.

"Both of you hands over your heads and interlock your fingers."

Fritz dropped one hand. "I have my ID in my pants pocket. If you'll let me—"

Braun didn't raise his hands and stepped toward the woman. "Cordy?"

She shot him a look that caused Braun to stop in his tracks. "That's Officer Cordelia to you."

"Right, officer. He's with me." Braun smiled that crooked smile of amusement as he continued to hobble toward the patrol car. "You remember Fritz, right? Like me, he's ex-FBI."

Officer Cordelia rose swiftly, arm extended with gun in hand. "Keep them covered," she said to her partner.

"Really? Cordy, we're on the same team. Don't you remember? Oh, right, you were unconscious. I guess you never met Fritz in person." Braun pushed past her partner and whispered, "Try not to shoot me in the back."

The partner turned to Cordy, who shrugged. "He means well—let them go." She jerked to attention. "Get down. Someone's out there in the woods."

Braun ducked behind the car and reloaded his pistol.

Fritz dove for his gun and moved for cover. He watched Cordy, still holding the weapon, as she dropped behind the car's fender and swung her arm toward the gardens in a 180° arc.

"Don't worry," Braun said. "I have your back, Cordy."

She nodded, then crouched over the downed man in the driveway and checked for a pulse. "Dead." Cordy shifted behind the car's hood in one fluid move.

Braun gave a hand gesture.

Cordy nodded, and Braun dashed toward the woods.

Fritz could tell Cordy and Braun had worked together in the past. They seemed to read each other's signals with just a nod or slight movement of their hands. Yet, there was something else going on between them.

Cordy motioned for her partner to follow Braun in the shadows.

A crackle of Cordy's radio split the silence. "Two men down at the gate. One's dead. Other is in critical condition. Gunshot wound to chest. Rescue squad's en route. Any injuries up there?"

Braun paused, nudged his boot against the man Midget had shot, then knelt beside him and felt his neck. "Make that another dead."

Cordy reached for the radio, "Two more dead at the house. One got away in the woods. Send ME." She turned toward Fritz. "Any other attackers?"

"I only saw the three." Fritz turned on his flashlight. "I'm sure Midget's long gone."

Cordy flinched. "Midget Corenelli?" At Fritz's nod, she asked, "How'd he get out of the mental asylum? I thought they locked him away for good."

Fritz reloaded his gun. "Must have escaped somehow—guess Vinny sent him."

"No wonder Braun's here. You sure hit the mother lode of scumbags."

Fritz moved toward the woods. His light caught a dark red splash along the trunk of a cottonwood tree. Tiny droplets of blood made a path for several feet and then disappeared. "Midget's been hit. Blood splotches for a short way, but I lost his trail."

An ambulance pulled up to the garden, and two attendants got out. An EMT approached. "ME's on his way. What happened? Any injuries?"

Fritz motioned to Cordy. "She's in charge. Talk to her."

Cordy pulled a phone from her ear. "Fritz, Braun, don't go anywhere. I have a few questions." She went back to giving orders.

Braun limped back to the house.

"Were you hit?" An EMT asked Braun.

"No, my ankle flares up whenever I crouch too long in one place."

"Maybe the metal's getting rusty." Fritz smiled. "It could be telling you it's time to retire."

Braun scowled. "No way. We have work to do."

Fritz climbed the stairs to the veranda. His boots scraped against chunks of wood and broken glass scattered across the deck. "I'm glad Laura and Marta left when they did. I'd better clean up this mess before she comes home. She'll have a fit. We love sitting out here on moonlit nights."

Braun's shoulders slumped as he followed up the steps. "Not tonight. You'll have to leave it as a crime scene." He glanced over his shoulder at Cordy. He turned and leaned against the railing. His long arms folded over his chest, and he watched her every move. That crooked smile blossomed once more.

"Is something going on between the two of you?" Fritz whispered. "You have a ditzy look on your face."

"I only wish." Braun swallowed. "Yeah, we were once a couple. I loved running my fingers through those silken locks. Look how her long, strawberry-blonde hair glistens in the moonlight."

"How can you tell? Her hair is piled under a cap."

"Memories, such memories…" That ditzy look stayed plastered on Braun's face. "She cut me loose last year. I have no idea why she kicked me out. It wasn't pretty. I haven't seen her since."

So Braun used to date her. That explains a lot. "Earth to Braun!" Fritz whacked him on the shoulder when he didn't move. "Where's your car? I thought it was you driving up to the house."

Braun rubbed his arm. "Someone tampered with it."

"How could you tell?" Fritz asked.

"I was in the car when the SUV crept along the drive. I thought I'd follow with my lights off, but when I turned the key, it clicked, and then there was a grinding sound. I recalled the last time I'd heard that sound and dove from the car, expecting the worst."

"Rigged for an explosion?" Fritz asked.

"I'd bet on it." Braun gave a visible shiver. "Don't know why it didn't blow, but I got the hell out of there. Then I heard shots and called 911."

Cordy ran up the steps toward the men. "I'm assigned to investigate the scene. My department will handle this case, so don't get any ideas."

"I understand that, Cordy, but you're in over your head under these circumstances." Braun stepped forward and straightened to his full height. Cordy barely came up to his armpits. "We have a major case probably involving the mafia. You'll need to work with the feds on this one, and they're working with Chief Jackson."

"Yes, I figured as much, Braun, and don't ever assume anything is over my head. It'll only get you into more trouble." Cordy stepped to the front door, faced the men, and made it perfectly clear that she took point for tonight. "I'll gladly work with the chief, but for now, **I'm** in charge. I'll talk to the feds first thing in the morning. Give me the facts. What just happened here?"

"Come inside." Fritz opened the front door. One look at Braun's scowl, he added, "I have a feeling it's going to be a long night."

Cordy nodded. "Count on it. I want to know everything. If what I learned from Dad's files is accurate, this is just the beginning."

NIGHT VISITOR

Tuesday, June 10 – 0410 MDT, Loveland, Colorado

Officer Joshtine Cordelia's world was one of long hours filled with split-second decisions. Often, they led to unforeseen consequences and created new challenges, yet she loved her job, even with its frantic schedule. Wrestling street thugs or arresting drug dealers was nowhere near as tough as fighting her worst nightmare. Having the mafia back on her turf threw her into a fitful sleep. Or maybe it was meeting Braun again.

She shook her head to focus. The underworld syndicate had attacked once and missed its mark. She knew they'd be back, but that wasn't her greatest worry. Braun was back in her life. It had taken months to forget him if she had ever succeeded in doing that. What could she do about it? Oh, she'd think of something. She always did, but… She blew out an exasperated breath. *What time is it anyway?*

Checking the digital clock at the head of her bed, the display blinked 12:00. *The electricity must have gone out sometime during the night.*

Cordy flipped on the light and glanced at her watch. *Ten minutes past four. I can't sleep, so there's no reason to linger in bed.* She went downstairs to the kitchen, ground some java beans, and brewed coffee.

A long, hot shower was what she needed. Usually, her mind cleared as the water washed over her body, but not today. The water turned cold—still no answers. After shutting off the faucet, she noticed her home phone ringing from downstairs. She stepped out of the shower and wrapped a towel around her.

The message went to voice mail before she could answer. "Cordy, it's Braun. Stay out of the line of fire, and let me handle this. Fritz is giving a live TV interview this morning, and all hell could break loose. Now would be a good time to take a vacation."

"Vacation? Yeah, right!" Her blood boiled at Braun telling her what to do—*again. And how did he find my new unlisted home phone number?* She thought she'd gotten over the man, but his memory lingered. Seeing him last night had nearly brought her to her knees. After slipping on her fleece robe, she sprinted downstairs for a hot cup.

At the bottom of the stairs, she remembered how he would catch her for a morning hug with coffee in hand. He knew just how she liked it, hot like his melting kisses. She savored the flavor. Her coffee needed no sugar, just enough cream. How she wished—*No! Stop it!*

She searched the cupboard for her favorite mug. It was white with two red hearts woven together. She realized Braun had given it to her on Valentine's Day. Why had she kept it? The cup was nowhere in sight, so she grabbed another and filled it. After adding a splash of milk, she returned the carton to the fridge.

It was too early for the morning news, so she picked up her tablet to hear the latest updates and headed for the dining room. The navy blue drapes were closed except for a small crack letting in filtered light from her outside floods. *I could have sworn I shut them off before going to bed.*

Her L-shaped desk had a flat screen on each end. The desktop computer on the right was turned off. The laptop on her left had a screensaver of fish swimming along a reef. *I know I shut down both computers.* Cordy scanned the desk. Nothing seemed out of place, but her gut knew better. She touched the corner of the laptop cover to shut it down, then paused and glanced around the room.

The Valentine's cup sat upside down on the dining table. *How did it get there?* She dropped the tablet onto the chair, set down her coffee mug, and returned to the kitchen for a pair of tongs.

She used them to lift the cup. A gasp escaped her lips. Under it was a pink heart-shaped sticky stabbed to the table with a steak knife. Not just any knife—it was her steak knife. The one with the ivory handle—the gold letters JC etched on it, for Joshtine Cordelia. Her parents made her their namesake, Josh, after her father, and tine, after her mother, Christine.

Cordy didn't touch the knife but lifted the edge of the paper using the tips of her fingers. In bold letters, the note read, "Have heart. You're next."

She got her gun and then paused, knowing she would be called to the scene if this happened to anyone else. *What would I do? What should I do?* Her fingers shook as she dialed the first person who came to mind—Braun.

It rang once, and then she disconnected. *That was dumb. Why call him, of all people? Besides, he's leaving for the TV station soon. At least he won't recognize my new cell number.*

Who did this? Midget? Vinny? Are they anything like Frank? Flashes of four years ago tore through her like a knife cutting out her soul. Intermittent images of Frieda left unconscious and barely breathing— lying nude on the cement floor and assumed dead. These alternated with scenes of a monster, the burly thug responsible for Frieda's raped and battered body—Frank Corenelli—the same Frank, who had captured Cordy during a failed FBI stakeout. He stood in the shadows, towering over her—fists ready for another punch. Anger flared, and she had fought hard until something slammed against the back of her head. She woke up shackled to the floor next to Frieda.

Those images were so crystal clear it was as if the attack had happened yesterday. Frank vowed to do the same to Cordy if she didn't tell him where Fritz was hiding. Frank hit Cordy again during one of his torture sessions—knocking her out for three days. When she came to, she was in ICU. Her father, Braun, and Fritz had rescued her, but Braun suffered a busted ankle and Fritz a gunshot wound to the shoulder. He had a collapsed lung and lay in an ICU bed next door. Frank didn't survive to go to trial.

Cordy's legs wobbled at the thought. She couldn't go there. The pain was too raw. *Think! What am I missing?* Instinct took over as she checked the windows and doors. Her security system was still on, so her unwelcome visitors must have stopped by when the electricity went off. *Or did they cut the power to gain access? When was that? Why didn't they go upstairs? I would have been at their mercy—maybe this is just a warning, but someone invaded my home.*

She ran back upstairs and threw on some clothes. Her fingers shook so much that it took three attempts to call Loveland's Chief of Police and the crime scene investigators. Within minutes, her quiet home was reinvaded, but this time by officers, and she had called the shots. Feeling more in control, her gut twisted. The mafia would be back soon—she knew it.

A DATE WITH THE WORLD

Tuesday, June 10 – 0445 MDT, Loveland, Colorado

After a sleepless night, Fritz Von Schlegen felt tired and wired so tight that all his senses were on hyper-alert. He was worried about his family's safety and frustrated that he had no control over his life.

Knowing he was the bait to lure Vinny, Fritz checked in at the TV studio's main desk, received a pass, and swiped the card through a reader. The door clicked.

His annoying partner followed behind. Braun had helped rehearse the speech at least ten times over the past three hours, making sure Fritz had memorized the little speech to be delivered over the early morning news.

Fritz opened the door and asked, "What's it like going on national TV?"

Braun smiled and followed him through the door. "How should I know? I'm just a peon here."

Fritz tugged at the collar of his dark blue shirt. "It's hot in here." The Kevlar vest beneath his shirt only made it worse.

"Tell me about it." SWAT Commander Russ Bracken, dressed in full body armor, complete with an assault rifle slung over his shoulder, stood guard at the newsroom door.

"The chief called in SWAT, really?" Fritz asked. "I thought you were exaggerating, just to get my attention."

"I told you, we're serious about Vinny. Chief has called in every favor ever owed him. Sharpshooters are in position throughout the building." Braun's cell phone rang once. He pulled it out of his pocket, but whoever called had hung up.

"Who's calling you at this hour?" Fritz asked.

Braun checked the caller ID. "Must be a wrong number."

Fritz felt his heart trip. *Could it be Vinny?* "Why do I have to do this live?" Sweat dripped down his spine. "I hate being a show pony with a target on my back. He's going to hear about this and go nuts."

"That's the point," Braun said. "Vinny will pay for ears to listen for leaks about you, but he won't strike here."

"Yeah, right," Fritz scoffed. "Like last night?"

Braun's lips pursed, and his eyes narrowed. "I mean it, Fritz. He won't dare attack. Not when he sees how well protected the place is."

Fritz shook his head. "That's what you said last night, and Midget still wormed his way in for an attack."

"We weren't prepared then, but we are now," Braun assured him.

"Will we ever be prepared for Vinny? He's always one step ahead of us. I have to admit, he's smarter than I remembered and meaner than a rattlesnake."

Braun shrugged. "Give your message as we rehearsed it. Remember to gaze into the camera as if you're talking directly to Vinny. We expect results. Perhaps not immediately, but this will get his goat."

"Vinny is far from a goat, and I hate being the red flannel shirt used as bait to get his center of attention. He's more like a vampire who wants my blood." Fritz felt a buzz like an annoying insect nibbling his nerve endings. It started with his fingers and toes and then clawed at his insides. "Let's just tape this and get out of here."

Braun tried one more ploy to reassure him. "We have a chopper on top of the building waiting for your escape if needed."

"A chopper—on the roof, as if I could race up five flights of stairs in time to reach it," Fritz muttered as he paced, a habit he indulged when stressed.

"Okay, I'll talk to the station manager to record this message, but it will be released at the top of the hour." Braun went in search of the person in charge.

The news reporter glanced up. The shoulders of his dark blue, Italian-made suit had a snappy, straight line over his shoulders. The pin-stripes lined up precisely at every seam with a crisp crease pressed down each sleeve. "Nervous?"

Fritz nodded.

"That's a good sign. It'll add tension to your message. People will take notice."

"Yeah, they'll take notice, all right. All I have to do is say my lines." Fritz closed his eyes and rubbed his forehead. Braun and Chief Jackson's lines were so carefully written to create a response. *It's all bullshit. It won't get the results I need. I want this over with once and for all.* "Then all hell could break loose."

The reporter didn't seem to notice the comment and attached a mic to Fritz's collar. He tugged at the suit lapels to make sure they were even, tucked a corner of the shirt inside the coat, and smoothed down the jacket pocket. "I guess you're presentable."

Fritz glanced down at his shoes. They were a bit scuffed. "It'll have to do."

The reporter placed a finger on his earbud and nodded. "I got word we plan to tape this instead of going live. It'll only take a moment to make a few adjustments. Then, you're out of here. You don't want these guys to find you, right?"

Braun returned and laid a hand on Fritz's shoulder. "It's taken care of."

Fritz jumped like a scared rabbit. "Vinny moves like a locomotive—once steamed up, he won't stop."

The cameraman motioned to Braun. "What if they attack after your protection leaves the building? Are we in danger?"

"We'll have extra security assigned for the rest of the day after we leave." Braun motioned to a corner away from the camera. "I'll watch from over there."

Fritz imagined how it felt to spit in the devil's eye and hoped he'd live long enough to tell about it. Slightly winded, he turned to the camera and blew out a deep breath.

The director raised his arms. "Bring up the lights."

The bright overhead spot bulbs illuminated Fritz. He squinted.

Braun watched outside the studio next to the window. He grinned as if he sat in a box seat of a grand theater, waiting for the greatest show of his life.

The floor director caught Fritz's attention. "You're on in three, two…" he held up one finger and then pointed, indicating they were recording.

The reporter seated next to Fritz introduced himself. "Let's get straight to the issue. Vinny Corenelli was released from the Texas Federal Penitentiary a week ago. You were the undercover FBI agent who put him behind bars. How do you feel about his early release? Be as direct as possible."

Fritz leaned forward and glared into the camera. "He should have served the full forty years of his sentence. Vinny started stealing by the age of five. He hijacked vehicles, ran an auto chop shop in his early teens, and then managed several gambling houses before his twenties. By twenty-one, he was in line to head the Corenelli crime family, killed his rivals, and was responsible for some of the largest jewel heists in US history."

The reporter leaned closer. "What would you like to say to Vinny?"

"Listen up." His thoughts turned to Diane. All fear turned to hatred. "Last night, members of the Corenelli gang attacked my home. Vinny, you may have done your time for that jewel heist, but I have a list of deeds you haven't paid for. This one is personal. You would have murdered my wife and the rest of my family. Fortunately, I survived to hunt you down as you planned to hunt me."

Out of the corner of his eye, Fritz saw Braun pop out of his seat, shaking his head. Fritz knew this message wasn't what they'd rehearsed, but it didn't matter.

The camera panned closer.

Fritz glared into the lens. "After twenty-five years, I'm still your worst nightmare. You thought you'd scare me off by having your boys kill my daughter. Well, you're wrong. I'm on your case, and I'm bringing you down. Nothing will stop me. Long story made short. Your days are numbered."

"Think of Diane. I want you to remember this name. Of all the murders you're responsible for, this will be your downfall. Wherever you are, wherever you go, look over your shoulder cuz I'll be in the shadows. Now you know why."

Fritz sat up straight, raised his index finger at the camera like a pistol, and slowly moved it to dead center. "Bam." He jerked his finger, blew on the tip, and slid it to his side as if he'd just holstered a gun. "You fine people out there will soon be rid of this scumbag. Trust me. This is Private Detective Fritz Von Schlegen. A man with a mission."

The director slashed a finger across his throat, signaling the interview was over. His flushed face glistened with sweat beaded across his forehead. When the cameraman stood frozen in place, the director called, "Cut!"

The cameraman flinched, and the red light of the camera disappeared.

* * *

Braun stormed through the studio doors. "Holy shit, Fritz. What have you done? You had a script. Why didn't you follow it? Rerecord—"

The director struck the desk with his fist. "My God, what happened? That went out live. We have to retract the statement."

Braun turned to the director. "That was live? You said you were recording the message."

"Boss said it had to go out live," the director swore and picked up the phone. "Get me the station manager!"

Fritz got up and strode across the room. "I'm out of here."

"Fritz—" The door slammed before he could finish. Braun turned to go after him when the director grabbed his arm. Braun's jaw clenched.

"What the hell am I supposed to do now?" Sweat dripped down his cheek. "Get that SOB back in here. I'm not going to lose my job over this."

"We can't stuff it back into the bottle." Braun stared into the still-lit room. "What's spilled can't be mopped up with a few words."

The station manager burst through the door. "The phones are ringing off the hook. We haven't had this much action since we miscalled the next president of the United States. Well done."

Braun scurried out of the studio after Fritz. "You just challenged an entire mafia family to a showdown!"

Fritz kept walking, nearly colliding with a guard who stepped into the hallway.

Braun grabbed Fritz's shoulder and spun him around. "Are you crazy?"

Fritz had the gall to smile. "I'm fine, but thanks for asking."

That calm attitude sparked Braun into apoplexy. His breath came out in short pants, and he clutched his hands into fists to restrain himself from slugging his partner.

"I made a mistake and let Diane get in the way of Vinny's revenge. Vinny was still in the PEN then, but I'm sure his boys are behind her death…" Fritz started, then heaved a sigh. "I'm not letting anyone near Laura and Marta."

Braun swallowed and then ran his hand over his brow. "You didn't follow the script."

Fritz's eyes narrowed. "No shit, I didn't follow that stupid canned speech! Once I got in front of the camera, that script got lost in my head."

Braun said, "That's why we rehearsed—"

"I should never have called you when Frank kidnapped my sister, but I did. Vinny's brothers knew I would do anything to rescue her. Vinny could get his family to fight his battles, even while in prison."

Braun wrestled with his conscience. His cheeks burned with anger as adrenaline pumped through him.

"At the time, I couldn't think straight. Desperate to get Frieda back, I needed help from someone I could trust." Fritz held up his hands, palm out. "But this is personal." Then he pointed at Braun. "You took away my whole family. I don't even know where to find them. We end it now."

"But they're safe! You can trust the chief, and our team will make sure they stay that way." Sweat dripped from Braun's forehead as he tried to swallow his anger, nearly choking on his words.

"Fritz muttered, "Calm down before you have a coronary."

"We planned every detail," Braun spat out. "And look how you showed your gratitude. Our team trusted you to deliver a challenging message."

"What?" Fritz poked Braun in the chest. "That wasn't," another poke, "challenging enough for you?" His finger stabbed once again, hitting Braun's sternum.

The guard backed away as the tension between the two men built.

Braun grabbed Fritz's finger and pulled him into a private room. "You asshole. You went rogue and put everyone's life in danger. That's not what we bargained for."

"Okay," Fritz shrugged away from Braun. "I'm on my own. Fine."

"It's not that." Braun crossed his arms and held them tight to his chest, as if not wanting to be poked again. "I want vengeance, too, but it would have been nice to have a choice of how and when we hit."

"That's rich coming from you. When did you ever give me a choice? You yanked my family from me in the middle of the night. Not knowing one's fate is the worst. Now you know how it feels."

Braun was ready to explode, but he couldn't afford to. "We'll talk more later—the clock's ticking. Let's get out of here. We may not have much longer to live."

HIDEAWAY

Tuesday, June 10 – 0700 EDT, Lewisburg, West Virginia

Laura never dreamed she would be ripped away from her husband's arms, and whisked away with her granddaughter, Marta, on a private jet headed for God only knows where—all under the guise of safety. She'd never felt so afraid and alone, yet she had to remain calm for Marta's sake. The little girl had been through enough, losing her parents, being uprooted from her country home, and settling into a new routine at the candy factory.

It was seven in the morning when the private jet landed near a small town in West Virginia. Laura and Marta climbed from the plane.

A blond-haired man dressed in a blue pinstripe suit appeared. He towered over Laura and reached his paw for her hand. "Morning, ma'am. I'm Special Agent Usher Hastings. You must be Fritz's wife. I'm glad to meet you, Mrs. Von Schlegen."

Laura gently pushed Marta behind her. The name had briefly thrown her. "So that's his last name. Do you have any ID?"

Usher held his palms face out. "Of course." He plucked out his ID with two fingers and placed it in her outstretched hand. "It's legit."

Laura's cheeks heated. "Sorry. I'm a little spooked at the moment." She handed the ID back and shook his hand. "I'm Laura Konig, and I've been married to Lars for 24 years." Gnawing her lip, she lowered her voice to a whisper.

Marta placed her fingers over her mouth and stretched her neck to see him. "You're taller than Mr. Brown." She stepped back but never dropped her gaze. "Your eyes are gray and have that same twinkle, too."

"You must be Marta." Usher knelt beside her. He pulled a Snickers Bar from his pocket. With a wink, he opened his fist. "Hope your grandma doesn't mind. Don't spoil your breakfast."

Marta smiled and pocketed the gift. "I ate breakfast on the plane. Right, Gramma?"

"Just this once," Laura warned.

"Chocolate is 'portent to our family. Gramma loves to 'speriment. She makes new candy for our store."

Usher cleared his throat. "Tell me, who's Mr. Brown?"

"That would be Lars', I mean Fritz's ex-partner," Laura said. "His real name is Braun, but you already know that, don't you?"

The special agent let out a chuckle. "I've never heard him called Brown before." He stood and nodded for the attendant to load the luggage into his black SUV.

"You must be related to him," Laura said. "I can see the resemblance."

"You're observant. I'm his older brother. Braun refused to let just anyone take this assignment. He wanted someone he could trust, so here I am. We'll protect you and Marta." He opened the back door. "I'll take you to the hideaway. You'll love the mansion and Maggie. She's the owner, caretaker, and a retired FBI agent. She'll keep you safe."

"What's an FBI agent?" Marta asked.

"It's like being a cop," Usher said.

"Oh. I've seen cops on TV." Marta studied the back seat of the car before climbing inside. "This car looks safe. Feel the soft seats. Gramps would say they feel smooth as our buttercreams, but they won't melt in your mouth." She giggled and scooted over to allow Laura to slide in next to her.

The mention of Gramps left Laura with a twinge of worry, but she smiled and kept her feelings hidden.

Usher climbed behind the wheel. "I know the cushions seem at odds with the armored exterior. Dark-tinted windows, shatterproof glass, and bulletproof tires make this car one of the safest in the nation."

The radio played in the background. Someone was saying, "… I'm still your worst nightmare."

Laura recognized the man's voice over the speaker. "That's Lars. Turn up the volume."

Usher cranked the radio up. "Nothing will stop me. I'm bringing you down. Long story made short. Your days are numbered."

Laura gasped. "What is he doing? At this rate, he'll be dead by the end of the day."

"Not if I have anything to say about it." Usher drove forward.

Marta placed her hand over Laura's closed fists. "Gramma, what's wrong? You're crying. Is it because of the bad man?"

Usher flipped off the radio and handed Laura a tissue. "It gets dusty back there. Let's get you to the mansion. I have some work to do."

Laura took the tissue, wiped her face with one hand, and wrapped her other arm around Marta. "I'm fine. I miss your Gramps, but we'll plan to talk to him tonight."

Marta scooted closer and patted her Gramma's hand. "And I'll draw him a picture."

PATCH WORK

Tuesday, June 10 – 0705 MDT, Fort Collins, Colorado

It had been a rough night for Midget Corenelli. The attack on Fritz had failed miserably. Raw pain was all that kept him alive. His arm throbbed, his muscles ached, and his brain was fuzzy as cotton. He didn't know how long he'd been passed out in the woods. Somehow, he managed to drag himself to the roadside and hitch a ride, but it was a miracle that he'd gotten here.

He blew out a deep breath and tried to climb up the steps to Doc's front door. That first step reached nearly to the kneecap of his stubby legs, so he pulled himself up by using his right arm to claw the railing and inched himself forward while his left arm dangled at his side. Blood dripped down his arm and off his elbow onto the porch. "Doc, open up!"

No one answered, so he leaned against the door kicking and shouting, "Doc! It's me. Open this damn door."

The porch light flicked on, and the deadbolt clicked. Doc pulled open the heavy wooden door and stood inside the screen. He was still in his PJs. "What happened to you? Vinny's gonna have a fit."

"Just patch me up." Midget moved aside as Doc pushed open the screen door. "This burns like the fires of hell. Got any painkillers?"

"I'll see what I can do." Doc's slippered feet padded his way to the exam room.

Forty minutes later, Midget slid off the exam table with a fresh bandage over a shoulder wound and his left arm in a sling. "Thanks, Doc." He moved into the lounge and climbed into a recliner. "Those painkillers are the best. I feel like I'm floating. Think I can be of any use to Vinny? After all, he broke me out to hunt."

"Take those magic pills, smoke some weed, and you'll be fine." Doc cleaned up his temporary treatment room.

Midget grimaced. "Yeah, but I missed my mark."

"We'll get him." Doc's cell phone snagged his attention. He answered and walked into the hall. "Vinny. Good to hear from you. The boys are anxious. They want their orders."

Midget made himself at home and flipped on the TV. Fritz came into view. "Hey, Doc! Listen to this." He turned up the volume. "Nothing will stop me. I'm bringing you down."

Doc's eyes bugged out as he stood in the doorway. "Vin. You near a TV? No? Then listen, Fritz is on the air." He held his phone closer to the TV. "Long story made short. Your days are numbered."

Midget scratched the stubble covering his chin. "That guy's got chutzpah."

"Or a death wish." Doc pocketed his phone after the interview was over. "Vinny says there's a change in plans. He'll be here in an hour. Are you up for another round with Braun and Fritz?"

"Got any crack?" Midget asked. "I'll be ready by then."

LETTER OF DARKNESS

Tuesday, June 10 – 0938 EDT, Lewisburg, West Virginia

Laura leaned forward and peered through the darkened car window. A flicker of fear combined with anxiety rushed through her. They drove around high concrete walls topped with razor wire surrounding a compound. From this view, it looked more like a prison than a safe house.

FBI's Special Agent Usher drove to a double set of steel gates. A security camera pointed down from above the left side of the entrance, and the gate swung open. A German shepherd walked into view with its head held high, sniffing the air, and then stood motionless as a security guard exited behind him. His alert eyes scanned the area before heading toward the car.

Marta's jaw dropped in wonder. "Gramma, that man has a dog. Isn't it beautiful? And look at all the trees."

Usher lowered the car window. "Morning, Jake. As we discussed, I'm here with a special package."

The armed guard saluted. "Sorry, I can't let you inside until I check out the car and trunk. You know the rules."

"Absolutely." Usher pulled a badge and electronic card from his shirt pocket for inspection, popped the rear hatch, and turned toward Marta, "Do you like dogs?"

"Oh, yes," Marta scooted toward the window. "Can I pet it?"

Usher smiled. "Jake will introduce you shortly. First, he needs to clear the car."

Jake snapped his fingers twice, and the dog walked around to the rear of the SUV. The guard lifted the trunk lid, and the dog sniffed the luggage. "Clear." Jake closed the trunk and opened the front passenger door. He snapped his fingers twice again. "Pepper, search."

The dog placed its front legs over the passenger's door ledge, sniffed the floor, the dashboard, and poked his nose over the middle gearshift. Jake held the dog's leash. "All clear." The dog backed out of the car, and they walked around to Marta's door.

Jake asked, "Would you like to meet Pepper?"

"Uh-huh." Marta moved closer to Laura. "Can I pet him?"

"Let's introduce you first." Jake said, "Pepper, break. Now hold out your hand and let him sniff your palm like this."

"He's so big!" Marta hesitated but slowly moved her fingers closer.

Jake loosened the leash. "Here, boy." Pepper lifted two paws over the rear seat's ledge. The German shepherd craned his long neck to nudge the little girl. He sniffed Marta's outstretched palm and then licked her hand.

Marta giggled and ran her fingers through the black and brown fur around the dog's collar. "You're a good dog."

Pepper moved to sniff Laura and her purse, pausing at Marta's pocket, which held the Snicker's Bar. He sat with his head in Marta's lap.

Marta scratched Pepper's ears. "He's so soft." She glanced at her Gramma. "I always wanted a puppy."

"Don't get any ideas." Laura smiled, but she wasn't ready to commit to getting an animal anytime soon.

"You'll see a lot of Pepper while you're here, but we have to get back to work." Jake snapped his fingers, and Pepper hopped from the car. They walked back to the gate and motioned to Usher. "All clear. Maggie's waiting."

Usher nodded, drove along a driveway lined with oak trees, and parked in front of a white arbor. "This is your new home."

Laura sighed. *Home? No. Her home was with Lars.* A gentle breeze wafted the earthy aroma through her senses. It did remind Laura of the old farmhouse where she grew up. The thought comforted her soul.

Usher climbed from the driver's seat and opened the back car door.

Marta slid from her seat. "Look at all the pretty red and pink roses, Gramma. I can even smell them from here."

Laura stepped from the car, shielding her eyes from the sunlight. "Yes, they're beautiful, but where's the house?"

Usher unloaded the bags. "Follow the walkway. You'll see the mansion hidden behind a group of maples."

Marta bounded forward and stopped to check out another patch of flowers. "Look at the pansies. They're yellow and purple. Momma's favorite."

Marveling at the colorful flowers that lined the sidewalk, Laura felt relief flow through her. This would be a safe place for Marta—fenced-in, and the yard was inviting. As they rounded the trees, the front steps of a wide veranda came into view.

The oak front door had an oval window with etched stained-glass red roses and green leaves. To the left of the door was a large bay window where an open laptop computer sat on a wicker table. A steaming cup of brew sat next to a silver coffee pot. Someone had been at work recently.

The door opened, and a dainty woman with a sassy flip of wild red curls emerged. A confident hand reached out and clasped Laura's palm. Her emerald-green T-shirt read, "Invisible to all but the blind." Pink polished toenails peeked from her leather sandals as she knelt beside Marta. "Welcome. I'm Maggie. My house is your home for as long as you need."

Marta's smile blossomed. "You're pretty."

"Thank you. What a nice compliment, coming from such a sweet sprite."

Marta blushed. "She called me Sprite, just like Momma." She turned toward Usher, who walked behind carrying their luggage. "Are you sure she was a cop?"

"Don't let her size fool you. She could throw me to the ground in a blink of an eye." Usher entered the house. "Where should I put these bags?"

"The Lavender Suites. They're at the southeast corner on the third floor." Maggie turned to Laura. "It's my favorite wing, and we don't have anyone else staying here now." She motioned for everyone to follow. "Sorry, we don't have an elevator. It wasn't a priority in 1878, when Great-Great-Gramps built the place. We did spring for a little luxury last year and added air conditioning. There's WiFi throughout the house, but all messages go through me."

Usher took the luggage upstairs while Maggie showed Laura and Marta around the first floor. "These rooms are open for your use. My rooms are private and are on the second level, but you're welcome to use the library and the poolroom."

When they got to the kitchen, Laura was in awe. "This is wonderful. I love to cook. Well, it's more like an experiment. I make candies for our factory and create a new recipe every few weeks." She ran her hand along the milky ceramic tiled countertop. A set of Oriental blue and white porcelain canisters in increasing sizes sat beside the four-slice silver toaster.

"Feel free to whip up whatever you want," Maggie said. "Cooking isn't my forte, but I do my best. Help is always welcome."

They stepped to the back door. Pepper lay on the deck, sunning himself.

Marta ran to the screen. "Oh, can I play with Pepper? I met him earlier, but he had to go to work. Is he on his lunch break? We get lunch breaks at the candy factory."

Maggie opened the door and called, "Here, boy." The dog got up and lumbered toward them. "Sit."

Pepper sat next to Marta, who held out her hand. Pepper sniffed her palm and licked it. Marta asked, "Will he obey me, too?"

"Yes, I'll teach you the commands." Maggie motioned for Laura to step over to the dog. "He's well trained."

Laura knelt beside the shepherd. "Hello, Pepper. Marta's always wanted a dog."

"Lie down." Marta clapped her hands when Pepper dropped to his belly. "Good boy." She petted the dog.

Maggie stood and went back into the kitchen. Laura followed. "Marta, what do you like to do?"

The girl patted Pepper again and went inside. "I like to draw. Momma's an artist. She's teaching me to paint."

Maggie paused, glanced over to Laura, and nodded at the girl. "Wonderful. I have the perfect place for you to work."

"Goodie." Marta beamed. "Can you show me now?"

"Okay," Maggie said. "Let's see if Usher has found your suite yet."

"I'll find him." Marta ran out of the kitchen and up the steps where she had seen Usher go with the bags.

The women followed her into the hallway. Laura pulled Maggie aside. "I think you should know that Marta's mom died two weeks ago. It's been hard on all of us, but she hasn't quite grasped that her mother isn't coming back. She talks to her as an imaginary friend, so don't be surprised—"

Marta leaned over the spiral staircase railing and called down from the top landing. "Are you coming, Gramma? You have to see this place. I have a room of my own with tables and chairs, just like at home. Only these are white instead of red."

"I'm on my way," Laura said as she darted after their hostess, who took the steps two at a time.

They met Usher on the landing. "I showed Marta to her room, and she was already unpacking. I think she likes the playroom. She calls it her studio and says she's going to paint a picture for her Gramps. Laura's rooms are across the hall."

Inside the suite, the sun shone through a set of French doors that led to a balcony. Laura's bedroom was to the left, a master bath to the right, and a spacious sitting room between. "This is lovely. Thank you for letting us stay with you."

Usher motioned to Maggie. "I need a word. Then I have to leave."

"Go ahead." Laura followed them into the hall. "We're fine. I'll unpack and meet you downstairs. Thanks for the ride, Usher. It was nice meeting you."

"If you need anything, let Maggie know. We'll make arrangements to get whatever you need." Usher headed down the stairs.

Maggie followed. "We'll have a cup of coffee on the patio and chat."

Laura returned to her suite to unpack her bags when Marta burst into the room. "Gramma, come quick. Momma left me a note on the table, but I can't take it out of my room."

"It can't be from your Momma," Laura said. "And why can't you bring it here?"

"Uh-huh," Marta insisted. "I know it's from her. It has pretty hearts and a kiss in the corner, just like always."

Laura darted to the doorway and scanned the stairway to see if anyone else heard Marta's remarks. She blew out a deep breath. "You can't keep talking about your momma as if you can see her."

Marta grabbed Laura's hand. "Come on. I'll show you." She pulled Gramma to the studio across the hall. "See the paper on the table? It has letters on it, but I can't read them. When I pick it up, the letters go away."

Laura saw the print disappear as soon as Marta lifted the note from the table. "You're right. Put it back. I want to see what it says."

Marta laid the paper back on the table, and soon black letters formed. "What did Momma say?"

Laura sat on a little white chair and leaned forward to look closer. She recognized the airy, open flow of her daughter's writing—the flat-topped R's, the well-rounded M's and N's, and a heart-shaped dot above the I's.

"Read it to me," Marta begged.

Tears threatened to spill as Laura cleared her throat. *How did this letter get here?* Laura read in silence, but Marta insisted she read it aloud. "I sit under the tree of Paradise and watch over you day and night. You always play in the light. Then yesterday, everything turned gray. I sensed danger, but I didn't know what it was. Colors kept getting darker until I couldn't see you anymore. I knew I had to leave Paradise and come to Earth to warn you, but I can't stay. I can only paint with you as I learn the dangers. Do you have your acrylics? We'll start with black."

"Why black?" Marta ran to her bag and opened it. "Oh, no, Mr. Brown didn't pack my 'crylics."

"Wait, there's more to the message," Laura said.

"Black comes in many shades and textures—black night, smoke, and black silk. It's when there's no pure light. I'm here to add color. Gramp's life depends on it."

Laura frowned.

"Is that all that Momma wrote?" Marta asked.

Laura picked up the note to turn it over. The paper went blank. She quickly placed the note on the table as she'd found it, but the page remained blank. "I shouldn't have touched it. I better write this down before I forget."

"I need 'crylic paint." Marta bolted down the stairs. "Maggie…"

"No, wait!" Laura dashed after her, but Marta was already talking to Maggie and Usher.

THIS MEANS WAR

Wednesday, June 11 – 0645 MDT, Fort Collins, Colorado

"Two can play this game." Vinny leaned over the kitchen table and crushed out a cigarette, thinking he'd snuff out Fritz the same way. A well-deserved death sentence after all Vinny had endured. The blasted trial stole his status among the family, giving everything he worked for to his archrival and slimy, sleazy, scuzzball cousin, Joey A. While Vinny rotted in prison, Fritz had knocked off three more brothers. Frank's death still ate at him. If he were still alive, Frank would have been the boss. It would have been a cakewalk to take over from him. Vinny shoved the ashtray aside and added a few spoonfuls of sugar to his coffee.

"Keep that smoke away from me." Jules removed the ashtray from the table.

"You bleached your hair," Doc said. "You're as blond as Fritz. You always were the master of disguises."

"Yeah. My photo was blasted all over the media. Even Little Suzie Cupcake from across the street could recognize me just getting the morning paper from the driveway. I'll need a nose job and a few tucks by the end of the week."

"No problem. I can make any changes you need, but there'll be bruises for several weeks. You'll need makeup. Let me show you some of my rubber and plastic masks. I can even make you into your 95-year-old granny." Doc leaned closer. "What's the plan?"

"Fritz wants to take down our family, so I'm going after his— every last one of them."

Doc flashed a smile. "Do you know where they stashed his wife and kid?"

Jules' eyes darted between Vinny and Doc. "You're not going to hurt them, are you?"

Vinny gulped his brew and rolled his eyes. Ignoring Jules, Vinny nodded toward Midget, who lay on the couch, smoking weed. "He gonna be any use to us?"

Doc shrugged his shoulders. "Let him rest a day or two. He still has his shooting arm—he's always been a crack shot."

Vinny gritted his teeth. "Why'd he take the chance? I never asked him to."

"You won't hurt the kid, will you?" Jules asked again and fidgeted with the handle of his cup.

"Quit bugging me." Vinny heard the bitterness in his own voice.

"Count me out!" Jules slammed his cup onto the table. Good thing it was metal, or it would have shattered with the force.

"Don't you worry," Vinny said. "I don't expect you to pack a gun. I have other plans."

"Like what?" Jules asked.

Vinny was tired of his kid brother's attitude. "Change into some real clothes. I'm sick of seeing that blasted clerical collar."

Jules protested, "I don't own anything but these robes. You whisked me away from the center without packing."

Doc got up from the table. "Come with me, son. I'll deck you out in the latest fashion."

"Dress him in all black. At least he'll look like a man." Vinny's smile blossomed as he watched Jules reach for the collar and carefully remove it. He trailed behind Doc like a lost puppy. "And burn that thing while you're at it."

Jules turned around. "No. It might come in handy. You'll see. It got us out of trouble once already."

"Yeah, keep the collar." Vinny reached across the table and popped the last chocolate from the box into his mouth. "Maybe you could visit a few of my prison pals. They'd get a kick out of seeing my baby brother. Father Corenelli has a nice ring to it."

A few minutes later, Jules reappeared dressed in tight black Levi's, a T-shirt, and a pair of dark Reeboks.

"I have a black leather jacket to top it off." Doc pulled it from the hall closet. "What do you think of our young buck now?"

"Handsome," Midget spouted with a crooked grin on his face. "All he needs is a pair of aviators. Get the cool reflective kind."

Jules squirmed under the scrutiny of his brothers. "I thought you said I'd meet the rest of the family. Where are Walt and Mick?"

"They're in Michigan," Vinny said. "We should hear from them in the next twenty-four hours. Now, where are the rest of the boys, Doc?"

NOT AGAIN

Wednesday, June 11 – 0715 CDT, Ann Arbor, Michigan

Risa Grant closed her eyes and blew out a sigh. She regretted being the OR nurse on call. As usual, the University of Michigan Hospital was understaffed. It normally didn't bother her, but after sixteen hours, she couldn't wait to get home to a hot shower and soft bed. She was glad to see Vicky, the charge nurse for the day shift, arrive. All she had left to do was the narcotic count, a handoff between each shift to double-check that all narc doses were documented and accounted for before Risa could go off duty. The count was accurate, and she trudged to the locker room.

Her supervisor clocked in for the day. "Looks like you're off in time for the morning rush-hour traffic. Anything to report?"

"Morning, Sheila. We just finished in Trauma 2," Risa said. "Head injury—epidural bleed from a motorcycle accident. The kid is in recovery and scheduled for neuro ICU. Get an update from Frieda," she paused at the sound of her original birth name, Frieda. Four years with the new name of Risa didn't erase the oddity of calling someone else Frieda. "She's in PACU today. The kid should be in recovery for another half-hour."

Sheila wrapped a stethoscope around her neck and straightened her name badge. "Thanks, I'll do that."

Risa went straight to her locker, not waiting around for the morning gossip. It had been a long night, but it went by quickly with all the critical surgical cases. She ran through a mental checklist to be sure she hadn't forgotten anything vital as she pulled off her scrub cap and scooped her platinum curls into a ponytail. She was on her feet all night long. The new dictation system was a blessing in disguise, at least, for the penny-pinchers, who no longer paid overtime for charting nurses' notes. Risa could document patient treatments and outcomes as she worked.

Those few minutes taken to chart used to give her time to get off her feet. A pain shot up Risa's legs as she knelt to get her clothes from the locker, and it traveled all the way to her throbbing head. A growl in her stomach reminded Risa that the last decent meal she ate was breakfast—two days ago.

All this overtime so she could get two weeks off to spend with her husband when he came home from military duty overseas. They planned to take a honeymoon that they never had three years ago. She had planned to go away for a while, but Jim only wanted to stay home. She couldn't blame him. After all he'd been through—military life couldn't end soon enough for either of them.

It didn't take long to change into a gray T-shirt, sweatpants, and green sweater. She stuffed her dirty scrubs into the laundry bag on her way out of the building. The early morning air nipped her face as she headed for her car.

"Risa. Wait up." Frieda darted out the door and waved. "You still have the narcotic keys."

"No, I don't." Risa frowned.

"You sure? It was on a green wrist coil keychain."

"I'm sure I gave them to Vicky after counting." Risa searched her pockets. "Nothing."

"She doesn't have them, and neither do I," Frieda insisted.

"Then, I guess, they'd be in my scrubs." Risa motioned back to the hospital. "I threw them into the laundry hamper in the locker room."

Frieda grabbed Risa's arm. "Let's go back and look."

Risa sighed. Turning around, she tripped on a crack in the pavement, lost her balance, and landed hard on the tarmac. Her palms and right knee stung. A car backfired as she hit the ground.

Frieda flew backward and sprawled over the top of Risa. A cascade of sticky warmth gushed across Risa's face.

Tires squealed.

"Frieda?" Risa swiped at the stickiness to see more clearly and slid from beneath the woman. Risa's right knee had ripped a hole in her sweats, and blood dripped onto the pavement. She stood next to a larger pool of red that was rapidly growing. "What happened?"

"Can't breathe," Frieda gasped. Bright red oozed between her fingers, clutching her chest.

Risa lifted Frieda's fingers and quickly covered the wound with her own hands. "Help! Help!" she cried out. Risa shifted to autopilot, yanked off her sweater, and stuffed it over the chest wound. "Hold on. I need to apply pressure." She screamed for help again.

Dr. Peter Archer dashed from his car and wove his way through a row of parked cars. He dropped to their side. "I called the emergency department. They'll be here any second. Frieda, can you hear me?"

Frieda's wide eyes glossed over. Blood soaked through the sweater. Her breathing came out in small pants.

"Stay with me," Risa said. "Frieda, take a deep breath."

"I saw everything, but who would shoot her?" Dr. Archer asked.

"Shoot her?" Adrenaline flooded through Risa. Her heart raced. "I thought a car backfired." Blood caked her hands and knees, and her mind refused to focus. She scanned the parking lot for anything out of place.

The security guard, a nurse, and the emergency department doc ran toward them with a gurney.

"Get her inside, STAT!" The emergency doc took charge and grabbed his 2-way radio. "Prep a trauma room."

Risa followed the gurney into the ED. The security guard grabbed her arm and pulled Risa aside. "I'll need a statement, and the local police are on their way. Better clean up first. I know you've had a long night. It looks like it'll be another long day, too."

An RN greeted her at the door. "We'll take you to a treatment room."

"No, I'm fine," Risa said. "Just find me a towel so I can clean up."

"I'll get some dressings." She led her to the nearest sink to wash up and then went to the supply cabinet. When she returned, the nurse cleaned and dressed Risa's hands and right leg. She placed an ACE bandage around her knee. "I still think you should lie down and get checked by—"

"I know you do, but I can't. I need to find the keys." Risa hobbled on her bum knee and paced. "Frieda wanted the narc keys. I know I handed them off to the next shift—need to check. I'll be right back."

"No. Call the OR, but we need you to stay here until the police arrive and take your statement." The nurse held out the phone, but Risa just stared at it.

Dr. Archer moved toward Risa. "You're white as chalk. Why don't you sit down?"

"I can't. Not yet." Risa clenched her fists.

"She's fretting over some narc keys." The nurse picked up the receiver and dialed a number. "Risa, I'm calling the OR and will check with PACU. You have more important things to worry about. The police will be here soon."

"Check the OR laundry hamper." Risa became frantic and darted toward the hallway. "I need my old scrubs." She paused, recalling the horror of years ago. "Oh, they're coming again. Frank's coming again. I have to leave." Turning, she weaved and nearly lost her balance as she headed for the front door.

"She's going to faint." Dr. Archer rushed to her side, and half-carried, half-dragged her to the nearest chair sitting in the entry, usually used by discharged patients who waited for their ride. The security guard also rushed to her side.

She grabbed the guard's arm and tried to stand. "Quick. I must hide." Her legs wobbled, and she nearly toppled from the chair.

The guard knelt next to her, ensuring she wouldn't fall. "Were you injured?"

"Risa, this is Dr. Archer. You're safe now. You're in the Emergency Department. Can you hear me?"

Risa cried out, "Not again." Black dots floated before her eyes. Tears ran down her cheeks.

"What?" the guard asked.

Dr. Archer guided her head between her knees. "She's in shock."

The guard turned to Archer. "Should we admit her, too?"

"No." Risa stiffened and ran a hand over her face. "It's nothing. The shot just brought back bad memories." *It couldn't have been him. Fritz killed Frank. He can't hurt me anymore.* She still had deep scars across her back as a reminder.

Dr. Archer rested a hand on Risa's shoulder. "Maybe we should admit you."

"No. I'm okay—just a little scattered at the moment."

Her supervisor burst into the room. "I just heard. Are you all right? The guard moved aside as Sheila took his place. "You're pale. What happened?"

"Someone shot Frieda." Risa gulped for air. "A drive-by shooting. Chest wound. Punctured lung, I'm sure. She's on her way to surgery. Did you find the narc keys?"

"Keys?" her supervisor asked. "I don't know. Nothing was reported to me."

"There's only one set." Risa tried to get up from the chair.

The supervisor glanced up at Archer. She mouthed, "Shock?"

Archer nodded as they stayed on either side of her. Something must have passed between the two of them.

"Calm down," her supervisor said. "There's another set in pharmacy."

"I know how important it is to hand them off between shifts. I don't have the keys," Risa said. "See. Check my pockets. Look in my purse." She flipped out her pockets to prove there were no keys and held out her purse.

The guard watched as she emptied everything from the small black leather bag. "No worries," he said. "They're checking with laundry services."

An officer entered the Emergency Department and found Risa. "Can you tell me what happened in the parking lot?"

Risa choked back her fear and repeated the story as best as she could recall. Exhausted, she asked in frustration, "Why is this happening? Who would want to kill Frieda?"

IDIOTS

Wednesday, June 11 – 0850 MDT, Fort Collins, Colorado

"Ann Arbor police are searching for two men who shot a nurse at a University of Michigan Hospital in a drive-by incident early this morning. The victim is in ICU on life support and remains in critical condition following surgery. Suspects are presumed armed and dangerous."

Vinny snapped off the news and flung the remote. "I'm dealing with idiots. Can't anyone do as I ask?" He grabbed his cell and punched in a number to his brother. The phone rang.

"Hello."

"Mick. What are you still doing in Michigan?" Vinny asked.

"The job's not done." Mick's voice cracked like it always did when he got excited.

"No shit! You got the wrong nurse," Vinny said. "Now everyone is watching their backs. If we're not careful, Joey will be on my tail. He hates chaos unless it lines his pockets!"

"Don't get mad at me," Mick said. "I was the driver. Talk to Walt."

"No." Vinny stuffed a bar of cream chocolate into his mouth. "You're the responsible one. Get me Frieda, Risa, or whatever her name is today. You know who, Fritz's sister. Then hightail it back here."

"How we gonna do that?"

"Do I have to think of everything?" Vinny barked.

"The hospital is crawling with cops," Mick whispered.

"Find another way. She doesn't live at the hospital. Just do it." Vinny disconnected. "I'm surrounded by idiots and losers."

Doc smirked. "Except for present company, that Cary Grant nose job blunted the hook. Once the swelling goes down, the women will swoon."

"Yeah, Doc. You did good."

Doc handed the phone back to Vinny. "So what if cops infest the hospital? I'm sure Ace can find out where Risa lives. Give him a call."

WAITING GAME

Irritation gnawed at Fritz as the harsh fluorescent light in their office continued its low-pitched drone. He sat across from his partner's metal desk, making a list of Vinny's potential hits, when his sister Frieda popped into his mind. No, her name was now Risa, and he had no clue where to find her. "You have access to the Marshals overseeing the Witness Security Program, right?"

A frown etched deep across Braun's brow as he stared at his computer screen. His eyes didn't even blink. He seemed in the zone.

Fritz rapped his knuckles on the desk. "It's been twenty-four hours since the newscast and nothing's happened. What's Vinny waiting for?"

Braun chewed on his lip. "I have some bad news. I think Vinny's men visited Cordy."

"Why do you say that?" Fritz leaned over the desk and turned his partner's laptop in his direction. The morning's news was on the screen, "…a knife through a paper heart?"

Fritz frowned. "What does that mean?"

"A warning. Why didn't Cordy call?" Braun reached for the office phone. His hand hovered over the receiver then he slammed his fist on the desk. "He's toying with us."

"Does he know where to find Laura?" Fritz asked.

"She's protected." Braun repositioned his laptop.

"What about Risa?" Fritz asked. "Did you put a guard on her?"

"Vinny doesn't know where to find her. At least she followed Witness Protection rules."

Fritz glared. "Don't care. That's not enough."

Braun shook his head. "Not even you know where to find her."

"Vinny's no dummy. He knows Frank's attack on my sister drew me out of the Witness Protection Program last time. He'll try again. I want to be sure she's safe." Fritz grabbed the phone and speed-dialed *1. "I'm calling Chief Jackson."

"I'll handle this." Braun hit the speaker button as the chief answered. "Morning, Chief, got a moment? We need to talk."

"Perfect timing—meet us in my office at 0915?" Chief Jackson disconnected the call.

"Meet us?" Fritz asked. "Who else will be at the meeting?"

"Only one way to find out." Braun grabbed his laptop and pushed back his chair. "Let's go."

THE GANG'S ALL HERE

Out of habit, Cordy jogged up the two flights of stairs and paused at the doorway. "Morning, Chief Jackson. Officer Cordelia reporting for duty as requested." Peeling off her backpack, she hadn't even broken into a sweat.

Three pairs of eyes turned toward her as Cordy walked further into the room. Braun stiffened.

"Morning, Cordy," the chief said. "Fritz and Braun, the rest of the team's here now, so we can discuss your issues. I've pulled together members from numerous departments to create a special observation unit."

Feeling burning eyes sending daggers her way, Cordy knew her assignment to the team rubbed Braun the wrong way. Well, he'd just have to suck it up. She cocked her head in the direction of the detectives. "Morning, Fritz. Braun." That wasn't so hard. I managed to say his name in a civil tone.

"Are you lost?" Braun huffed.

Cordy opted not to reply and watched Chief Jackson's smile blossom beneath a trimmed mustache. Silver streaked the temples of his otherwise ebony hair. Those eyes, the color of fine whiskey, had a way of taking in a person. He possessed quiet wisdom and a deep awareness of people. She'd let him set Braun in his place.

"Glad you could join us." The chief glanced at Braun, who had frown lines fanning above the bridge of his nose. "I see you've already met."

Braun gave a sidewise glance at the chief. "You know we have."

The chief motioned Cordy to a table in the corner of his office, where neatly stacked files lined one end.

Braun stepped forward to block her. "Why is she here?"

Fritz pursed his lips, took the chair nearest the files, and picked up a four-inch folder with a purple stripe. He lifted the cover and leafed through it. "These go way back. My life since I was born."

"Not quite that far—only since your rookie days." The chief stood at the head of the table. "Let's get to work."

Braun snapped, "I still don't understand why she's here."

The chief scowled. "You made that call, remember? The other night, she was the first responder outside Fritz's house."

Cordy moved toward the table. If the shiver racing through her didn't confirm the room turning to ice, her cold fingers did.

Braun jerked out the chair across from her and stared as he sat down.

Although Braun was the only one with issues, she felt like a hunk of meat thrown to a hungry pack of wolves. Why do I allow him to do this to me?

"I heard someone broke into your house the other night." Braun worked his right thumb around the nail of his left index finger. Cordy recognized the old habit he used when he was upset. Braun continued, "That should warn you off the case. Guess, some people—"

Chief Jackson slammed his fist on the table. "This ends now! Set it aside, Braun. We're a team. I'm not putting up with any old business or love affair gone sour."

"He's right." Fritz glared, swung his foot, and gave a swift kick from under the table.

"Ouch!" Braun rubbed his shin. "I got the message."

"Shush, I want to know the plan." Fritz flipped through the pile, searching for his sister's file. It wasn't among the folders. "I'm worried about Frieda, I mean Risa. Do you know where she's located? I haven't heard from her since she entered the witness program."

"We've heard from her contact." Chief Jackson paced as he relayed the information about a shooting at the hospital where Risa worked. "We're not sure if it was a Corenelli contract, but we're putting an agent on her. Here's the case ID number. Look up the file. Everything in the last five years has been digital. We haven't taken the time to enter past data. That's strictly on paper."

"Who's the agent?" Fritz asked.

"It won't be you, so don't ask," the chief warned. "You've broken enough rules. At least your sister has the common sense to avoid family as ordered.

Fritz bristled. "Okay, fair enough, but I'm not asking. I'm telling you, I want my baby sister protected."

"Getting Fritz out of town might not be a bad idea." Braun was still rubbing his shin. "Vinny won't expect Fritz to be assigned to the case."

Chief Jackson shook his head. "I don't like it. My gut doesn't like it, either. I usually follow my gut. Let's see what it says by the end of the day."

Fritz stood. "In the meantime, I'll hire a private investigator to keep track of her."

Chief pointed at his vacant chair. "Sit down. I'll arrange everything. She'll have the best person for the job, so let me handle it."

Fritz paused and dropped back into the chair. "Right, chief."

Jackson clasped Fritz on the shoulder. "Don't worry. I know who to ask for."

"Thanks."

Braun turned to Cordy. "What did the Evidence Response Team find after the break-in at your home?"

She shrugged her shoulders. "They lifted a thumbprint, but I'm waiting on the final report." She didn't want Braun involved, especially when it came to her home.

The chief said, "I've divided the files into thirds and handed the stack out to the partners. Cordy's pile was half that of the other two. She raised her hand, but the chief read her mind and nodded. "Cordy, I also assigned you some electronic files."

"Can we take these?" Fritz asked. "It'll be a while before we can go through all of them."

"Keep them with you, but lock them up when you leave. Some sensitive data's in those records—especially yours."

Fritz nodded. "Okay, chief."

"Braun, you have the most recent experience," the chief said. "You're the team leader. Review the files, come back with a plan, and we'll touch base tomorrow at 4 p.m. I don't need to remind you, Braun, that I'm watching, so play fair."

"I always do." Braun slid his chair back and picked up his files. "Cordy, have you been assigned a desk?"

"Yes. It's across the hall from you and Fritz. I'll review these and be back tomorrow at four."

"I'll come up with a surveillance plan. You okay with that? We need to track down the whole Corenelli family." Braun stormed out of the room before she could answer.

Cordy counted four files and studied each name. "Are you sure you want me to take Midget's folder?"

The chief nodded. "Midget headed up last night's attack. All I know about him is that he's Vinny's half-brother and their father's oldest. Not the brightest child, and as you know, he's of small stature, so Poppy bypassed him to train Vinny to be the next mob boss."

"That must have pissed off Midget," Cordy said. "Maybe that's why he attacked before Vinny could take charge."

Chief Jackson searched his desk for a pen, found it, and jotted "Meeting 4 p.m. Friday" on a sticky note and pasted it to his calendar. "Could be. Figure out why Midget attacked and, most importantly, what he plans next."

"How about Midget's mother?" Cordy stacked her files and placed them into her backpack.

"She died giving birth. Vinny's mother raised Midget, but she's gone, too."

Cordy placed her backpack over one shoulder. "Thanks. I won't let you down. Anything else?"

"Get out of here." Chief Jackson motioned to the door with a smile. "Some of us work for a living." He picked up the phone and called the front desk. "Get me, Agent Kelly."

Cordy planned to get up to speed. She'd show the whole team what she was made of.

ORIENTATION

University Michigan Hospital's newest hire looked nothing like her real identity, an undercover FBI agent working with Chief Jackson. Her mousey brown hair belied the vibrant blonde of a few hours ago. Her training as a nurse was ideal for this position. Like the other nurses on duty, she wore green scrubs, white shoes, and a stethoscope around her neck.

The OR supervisor met her outside the office. "Come with me." They entered the locker room. "Jacqueford Kelly, I want to introduce you to Risa Grant. She'll be your mentor for the next two weeks."

Risa set down a half-drunk cup of java. Obviously, the coffee hadn't kicked in yet. Dark shadows pooled under her eyes. She dragged herself over and managed a smile. "Jacqueford. That's an interesting name."

"Call me Kelly. Everyone else does."

"I'm glad they finally hired someone," Risa said. "I was afraid they'd cancel my vacation."

The supervisor laughed. "As if that's an option. You'd quit work before missing your honeymoon."

"Are you getting married?" Kelly asked.

"No. It's a long story," Risa said. "I'm sure we have plenty of time to discuss that, but it's time to get a report from the day shift, so the nurses can go home."

"I'll see you later." The supervisor waved and then turned. "Oh, by the way, the narcotic keys are still missing. We had to get the spare set from pharmacy. Laundry didn't find them. Look in your locker. Maybe they fell out of your pocket when you changed clothes."

Risa shook her head. "I searched earlier today. I know I gave them to Vicky at shift change. How is Frieda doing?"

"She's on a vent in ICU. They removed part of her lung, but she'll live."

"What happened?" Kelly asked, although the incident was included during Jackson's briefing of her assignment.

Risa glanced toward the supervisor and then cleared her throat. "I hope this doesn't scare you off, but she was shot in the parking lot. No one knows why."

"Do you think the keys had anything to do with the shooting?" This was the first time Kelly had heard about them.

"I doubt it." "We're going to be late for report." Risa held the door open.

Kelly wondered if something else was going on at the hospital. "Who might have taken them?"

Risa shrugged. Kelly made a mental note to keep her eyes open and listen to the grapevine.

GRAY DAY

Marta spied Usher coming up the walkway with a canvas bag over his shoulder. The dog ran out to meet him.

Usher knelt and scratched the German shepherd behind his ears. "Good morning, Pepper."

Marta called from the open window of her studio, "Morning, Usher." The little girl didn't even wait for a reply before she headed downstairs.

Gramma stopped Marta as she passed in the hallway. "Remember, no talking about Momma. You promised."

"Okay." Marta twisted out of Laura's reach and ran down the steps. "Did you get some 'crylic paints?"

As Usher entered, Maggie glanced up from reading a book in the living room. "Hi, Sprite. It looks like you're on a mission."

Marta stopped next to her chair. "Mission?"

Usher motioned for Pepper to lie down and walked closer with a smile on his face.

"What do you mean?" Marta asked.

"It means you have something important to do." Usher scooped the canvas bag from his shoulder.

Marta's mouth opened in surprise. "Yes. I'm on a mission. I'm going to paint with Mom, ah, my new 'crylics." She grabbed the bag, looked inside, and pulled out a pink tube. "This is my favorite color! And Momma loves purple."

"I bought every color I could find, including pink, rose, purple, orchid, lilac, lavender, and blue iris. I hope she likes one of those colors." Usher smiled.

"Run along now," Maggie said. "We have work to do."

"Okay." Marta had business of her own.

Maggie turned to Usher. "I did some research as you asked. I'll grab a coffee and meet you out front."

Marta dashed upstairs and into the studio. She set the canvas bag on the table and put on a ruffled pink apron that Maggie gave her to keep her clothes clean.

Gramma paused in the doorway. "Need help?"

"No, thank you. I have work to do. I'm on a mission." Marta put a clean sheet of drawing paper on an easel and took out the tubes of paint. Eyeing Gramma still in the doorway, she asked, "Are you going to make candy today?"

Gramma nodded. "I think so. Call me if you need anything."

"Okay." Marta grouped the tubes, carefully selecting each by hue: black, gray, browns, yellows, oranges, reds, greens, blues, and then the purples. "Momma, I'm ready. What do I paint first?"

Momma didn't answer.

Marta sat on the chair and stared at the paper. "Are you going to write me another note?" No note appeared either. Marta frowned. She took out the gray paint and drew a rain cloud with small droplets falling into the dirt. "This is boring, Momma. I don't like being by myself. Can't you come and see me?"

The room remained quiet.

Marta put away the gray paint, carefully putting the cap back on so it wouldn't dry out. She set the paint tubes in a plastic pail and then took off her apron. Two dolls sat in the corner of the room. "I know. Let's have a tea party." She put the apron on the biggest doll and set her on a chair by the table.

Usually, her dolls cheered her up, but she couldn't seem to heat the water hot enough. Then her cup tipped over, and she spilled imaginary tea on her tablecloth. "Now I have to wash out the stain."

Marta removed the tablecloth and went to the bathroom to wash out the stain. She couldn't reach the faucets on the sink, but it was all right because she used make-believe water.

When she returned to her painting, someone had added a bouquet of brown-tipped, red roses. Marta glanced around the room. "Gramma? Were you in here painting?"

No one answered.

Marta went across the hall to the Lavender suites. "Gramma? Are you in here?"

The bedroom and sitting room were empty, the curtains were pulled shut, and the room was dark. The bathroom door was open.

"Momma?" she called as she went back to her studio. The painting still had the flowers, but now they had brown leaves and lay on the ground.

"Can you draw something else?" Marta asked. "These ugly roses stink."

Nothing more appeared. *If Momma hadn't made the painting, who had?* She let the picture dry while she went to find her Gramma. Maybe *she* could explain the roses.

MYSTERY BOX

Fritz worked the rest of yesterday, after his radio fiasco, and most of this morning scanning old photos of the Corenelli brothers into his laptop computer. He kept interrupting Braun as he printed each color photo and taped them across the top of a large white foam board, starting with Midget and Vinny. "We need another scanner printer. I'm tired of waiting while you run off data."

"Put it on the agenda," Braun said. "How are you coming with the profiles? I have notes on Alessandro and Leroy. And I see you have Lester and Leonardo—probably don't need to add much under their photos as they're all deceased."

"I remember going after each of them, but you're right. They won't give us much in this case. Now, Frank is another story."

"He's also dead," Braun said, "but you and Cordy each have a file on him."

Fritz posted information he remembered about the kidnapping of his sister, Frieda/Risa, under Frank's picture. Why are there two files on him and not the others? Shouldn't both be assigned to the same person?"

"Talk to the chief," Braun said, "but since Cordy is the IT guru, she has the more recent electronic reports, including your sister's. It also makes sense to have info on her kidnapper. I'm sure our partner will fill us in at the meeting." He emphasized *our partner*, to indicate his irritation.

Fritz knew Vinny had more brothers and didn't find their files in his stack or Braun's ever-growing reports. "I'll add Walt and Mick on the board. Cordy must have the info on them."

"Don't forget to add baby brother, Jules. Cordy must have him, too." Braun pulled a few sheets from the printer. "Juvie Court sealed his file, but the chief pulled some strings to access the record."

Fritz added Jules on the far right of the board. "He's of age now—anything else to add?"

Braun handed over three more names—Doc, Ace, and an old lawyer buddy from prison, Hatchet. Place these under Vinny. Our first task will be tracking down a few close inmates."

"Good idea," Fritz added them to the key contacts and task lists. "This is a work in progress."

"You can say that again," Braun tapped away at his computer. "Not as easy as I expected. It took until the wee hours of this morning and most of today, but I think we have a good start. Do you think we can meet ahead of schedule? I want to pool our knowledge, finish this board, and make a concrete plan. We'll never find Vinny while sitting in the office."

"Fine by me. I'll check with Cordy." Fritz stepped into the hallway.

A pudgy man in a brown suit came out of Cordy's office, whistling as he left.

Fritz stepped into his path.

The man jolted and glanced up at Fritz. "Ah, sorry. I didn't see you." The man tried to step around the detective.

"Do you have a pass? Where is it?" Fritz demanded. "I don't see one on your lapel. No one comes down this hallway unless they have one or work here."

The man stood straighter and huffed, "I work here. I'm the receptionist today. And who are you?"

Fritz narrowed his eyes. He'd never seen the man before, but this was his second day at this office. He hadn't paid enough attention to who was behind the desk when he came to work this morning.

Even so, the receptionist didn't usually come to the back. "Why were you in Officer Cordelia's office?" He peered around the man. Loose pages and stacks of reports were scattered over the table by her desk. Nothing else seemed out of order.

* * *

Cordy heard loud voices outside her office and went to the door. "Is something wrong?"

The receptionist darted around Fritz. "Ask her."

Fritz turned, glanced up, and then scanned the hallway. "Where did that plump man go?"

She shrugged and went back to her desk. "Did you need something?"

Fritz followed Cordy into the office. "Can we meet a little early? I'm done with my files."

"Yeah, I'll be there in a few minutes." Anxious to see what was in the box, she lifted it from the glass desktop. "Tell Braun thanks for the gift."

"He gave you a present?"

"Oops." Whatever was inside had spilled. Liquid dripped from the bottom of the box and hit the floor. She set the package back on the desk.

"Where did this really come from?" Fritz grabbed the pink form that had been taped to the right corner of the lid. "Deliver ASAP." He glanced back to the door. "Flowers? That man delivered you flowers? And you think they're from Braun?"

"I guess. I haven't opened it yet." Cordy snatched back the form from Fritz's fingers. "The receptionist called me from the front desk to pick up a special delivery." She noticed the puddle growing on her desk and grabbed a few tissues to soak up liquid around the box. "I told him I was busy, so he kindly brought it to me."

"When did Braun order flowers? I've been with him all day and most of last night. So that man was telling the truth?" Fritz turned the box and studied the Floral Express logo in the left-hand corner. "It looks legit."

"Why wouldn't it be?" Spying a note, she plucked it from the container. "The card's from Braun. I bet he thought he'd get on my good side before kicking off this meeting." A faint odor drifted into the room and irritated her nostrils.

"I'm not sure about that," Fritz's words faded as she noticed spots on the tile floor turn from gray to white where the liquid had spilled. She knelt on the floor to clean up the mess, then wiped her damp hand down her thigh. Her fingers tingled. She shook her right hand when she stood.

"What's wrong?" Fritz asked.

"My fingers feel funny." Cordy stamped her foot a couple of times, "and my leg burns."

Braun called from across the hall, "How long before we can meet?"

"Impatient, isn't he?" Cordy glanced at her watch. "Give me five minutes."

"I'll let Braun know." Fritz turned to leave as Cordy moved the box closer and flipped the lid open. Liquid splashed onto her face. "What the—" She shoved the container away, tipping it over. Brown-tipped red roses lay scattered on her desk, and decayed leaves spilled onto the floor.

"Dead roses?" Fritz asked. "They can't be from Braun."

"Can't breathe." The office smelled like sulfuric acid. Cordy's eyes watered, and her lungs burned. She darted around her desk, away from the box, and nearly collided with Fritz as she headed for the door. "Need air."

"Battery acid." Fritz smelled it, too. He caught Cordy as she staggered into the hallway. The dye on her navy blue suit turned white, where the liquid had splashed onto her pant leg. The material had frayed and looked as if eaten away. "Come on. Let's run your hands and face under water."

Cordy coughed and dashed for the restroom.

Fritz shoved the door open and called down the hallway, "Braun! It's Cordy. Call 911—acid burns."

Cordy croaked, "Got any baking soda in this joint?"

REGRETS

Thursday, June 12 – 1800 MDT, Loveland, Colorado

When Cordy awoke, she panicked. Something covered her face. "I can't see." She tried to touch her eyes.

"Don't move. You have bandages on your hands and an IV in your arm." Braun's voice sounded alarmed. The rush of words poured out with a hint of panic. She'd heard it once before when things happened too fast and weren't under his calm control. *The day I broke up with him.*

Braun continued his flurry of words. "You have patches over your eyes. There's an oxygen mist mask over your face."

"Where am I?" she croaked.

"The emergency department," Braun ran a hand over her hair. "Don't worry. I'm not going to let anyone hurt you."

Oh, now he wants to take control of my life again. I refuse suffocation by love. Cordy swallowed the lump in her throat. "What happened?"

"Someone sent you roses soaked in battery acid. You breathed it in and splashed it on your skin. There are first and second-degree burns on your hands and leg. Fumes irritated your eyes and lungs."

"Roses? Oh, that's right." Cordy brushed aside the mask. "I thought." She let out a hoarse laugh. "Well, I know it sounds stupid…I should have known better."

Braun's voice tightened. "You thought I sent them. Fritz told me." He moved the mask back in place. "Why would I send you flowers?"

Cordy coughed. Her throat felt raw as she choked back a sob. "Of course, you didn't send them." She was glad the bandages hid the tears forming in her eyes. *Why would I expect my former lover to send me flowers when we're barely speaking? How stupid of me.*

Braun brushed his finger along the side of her cheek. "Look, Cordy, I wish I had sent you roses. At least they would smell sweet and be safe. Why did you accept a box from a stranger? You know better. Especially—"

"Don't say it," Cordy said. "You're right. Whoever sent them had some nerve to deliver them to me at the agency. Now, what do we do?"

"Fritz is investigating as we speak." Braun moved his hand along her upper arm. "Did you get the name of the receptionist?"

She shook her head. "So you think I'm stupid, too, huh? Well, it won't happen again."

"I'll find him, Cordy. I promise."

Cordy grimaced. "We'll find him. We're a team now, remember?"

Braun ignored the comment and asked, "Do you need something for pain? I'll get the nurse."

"No. Don't leave. I mean, I can't see. What if someone is out there?"

"I'm not going anywhere." Braun gently squeezed her shoulder. "I pushed your call light. We'll get something for pain."

"Thanks." *At least he said, 'We.'* "Do you think the box came from Midget or one of the gang?"

"I'd bet on it." Braun let go of her arm as the nurse came into the room. "She's in pain."

"I'll check with the doctor."

A few minutes later, the doctor stopped by and examined Cordy. "Are you allergic to anything?"

"No," Cordy whispered. "My hands feel like they're on fire."

"We'll give you morphine IV," the doctor said. "It's fast-acting. You'll probably fall asleep." He turned to Braun. "So don't ask her a lot of questions."

It didn't take long for the morphine to take effect. Cordy felt secure, knowing Braun was at her side as she drifted into her comfort zone.

I KNOW NOTHING

Before Fritz went to the florist, he stopped at the reception desk. A weasel-faced, middle-aged woman leapt to her feet. "May I help you?" Her protruding nose stuck up in the air as if she'd smelled a putrid odor. Well, maybe she did. He could still smell the acid even after washing with soap and water.

Fritz peered around the lobby and behind the counter. "I'm looking for the receptionist."

Her beady black eyes bore into him. "You're looking at her. I've been here all day. I didn't even get a lunch break."

"No, I'm looking for a heavy-set man in a brown suit. Do you have an assistant?"

"Detective, I just told you I haven't had a break. Does that sound like someone who has an assistant?" She poked her finger in the direction of the lobby. "See for yourself. We've been busy. All that commotion in the back hasn't helped. I heard someone had collapsed. Then the ambulance arrived, followed by the news reporters, and now you. I haven't had time for a cup of coffee. Why aren't you securing the crime scene instead of hounding me?" She went back to work.

"The chief already took care of that." Fritz crossed his arms over his chest and refused to leave. "Were you here when they delivered the flowers?"

"You must be deaf," she snapped. "I was here, have been here, and am still here. And no packages, flowers, boxes, or anything else were delivered to this desk. So if some man claimed to be my assistant, he lied. Now, leave me alone. Number 18, you're next."

A young man from the lobby walked to the counter. "I'm 18. I mean, I'm 21, but my number is 18."

"Whatever," the receptionist said. "How may I help you?"

Fritz let out a groan of frustration and stepped into the lobby. "Did anyone see a guy in a brown suit carrying a white box?" He studied the crowd. A few people shook their heads, one person went back to reading a magazine, and others just shrugged. No one volunteered any information. "Thanks for your help."

Fritz left the building in a huff. "Should have nailed the sucker when I had the chance," he muttered as he unlocked his car door. He'd have to call a team conference to see if any other detectives had spoken to the man.

He had made several phone calls, searched the internet, and narrowed his search down to three floral shops. The rest denied any deliveries today. Although this delivery might not have been recorded, he had to try. There was no company named *Floral Express*, nor could he find a matching logo. The day was slipping away, and the shops would close soon. He headed to the first one in downtown Loveland.

A lady greeted Fritz with a warm smile. "We're about to close. How may I help you?"

"I called earlier and requested a list of today's deliveries." Fritz pulled a small notepad from his back pocket. "I talked with the owner."

"She's in the back creating a wedding arrangement that has to go out tonight. Will this take long? Maybe you can come back in the morning."

"No. I need to talk to her now." Fritz pointed to the small door behind the counter. "I'll go on back, and she can arrange it as she answers a few questions."

"Maybe I can help?" The lady pulled a sheet of paper from a shelf under the cash register. "Here's the list. What else do you need?"

"Who delivers your flowers?"

"My uncle drives his van. He had three stops today and was done by noon."

"What does your uncle look like?" Fritz pulled a pen from his pocket to jot down some notes.

"He's in his seventies, limps, and uses a cane. He has more hair on his face than on his head. Just a minute, I have a photo of my aunt and uncle's 50th wedding anniversary." She fished out a black handbag and flipped open a wallet. An elderly couple smiled as they cut a cake topped with golden wedding bells surrounded by frosted red roses.

"Is he the only one who delivers your flowers?" Fritz asked.

She nodded. "My aunt is trying to sell the shop. She's afraid they're getting too old. I love flowers but can't afford to buy the business."

"Thank you for your time." Fritz jotted a note, closed the pad, and slipped it into his back pocket as he left the shop.

The second florist wasn't as helpful as the first. As soon as Fritz entered the building, everyone clammed up. It didn't stop Fritz from asking, "May I see your floral delivery record for today?"

"Who wants to know?" a teenage female asked.

"I'm a private detective."

"Got a badge?" she asked. "Cause if you don't, we don't have to show you anything."

"Private detectives don't carry a badge," Fritz answered.

She turned her back on him.

"That's fine." Fritz took out his cell phone. "I'll call in the Loveland Police. Not only will they ask for your delivery records, but they'll check your license to do business, pull an IRS investigation, and—"

"Get him the form," an old man shouted from the rear of the store. "Only delivery today was for a funeral this morning. Check with Good Shepherd Church."

The teenager pouted as she ripped a sheet off a clipboard. "Satisfied?"

"Thanks for all your help." Fritz let the door slam on his way out. By seven, he reached the third shop. A white van parked outside had the engine running. A Latino teenager leapt from the driver's side. "Name's Carlos. May I help you? I just locked up for the night."

Fritz explained why he'd come.

"We have two drivers, but I wouldn't say I'm plump, nor is my dad. We made several deliveries today, but none to a detective agency. I'll get the list—mainly churches, funeral parlors, and three private homes. You can have the back copy. It's not as clear as the original, but I think it'll do."

Fritz took the copy and thanked the lad. He pulled out a plastic bag with the torn corner of the cardboard box delivered to Cordy. "Have you ever seen this logo?"

"Floral Express. I never heard of them, but I like how the flower's stem curves like it's being delivered quickly." Carlos studied the logo and ran his finger over it through the clear plastic. "That's custom-designed. See the raised ink? It's been printed using thermography."

"What does that mean?" Fritz asked.

"A thermographic printer uses high temperatures to melt powdered ink. They did a nice job. I wish I had a printer like that."

"Do many florists use this type of printing?"

"I doubt it," Carlos said. "We use an old-fashioned DeskJet printer. It's cheaper than engraving our logo onto letterhead. I want to talk to their designer. We could use a sweet logo like that one."

"Thanks for your help." Fritz headed for the car.

"Wait." Carlos dashed toward him. "Check with Kinkos."

Fritz pulled out his notebook. "Thanks for the tip."

The boy straightened and beamed. "You think it'll help? I've always wanted to be a cop."

Fritz grinned. "It's more information than I had when I got here. Keep studying."

"I will, sir." Carlos waved, climbed back into the van, and left.

Fritz got on his cell phone to look up the nearest Kinkos. As he drove away, a black sedan pulled in behind him. It stayed only two to three cars back. *Am I being followed?* Trying to remember if he'd seen the car earlier in the day, he sped up and turned the corner.

The car did the same.

Fritz slowed and waited for the car to pass.

It didn't. The sedan crossed the street and pulled up to a Starbucks.

Feeling paranoid, Fritz continued around the block and drove into the Starbucks parking lot. He climbed from the car and was standing behind the sedan, jotting down the license plate, when a man in a brown suit with a Floral Express logo on his lapel exited the coffee shop.

The man eyed Fritz and fled back inside.

Fritz dashed for the front door. The man had disappeared when he got inside the Starbucks. He scanned the shop and then rushed to the men's room, pushed open the door to each stall—no one. Fritz went back into the hallway to find a female to let him into the women's side.

"Hey, buddy. Watch it," a kid from behind the counter yelped.

Fritz rounded the corner as the back door slammed. He wove his way around the kid and shoved the door. It didn't budge.

An older man with a green t-shirt grabbed Fritz by the arm. "Hey. Employees only back here."

Fritz shrugged out of his hold. "I'm a detective."

"Well, I'm the manager, and I only allow employees back here, so either go to the counter and order or leave."

Fritz ignored him and shoved at the door again. It still wouldn't open. He ran to the front door and heard a popping sound. The black sedan squealed away. Fritz ran out to his car, but the back tire was flat.

The man in green stood in the parking lot, talking on his cell phone. "He had a gun. I saw him shoot out a tire." The manager pocketed his cell phone and stepped up to the detective. "I called 911. The cops are on their way."

"Great. I missed him again." Fritz cursed under his breath and dialed the crime scene investigation team.

MAGIC MOMENTS

Thursday, June 12 – 2000 EDT, West Virginia

Laura paused in the doorway of Marta's studio. Pepper sat beside her. His tail thumped the floor when Laura entered the room. "Want to try my latest creation? The candy melts in your mouth and leaves a fresh taste when it dissolves."

"Okay." Marta moved from the easel. A clean sheet of paper was fastened at the top. Her acrylic paints sat in a plastic pail on the table.

Laura knelt beside the girl and held out a plate with two candies. "I call them Enchanted Chocolates."

"Like magic?" Marta popped one into her mouth and closed her eyes. That's the way she always sampled Laura's candies. "Mmm." She smacked her lips. "They're good. Soft and creamy. Call them Magic Creams. It's easier than 'chanted."

Laura smiled. "I like that." She hugged Marta. "It's bedtime, and Pepper needs to go out."

Marta remembered the commands Maggie had taught her and motioned for Pepper to go downstairs. The dog nuzzled Marta's leg and left the room.

"Gramma, what if we made a special chocolate candy for the bad man? Would he like us better?"

"Are you still thinking about him?" Laura felt tears well up in her eyes. She missed Lars terribly. No, it's Fritz now. I have to call him Fritz. She sniffled and turned away so Marta wouldn't see. "Why the clean paper on the easel?"

"So, Momma can paint me a picture while I sleep. I miss her."

"I miss her, too." Laura kissed Marta on the cheek and held her close. *Out of the mouth of babes. Candy for villains.* "I wonder."

Marta stepped back. Her brown eyes twinkled. "Wonder what?"

"Nothing, dear. It's time for bed."

I NEED SPACE

Thursday, June 12 – 2124 MDT, Loveland, Colorado

"Thanks for bringing me home, Braun." Cordy still had patches over her eyes as they recovered from acid burns received earlier today. She felt her way into the living room and sat on the recliner. "I can take it from here. Please lock the door on your way out."

"I'm not leaving." Braun closed the door and reset the alarm. "Someone broke into your apartment the other night. You didn't see them, and that was before the eye patches. I'll make us some dinner. You must be starving."

Cordy hopped to her feet. "No. I'm not having you spend the night."

"No one said anything about spending the night." Braun's rapid defense raised a red flag.

"But it's what you meant. The answer is still no."

Braun sighed. "I promise I won't touch you. I'll sleep on the couch, but I'm not letting anyone break in to hurt you again."

"I'm not a child to be protected. I'm a grown woman. My father's offspring. A cop."

"Then grow up," Braun snapped. "Use your brain before leaping into dangerous situations. Accept a helping hand when offered. I'm not asking to move in permanently. We've already tried that. It failed miserably."

Braun continued to amaze her. She heard his words. First, he wanted to protect, yet those hot lips went on to utter such cold, brutal honesty that it stung—all the way to her heart. His voice changed from concern to a low-pitched animal warning, more like a growling bear. Cordy imagined the emotions on his face and was glad the patches covered her eyes. His dimples would deepen in his cheek as his lips tightened. As the inner conflict built, he'd have a slight nervous tic in his left eye. Unyielding, he'd launch into the real crux of the problem.

"Why do you hate me?" Braun's voice came in a whisper.

The words startled her. "I don't hate you. I hate the way you treat me."

Braun's finger brushed a curl behind her ear. "May I at least make us some dinner?"

Cordy felt her face heat.

"Your cheeks blushed. That means my invitation is for dinner and nothing more. Does that blush mean yes?"

His warm breath on her face had gone cold. "Yes, I guess we both need dinner. I could order a pizza."

"I don't think another delivery would be wise," Braun teased in that sing-song voice. "Anyone could watch the house, nab the food, and wait for you to open the door. I have a better idea—"

Cordy stopped listening. She could kick herself. *Of course, he was right. I can't think clearly, and since Braun reentered my life, I haven't had my act together. I better get my wits about me. He always does this to me. No, wait, I'm doing it to myself.* "Stop it."

"Stop what?" echoed from the kitchen. "Don't you want steak?" His voice was more precise now.

"Okay." Cordy held out her hand.

Braun took her arm and gently guided her from the living room.

"I'll fix a salad." Cordy noticed him pause, but then he moved her to the kitchen counter.

"Sure, with both hands wrapped in bandages?" He let go of her arm. "Want some iced tea? I'd offer wine, but not with pain pills."

"I'll get it." Cordy knew her kitchen. She ran her elbow along the counter to the right and found the fridge in the corner. She fumbled to open the door. "Dang it. Maybe you should fix the salad."

"You think?" Braun said. "What would you like in it?"

"Wow, you're asking my opinion?" Cordy chuckled. "That's a switch."

Braun's laughter lit up her soul. "I'm a male. I admit it. I like options as much as you do."

"What's that supposed to mean?" She couldn't let him worm his way back into her heart.

Braun pulled up a chair and nudged Cordy onto the seat. "Plan A. I'd love to take you in my arms and comfort you, but I don't dare. I don't think you'd allow it. Plan B. In all honesty, if I had my way, I'd take you upstairs and lock you in your bedroom until this whole thing blows over. And that I know you won't allow."

Cordy held up her bandaged hand.

"Wait, I'm not finished." Braun rushed to continue. "So, I'm on to plan C. You're my partner at work, for better or worse. In all honesty, I want to make you my partner in life, BUT I'm taking it slow here. Let's be partners in making dinner. What do you say?"

Cordy hesitated. "Okay. You make the steak and salad. I'll entertain you with stimulating conversation. We'll eat, and then you'll go home for the night."

"Right." Braun got back to work. "We are just two old friends having dinner together."

Okay, he did say friends, didn't he? Is that what we are? Her mouth watered—probably from the savory aroma of grilled meat filling her nostrils. Soon, they sat down to a relaxing dinner. A fresh, tossed salad with ranch dressing accompanied the rich, succulent steak. Cordy reached for her fork and knocked over her iced tea.

"I'll get it," Braun grabbed her napkin from her lap. "Would you like some help?"

"Yes, as much as I hate to admit it. If you cut up the meat and hand me the fork, I think I can take it from there and keep my drink to the left of my plate so I don't spill it again."

"My pleasure." Braun had cut the steak into small pieces, stabbed her fork into a slice, and handed it to her. They chatted together like the old times. Braun did the dishes while they caught up on the past year. After he put away the last of the glasses, he took her hand. "You're rubbing your thigh again. In pain?"

She nodded. "It still stings."

"One moment." A pill bottle rattled, and water ran from the tap. "Open wide." Braun placed two pain pills into her mouth and nudged a glass into her bandaged hand. "Can I at least tuck you in for the night?"

His familiar scent wafted toward her, a powerful, masculine, earthy aroma that reminded her of old times when his soft lips had caressed hers. "Thanks, but I'm fine. So, we'll move on to plan D. I'll escort you out. You set the security alarm, close the door, and go home. Then, I'll see you tomorrow when you pick me up for work. Be sure to call first and use that special knock."

"Plan D, it is. Call me if you need anything." Braun paused in the doorway. "You still have my phone number on speed dial, right?"

Cordy hated to admit that she could never find the time to erase his number. "I'll reach you if I need you, but don't count on it, and I wouldn't lose any sleep over it."

"Fair enough, but a slight modification to your plan, if you don't mind. I will walk around the building before I leave for the night." He guided her to the front door.

Cordy felt the door knob and the lock. "Did you set the alarm?"

"Yes. We're following plan D. Your plan, or did you change your mind?" Braun's warm breath washed over her face. He smelled of wine.

She almost forgot to breathe. "No. Thanks for everything." Cordy gently pushed him onto the front porch, shut the door, and quickly locked it before he could kiss her. She blew out a deep breath and leaned against the wall. Her heart raced. She'd taken control of her life, turned Braun out one more time, and regretted every moment.

A few minutes later, Braun called through the door, "Everything looks secure."

"Thanks. Good night." Cordy smiled. She probably should have let him sleep on the couch instead of watching her house all night from the front seat of his car. He thought she didn't know, but that was just like Braun. *Maybe I'll give him a second chance after all this blows over. Things would be a lot different—if he could just let me be me.*

HOSPITAL WOES

It was Friday the thirteenth. On top of that, there was a full moon. Risa had drawn the short straw and was stuck working the extra shift. Although she wasn't superstitious, it didn't surprise her that the twelve-hour night shift in the hospital's OR was busier than usual. She did her best to keep up with the load.

The night's surgeries started with a knife wound to the abdomen. Surgery didn't go well. The patient had a massive infection, was septic, and her blood wouldn't clot. Risa knew without even running a lab test that the thick, yellowish drainage was a staph infection. She recognized that sickly sweet smell immediately.

The surgical team treated the patient for D.I.C., a deadly clot disorder. The doc, torn between giving platelets to stop bleeding or heparin to prevent blood clotting, finally transferred the critical patient to the ICU.

Risa scrubbed in for three major cases in rapid succession. Two motor vehicle accidents and a stab wound to the chest, and it was only a little after midnight. She needed to set up for the routine surgeries that begin at five. If this continued to the end of the shift, she'd never get the rooms set up in time.

During the mad rush, Risa barely had time to say hello to Kelly, who she was supposed to orient. Thank God Kelly was an experienced nurse and fell into step alongside her mentor—she adjusted the bright overhead lights, attached the monitor cables to patients, and set up the equipment. Then Kelly scrubbed in, handed off instruments, and sutured incisions as needed.

At ten past three, "Code Blue, ED3, Code Blue…" blurted over the intercom system. The phone rang at the main OR desk.

"I'll get it." The circulating nurse left the room. A few minutes later, she returned. "Risa, can you take this call? The ED has a massive head trauma. They need to bring her down for surgery, STAT."

"One moment." Risa pulled off her gloves. "Kelly, you're on your own. You know what to do. If you have any questions, flag me down."

"Okay." Kelly helped close the incision and then took on her own cases. As usual, too much work and too few hands to carry the load.

A dark-haired male tech dressed in a white lab coat stopped to draw labs for the fourth time in the last hour. "I need another syringe." He entered the unlocked med room.

Risa restocked meds on the head trauma cart, preparing it for the ED patient. She watched as the lab tech dug through the cabinet, stuffing a few needles, syringes, and alcohol wipes into his plastic carrier tray.

Kelly must have seen the tech, too. "Don't they furnish enough equipment in the lab?"

The man glanced up. "Oh, hi. You must be new here. We never get enough supplies to last the whole shift. If I had to run back downstairs every time I ran short, I'd never get my work done."

For some reason, this guy irked Risa. Maybe it was his nasal voice.

"So they let you into the med room whenever you want?" Kelly asked. "I thought you had to have a code to open the door."

"You do, but the night shift never locks it," Risa said.

Kelly plucked the med key ring from a nail above the sink, where the night staff stashed it, so it was available to all the nurses to open the narc cabinet. She turned toward Risa with a questioning look. "Won't your supervisor get in trouble knowing you leave that key out in the open like this? It's a huge no-no where I came from. One person has to be responsible for the keys at all times.

Risa shook her head. "I know, but it's too busy. You'll see."

Kelly moved to the med cart and was about to unlock it, then turned to the tech. "What's your name?"

"I'm Dave. I see your nametag says, Kelly. Glad to meet you. I hope you stick around. The turnover rate is atrocious."

Kelly frowned and pocketed the narcotic key. "I'd appreciate it if you'd ask for equipment from now on." She motioned him into the hallway.

"No problem. I have enough to last through the shift, but watch out for Bertha." Dave slid his index finger along the bridge of his gold wire-rimmed glasses and scooted them up his narrow nose. "She won't be happy."

"I haven't had the pleasure of meeting her yet."

"Pleasure. That's a good one." Dave wheezed out a laugh.

"I need some help down here," a doc yelled from the neurotrauma room.

Risa glanced up. "Coming." She turned to Kelly. "You okay on your own?"

"Don't worry. I'll be fine."

Risa dashed toward trauma when the doc poked his head out of the room again. "Valium, STAT." She turned around and flew toward the med room as Kelly closed the door.

"Wait." Risa reached out, but it was too late. "It's locked." She punched in the code, but the door wouldn't open.

The doc yelled again. "Hurry. She's seizing."

"I'm trying!" Risa called back and poked in the code once more. "Dang door. It never works!"

Kelly flushed. "Sorry. Let me. It worked earlier." She entered each button until it beeped and the door opened.

"Thanks." Risa glanced up at the bare nail, dug through her pockets, and came up empty-handed. "Where's the narc key?"

Kelly fished it out of her pocket and opened the drawer. "Valium, right?"

"Yeah, and who knows what else?" Risa took the med and dashed down the hall.

* * *

Kelly called after her. "You didn't sign for that."

Risa disappeared into the trauma suite.

Kelly jotted down the med and the time, leaving the dose and signature line blank for Risa to sign when she had time, and locked the med drawer. She brought the clipboard to the trauma room. "What's the name of the patient?"

"Jane Doe," the doc said. "I need a hand. Suction."

Kelly dropped the board on the counter, grabbed the suction tube, and cleared the airway. The patient bucked and went back into a full-blown seizure.

"More Valium," the doc called out.

"I'll get it," Risa grabbed the narc key from Kelly and dashed from the room.

Dave stood outside the locked door with a sly grin on his face. "I found it open and knew Kelly forgot to lock it, so I closed it."

Risa groaned and punched in the code. The door remained locked. "This is ridiculous." Risa paused after each number and waited for a beep before entering the next. The fourth number beeped, and the door opened. She unlocked the med cart and grabbed more Valium. Then she wheeled the med cart down the hall and parked it just inside the trauma room door.

"It's about time," the doc said. "What happened to the trauma stock?"

Risa blew out a deep breath and pushed the Valium into the IV line. "Pharmacy supplies each room, but it's been too busy to replenish the meds."

"It happens all of the time," the doc said. "I'm tired of it."

The patient became quiet. The blips on the monitor slowed— and slowed again, reaching only 32 beats a minute.

"Atropine STAT," the doc shouted.

Risa broke open the crash cart and got the med, but the monitor straight-lined before Risa finished giving the drug. "She's arrested."

A circulating nurse called from out in the hallway, "Risa, you're needed in OR 2 STAT!"

"Go ahead. I'll take it from here." Kelly hit the OR Code Blue button.

Risa darted out of the room as the whole place turned to chaos.

"What was in that syringe Risa gave her?" the doc asked.

Kelly grabbed the vial and showed it to him. "Valium, like you asked."

The team jumped into action. The circulating nurse started CPR, and the anesthesiologist intubated the patient.

"Should I give Narcan to reverse the effects?" Kelly asked.

"It wouldn't hurt." The doctor checked the monitor. "And give her some epi."

Kelly drew up Narcan and gave it IV, followed by a saline flush and epinephrine.

Blips appeared on the monitor as the patient's heart rate picked up, and her vital signs stabilized.

"Okay," the doc said. "She's in the clear for the moment. Everyone take your places—anyone not here for surgery, leave."

Risa poked her head into the room and motioned to Kelly. "Can you get the routine rooms ready?"

"Sure. We need to talk to the supervisor. The med situation is dangerous."

* * *

Risa nodded. "Tell me about it, but not now. I'm due in OR2—another gunshot wound." She darted into the scrub room, pulled out a Betadine sponge, and bumped into a man at the sink. He wore wrinkled scrubs with bulging pockets. Dark strands of hair hung below his surgical cap. "Are you an intern?"

"No. I'm assisting on a chest case." The man leaned in to grab a sponge of his own. A stethoscope and penlight fell from his pocket into the sink. He scooped up his gear and squinted at her nametag. "Risa. That's an unusual name. Have you worked here very long?" His eyes darted toward the rear door, going to the supply room and then back.

"Long enough." She didn't like to chit-chat during any crisis.

The man moved, accidentally stepped on the floor pedal, and sprayed water everywhere. "Oops. I'm a little nervous. It's my first head case."

Risa moved away from the man to stay dry. I wouldn't doubt it's your first case ever. "I thought you said you were scrubbing in for a chest wound."

"Ah, Right, a gunshot wound. I'm Dr. Staples," he mumbled.

Risa moved to the far end of the sink to continue scrubbing. "Where's your name badge?"

Staples' hands dripped with brown suds from the Betadine. He reached into his pocket but came up empty-handed. "Where'd I put that badge? I used it just a minute ago to swipe myself into the OR." He moved toward Risa. "Do you have a towel?"

Risa frowned. "You haven't finished scrubbing yet."

Staples leaned closer and crowded her away from the sink and into a corner by the supply room door.

"Excuse me." Risa nudged the man with her elbow.

Dr. Staples pushed back. The supply room door swung open. A second man's hand flew across her mouth, and a strong arm pulled her behind a metal rack of supplies.

Risa rammed her elbow into the man's gut and stomped her heel into his instep.

"Get her, Walt," the second man groaned as he released his grip.

Risa screamed with all her adrenalin-induced might. "Help!"

The lights went out in the storeroom.

Risa kicked out at anything near her. "Stay away from me." She grabbed her stethoscope from around her neck and swung it over her head. It hit something.

"Ouch, that hurts," a man cried. Footsteps ran across the hall floor. There was a scuffle in the darkness. "Leave her! We'll get her next time."

A door opened, and a sliver of light shone from one of the general OR doors. Risa heard a thud, and air rushed from someone's lungs.

Another door opened. When the light turned on, Dr. Staples was spread-eagle on the floor. Kelly stood over him with a gun to his head. Blood dripped from his forehead.

"What happened to the other guy?" Risa asked.

"I want a lawyer," Staples yelled as Kelly wrapped catgut suture around his wrists.

Risa grabbed Staples by the arm and yanked him around to face her. "Who are you, and what are you doing here?" She wanted to kick him, but Kelly stepped in her path.

"Come on," Kelly grabbed his elbow. "Your friend wouldn't be Mick, by any chance, would he, Walt?"

"You know these guys?" Risa asked. "He said his name is Dr. Staples."

"He lied. This is Walt. I've been waiting for Vinny's brothers to strike. I didn't think they'd attack so soon after the last one."

"You mean they shot Frieda? Oh no." Risa's flushed cheeks paled. "They weren't after me, were they?"

"I'm afraid so. Mick won't get far." Kelly shoved Walt up against the wall and picked up the phone. "Call the supervisor. I'm calling security. Someone else will have to scrub in for these cases. We need to talk."

BLUEBIRD

Saturday, June 14 – 0322 EDT, Lewisburg, West Virginia

Marta lay awake in her bed. She didn't have a nightlight like at home, so she opened her drapes to let the full moon beam through her window. *Everyone else must be asleep by now. The stars are out.* One star seemed brighter than the rest. "Momma, is that you watching over me?" she whispered.

The light twinkled.

Marta knew it answered her. "Come paint with me." She climbed out of bed and tiptoed to the door. It was dark in the hallway. Her gramma had given her a flashlight so she could find her way to the bathroom, so Marta went back to the bedstand to get it. "Okay. I'll meet you in the studio."

The beam was too bright. Marta put her fingers over it to shine a narrow path in front of her as she crept down the hallway, entered the studio, and closed the door. When she turned on the desk lamp, the yellow tube of acrylic paint sat on the table.

Marta squeezed a dab of yellow onto her palette. "What will we draw today?"

The brush lifted, and Momma said, "We need brighter days ahead." She painted a sun. "I will need a light blue, brown, green, and a little red added to the palette. You pick the hues you like best and paint a pretty tree."

Marta pulled the paints from the pail and used a dab of each color. She drew a brown tree trunk loaded with green leaves.

Momma added blue to the sky.

Marta colored in the grass along the bottom of the paper. "What's the red going to be?" Marta asked.

The brush lifted, and Momma painted a red bird high in the tree. "Mix some blue with the red. What color will it make?"

Marta smiled and mixed the paint. "Silly, Momma. You know it makes purple. It's your favorite color."

A warm breeze blew through the little girl's hair. "You remembered." Purple flowers appeared in the grass, and a smear flicked across the bird's wing. "What should we name her?"

Marta thought for a moment. "Bluebird."

"Why bluebird? It's red." a rustling noise sounded like a light laugh.

"I know, but the wing has a purple stripe," Marta said. "The secret is in the blue paint we added. I like secrets."

"Oh, sweetheart, I love you and your brilliant imagination." Momma put down the paintbrush. "So, Bluebird it is. This secret bird will keep you safe. Listen for its chirp."

Marta heard a tweet, tweet, tweet, followed by a shrill noise. "It sounds like a whistle at the end."

"It does. Remember, when you hear that sound, there is danger. You must call me. I'll protect you."

"How will you do that?" Marta asked.

"I'll hide you so the bad man can't see you, but I can't hide Gramma, too. We have to keep her safe."

Marta peered around the room. "Are we going to be in danger?"

"I'm afraid so, Sprite."

"What about Gramps? Is he in danger, too? Can you hide him?"

"Sorry, honey. I'm your angel, and I can only protect you, but we can warn the others."

NEED A LAWYER

Saturday, June 14 – 0405 CDT, Fort Collins, Colorado

Vinny wasn't in the best of moods. His brothers had failed him, and Risa was still free. Even the great hacker, Ace, couldn't find Fritz's wife and grandkid. Without one of them, he'd never lure Fritz into the open. Vinny would give them another twenty-four hours. If they still had no results, there'd be hell to pay.

It was a little past five in the morning, and the second phone call went to voice mail. Vinny dragged himself from bed on the third call, leaned over the stair railing, and yelled downstairs, "Answer the damn phone."

It was Doc's home, but he wasn't obligated to answer. Besides, he'd only been in bed for an hour. He'd spent the night with an old friend, who vowed to retire from the floral delivery business after Fritz nearly caught him at Starbucks.

The phone stopped ringing. "It's about time." Vinny headed back to his room.

Jules bounded up the stairs. "It's Mick. He has to talk to you."

"At this hour?" Vinny snapped.

Jules shoved the phone in his face. "He's frantic."

Vinny rolled his eyes. "Put him on speaker."

Jules hit the button. "Mick? Here's Vinny."

Vinny squinted at his watch. "Geez, do you know what time it is?"

"Early morning," Mick said. "I'm having breakfast."

"Well, it may be breakfast time in Michigan, but we just got to bed. This is getting out of control. Do you have Risa?"

"Not yet. Now, don't get angry. Let me tell you what happened." Mick made a loud gulp. "They nabbed Walt. He needs a lawyer."

"A lawyer!" Vinny's blood pressure skyrocketed. "How did Walt get caught?"

Mick told him about the attempted kidnapping of Risa at the hospital. "There was an inside agent."

Vinny clenched his fists and gritted his teeth. "I don't believe this. You guys are the dumbest SOBs on the planet. How'd you get away?"

Mick told of his narrow escape. "Walt needs a good lawyer. Not one of your shyster buddies."

"How long has Walt been locked up?" Vinny ran a hand down his face. He thought about a few attorneys who owed him a favor, but this one had to be top-notch.

"An hour or so."

"Do you think he'll keep quiet?" Vinny asked. "He's not the brightest penny."

"He's our brother!" Mick yelped. "You can't bail on him now. After all, he wouldn't be here if it weren't for you."

"Yeah, yeah, I know. Don't rile me. I can't believe you broke into the hospital. Couldn't you come up with a better plan?"

Mick's voice cracked. "I thought we had to snuff out Risa ASAP."

"Snuff her?" Vinny shouted. "How the hell can I lure Fritz out if his sister's dead? I need her alive."

"You didn't exactly make that clear." Mick's voice trembled. "If we had a week or two, we'd come up with something better."

"Then you're a moron." Vinny grabbed the phone and paced down the hall. "Walt's even worse. I'll call you back by noon. Don't do anything stupid in the meantime." He threw the phone against the wall, ending the call.

Jules stood at the top of the steps with his mouth agape. "You can't harm her. She's a nurse. She helps people, and she's innocent."

Vinny glared. "I can, and I will if necessary."

Doc came out of the bathroom. "So your brother needs a lawyer. What about Hatchet from the PEN? He knows more than all those country bumpkins combined."

"Hatchet?" Jules looked as if he'd faint.

"It's his last name," Vinny lied. "We all called him that."

Doc scooped up the phone. "Hope you didn't break it." He headed downstairs. "I need coffee before we make this call. He owes both of us. I'm sure he'll find a way around the system. If not, he'll break Walt out. Do you have enough money for bail? It'll cost you."

"Yeah, I still have a stash."

"If the lawyer is from the PEN, isn't he a criminal?" Jules asked.

"Aren't they all?" Doc answered.

"Don't worry your pretty little head over it." Vinny wrapped the robe's tie tighter around his waist. "You just stay innocent. I might need divine intervention in the future."

Jules crossed himself and crept downstairs.

"Doc, get a private jet while you're at it." Vinny scratched the stubble on his neck. "Let's take a fishing trip on Lake Michigan. I need some bait."

LOST IN THOUGHT

Saturday, June 14 – 0555 CDT, Loveland, Colorado

Fritz arrived at the office early. He sat inside his car and reread the letter he found tucked in his file. It was from Vinny, sent to him the day after his release from prison.

Fritzy old boy,

I heard about the terrible car accident that took your daughter's life. I want to say how sorry I am that it was her and not you. Of course, I had nothing to do with her death, but I promise to put every effort into yours. For years, I thought you died in the jewel heist. Now, you're in my thoughts daily. How distressing to discover you're still alive and free to live your life as a private citizen. I can't wait to see you again.

Vinny C.

Questions rolled through Fritz's mind. *How did Vinny know about Diane's death unless he caused it? But then again, how did he arrange the accident while still securely locked away at the PEN? The same way he sent Frank to hunt down my sister.* His stomach flipped and nearly made him gag. Fritz wondered who found the letter and if Braun had already seen it. If so, why hadn't he shared it earlier? Now was the time to tackle the past. He'd prove Vinny was behind the murder of his daughter—or was it one of his brothers? Either way, he would find the truth.

Fritz refolded the note and stuck it in his pocket. The sun reflected off the snowcaps of Longs Peak. Lost in his thoughts, he remembered hiking the mountains with Diane on her sixteenth birthday. They stopped at the ranger's station on the way down and had a picnic lunch. She was so vibrant and talked non-stop about her future. Fritz climbed out of his car. His fists clenched. He reached into the hollow place where the joy of his daughter forever lived. He felt his heart shatter. That bastard snuffed out her bright future. *I'm going to make him pay!*

Chief Jackson walked toward him, holding his briefcase. A deep crease ran across his forehead. "Are you going to stand out here all day?"

"No. Why the frown?"

"I got an urgent message from Michigan," the chief said. "Something's going on that involves Risa. I called her Witness Protection Agent. He couldn't confirm anything, but my gut tells me so, and it rarely fails me. After a fitful hour, my gut and I agreed to send you out to protect your sister after all. You'll team up with Agent Kelly, the best agent I know. She was guarding Risa during the last attack."

"Last attack?" Fritz startled. "Has there been another? Did something happen to Risa? Is she safe?" Like a bulldog, he followed close to Chief Jackson's heels as he strode into the building and down the hall.

"Hard to say. Come into my office. After several phone calls, I was told to stay out of this, or I'd lose my detective license. I had to research the latest events on my own."

"What did you find?" Fritz paused while the chief unlocked the door. Then they went inside.

"It's all here." The chief opened his briefcase and handed him a manila folder. "Log in to our system for updates—the file number is on the tab."

Fritz snatched the folder. "Give me the summary version."

"A kidnap attempt while at work," the chief said. "I hate not being the boss anymore. I had to pull every string available at the bureau to get Agent Kelly assigned to go undercover. I knew she was the best. Call her for more details."

"Won't you get into trouble if I—"

"The hell with those guys. I don't trust them. They don't give a damn about your sister. They only want to grab Vinny."

"Do you trust Agent Kelly?" Fritz asked.

"She's different," the chief said. "Almost like a daughter to me, and I'd trust her with my life. Catch the next plane to Michigan, work with Agent Kelly, and protect Risa. Keep in contact. You know the routine."

"Thanks, Chief." Fritz took the folder back to his office, closed the door as he always did when he needed to concentrate and studied the case. He called Agent Kelly, but she wasn't available. He left a clipped message. Fritz hung up, desperate to catch the first flight to Ann Arbor.

Braun burst through the door as Fritz finished making airline reservations. Braun's usual pressed suit looked as if he'd slept in it. "I just spoke to the chief." Braun pulled up a chair. "What did you find out about yesterday's delivery to Cordy?"

"I got a tire blown out at Starbucks, but I have the guy's license plate number. I'll let you follow up. Also, I stopped at Kinkos. They printed the delivery box logo. Here's the company's address. Probably bogus. Why the wrinkled suit?"

Braun's crooked grin told Fritz everything he needed to know. "Cordy wouldn't let you sleep on the couch, so you camped out in your car to keep an eye on her."

"Pretty much. We followed Plan D, her plan, so I tried other options, but she refused to stay home this morning. She just got word that she's been accepted as an FBI agent and will start in two weeks. I've never seen her so elated. She's in Chief Jackson's office, making arrangements as we speak. I had hoped he would talk some sense into her and make her stay home until she recovers."

"Don't count on it. Remember how excited you were when you got accepted?"

"Yeah. Nothing will stop her now. I mean, I'm happy for her, but this will change everything. What if she's transferred?"

"Have faith and give her time to reflect. Cordy will make the right decisions. While you're here, have you seen this before?" Fritz slipped Braun the letter from Vinny.

Braun perused the note and handed it back. "So this is why the chief wanted me to track you down. It's the first time I've seen it."

"I wondered." Fritz tucked it back into his file. "I know Vinny's behind Diane's death, and if not him, one of his brothers did the job. I'm not going to let anyone take out another family member. My plane leaves in five hours. I'll barely have time to pack and drive to Denver before boarding."

Braun nodded. "I thought you should know that I heard from my brother. He took the assignment to watch over Laura and Marta. They're safe, but…"

Fritz jumped up from his chair. "But what?"

"I said they are safe. Usher will be sure they stay that way. It's just that Marta showed him an interesting picture. It seemed to be a warning."

"Warning of what? Spit it out, Braun. I don't have any patience."

"I see that. Usher sent this to me." He pulled out his cell phone and showed Fritz a photo. "It's a picture of dead roses, red ones with brown tips and leaves. Does that sound familiar?"

Fritz ran his hand over his face. "Did Marta say why she drew them?"

"Actually, Usher said something odd. Marta told him that an angel drew them." Braun shook his head. "I'm not sure what to think about this, but we'll want to know if she draws anything else. Usher agrees."

"If you hear anything else from Usher, call me." Fritz headed for the door and turned, "I'm counting on your brother to keep my family safe."

THE PROTECTOR

The cagey, old defense lawyer glanced at his gold pocket watch. It was nearly 7 a.m. on a Saturday. What luck that Judge Rocani agreed to see him in his chambers on the weekend. When Hatchet slid the watch back in place, his hand bumped the hidden revolver. The piece felt more like a toy than a deadly weapon, made from a 3-D printer, so it wouldn't set off the front door alarm. He hoped he wouldn't have to use it. The elevator door opened, and he stepped into the hallway.

A man with a crew cut, dressed in a Marine uniform, limped stiffly up the hall toward the courtroom. He paused. "Morning, Mr. Hatchet."

"Good to see you again, Bobby," Hatchet straightened his maroon tie and tucked the ends into his three-piece, gray pinstriped suit vest. "Home on leave?"

"Yes, but if my father sees fit to take me on as his clerk, I'm sure it'll be my last tour overseas."

"You can count on it," Hatchet was sure Bobby would replace that uniform by the end of his leave.

"The judge is trying to catch up on last-minute details before Monday's hearing." Bobby opened the door and motioned for Hatchet to enter the courtroom.

"Thanks. Your father is a busy man. I can't keep the judge waiting."

"Yes, sir. Have a good day." Bobby stood in the doorway and saluted while Hatchet entered.

Judge Rocani's heavily accented English came out slow, strong, and deliberate, "That'll be all for today, son. Enjoy your breakfast with your old Marine buddy. I'll see you for supper."

Bobby nodded and hobbled back into the hallway.

The judge raised his spider-veined hand in greeting, "Welcome, Maggio. Do you still go by that name?"

"Judge Rocani. I go by Hatchet now, but you, honorable one, may call me by my given name."

"What can I do for you?"

"I'm not really here on business—just a little job for V. C. You know who I mean?"

"We'll talk in private." the judge rose and motioned for Hatchet to follow him into his chamber. He latched the door behind the lawyer and eased his bones into a high-backed leather chair. "You want me to find a way to free his brother, Walt."

Hatchet sat across from the judge. "I didn't say it."

A smirk flashed across the judge's lips. "You know the litigation process."

"I do." Hatchet reached into his pocket, pulled out a knife, and cleaned his fingernails.

The judge frowned. "It won't be easy."

Hatchet narrowed his eyes. "Walt was simply in the wrong place at the wrong time."

"Still playing the protector, I see. Well, I could pull a few strings. No guarantees."

"Never is." Hatchet folded his knife and slid it into his pocket. "I'm sure you have a favorite charity."

The nod was slight. "Same as last." A chair scraped across the floor in the main courtroom. "I smell a rat lurking." The judge got up and opened the back door of his chamber leading outside. "Go! I never saw you."

ALARMED NEIGHBOR

"Someone's breaking into the house next door," Risa's neighbor shrieked over the phone. Terrified that the intruder might hear her, she stifled her cries with her a hand over her mouth and slid to the floor. Her body trembled, wracked with silent sobs.

"Ma'am, calm down," the 911 operator said. "Tell me—"

"Send the police," she whispered.

"Are you in a safe place?" The 911 operator asked.

"I hope so," she whispered. "I think he's cutting away the screen to her bedroom window."

"Where are you now?"

"I'm hiding behind my curtain. It's dark in here, so I hope they can't see me."

"Is there more than one intruder? You said they," the operator asked.

"I don't know for sure, but it looked like someone was in the car and a driver who can barely see over the steering wheel."

"What is your name? I need a phone number and address?"

"In…Inga. My name's Inga." She gave her number and address. "But it's my neighbor that needs help." She gave Risa's address.

"What does the man breaking into the house look like?"

"He's wearing a black hoodie," Inga said. "I can't see his face."

"Who is your neighbor?" the operator asked.

"Risa. She works nights and is probably sleeping." Inga crouched on her knees and peeked around the curtain. "The man's lifting her bedroom window. Oh my God. There's another one—a guy from the car, and he has a gun. Hurry!"

"The police are on their way. Inga, I need you to stay on the line and explain what you see."

"I have to call Risa and warn her."

"No. Stay—"

Inga hung up and speed-dialed Risa. "Pick up. Pick up, pick up. Hurry."

The man in the hoodie had lifted the window and was crawling over the sill.

The phone must have gone to voice mail. "Risa, hide." Someone's breaking into the house. Hide now." She hung up.

Inga ran to her office at the back of her house for a peek in the alley, hoping to get a better view and see who else might attack. At least two men and a driver, but were there more?

A green jeep pulled up and parked along the curb at the alley's entrance. A man in a gray camo uniform climbed from the passenger's side. The soldier opened the rear door and pulled out a duffle bag. "Thanks for the ride, Bobby. See you later." He waved to the driver, who drove away from the curb.

Inga's heart sank. She raced down the stairs to the backdoor. Thank goodness she'd pulled the drapes to the patio window between the houses. She nearly fainted when her cell phone rang.

It was the 911 operator. "I need you to stay on the line."

"Hang on. Jim is home. Risa's husband is walking into danger." Inga dashed across the patio to the back door. Her fingers fumbled with the lock, but she finally cracked the door as he walked in the back of her house.

"Psst, Jim," Inga whispered and motioned with her hand to come inside. She raised her voice, "Jim! Watch out!"

He didn't pay any attention and continued walking.

The operator asked, "What's happening?"

Inga held the phone between her shoulder and her ear. Her voice shook. "Jim! Come here," she shouted.

Jim stopped in his tracks and glanced toward her.

A shot rang out.

Jim dropped to the ground.

"God no, the shooter must have heard me," Inga cried. "I think Jim's hit."

"Tell me what you see." The operator's voice wasn't as calm. She was demanding.

"Someone shot Jim. No, wait. He's rummaging through his duffle bag. There's blood smeared on his thigh. He's been shot, but he's alive."

The green jeep pulled up again behind her house. Bobby yelled, "I heard gunfire!"

"Take cover, Bobby," Jim shouted.

"You're wounded!" Bobby dropped to the ground behind the vehicle. He limped as he zig-zagged toward Jim.

"His friend is back." Inga saw a flash of metal in the driver's hand.

Another shot, and Bobby pulled Jim toward the jeep.

Inga locked the back patio door as she lost sight of both Jim and his friend. "Anyone else injured?" sounded in her ear.

"I can't see," she whispered. Inga moved into the patio and crept closer to a screened-in window.

"Talk to me. What do you see?" The 911 operator practically shouted.

Inga's hand shook as she knelt closer to the window. A bullet cracked through the screen and whizzed past her head. "Oh my!" Fear overtook her. Sprawled on the floor, she crawled to the back door of her house. The lock clicked as she slithered over the threshold and slammed the door.

"Inga, what's happening? Where are you now? Are you safe?" The operator wouldn't shut up.

Irritated, Inga said, "I'll call you back." She shoved the phone in her pocket and darted back upstairs to look for Jim.

The phone rang again. Inga picked up and told the operator what she'd done. "Jim's out there. He's been shot. Where are the police?"

"The police are on their way," the operator said.

Inga's heart thumped wildly in her chest. Her armpits felt damp, and her fingers were like ice. She couldn't stop shaking. Her voice trembled, "Do I have to meet them?"

"No. Don't go outside. Stay on the phone with me," the operator warned. "Let the police handle this."

"I would if they'd ever get here."

Sirens blared in the distance and were drowned out by more gunfire.

"I hope they're here in time. What if they killed Jim? Hurry. Please, hurry." Inga felt lightheaded. Her breathing came out in pants. Holding a hand over her mouth, she gagged, "I'm going to puke."

"Don't hang up again," the operator warned. "Inga, stay on the phone."

Inga stumbled to the bathroom. She barely made it to the toilet before she heaved.

BREAK-IN

Risa's breath hitched when she awakened from a deep slumber. Still sleep-deprived, it took a moment to realize it was her blasted phone ringing. She hated calls in the middle of the day. *Why didn't I turn off the ringer?*

The answering machine came on. "…Pick up. Pick up! Hurry." The woman's panicked voice startled Risa. It sounded like her neighbor, but what could be so important that Inga would wake her? She knew Risa worked nights and slept during the day.

Risa held her breath to hear the rest of the message, "Quick, hide. Someone's breaking into the house. Hide now." Confused, Risa wondered whether she mean my house or Inga's? She grabbed her robe at the end of the bed and slipped it on. She'd better answer the phone and see what was causing such an alarm.

A breeze blew the curtain from her bedroom window, and the shade moved. A scraping sound startled her, and a leg quickly slid over the sill.

My house! Risa dropped to the floor and searched for a weapon. Panicked, she grabbed her high-heeled shoe—the only thing she could find within reach to defend herself.

A man in a black hoodie lunged toward her. "Don't move."

She swatted the heel spike at his head, but it didn't stop him.

He caught her arm and pulled hard, making her lose the shoe. "I got you."

"Getaway, you bastard," Risa's heart pounded as if it would burst from her chest. "Help. Help me!" Knowing she was alone, she batted at him with her fists, twisted away from him, and yelled again, "I mean it! Get away from me."

"Don't scream. It'll only make things worse." His voice dripped with menace. "You won't get away this time."

Filled with rage, Risa kicked the man in the groin.

Crying out, his hands flew to cover himself as he crumpled in pain.

Risa scrambled to her feet and raced down the hall, moving anything she could into his path—a picture from the wall, a clothes' hamper, then the mirror, shattering it into tiny shards of glass, hoping to slow him.

"Frank said you were slippery as an eel."

His words bit through her courage—nearly paralyzing her. *Not Frank again!* Her mind flashed back four years. How he'd whipped, tortured, and raped her. *How can this be happening? I can't live like this.* A burning fury, hot and seething, bubbled to the surface. *What can I use? My gun—No, it's in the bedroom closet.*

The man grabbed for her and snagged her robe.

Turning, she smashed her elbow into his chest, ripping the house coat from his grasp.

"Feisty little thing, aren't you? But you don't have a chance." The man reached for her again, snagged her gown, and tried to get a better hold.

Adrenaline spurt through her system, adding a burst of energy. Yanking her gown away, she tore the lace from his fingers and ran. Her foot caught on a scatter rug. She slid, crashed into the wall, and lay sprawled across the floor.

He sprang forward, but Risa rolled away, leapt to her feet, and sprinted for the bathroom, hoping to escape through the window. Risa dove for the door and froze instantly when a popping sound exploded. *He's going to kill me.*

Her fingers fumbled for the lock when it dawned on her that she felt no pain. *There must be two men. If the intruder had a gun, he would have shot me by now.* Tears blurred her vision. She shoved harder but couldn't latch the door.

Hoodie guy's foot had blocked it. "You're mine."

She stumped on his foot, but he was too strong for her, forced the door open, and slapped her hard across the cheek.

Risa flew backward and saw stars. Without thinking, she lowered her head, rammed him in the gut, and pushed him toward the shower.

His foot caught on the shower lip, and he fell backward onto the tile.

Risa fled the bathroom, ran down the hall, and opened the back door. Catching a glimpse of Walt standing outside near the window, she gasped when she saw the gun in his hand. No longer able to think clearly, she darted back into the hallway. Fear took over.

Clanking came from the bathroom—"Damn shower curtain." Another rustling sound and Vinny swore again.

Hide! In her haste to close the back door, it didn't fully latch as she backed into the hall closet. Using both hands, she covered her mouth to keep from screaming and watched through a crack. Pure survival skills guided her to grab a coat hanger. She bent it into a claw and pulled a coat around her, ready for the next attack.

The hooded man must have gone into the kitchen. She heard banging and muttering as drawers opened and closed, and then he darted toward the back door, holding a kitchen knife in his hand.

Why didn't I think of that?

His head jerked from right to left, searching. He must have seen the back door ajar and dashed outside. "Did you see the woman?"

"No, Vinny. She didn't come out here," Walt said. "I would have nabbed her."

"Go back and have Midget drive the car around to the front," Vinny yelled.

Oh no. Fritz's Vinny! Risa debated if she should run to the door and bolt it but hesitated when another shot fired. The back door window shattered. Crouching further into the closet, Risa expected him to shoot her, but no bullet came. *Maybe he plans to stab me.* He came closer. Sweat dripped from his brow. His neck veins bulged, and blood oozed from his temple.

The closet door flew open. Vinny's mouth twisted in rage—a demon-possessed. He parted the coats. "Aha!"

She raked the hanger's hook across his face. It caught his cheek and sliced into his flesh. Unable to prevent it, a scream escaped her lips.

Vinny yanked her arm and forced the hanger from her fingers. "If I didn't need you for bait, you'd be dead by now." He pulled her from the closet and shoved her in front of him.

Something hit the back of her head, enveloping her in darkness.

SET-UP

Saturday, June 14 – 1308 CDT, Ann Arbor, Michigan

"Help her, please, get the police here before it's too late," Inga shouted once again at the 911 operator. "They may have already killed Jim, and that thug is still inside the house doing, God only knows what to Risa!" Fighting for control, Inga felt beyond panicked—nearer to hysteria. All her senses were on hyper-alert.

She caught a glimpse of a vehicle driving up the street. A shot rang out, and a woman screamed.

"That's Risa!" Inga could hardly breathe as she moved to a window at the front of the house to get a better view of the car. "A brown SUV just squealed to a stop in front of Risa's. A man in a dark jacket is getting out of the passenger's seat. He's opening the back door—"

"Are the police there yet?" the operator asked.

"I don't see any," Inga pulled the curtain back even further to check. "No, police. Wait! That guy in the hoodie who broke into Risa's is heading for the car. Oh no! He has Risa. She's lying over his shoulder, and she's not moving. I hope they didn't shoot her."

"Where is he taking her?" the operator asked.

"Hoodie guy just shoved Risa into the backseat and slammed the door. Where are the police? They have Risa! What's taking so long?" Inga cried.

"Is the man in the hoodie still there?"

"Hoodie guy is arguing with a man in the black jacket." Inga stood up and strained to hear what they were saying. "Bang!" Inga jumped at the sound, and her heart thudded in her ribcage. The jacketed man toppled to the ground. "He's hit!"

"Who's hit?" The operator cut in, "What just happened?"

"A shot fired from somewhere in the yard. It hit the bad man— the one in the black jacket. I think he's Hoodie guy's partner." Inga went to a side window to glance around the yard. She saw movement by the hedge. Someone in camo gear was on the ground. "Is that Jim?"

The car's engine revved, and Inga darted back to the front window. "Hoodie guy just kicked his partner away from the car, stepped over him, and slid into the passenger's side."

Tires squealed, and Hoodie guy yelled, "Step on it, Midget!"

"They're getting away!" Inga gasped. "Stop them!"

"Can you see the license plate number?" came from her phone,

Inga caught a glimpse of the car. "It ends in 413, but I can't make out the rest. Why are the police taking so long."

"They should be there any minute. What happened to the man in the black jacket?" the operator asked.

Hoodie guy just left the jacketed man lying on the ground, and I know another partner was inside Risa's house. He was the one with the gun. I didn't see him leave, and I don't know what happened to Jim."

Red and blue lights flashed as two patrol cars came into view.

"Now, they arrive, but it's too late. They're too late! I'll talk to the police." She dropped her phone and raised the window.

An officer climbed from the car, drew his gun, scanned the area, and crouched by the man in the black jacket. He checked the man's neck and shook his head. The cop's partner got out of the patrol car and raced up the steps to Risa's apartment as a second cruiser pulled to a stop.

Inga yelled out through the window. "Be careful. There's another bad man out there, and he has a gun. He didn't leave in the getaway car and check on Jim. They shot him in the leg."

"Shut that window and step away," an officer shouted. "Stay inside. We'll come to your house and talk to you soon."

Inga closed the window and backed away. A flashlight beamed over Risa's bedroom window.

"Inga! Are you there?" came from the cell phone. She'd forgotten about the operator.

The officer, who had shouted at her, inched his way along the hedge. "Drop your weapon!"

Inga couldn't see the officer when another shot rang out.

An ambulance drove up to Risa's. There seemed to be a flurry of activity next door. Someone yelled, "Two guys down."

Inga felt dizzy. Black dots floated before her eyes, and she woke up sprawled on the bedroom floor. Her cell phone was still in her hand. The operator hung up, or had she disconnected again? Her mind was in a fog.

She flinched when someone pounded on her back door. "Police. Open up."

"Finally." With all her adrenaline used up, Inga dragged herself down the steps and to the back door. *How'd he get through the patio? I know I locked that door after talking to Jim.* "Show me your badge."

The officer stepped closer. A police emblem was embossed on his uniform. He removed his cap and held his ID up to the glass in the back door. His thumb was over the photo, but it looked legit.

Inga unbolted the lock and let him inside. "Thank God. I was so afraid. Is Jim going to be all right?"

The officer pushed inside and shut the door. "Don't know. The paramedics are working on him."

Befuddled, her mind still spinning, Inga's vision seemed to clear. Blood dripped down the officer's shirt. "You've been wounded. Shouldn't you see the paramedic, too?"

"It's just a scratch, but thanks for caring. What's your name?"

"Inga. What's yours?"

"Call me, Officer Walt."

Someone banged on the front door. "Police."

Confused, Inga opened her mouth to answer.

Walt shoved a gun under her chin. "Shut up, and no one will get hurt. Give me your phone."

HINT

Fritz couldn't wait to get to Ann Arbor to protect his baby sister, Risa. Vinny's gang had attacked twice in two days, but she had survived. She may not be as lucky the next time, and Fritz wasn't about to lose another family member. Memories of rescuing her four years ago from Vinny's younger brother, Frank, burned deep in his soul. He found Risa barely alive after being beaten and raped. His emotions seethed within, driving him to avenge her.

At 0930, Agent Kelly texted, "The police arrested Walt, but some judge found a loophole. Walt's already back on the street. I can't wait until you get here. I'll watch Risa while at work, but what if someone tries to reach her at home? See you soon." The text raged the intense flame within, setting fuel to fight once more, to the death if need be, but it wouldn't be Risa's death—it would be Vinny's.

When Fritz's plane touched down in Detroit, Agent Kelly was waiting for him. The first words out of her mouth devastated him.

"Risa's missing. A fellow Marine brought Jim home. He got off a round and killed Mick, but Jim's been shot."

"Shit." Fritz grabbed his bag from baggage claim. "I knew I should have come yesterday. Let's go. I want to talk to Jim."

Agent Kelly's phone rang. Ann Arbor police department ID flashed. "Yes, Officer McCoy." She paused. "One moment." Kelly handed Fritz the phone. "It's for you."

"Detective Fritz Von—"

"I know who you are. We need your help. Our officers arrived at your sister's house a few minutes ago. Risa's neighbor called 911 to report the kidnapping but now refuses to answer the door. The investigator reported blood splattered across the back walkway, and the patio door was broken. We suspect a hostage situation. Chief Jackson wants you on the scene ASAP."

"What about Risa?" Fritz headed for the exit. "That's why I'm here. Where did they take her?"

"Our best bet is to find out what the neighbor and possibly the hostage taker knows."

Fritz paused at the doorway, wondering where Kelly had parked. "Which way?"

She pointed across the street. "Car's on the next level down."

Fritz returned his attention to the phone call. "Who's holding the neighbor hostage?"

"We think it's Walt Corenelli," McCoy said.

Fritz stumbled. "Wait a minute. If Walt's holding the neighbor hostage, and Mick's dead, who has Risa?"

"I thought you knew," the officer said. "Vinny is in town. Midget drove the getaway car."

"We're on our way." Fritz handed Kelly her phone and raced down the steps. "Got any ideas?"

"About how to rescue the neighbor from Walt? A few." Kelly punched a button on the key fob. Two small beeps unlocked the car doors.

"No, I meant, about where they took Risa?" Fritz opened the hatch, dropped his bag in the back, and unzipped it. He dug his fingers along the edge and came up with his gun. After loading it, he closed his bag and slammed the hatch.

"None." Kelly climbed into the driver's seat.

A red bird with a purple-striped wing landed on the roof of the car. It dropped something from its beak. Fritz watched the bird fly away. He climbed into the car as a breeze blew a business card onto the windshield.

"I hate it when people leave trash floating around." Kelly got out, snatched the card, and threw it into the ashtray. She backed out, flipped on her flashers, and sounded the siren.

Fritz glanced at the card and recognized the florist's logo. Not sure if it was a clue, he pocketed the card and called Braun.

NEWS FROM MARTA

Saturday, June 14 – 1330 MDT,
Fort Collins, CO/1430 CDT, Ann Arbor, MI

Cordy's eyes still were sensitive to the light after the splashed acid incident, but she refused to let it get in the way of work. Braun had been kind enough to pick her up for work today, although, in her hurry to meet him, she'd forgotten her cell phone on her dresser, so they were sharing Braun's. He'd just stepped out of the office when Fritz called, so she answered, "Officer Cordelia. How may I help you?"

Fritz shouted over a siren and sounded pissed. "Why are you answering Braun's phone? You should be at home, resting."

"My bandages are off. I can see again." Not wanting to create more chaos, she called out, "Braun, it's for you. One moment, he's heading my way." She held the phone out to Braun. "It's Fritz."

Braun took the phone. "Sorry to hear about your sister. Let me put you on speaker. We've been following Risa's kidnapping on the police scanner."

"You know more about the case than I do." Fritz buckled his seatbelt. "I just landed and heard the news from Agent Kelly. We're heading into a hostage situation now."

Kelly drove like a madman. The traffic shifted out of her way as she sliced across the lanes and pulled up the police scanner for an update. "I hope Inga's okay. There must be a shooter still on the scene. The police have blocked off the area for at least six blocks."

"That poor neighbor," Cordy said. "I'm sure she's scared out of her mind."

"What else have you heard?" Fritz's words were clipped—impatient as usual.

"The police are on the scene," Braun reminded him. "On a brighter note, I heard from Usher. He said Marta's still painting. Her latest was a bluebird."

"A bird? I don't know anything about a bluebird, but a red one landed on our car at the airport." Fritz noted. "That reminds me. It dropped a business card with the same logo as the florist that sent Cordy those flowers."

"Whoa," Braun said. "Did that red bird have a purple stripe on its wing?"

"It did. Why?" Fritz held his breath.

"It's Bluebird," Braun said. "It's too much of a coincidence to be anything else." He explained Usher's phone conversation about the painting. "Marta says that red bird protects her, but it can only warn you."

"Don't let anyone deliver flowers to Laura," Fritz said. "I can't dwell on this, but there's an address on the card. Check it out." He gave the information. "Let me know what you find."

"I will," Braun promised.

"Fritz, I don't usually put stock in any of this, but after that acid attack, I'm a believer—if Bluebird flies your way again—pay attention." Cordy added, "It might save your life."

"I will," Fritz said. "Oh yes, congratulations on your promotion as an FBI agent."

"Thanks—"

"I'll talk more later. We just passed the roadblock in Risa's neighborhood, so I have to go. Keep in touch."

HOSTAGE

A chill raced up Fritz's spine, warning him that something was off-kilter, as Kelly drove her Lexus past the roadblock on Risa's street. "I thought we were the backup." two police cruisers had parked hastily at odd angles near the curb. The roof rack beacon of one car still flashed red and blue. Both front doors were wide open, but no one was in sight except a body crumpled at the end of the sidewalk. It was too quiet—a dead silence.

Kelly pulled in back of the blinking patrol car and kept her head low behind the steering wheel. "I don't see any cops around."

"Stay down and call the person in charge." Fritz grabbed his Glock, stepped from the Lexus, and dodged between the houses. Glancing down the hedgerow, Fritz spied two officers lying in a heap.

One officer's cap and jacket were nowhere in sight.

Braving possible gunfire, Fritz led with his weapon, put his head down, and dashed across the exposed area to that officer's aid. He knelt to check the man's carotid. *No pulse.* Fritz paused when voices came from the neighbor's house.

A woman sobbed. "Please, don't shoot. I won't tell a soul."

A man's voice was matter of fact, "I don't want to hurt you, but this is business." There was a scream, but no gunshot followed. Then silence.

"Fritz glanced back to the curb. Agent Kelly had gotten out of the car and kneeled over another cop in the neighbor's front yard. Why hadn't he seen that victim? Tunnel vision?

Sirens echoed in the distance. Kelly made eye contact, shook her head, and dashed to the blinking patrol car.

Fritz crept along the hedge on Risa's side to the second officer. Something grabbed his leg. Peering down at the cop's hand clenched around his ankle, he saw a pool of blood flowing from his neck, soaking the front of his shirt.

His face shone gray as granite. "Help." Blood spewed from his lips as he spoke.

"Help is on the way." Fritz knelt closer, grabbed the cop's cold, clammy hand, and squeezed it gently. "Hang in there." Fritz's eyes filled with tears as he applied pressure to the hole in the man's neck, trying to close the gap.

"I'm," the man coughed, "dying." A guttural whisper escaped. "Save her," bubbled from his lips. He sighed. The cop's hand fell limp, and his eyes glassed over.

Fritz's mind knew it, but it took a few seconds to register the man was dead. He ran in a low crouch to the end of the row. The patio door of the neighbor's house swung in the wind. Drops of blood led up the walkway to the steps.

About to bolt through the back door, Fritz heard screams from out front. "Run, Fritz!"

"Kelly." Fritz darted around the corner of the house as two shots popped like firecrackers and blew off part of the hedge.

Sirens grew louder. An ambulance drove into view.

Fritz abruptly stopped when he saw Walt holding Kelly with a gun at her temple.

"Drop the gun," Walt yelled.

Fritz lowered his Glock, but before he let go, an ambulance pulled in the back of Kelly's car, followed by another patrol cruiser, blocking the road.

Walt's eyes grew wide as they darted between Fritz and the cop car heading his way. He swung the gun and pointed it at Fritz.

Kelly rammed her elbow into Walt's gut, twisted his arm, and wrestled the gun from his hand.

The previous wound burst open. Walt hunched forward and dropped the gun.

"Get away from him, Kelly," Fritz yelled. "I have him covered." He leveled his Glock at Walt. "Where did Vinny take Risa?"

Walt shrugged. "Don't know. Don't care. Vinny left me here alone to die. He never talks to me directly. Only through Mick, and now he's dead."

Fritz yelled to the paramedics, climbing from the ambulance, "Check on the woman inside. I haven't heard from her in a while. There are two cops along the side of the house near the hedge, but both are dead."

Kelly handed Fritz Walt's pistol. "So is the officer by the front door. I'll check on Inga."

Two officers ran toward Fritz. One held out his hand for Walt's gun. "You must be Detective Von Schlegen. I'm Officer McCoy. I talked to you earlier. We'll take it from here."

"Any word on Risa?" Fritz asked.

McCoy shook his head. "Sorry. Nothing yet. Go down to headquarters. Maybe the captain knows more. Tell him I sent you."

Agent Kelly came back a few minutes later.

"She okay?" Fritz asked.

"He slugged Inga on the back of her head," Kelly said. "She's unconscious. We'll have to talk to her later if she comes to."

"No more news on Risa," Fritz said. "We need to check at police headquarters."

Kelly dug through her pockets for her keys. "I know the way. I'll drive."

TRAPPED

Saturday, June 14 – 1612 CDT, Vinny's hideout

A bone-rattling tremor vibrated through Risa's body as she bounced from the rear seat of Vinny's car and landed on the floor. Memories flooded back to the last time she was kidnapped. Cold metal cuffs cut into her flesh—her arms raw, bloody, and scarred. Holding up her hands, she realized the only thing binding her wrists today was the tie from her robe, yet that unforgotten fear coiled through her, waiting for the snake to pounce.

Vinny's car rolled to a stop. He flicked his lighter, but it wouldn't keep its flame. He flicked it again, lit a stogie, and then kicked open the front car door with a booted foot. The rusty metal hinge grated in protest, but in Risa's mind—the lock clicked, followed by a high-pitched squeak of the heavy soundproof door, opening to let the monster inside her hidden cell. Frank reeked of tobacco and knew he lurked in the shadows wielding that rawhide whip.

The door slammed, jolting her back from the past. Swallowing back the bile rising in the back of her throat, she vowed, *Never again. Show no fear. Submit. Create no waves. I must survive until Fritz finds me once again.* Closing her eyes, the loneliness crept back and threatened to overtake her—seconds turning to minutes, to hours, and then to weeks...

* * *

Vinny threw open the rear car door. "What the heck? What are you doing on the floor?"

Risa lay there frozen like a trapped animal. Her wide blue eyes stared through him in a glazed horror. Tears trickled down her face. Her breaths came out in small pants.

"You can't hide from me." Vinny smiled and gave her the better part of a minute to stare at him and take in her situation. With slow, deliberate movements, he leaned into the car and grabbed her arm. "There's no place to run, honey, so behave, and we'll get along just fine. I want to get to know you better. Every part of you."

Recoiling, she scrambled onto the back car seat and watched his every move. Her nostrils flared. If looks could kill, his blood would spew. She'd step over his lifeless body and never look back.

Vinny grabbed her ankle and dragged her closer. "I'm not going to hurt you." Her eyes darkened as he held her leg in a vice-like grip and ran his other hand over her calf. "Not yet, anyway."

A jagged sob escaped from her lips. "Please, don't." Risa pulled her robe tighter around her body.

Vinny let go of Risa's leg. Kidnapping Risa wasn't as rewarding as he'd imagined. She did not fight. *Maybe that will change.*

Midget shuffled up to the car. He rubbed his pudgy paws together and had an idiotic smirk. "I haven't had a broad in twenty years—at least, one I didn't have to pay for."

Vinny glared at his brother. "She's not to be touched. Do you hear me?" He pushed Midget away from the car. "So, don't get any ideas."

Midget groaned and grabbed his shoulder. "Hey, watch it. I'm running low on painkillers. Have you called our supplier?"

"He works tonight," Vinny blocked Midget's second attempt at grabbing Risa.

He stepped back but didn't go far, needling Vinny. "Who's going to watch her? Feed her? Bathe her?" Midget chuckled. "Not you. You'll be hunting."

"She's safest with Jules. He hasn't discovered his dick yet. Besides, you'll be driving right next to me."

"Only during the day. Can't drive at night." Midget licked his lips.

Another tremor ran through Risa's body. A pulse in her neck beat wildly. She drew her knees up to her chest and rocked silently.

Vinny pulled a pair of handcuffs from his pocket. "I don't want to do this to you." He smiled. "Damn it. There's no other way."

"What's this?" Midget asked. "Compassion? You're freaking me out, bro."

"Hell no." Vinny motioned for Risa. "Get out of the car and don't make a run for it, or I'll sic Midget on you."

Vinny had to give her credit. He expected her to leap forward and fight him with every ounce of her life.

Instead, her tiny hand reached toward his chin and gently brushed away a smear of blood from the gash she'd raked across his cheek with a coat hanger earlier that day. "That's a deep cut. It'll need stitches."

"It'll be fine. Just get out of the car."

Risa lowered her eyes and scooted toward the edge. "Give me a moment. Everything's spinning." Her hand flew to her mouth.

Vinny bent over her and held her hair away from her face as she leaned over the car and puked.

Midget gagged and backed away. "That's disgusting."

"Unlock the front door. I'll bring her inside." Vinny wiped her mouth with the edge of her robe. "Better, doll?" He took her wrists and snapped on the cuffs. "These are to protect you. If Midget thinks you'll run, he'll shoot you in the back. Do I make myself clear?"

Risa didn't answer. She'd passed out.

Vinny lifted her from the car, carried her downstairs, and placed her in a prepared cage. "I'll get to know you later, when you're awake, and we're more comfortable. Rest up."

SKELETON KEY

Fritz tapped his fingers on his thigh and bounced his knee, making the whole car vibrate with his nervous energy. "What's taking so long? Can't you drive any faster? Risa is fighting for her life. I need to find her ASAP!"

"Two more minutes, and we'll be there," Kelly rounded a corner, passed the precinct's parking lot, and pulled up to a gray-cement multi-storied building. Large black letters overhead read Ann Arbor Police Department.

"Thanks. This shouldn't take long." Fritz climbed from Agent Kelly's Lexus before she came to a complete stop, then grabbed the door, and leaned inside, snapping off orders, "Park and see if McCoy's arrived yet, while I track down the captain." He didn't wait for a reply, slammed the door, and headed inside. He was greeted by a busy reception area. An array of smells hit his nose—sweat, cheap perfume, and stale tobacco all wrapped into one—a very different aroma from his office, usually a combination of coffee, sugared doughnuts, and gun oil. He bulldozed his way past a teenager to the front of the line. The teen grumbled and flagged down another receptionist.

A petite black woman stepped up to the counter. She stiffened at the sight of him. "Hey, hotshot! No cutting in line. You think you're FBI?"

Fritz knew that look. He was the outsider. "No. I'm a private detective. Officer McCoy sent me. Is the captain in?"

Her head nodded toward the clock.

Fritz didn't wait for her refusal. "Look, I know it's after five, but a few thugs kidnapped my baby sister. I must talk to the captain."

The clerk placed her hand over her chin, frowned, and nodded. "Used to be FBI?"

"You're good." Fritz noticed she was smiling now, and it wouldn't hurt to give her kudos. A little praise can go a long way, and he may need her help in the future.

"Sorry to hear about your sister." "I'll check with the captain." The clerk reached for the intercom.

"Thanks."

"Next time, lose the suit. Slump a bit and wipe that attitude from your face before cutting in line." She leaned closer and lowered her voice. "It'll get you in the door without the hassle."

"Okay—next time." Fritz slouched a bit.

She chuckled and punched the button.

A few minutes later, she directed him to the captain's office.

Fritz knocked and opened the door. "Evening, sir."

The captain motioned him inside. He was on the phone and didn't bother getting up when Fritz approached the cluttered desk. Like most offices Fritz had passed along the hallway, this one had no view. The dusty window overlooked the parking lot. The captain hung up. "Have a seat."

"I appreciate you taking the time to see me." Fritz pulled up a battered wooden chair. "Any news on Risa's kidnapping?"

"It's still early." The captain ran a hand over his dark crew cut. "Do you expect a ransom demand?"

Fritz frowned at the question. "I hadn't thought of that. If anything, Vinny will demand a trade. My life for hers."

"If it's an option, are you willing to take the risk?"

Fritz nodded. "It's me he's after. If you knew Vinny as well as I do, you'd know he lies. He'll never let her go. He'd swear on his mother's grave and then shoot her in the back. I'm afraid we'll have to track him down and free her the hard way."

The captain turned the computer screen so Fritz could see it. "Here's what we have so far." A photo of Mick lying on his side next to the curb in front of Risa's house popped up. "The ME has him down at the morgue."

"Did he find anything interesting?" Fritz asked.

"Nothing in his pockets. No ID. Not even a driver's license."

"I can ID him," Fritz said. "That's Mick Corenelli. He's Vinny's younger brother. Age 41. Born in 1980. Married three times and is currently divorced. Four kids. Youngest is nine and lives with his mother in upstate New York."

"You're a walking textbook," the captain laughed.

"His brother, Vinny, has been my nightmare for nearly thirty years. I've studied his family for a long time." Fritz pulled the screen closer. "Something is hanging out of his jacket pocket—looks like a piece of paper. Are you sure they didn't find anything else on the body?"

The captain squinted at the photo. He moved the cursor over the pocket and enlarged the area. "That's the info I received. Maybe the card fell out of his pocket. I'll check with our criminal investigator.

"Mind if I have a chat with him too?" Fritz asked.

"No. All I ask is that you keep me informed."

"Where's his brother, Walt?" Fritz asked.

"The ambulance took him to the hospital with a police escort to check out his wound. Once the doc gives the okay, an officer will lock him up. You can come back in the morning to interview him."

Officer McCoy poked his head in the door. "Detective, I'm heading to the ME's office if you'd like to ride along."

Agent Kelly was at his side. "You won't believe what the ME discovered."

"So they did find something," Fritz said.

"A skeleton key in the deceased's shoe," Kelly said.

"Any idea what it might open?" Fritz asked.

The captain shook his head. "No, but why would he keep it in his shoe?"

Fritz shrugged. "Do you remember that business card Bluebird dropped on your windshield? Look at this photo." Fritz pointed out the small card peeking out of Mick's pocket. "The logo is the same as Cordy's floral delivery. Let's see what else the ME found."

SECRET HIDING PLACE

Sunday, June 15 – 0552 EDT, Lewisburg, West Virginia

Laura got up early the following day, enjoying the silent dawn growing into a gorgeous apricot sunrise. Yesterday, she discovered an herb garden planted beneath her deck. A new recipe flashed in her mind—fresh mint added to dark chocolate fudge. Her mouth watered at the thought of testing a small batch of the homemade delicacy. Her husband was a confirmed chocoholic. Fudge was Fritz's favorite candy. She wished she could whip up a batch and deliver it to him in person, but Usher had already refused to send her Magic Creams to the candy factory. He certainly wouldn't ship fudge directly to Fritz.

Laura peeked into the studio. Marta was already up, dressed, and at the easel. The tip of her tongue was trapped between her lips as she concentrated on drawing. "Morning, Sprite."

Marta didn't even look up. She just nodded. "Morning, Gramma."

"Have fun." Laura backed out of the room without disturbing the busy girl. She hummed to herself as she harvested the youngest mint leaves.

Pepper nudged Laura's leg, begging for attention as usual.

"Where did you come from?" She petted the dog and then went inside with a handful of sprigs.

Maggie met her at the kitchen door. "Do you need anything? I'm getting low on groceries, so I'm running into town. Usher is at the front gate with Jake, so you're not alone."

Laura checked the fridge. "I'll probably use up the whole milk and butter." She checked the cupboard. "Add some cocoa to the list. I need the real stuff, not the hot chocolate blend."

Maggie rubbed her stomach. "Making more candy? If I keep sampling your inventions, I'll need to work out soon."

"I'm not forcing you to eat any." Laura chuckled. She took out a mixing bowl and a heavy-duty wooden spoon and poured cold water into a measuring cup.

"There's an electric beater in the drawer to the left of the sink," Maggie said.

Laura shook her head. "Thanks, but I prefer a big wooden spoon and a lot of muscle. I guess I take after my mother. I can still see her sitting in a kitchen chair, holding the bowl on her lap. The spoon made a wonderful drumming sound as she beat the thickening candy. Her fudge was perfect every time."

"Sounds like a lot of work to me. What is Marta doing today? I haven't seen her this morning."

"She's in the studio painting." Laura beamed. "Her pictures are getting better each day."

"I'll run up and see if she needs anything from town." Maggie called back from the hall, "I won't be long. I should be back in an hour or so."

"That's perfect." Laura heard Maggie climb the steps. She didn't pay much attention and turned on the faucet to wash the mint leaves.

Sometime later, Maggie burst through the door. "Did Marta come down here?"

Laura looked up from her mixing bowl. "No."

"She's not upstairs." Maggie's eyes flew from right to left before returning her gaze. "I checked the third and second floors, then went outside. I even called Usher to find out if he or Jake had noticed her playing outdoors. They hadn't, and Usher is still searching the grounds. I can't find her anywhere."

Laura set the bowl on the counter and dashed upstairs. "Marta? Where are you?"

The studio looked the same as it did earlier, but Marta was gone. Laura noticed the paper had a painting of a bookcase at an odd angle. A few books were on the shelf, but no notes.

An echoing voice came from downstairs as Maggie called for the girl. "Yell, if you can hear me, Sprite."

Laura went through her suite. She threw open the balcony door. A red bird with a striped purple wing chirped loudly. It circled Laura and then sat on the railing.

Maggie stepped into the room. "Did you find her?"

"No, but I think that little red bird is Marta's Bluebird. See the purple stripe on her wing. Marta called her Bluebird because she had to mix blue with red to make purple." Laura moved onto the balcony and held out her hand. "Is Marta safe?"

The bird hopped onto Laura's outstretched arm and bobbed its head.

"Where is she?" Laura asked.

Bluebird flew into the hallway and down one flight of stairs. It hovered while Laura and Maggie caught up, and then it flew into the library on the second floor and perched on the fireplace mantle. The bird chirped and then gave its warning whistle.

A bookcase to the right of the fireplace slid open. Marta poked her head out and turned off her flashlight. "Hi, Gramma. Maggie. Look what I found."

Laura dropped to her knees and hugged Marta. "We've looked everywhere for you. Why didn't you answer?"

"I didn't hear you." Marta brushed off her dusty knees. "Momma said this is a great hiding place for when the bad man comes."

"Man? Is there a man coming?" Maggie took out her cell phone. "We better warn Usher and Jake." She walked over to the window to talk.

Laura remembered the painting. "Books. Is this what you painted in the studio?"

Marta nodded. "Where's Bluebird?"

Laura glanced around the room. The bird had disappeared. "She led us to you, but I guess she flew away."

Maggie spoke into the phone. "We found Marta. You'll never guess what she discovered. Come check it out." There was a pause. "No, I'm not leaving for the store. Not today. Send someone else to get the groceries." She paused again. "Yes, see you in a few minutes. Oh, Usher, be sure, and lock up after they go."

Maggie pocketed the cell and peeked around the bookcase. "I never knew we had a secret hiding place." She crouched behind the shelf. "I wonder where it goes."

Marta wrapped her arms around herself and rubbed her shoulders. "I went a long way into the cave, but it's cold."

Laura moved into the hallway. "I'll go upstairs and make sure the doors and windows are locked."

Maggie nodded. My rooms are locked, but I'll check the main floor."

By the time Laura came downstairs, Usher was at the door. He knelt beside Marta. "Let's check out that hiding place and see where it goes."

Marta squealed with delight. "Coming, Gramma?"

"No. You go ahead. I'm in the middle of making fudge."

"Okay." Marta grabbed Usher's hand and glanced at his wrist. "That's a fancy watch."

"It's a magic one," Usher said. "Let's go upstairs, and I'll show you how it works."

"Okay. Follow me," Marta chatted on, "see here? You have to push on this rock in the fireplace…"

CAGED

Sunday, June 15 – 0802 EDT, Ann Arbor, Michigan

Risa awoke in a heap, cramped and unable to see clearly. Shivering in the damp room, her head felt like it was ready to explode. A noxious stink of mildew mixed with a sickly, sweet, earthy stench filled her nostrils. *Gardenias. Oh, how I hate the smell of gardenias.*

Trying to sit up, she discovered her wrists cuffed in front of her. Memory trickled back. Something or someone had hit the back of her head, and everything went dark. A shudder ran through her.

Risa tried to figure out how she got here. *How long ago?* Then, snippets of her arrival eked through her consciousness. She scanned the room. A narrow, broken window filtered dingy light near the ceiling on the other side of the room. *I must be in a basement.*

An irritating drip, drip, drip came from her left. It sounded like a splash into something metal. The thought of water made her thirsty. She rose on her knees for a closer look and nearly gagged. A leaky faucet dripped into a rusty pail. Dead leaves floated in the stagnant water.

Trying to sit up higher, her head banged against something metal. Her eyes were so swollen, that she could barely see. Feeling along the top and sides of her confined area, she realized she was in a large metal cage, locked with a padlock. Not again. *Is this the same cage Frank put me in?* It was too dark to tell, but her throat tightened with growing fear.

Clear your mind, Risa. Think of something else. She tried to lie down. A cloth lay beneath her, but it was not thick enough to prevent something sharp from cutting into her flesh. Her back ached, and her neck muscles tensed. She flexed her neck to work out the kinks. Tightly confined, her legs bumped against the metal bars surrounding her.

Willing her vision to clear, she noticed cardboard boxes lay scattered along the floor. Several pots with shriveling plants sat on a wooden table beside the cage.

A wave of nausea flirted with her insides. Bile pooled in the back of her throat. She took several deep breaths, swallowing hard to prevent throwing up. Goose bumps rose on her bare arms. She wore only her underwear. *Where's my robe?* A flash of dark green caught her eye. It was her robe lying beneath her, and it didn't give much padding. *No wonder the bars of the cage cut so deep.* She grabbed at a robe's corner and pulled the hem around her. The effort was exhausting. Covered in bruises, she ached all over.

The steady drip, drip, drip marked off the seconds. Risa strained to listen for any unwelcome visitor but seemed to be alone, hearing no one.

Where was the hooded man? His name was Vinny, right? She held her breath and listened again. There were no footsteps above her. No voices and no sound of a Like an insidious cancer, fear flooded her mind, built like a tsunami, and threatened to drown her. *Vinny left me here to die. He'll torture me first, and then I'll die. Fritz won't rescue me this time. He doesn't even know I'm missing.*

ACE

Sunday, June 15 – 1017 EDT,

Ann Arbor, Michigan/0917 MDT, Fort Collins, Colorado

Vinny phoned Ace. "What do you have for me? It's been over a week. Have you located Fritz's wife?"

"Not yet, but I'm working on it." Ace tapped away on his computer. "I need more time."

"There is no more time," Vinny said. "I need to act now. Get those wheels in motion, Braun, Laura, and the girl. We have to nab them while Fritz is still spinning over Risa's kidnapping."

"So you haven't snuffed her yet?" Ace asked. "I thought Mick's orders were to dispose of the sister."

"Well, Mick's no longer the mastermind, is he? He's dead," Vinny blurted. "I need Risa as bait to lure out her brother. It feels like I'm only one step ahead of Fritz, so get a move on this before he tracks me down. You told me this was right up your alley. I feel like you've taken a detour. I'll give you twenty-four more hours, and that's final."

"I haven't heard from my contact in the FBI." There was a pause, then some clicking on a keyboard. "Oh, wait." Ace laughed. "We're in luck. I just discovered he was transferred to Washington, D.C. Once you have the wife and kid, how will you lure out Fritz?"

"That's the easy part," Vinny said. "He'll do anything to save them. What a pleasure. Then I'll get my revenge, take on an alias as Fritz did, and live happily ever after."

"Ahh, there's a little problem we need to handle," Ace mumbled something under his breath.

"Speak up, man. What did you say?"

"Money," Ace spit out. "There's a little problem of money. Joey A is demanding his usual cut. He claims you went around his boys and stiffed him. Now, you're doing the same to me."

Vinny's temper flared. "Joey! How did he find out about this? It doesn't have anything to do with him."

"He's better than a bloodhound. His scarred face is uglier every day, and his grapevine grows with each passing minute. It's filled with suckers who'll pass on whatever he asks for," Ace said. "You really scarred him for life."

"Are you one of those suckers?" Vinny asked.

Ace cleared his throat. "Naw, I just want my money."

"I never could trust the bastard," Vinny swore. "I'll take care of Joey. You do what I asked. Find the Mrs. and Fritz's granddaughter."

"You promised me half upfront—in cash. All I've seen is two hundred grand. We agreed on five now, and I expect the rest as soon as the job is done. I'll need to fly out to D.C. to meet with my contact. That'll cost more."

"Okay," Vinny snapped, "I'll deliver the whole million upfront to get the information in my hands today, but I need until Tuesday to get that much cash. I'll wire funds by noon. It'll be divided into three different accounts. By the way, don't waste it on drugs. Your habit better not become my problem."

"Don't worry, Vinny, a little buzz helps me concentrate on my hacking skills." Ace chuckled. "Okay, I have until Tuesday. I'll see what I can do. Later."

"No, I gave you 24 hours. Better get it before Tuesday." The line was dead. Vinny pocketed his cell and made a chuckle of his own. *I have a cure for addicts and mob bosses. Right now, Joey would have to wait.* A shudder raced through him. He hoped never to see Joey's scarred face again. Vinny vowed it would be a fight to the finish if he did. One of them would be dead, and it wouldn't be Vinny.

ROADBLOCKS EVERYWHERE

Sunday, June 15 – 1323 CDT, Ann Arbor, Michigan

"Call me ASAP!" Fritz tossed the cell phone back on the desk, jotted a note, and muttered to himself. Picking up the phone again, he glanced at a text message. "Why is everything closed on Sundays? I can't reach CSI, the ME, or even Officer McCoy!"

By noon, his frustration grew into anger. He'd spent most of Sunday morning typing. No, actually, his hunt-and-peck system was nothing like typing. He'd punched in a sentence or two with his index fingers, then hit delete instead of backspace, wiping out a whole line in one stroke.

"Calm down," Agent Kelly said. "You're going to pop the keys off that board."

"The damn delete button is on the upper right row of this blasted keyboard. It's the same spot where backspace is located on my old HP. I can't do this anymore. "You're in charge of the data searches. I'm going to visit Risa's neighbor at the hospital. Inga should be awake by now."

"Good idea. Maybe I can finish some work without hearing you mumbling every two seconds."

Fritz pulled on his jacket and searched the pockets. "Oh yeah, I forgot. No keys. No car. Can I borrow your Lexus? I need a rental of my own."

Kelly fetched her purse from the bottom right drawer of her desk and dug out her keys. "Not a problem. I'm not going anywhere. I can't believe how many properties are associated with Vinny and his family."

"Risa's been missing for two days. Any luck finding out where that skeleton key came from? It might open Vinny's hiding place where he's keeping Risa. Why else would Mick still have it on his person? It was in his shoe of all places."

"Like I said, I'm still looking." Agent Kelly typed away on her laptop computer. Her fingers eloquently tapped each key—using all her fingers on both hands. She managed to type half a page in the short time Fritz took to gather his notes, stuff his cell phone into his pocket, and walk to the door. "Maybe I'll have more news by dinner time. We can share our notes over some Italian food."

"Sounds great." Fritz left the office, found Kelly's Lexus, and then remembered he wanted to replay Inga's 911 call. He trekked back up the two flights of stairs to retrieve the file.

"Why didn't you just call me?" Kelly asked. "I could have sent it to your phone."

"I wouldn't even know how…oh, never mind. I found what I came for, but thanks. I'll think of that next time."

Kelly smiled. "We'll get you back into the 21st century before the end of the week."

Fritz grumbled the whole way back to the car. He replayed the 911 call several times and nearly drove past the hospital. It took two passes through the visitors' lot before he found a parking space, and no one was at the information desk when he arrived. Instead, there was a touch screen and a black box on the corner of the counter. Fritz wondered what he was supposed to do when he spied a security guard. "Good afternoon, Officer."

The guard nodded and kept walking.

Fritz moved into the guard's path. "Sorry to bother you. I'm here to visit a patient and need to find out what room she's in. Can you help me?"

The guard tapped the touch screen. "Jeannie, we have a visitor who's lost."

A teenager, at least she looked that young, poked her head around an office door behind the counter. "Thanks, John." Her half-pink, half-black ponytail bounced as she turned toward Fritz. "How may I help you?" Her long, black, polished fingernails were poised over a keyboard, waiting for his reply.

"I'm here to see Inga Freeman. What room is she in?"

Jeannie typed in the information and frowned. "John, can I talk to you?" Her eyes scanned Fritz, then the waiting room. The two whispered for a moment.

John stepped up to Fritz. "I'm sorry. We can't give out that information."

"Why not?" Fritz asked.

"She's in protective custody," John said. "Only the immediate family is allowed to visit."

"Wait." Fritz dug through his wallet, pulled out his ID, and showed it to Jeannie and the security guard. "I'm a private detective. I have permission from Officer McCoy to follow up on her case."

After more explanations and hassle, John agreed to escort Fritz to Inga's room and took the elevator to the third floor. The officer, who stood guard outside her room, noted that Fritz's name was on McCoy's approval list, so John returned to work.

"The patient is still in a coma." The police officer flagged down a nurse to answer Fritz's questions. She wasn't much help but admitted that Risa's neighbor had not regained consciousness since her injury.

So, Fritz went back downstairs to track down his brother-in-law, Jim. This time, he spoke to the touch screen, but no one answered, so he walked behind the counter and knocked on the door.

Jeannie appeared. "Did you get lost again?"

Fritz blew out a deep breath. "No, I found Inga. Now I'm looking for Jim Grant."

"Why didn't you use the intercom?"

"I tried the screen, but you didn't respond. Anyway, what room—"

"Old people today," she muttered under her breath. "Jim Grant, right?" She tapped the keyboard and gave him the room number. "Next time you need me, press this button." She pointed to a large red button at the bottom of the screen.

It was the first time Fritz noticed the large circle. "Okay. Thanks."

It shouldn't have been a difficult task to find Jim. However, he wasn't in his room.

Spying a nurse passing Jim's door in the hallway, Fritz dashed after her. "Wait up. Where's Jim? The patient was assigned to this room. Has he been moved?"

The nurse checked a clipboard hanging outside the door. "He's in X-ray, and then he's scheduled for surgery. He'll be there for a few hours, and then he'll go to PACU."

"What does that mean?" Fritz asked.

"You'd probably know it as the Recovery Room."

"Thanks. Tell Jim I'll come back this evening." Fritz glanced at his watch—5:57 p.m. Time was flying by too quickly.

"I'll leave word with the next shift." The nurse hurried into a room two doors down.

Fritz waited until the hallway was empty before checking the clipboard. *What's going on? No security guard on duty? Inga gets one, but not Risa's husband?* His anger spurred him into motion. Grabbing his cell, he called Officer McCoy one more time. He clenched his fist when, again, he couldn't reach the man in charge of this case. His message was curt. "I want a security guard for Jim Grant. Remedy this ASAP." He swore while heading back to the office.

* * *

It was nearly 7 p.m., and Agent Kelly wasn't having much success either. Instead of a relaxing Italian dinner, they went to a fast-food joint and updated each other on their progress. In a hurry, Fritz downed his burger in four bites. "Jim must be out of surgery by now. I want to find out what he saw and heard during Risa's kidnapping."

"Did you find out who the friend was that drove Jim to the hospital?" Kelly asked.

"I thought the ambulance brought Jim there," Fritz said. "No wonder no officer was outside of his door."

"I'm sure Jim will tell you his friend's name, but in the meantime, I'll review the police report once more before turning in for the night." Kelly drove to her home and parked the car. "You can borrow the Lexus and pick me up early. I need a few paper records from the courthouse, and they open at eight."

"Thanks. I'll see you at 6:30 a.m. It'll give you enough time to drop me off at the office before heading downtown."

Kelly agreed, and Fritz drove across town to visit Jim. To his surprise, another patient was in Jim's old room. He checked at the nurses' station.

The nurse replied, "Jim was moved to intensive care after surgery. The ICU is on the second floor. Turn right when you exit the elevator, but they have limited visiting hours."

Fritz thanked the nurse and took the elevator down one flight. He argued with the ICU nurse about allowing him to see Jim even for the allotted five minutes. She finally relented after inspecting his private detective ID. *Still no security officer, but that nurse won't let anyone near him. I'm giving McCoy an earful next time I talk to him.*

Unfortunately, Jim had been sedated and floated in and out of consciousness. He didn't even know Fritz was in the room.

Fritz jotted a quick note and placed it face up under the water glass so Jim could read, "Fritz was here at 9:48 p.m. I'll come back tomorrow." Fritz stopped by the ICU nurses' station and delivered the same message before exiting the hospital.

CLEAR DREAMS

Monday, June 16 – 0417 EDT, Lewisburg, West Virginia

In that hazy zone, just before sleep stole consciousness, Laura drifted in fear for her husband's life. It had been a week since she'd left him. Not a word from him since, except for that dreadful radio broadcast. He popped into her thoughts frequently, and she wondered what he was doing at that moment. How could she help bring this nightmare to an end?

Dwelling on that thought, she reflected on something Marta had said in passing. "Gramma, what if we made a special chocolate candy for the bad man? Would he like us better?"

As morning approached, she'd mulled over an unforgivable idea and made up her mind. Everyone loved chocolate. At least, she hoped that Vinny did. What if she made a special recipe—one with poison? Oh, not a lethal poison. She couldn't bring herself to that, but one that would incapacitate him. She didn't have a clue how or where to start or even if she could go through with that, but she'd research the matter.

Laura got up, threw on her robe, and went downstairs to the library.

The little red bird sat on the mantle. She chirped when Laura turned on the light.

"Morning, Bluebird." Laura glanced around the room. The bookshelf was along the wall as usual. No one would know there was a secret hiding place in the room. She closed the door. "I'm looking for a book on poisons," Laura whispered more to herself.

The bird raised its striped purple wing, pointing across the room.

Laura moved to the shelf. There were three books on the subject. Maybe she wasn't the only one interested in the topic. "This is our little secret."

The bird flew off the mantle and landed on Laura's shoulder as if glancing over the first book she pulled out for review. "Let's see. It has to be odorless, colorless, and tasteless." Leafing through the pages, she shook her head. "I'll need to spend more time."

Bluebird flew toward the door, tweeted a warning whistle, and landed on the table.

"Is it time to go?" Laura asked. Then she heard footsteps outside in the hallway. "Maggie's up." She shoved the book back onto the shelf.

Bluebird knocked a small magazine from the table and flew to the ledge above the hallway door.

When Maggie opened the door and walked into the library, Laura bent down to pick it up. "Good morning. I thought I heard someone in here."

Bluebird dropped from the door ledge and flew into the hallway.

Maggie didn't seem to notice. "I'm going downstairs to put on some coffee. Usher will be here at ten. We need to make a plan in case someone infiltrates the house."

"Yes, I agree we need a plan." Laura set the magazine on the table. An article on forensics caught her eye. "I'll get dressed and meet you downstairs." She stuffed the journal under her arm and headed back to her room. The more she thought over her plan, the less she liked it. *I'm losing my mind. This is crazy.* Her heart ached at how she treated Fritz when he finally told her the truth. *I'm beginning to understand how Lars got hooked on those 'fishing trips' that were really special ops missions with the FBI. He was trying to save us.* She had to admire the extremes he went to keep them safe.

Laura shook her head at the thought of her idiotic plan and returned the magazine to the library after she got dressed.

NAILED

Monday, June 16 – 0648 MDT, Fort Collins, Colorado

The address on the florist's box delivered to Cordy was bogus, but Officer Cordelia ran the numbers through an algorithm her father had shown her years ago. Bingo. A promising location popped up on the outskirts of Fort Collins. It was barely fifteen miles from the agency. The property was an abandoned factory with a large warehouse made of gray cinderblock. It wasn't much to go on, but Chief Jackson agreed to send in teams to stakeout the factory around the clock.

Cordy arrived early at the office to meet her partner for the stakeout. A message lay on her desk. 'Need to run an errand. Get another partner until I meet you.' He left specific details: 'If you see anything suspicious, call for immediate backup. Do not venture out on your own. Stay put. Stay safe. Braun.'

Cordy crumpled the note. After conducting an investigation, the owner of a business located across the street stated that a flower truck had been spotted in the area at times, but they were unable to confirm the logo associated with it. After the report from the previous team, Cordy planted herself in the driver's seat. With a steaming cup of coffee in hand, she settled in for her stint of watch and wait at the warehouse. Six-hour shifts made a short day, but they dragged on forever. She preferred to run, work out, or even do paperwork instead of this tedious stakeout.

Ninety minutes into her shift, Cordy hadn't seen anything unusual, and another hour ticked by. After drinking nearly a full thermos of coffee, a potty break was a necessity. The thought of doing a manicure wouldn't have crossed her mind, except she'd stationed herself under a tree in the back alley of a nail salon located across the street from the warehouse. Unlikely to find a restroom in the old abandoned factory, she became a customer at the salon. She'd take the opportunity to gather some information as well. In desperate need of a bathroom, Cordy sprinted to the front door. A little bell dinged when she walked into the shop.

"Good morning. May I help you?" the clerk behind the counter asked.

Cordy's eyes roamed around the room and targeted the restroom in the back of the salon. A stand filled with bottles of nail polish lined the wall in front of a window facing the warehouse. "I'm just looking for now." She rubbed her index finger. "The tips keep breaking."

The clerk's smile brightened. "I have just the cure. It would help if you trimmed your nails regularly. Round them with an emery board and avoid harsh soaps. Keep your nails polished so they don't split. Her eyes frequently darted toward the window, but there was still no activity outside to pique her interest.

The clerk searched the rack for something.

"Mind if I use the little girl's room while you look?" Cordy asked.

"Sure. I know it was here yesterday."

Cordy didn't wait. When she finished in the bathroom, she thanked the lady and was about to leave.

"I found it," the clerk said, holding up a bottle of clear polish. "I guess I set it down when the alarm went off at the factory yesterday."

"What alarm?" Cordy asked. "I didn't hear about that."

"I thought everyone knew about the fiasco," the clerk said as she took the nail polish to the check-out counter. "Well, it was a false alarm. The real racket came from those fed cars. Even old Miss Gardner hobbled out the back door to take a look." She chuckled. What a sight she made. Small tufts of shampoo bead up from all fifty strands of gray hair."

"Fed cars?" Cordy asked. Why hadn't she been aware of this? Did the chief know? "Thanks. I'll take the polish." She paid in cash.

The clerk put a free emery board in the bag with the purchase. "Would you like to schedule a manicure?"

Cordy glanced at her watch. "I can't today. Maybe later." She dashed back to the car and called Braun.

He didn't answer, so she called radio dispatch. "Where is Agent Braun Hastings?"

"In a meeting with Chief Jackson," the operator began.

"Is Chief Jackson in his office?"

"No. Can I put you through to his voicemail?"

"I actually need Braun," Cordy said.

The operator cleared her throat. "Do you need backup?"

"No. I'm fine. Just have Braun call me."

Cordy heard the crackling of paper, and then the operator said, "Braun left word that if you called, you are to sit tight."

"What does that mean?" Cordy huffed, "Never mind. There's nothing to report."

"Are you sure? Braun said to tell you—"

"I'm sure he did." She hurriedly disconnected the call, fuming at Braun's constant bossy behavior. She hated being told what to do, how to do it, when and where to go, or how much she could handle.

By 12:15 p.m., Cordy became more concerned. Braun said he'd meet here at noon, and there was still no word from him. He was never late. Punctuality was mandatory in his book. Every second seemed like an hour. After all, she only had ten fingernails to trim, buff, and polish. Cordy finished the job in less than ten minutes. She felt ridiculous spreading clear goop over her nails while wearing running shoes, jeans, and soft body armor beneath her blouse.

She lifted the binoculars from around her neck and scanned the area. A red Beamer caught her eye as it inched along the railroad tracks near the rundown warehouse.

Her handheld radio crackled to life. "See anything suspicious?"

Cordy grabbed the radio and nearly responded when, "Nope. All clear. Let's go," came back as an answer. Confused, she checked the radio. *Was someone using her frequency? No, it must be bleeding over from another.*

"Are you sure we should try again so soon? They nearly caught us the other day." The red car came to a stop.

"That's why you're driving a hot shot Beamer instead of a boring black sedan. If anyone's watching, it'll distract their attention from the real action."

That's when Braun's car appeared on the warehouse ramp.

Why now? Cordy ducked behind the steering wheel and peered once more through the binoculars. The chief was with Braun. *Had they used the radio? No,* she decided. *The voices didn't sound like either of them.*

A dark SUV drove around the side of the building and parked so it was out of Braun's view.

Cordy bolted upright, bumped her cell phone perched on the dashboard, and had to stretch to reach it. She speed-dialed Braun while she checked the area through the lens for the SUV. The call went to voice mail. "Someone's bleeding over our radio frequency. I think they're—"

Braun's redial call interrupted. She hit the speaker. "Braun here."

"You're being watched."

"What?" Braun asked.

Cordy saw another car drive down the alley. The passenger window zipped down, and she had just enough time to yell, "Gun! Duck, now!"

The back window of Braun's car shattered, and she heard a gun blast. The SUV pulled in behind Braun's sedan and blocked him.

Cordy watched helplessly as two men in full body armor got out of the SUV. One man pulled open the passenger door, and Chief Jackson fell onto the pavement.

The other man flew backward as Braun fired and jumped from his car. The body armor protected the man from Braun's bullet.

The armored man opened fire.

Braun stumbled and lay crumpled, motionless on the ground.

Unsure about using the radio, Cordy dialed 911 with one hand and grabbed for her Glock with the other. "Agents down. Need ambulance and back up." She gave her location while steadying her aim.

The red Beamer screeched to a halt and blocked her shot. A man leapt from the car.

Something about the man was familiar. Cordy grabbed her binoculars for a closer view. It was the receptionist who delivered her dead flowers floating in acid. The man opened the hatch of the SUV and ducked, shielded from her. He returned with a rifle in his hands.

Cordy opened her door, and everything seemed to happen at once. A bullet sliced through her fender. Cordy steadied her gun against the door frame and fired back, but he was too far away. Sparks flew as another bullet ricocheted off the pavement. She climbed back into her car and started the engine.

The man in the red beamer raced back to his vehicle with the rifle in hand and drove out of sight.

The second man from the SUV covered the driver, who had Braun over his shoulder. He placed Braun into the back, climbed into the driver's seat, and slammed the door. The SUV's engine roared to life, and the two men took off with Braun.

"We have company," the radio crackled again.

Cordy ducked behind the wheel and floored the gas pedal. The car rocketed over the curb and zigzagged, hitting the corner of a trash bin next to the nail salon.

Her windshield cracked under the weight of a fallen tree branch before she heard a rifle pop. Cordy swerved, knocking the branch from the hood of her car, and kept driving while fishing for her cell phone. Her fingers found 911, and she shouted, "Agent down. Get me back up and an ambulance. I'm in pursuit." She hoped the 911 operator could hear her above the din of bullets slicing through her car's back end. Unable to see clearly through the cracked windshield, she nearly missed the side street and made a wide turn to get out of the line of fire.

The black SUV also rounded the corner, but it wasn't the only threat. Cordy saw the red Beamer advancing in her rearview mirror at top speed, poised to ram her.

Cordy wrenched the wheel and turned again, managing to lose the SUV for the moment. Sirens grew louder. She raced around the block and heard an alarm, a growing wail of a patrol car approaching.

The driver of the Beamer must have heard the sirens, too. He pulled away and disappeared into a cloud of dust.

Cordy headed back toward Braun's car to check on the chief. She grabbed her Glock, threw open the door, and crouched behind the trunk of his car.

Chief Jackson was still on the ground, not moving. No one took a potshot at her, so she crept to the chief's side. Blood soaked the back of his head.

She felt for a pulse. If there was one, it was very faint. His chest didn't move for the longest time. Then he heaved a sigh.

"Chief, can you hear me?"

He didn't answer.

"Don't give up. Help is on the way." Cordy brushed a clump of hair from his eye. "What happened to Braun?" She didn't expect an answer. None came. She let out a breath she didn't know she was holding. The chief, for now, anyway, was alive.

She glanced under the car and saw droplets of blood under the driver's side. It must be Braun's. A popping sound surprised her. A stinging pain slashed across her forehead. She dove beside the front car wheel and caught a flash of red as the returned Beamer took off.

An ambulance running red lights and sirens pulled to a stop. Paramedics raced toward her.

Cordy motioned. "Over here. It's the chief."

One paramedic dropped to his knees beside the chief. "I'll take over."

His partner ran to her side. "You okay?"

"Take care of the chief." Cordy felt the adrenaline escape her. She shook. "They must have left him for dead." Tears blurred her vision. She swiped a hand across her face. It came away bloody.

The next thing she knew was waking up in the hospital with a terrible headache. Usher Hastings was at her side.

"Thank God you're okay." Usher squeezed her hand. "I need you to tell me everything that happened."

Cordy tried to sit up, but the room was spinning, and she couldn't find the strength to lift her head. "Where's Braun?"

"I had hoped you knew where to find him." Usher's voice held a tinge of urgency to it. Not fear—not even anxiety, but she could tell he was concerned.

"When did you get here?"

"I flew in last night and met with Braun and the chief early this morning. I missed my flight back when the call came in, so I rushed right over, hoping I'd see Braun."

"How's the chief?" Cordy asked.

"I couldn't tell. There was a whole room full of medical personnel. They pushed past me as if I wasn't there. Everything was chaos. I heard it could go either way. I barely got out of the way before they wheeled the gurney into the corridor heading for the OR. The chief was pale as the sheets. They hauled him to the elevator, and the doors closed, so I came to find you."

Cordy squinted at her watch. Her vision was blurred. "What time is it?"

"After 6 p.m.," Usher pulled out his cell phone. "I have to call Fritz and let him know what's happened, especially since I was assigned to watch Laura. Oh, she's safe. My team is by her side, but with the Chief out of commission, our plans have changed, and I need to find Braun."

"Fritz has enough problems." Cordy held out her hand for the phone. "I'll call Agent Kelly. Chief Jackson is like a father to her. She'll want to know."

Usher glanced at the phone. "No service. We'll have to go out of the building. One moment." He left the room for ten minutes and returned with a wheelchair. "No more than five minutes. Doctor's orders, and someone needs to be with you." He flashed a smile. "I volunteered."

"Fine." Cordy dropped her legs off the cart and grabbed his arm. "The room's still spinning."

"Should I call for help?" Usher offered.

"No." She dropped into the wheelchair and pulled a sheet over her legs. "Just get me out of here."

Ten minutes later, she changed her tune. Making a call to Kelly took all her energy. She barely remembered Usher wheeling her back to the emergency room.

He lifted her onto the cart. "You're not ready to go home. Rest like the doctor ordered, and I'll see you in the morning."

AFTER VISITING HOURS

Fritz wanted to find Risa ASAP and needed more answers. Her husband, Jim, might know something that could lead Fritz in the right direction, but Jim had been shot in the leg while trying to rescue Risa from the kidnappers and was in the hospital. *What did Jim see? Did he hear where Vinny was taking Risa?* Fritz had visited Jim once, while he was in ICU, but he faded in and out of consciousness. Yesterday afternoon, they moved Jim to a surgical floor. Today, he seemed more alert on the phone, so maybe he could answer a few questions in more detail.

Fritz knew it was way past hospital visiting hours, but he refused to wait any longer to talk to Jim in person. The deserted hallway seemed to go on forever in the dimmed lights. This was an older part of the hospital that needed renovation. Every time Fritz turned a corner, he expected to see someone, a doctor, nurse, patient, or security guard, but there was no one. The sound of his footsteps echoed on the stained tile floor.

Fritz paused to check for room 218, but he hadn't gone far enough because a faded 207 was above the door in front of him. Something caught his attention. Another set of footsteps. They continued for a split second, then they, too, stopped.

Odd, but Fritz felt uncomfortable—unsure if anyone followed him. Fritz checked his watch. It was after eleven. *No wonder the halls are empty. It's change of shift, and most patients have turned in for the night.* Still uneasy, he glanced up and down the hallway. *No one.*

That old gut feeling had saved him more than once. *As a precaution, I need to get out of the hallway, wait, and watch just to be sure I'm alone.* He had no idea if anyone was in room 207, but he didn't want to startle an innocent patient, so he knocked on the door frame. "Hello."

No one answered his knock. The door squeaked as he slipped inside and ducked away from the opening.

A nightlight reflected a shadowed body lying in bed on the other side of a curtain.

Light steps shuffled in the hallway, paused, and then Fritz heard a whispered voice too muffled to understand coming from outside the door.

Fritz's heart raced as he ducked into the bathroom and quietly closed the door. An automatic light flicked on. The bathroom had two entrances, one on each side of the room, so rooms 207 and 209 shared the same facilities. He leaned against the bathroom door and heard a squeak as room 207's main door opened wider. Faint footsteps passed the bathroom, and then Fritz heard a swishing sound as a curtain slid along the metal runner.

"Who's there?" a sleepy, frightened voice called out. Her panicked voice sent a chill down Fritz's spine,

"Can you get me something for pain?" *It must be a patient.*

"Did a man come into your room?" A low whisper sounded like a male's voice. *Probably a nurse.*

"I didn't see anyone except you," the female patient said.

"Were you sleeping?" the male asked.

"Off and on. What are you doing? I told you, I didn't see anyone."

Fritz didn't wait around. He snuck across the bathroom and entered room 209, where another patient snored softly. Inching the main door open, Fritz spied a nurse heading toward him, pushing a cart. She passed his door and entered room 207, where Fritz had left moments earlier.

A red light popped on over room 207's door, and someone yelled, "Code Blue! Get the cart."

Three chimes bonged overhead. "Code Blue, room 207, code blue…"

A flurry of activity emerged in the hallway that was vacant seconds before. A man in a white lab coat shoved the bathroom door open and fled past Fritz, nearly bumping into him as he ran into the hallway and headed in the opposite direction of the traffic flow. *Was he the man following Fritz? What did he do to the woman?* She was talking when Fritz left the room. Fritz decided to follow the guy in the lab coat, but as he stepped into the hallway, he almost got run over by the Code cart.

"Watch out." A nurse swerved the cart around him.

Fritz dashed after the guy in the lab coat. "Stop. I need to talk to you."

The man turned, his eyes widened, and then he high-tailed it down the hallway, opened a door, and fled down the steps without another word.

Fritz lost the man in the lab coat when he disappeared into the stairwell. He needed to find Jim now.

Disappointed, Fritz turned to continue his search for room 218, which he found at the end of the corridor. He stepped over what appeared to be stuffing from a pillow. It led a fluffy trail to a back elevator. Fritz slammed through the door. "Jim, are you in here?"

The bed was empty, and the room was in shambles. Covers draped over the foot of the bed and a torn sheet cluttered the floor. Another pillow lay on the chair, and the pillowcase was missing. There was no sign of Jim.

Fritz threw open the bathroom door and gasped.

An officer's body lay sprawled on the floor. No apparent wound, yet his glazed eyes stared at the ceiling. The bathroom emergency cord lay in his hand. Someone had cut the string.

Fritz knelt beside the officer to check for a pulse but found none. *What happened? No time now. Find Jim!* Fritz pressed the room call button to notify the nurse. He didn't wait around. He speed-dialed the criminal investigative team as he ran down the back stairs, and paused long enough to deliver a message. Then he hit the main floor running. After exiting the hospital, he darted for the parking lot. There were no signs of Jim, no cars speeding away, no black skid marks, and no commotion of any kind. Out of breath, coughing, and wheezing, Fritz went back inside the hospital lobby.

The guard on duty at the front desk denied seeing anything suspicious.

Fritz's mind whirred with more questions now than when he came to the hospital. *Who took Jim? Where did they take him, and why? Had that guy in the lab coat caused a Code Blue as a distraction? Was he one of Vinny's men?* Fritz sprinted back to the elevator. *Maybe his nurse will have some answers.*

NO ANSWERS

Tuesday, June 18 – 0019 CDT, Ann Arbor, Michigan

When Fritz returned to room 218, it was swarming with hospital personnel. A doctor knelt over the downed cop with defibrillator paddles in hand. A straight line ran across the attached cardiac monitor. "Three shocks and no response, he's gone." After a quick search of the body, the doc ordered, "Call the ME."

Police officers gathered outside of the room.

Fritz stood just inside the doorway, listening to the commotion coming from the hallway. "Better clear out. This is a crime scene." Fritz ran a hand over his face. *Crime scene—it didn't seem possible that someone broke into the hospital, downed a cop, and took Jim. Word would spread rapidly.*

A woman stepped into the room and flipped her badge toward Fritz. "CSI. Name's Erin. Did you call this in?"

Fritz nodded. "Yes. Jim is my brother-in-law. He's missing."

"I'll talk to you in a few minutes, but I want to secure the scene." She motioned for the photographer to take photos, then as an afterthought, she added, "Sorry for your loss."

Loss? She said loss. Fritz had seen how fragile life could be, but he didn't expect those words to cut to the core. *First Risa, now Jim. What next?*

An officer, who must have been fresh out of the police academy, bulldozed his way into the room. His name badge read T. Higgins, and his nervous energy pulsed through the room as he stepped up to Fritz. "Did you see what happened?"

"No." Irritated, Fritz asked, "Who's in charge here?"

Higgins' eyes widened as he scanned the room, then turned back to Fritz. "You must have heard a commotion."

"Yeah." Fritz put a hand on the officer's shoulder, trying to calm the man. "There was a commotion, but it was down the hall. You shouldn't be in here."

The officer shrugged off Fritz's hand. "Back off. You're not one of us." Higgins moved to the bathroom and must have seen the officer on the floor. His face paled. "Tony!" Higgins dropped to his knees and then asked the doctor. "Is he going to be all right?"

A hush fell as if in reverence to the fallen cop.

Officer McCoy stepped into the room. "Morning, all." He rubbed a hand down the sleeve of his rumpled uniform. "Can I have a word with you, Fritz?" He glanced over at the rookie, who was whiter than the roll of toilet paper he held in his hand. "One moment. Officer Higgins?"

Higgins hung his head over the toilet and puked.

McCoy squared his shoulders and approached the officer. "Higgins, what are you doing here? Go home. Your shift ended hours ago."

Higgins wiped a tissue over his brow. "What about you?"

McCoy frowned. "I barely got home before being called in to meet the media."

"What about Tony?" Higgins' voice cracked.

"The ME will take over." McCoy motioned to a man in blue scrubs.

Higgins didn't move, so McCoy wrapped an arm around the young cop's shoulders. "Let's get some coffee. I saw your partner in the hall. He'll take you home."

Higgins' partner stepped into the room. "I told him we didn't need to be here. I think it's his first…you know." The partner nodded his head toward the body. "A shame it had to be one of us."

"Take him home," McCoy said.

"Will do." The partner guided the glazed-eyed Higgins to the elevator.

Erin, with CSI, motioned for McCoy and Fritz. "Tell me everything."

Fritz spent the next hour answering questions and asking many of his own. When Erin and McCoy had nothing else to tell Fritz, he went down to the cafeteria for a cup of coffee and phoned the chief. It was well past midnight, so he wasn't surprised when the call went to voice mail. He tried to stay calm, but questions kept popping up—questions that he had no answers to.

The coffee tasted stale, bitter, and cold, or maybe it was his life. This month had been one disaster after another, starting with Diane's death. Vinny got out of prison, and Fritz's life went to shit after that. Laura and Marta had been whisked away and relocated to an unknown place, and hopefully, they were safe and would stay that way. A miserable flight was delayed due to a weather pattern over the Rockies, and then he landed only to find out Vinny had kidnapped Risa. A hostage situation was finally resolved, but the victim remained unconscious, Mick was dead, and three cops were killed. No, make that four cops killed—the latest guarding Jim, and he still went missing. At least Walt was in custody.

"Officer McCoy said I'd find you here." Agent Kelly's green eyes were bloodshot. She wore faded black jeans and an emerald sweater. A streak of mascara smudged at the corner where she'd rubbed away a tear.

"What are you doing here?" Fritz pulled out a chair. "You're not on duty."

"No, but I couldn't sleep after I heard about the chief and Braun." Kelly heaved a sigh and sat down. "I'm sorry about Jim. Vinny must be working overtime."

"Back up a minute," Fritz said. "What about the chief and Braun?" His mind went into overdrive. It couldn't be good. Why else would she be here?

Kelly straightened in the chair. "You haven't heard? I hoped that I wouldn't be the one to break the news."

"News?" His voice rose in pitch. "What happened, Kelly?"

She swallowed, and a sob escaped her lips. "I don't know the exact details."

It wasn't the answer Fritz wanted to hear. "What do you know?"

"Someone shot him. He is hanging on by a thread."

"Shot who?" Fritz shouted, then tamped down his anxiety. "Who was shot? The chief or Braun?"

Kelly lifted her head. Tears streamed down her cheeks. Her eyes widened. "Head injury. On the vent."

The look was nothing new to Fritz, a doe in headlights. "Chief Jackson?" He already knew the answer. Of course, it was the chief. He was Kelly's godfather and mentor.

Kelly nodded. "Who would want to kill him?"

Vinny, of course, his mind screamed. Kelly wasn't thinking clearly, so he better keep his wits about him and calmly asked, "Where did it happen? In Michigan, or were they still in Colorado?"

"Colorado, of course," Kelly said. "Why would the chief come here? He sent you. Braun couldn't protect him, and Vinny shot Chief Jackson."

Fritz leaned forward. "What about Braun?"

"Wait. Vinny was here in Michigan," Kelly said. "He took Risa. Could he have flown back to Colorado?" She shook her head. "No. Not enough time. Someone else shot the chief."

"Kelly!" Fritz gritted his teeth. "What happened to Braun?"

"Oh, Braun's missing." Kelly picked at a fuzz ball on her sweater.

"So he's alive?" Fritz felt his heart calm down. "How did it happen?"

"Stakeout." Kelly gathered her strength. "Braun was supposed to meet Cordy at a warehouse, but they were delayed because they had a meeting with Usher. Afterward, Braun drove to the warehouse with the chief. Someone shot at Braun's car. Cordy was alone on the stakeout, but she was the next target. She managed to get away, but

Braun was gone when she returned to Braun's car. They'd shot the chief and left him for dead."

"What about Cordy?" Fritz asked. "Is she all right?"

"A bullet grazed her forehead. The paramedics took her to the emergency room, but she sounded okay. She's the one who called me."

Fritz's mind went into overdrive. "At least Laura and Marta are safe. Let's get some real food and make a plan. I haven't eaten since breakfast."

"I'm not hungry." Kelly stared into space. Tears brimmed her eyes.

Fritz put his hand on her shoulder. "I'll take you home."

"I don't want to go home. We have to stop this bastard," Kelly swiped a sleeve over her face. "What if the chief doesn't make it?"

"He's strong. He'll put up a good fight," Fritz said, lowering his voice. "Let's get Vinny."

"We'll be next," Kelly said. "As your partner, I'll be in the same line of fire as you."

"Maybe, but I'm not going down without a fight." Fritz shoved back his chair and headed for the door. He turned. "You coming?"

DIGESTING THE DAY

Tuesday, June 18 – 0310 CDT, Ann Arbor, Michigan

By 3:10 a.m., Fritz pigged out in front of Agent Kelly at an all-night café while reviewing the latest details. He set aside his fourth rib and licked Bar-B-Q from his fingers, hoping no sauce smeared the crime scene photos spread across the table.

Agent Kelly replayed the 911 tape of Inga's call during Risa's kidnapping. "A lot of information, but we barely made a dent." She sipped her cola. "Are you sure it was Vinny that took Risa? Who shot the chief? Maybe Vinny never left Colorado."

"McCoy said, 'Vinny took Risa.' So he's here in Michigan. We have a date with Walt at 9:30 this morning. Let's discuss what we know so far."

"Okay." Kelly took out a pen from her black leather purse. "Vinny got out of prison two weeks ago. He and Father Jules drove across Texas. They were pulled over by the local police later that day."

"Right." Fritz popped a fry into his mouth, chewed, and swallowed with a swig of coffee. "His brother, Jules, was with him, but he's no priest. He's just a kid wearing a clerical collar. He's barely of age."

"Where is Jules now?" Kelly asked. "He may be our linchpin."

"I wouldn't count on it."

"What happened next?" Kelly asked.

Fritz listed the events from the time Braun popped back into his life. "My family had to relocate to safety, Midget attacked our home, someone broke into Cordy's, and a day later delivered deadly flowers to her at the office. There were three attempts on Risa's life before they kidnapped her, then a hostage situation with Risa's neighbor, and an attack on Chief Jackson. Now they have Jim and Braun. A lot has happened over the past two weeks."

Kelly asked, "Where would they hide three people? Two are in Michigan, and Braun is in Colorado. Would they move them all into one place?"

"I checked out real estate," Fritz said. "Tracked down every home, apartment, and condo Vinny or his family ever owned—nothing in Michigan. So where is he?"

"The chief was probably in the wrong place at the wrong time." Kelly clenched her fists. "The hitman probably got a bonus."

Fritz rubbed his chin. "I wonder how long Jim had disappeared before I discovered his absence. The cop's body was still warm."

"There must have been some commotion," Kelly said. "Why didn't the nurses hear anything?"

"It was so quiet in the hallway until the Code Blue." Fritz pulled his hand away from his chin and stared at Kelly. "You don't think that was intentional, do you?"

Kelly frowned. "What do you mean?"

"The patient in 207," Fritz said. "She was talking a few minutes before the nurse found her and called the Code Blue. You worked there. Call and check on her condition. Did she suffer a stroke or a heart attack? If not, we may have another murder case."

"I can do better than that. I'll go over and see for myself. I'm sure I can get her record. What was her name?"

"I don't know," Fritz said. "There's a guy who wore a lab coat. I think he's a lab tech. I'd like you to check on him for me, too."

"Okay. Do you have a name?" Kelly picked up her pen, poised to write.

"No. I don't have his name either. He worked the evening, or maybe it was the night shift since it was around midnight. Or, maybe he doesn't work at the hospital at all."

"What does he look like?" Kelly asked.

"Lean male, white coat, dark hair. I think he wore glasses."

"A lot of techs fit that description." A smile crossed Kelly's face. "I was hoping you'd say big Bertha. I haven't met her yet, but someone warned me about her."

The waitress stopped by. "May I get you anything else?"

"Just the check." Fritz scraped the last of the baked beans onto a fork and popped it into his mouth.

The waitress pulled the bill from her pocket and handed it to him.

"Good food, good service." Fritz paid the bill.

Kelly stifled a yawn. "Should we go back to the hospital now?"

"No. You need a few hours of sleep before we meet with Walt. I'll drive you home and pick you up at eight-thirty."

SAIL AWAY

Tuesday, June 18 – 0652 MDT, Loveland, Colorado

Cordy relived the horrific scene: the popping gun and a man flinging open the passenger's door. The chief toppled to the ground and lay in a blossoming pool of blood. He hardly breathed. His face was slate-gray. Spying a doctor in the hallway, she blurted, "Chief! Check on the chief."

The doctor grabbed a clipboard and walked away.

"Wait!" Cordy scooted from the gurney of the emergency department. A bout of dizziness made it difficult to stand. She eased herself to the door, took a few deep breaths, and left her room. "Where is Chief Jackson?" she asked the first nurse she met.

"He's not here."

"Where is he?" Cordy looked in each direction.

"Surgery," the nurse said.

Another employee walked past. "No. I'm sure he's out of OR by now."

The secretary behind the desk called out, "ICU."

"Which is it?" Cordy glanced up as another doctor approached. "Is the chief going to make it?" Her legs trembled. Black spots floated before her eyes.

"Miss, you need to calm down," the doctor said.

"She's having a panic attack." A man in blue scrubs darted for her from the doorway. "I'll take over. I'm her doctor's partner."

Another male in a white lab coat walked through the entrance. "Do you need some help?" His voice was an irritating, raspy quality that grated at her senses.

She assumed he was a nurse.

"Take her back to her room." The doctor moved with authority. Everyone else seemed to go back to work and didn't pay any further attention.

"Don't faint now." The nurse helped her into a wheelchair. "Let's get you back to bed."

The doctor followed. When they reached her room, he closed the door while the nurse laid her on the cart.

"Will the chief live?" Cordy asked.

"His life is in the surgeon's hands, and you're in mine." The doctor pulled out a syringe. "This will help relieve your anxiety."

"I don't need any medicine," Cordy argued. "I'm fine. I just want to know how the chief is. No one will give me a straight answer."

The doctor nodded and then laid his hand on her arm. "It's a light sedative. You'll calm down and drift off to sleep. When you wake up, you can go home."

"Tell me the truth. Is the chief still alive?" She jerked when he pricked her arm and injected the medicine. "Wait, I didn't give you permission to give me a shot! You'll hear from my lawyer. I'm a cop."

The nurse stared at the doctor. "Are you sure, Doc?"

"It'll be fine, Ace. She won't remember a thing." The doctor leaned closer and spoke softly in a calm voice. "You will listen only to my voice. Everything is okay. It's time to rest. As I count backward from ten, you'll go deeper into a relaxed state. Close your eyes, Cordy. Ten. You're walking in the forest by a deep blue pool. Nine… Breathe in deep and let it out."

"I want to go home." Cordy felt her willpower slipping away. "What did you give me?" Her voice sounded slurred even to her ears. A heavy wave overpowered her. She took a lung full of air and slowly exhaled.

"Eight…" The doctor's voice continued to fill her senses. "Seven. Everything is beautiful. The sun bathes you with warm light."

Her body went limp. She tried to fight his words, but they filled her mind.

"Six. Close your eyes and relax."

Her eyes drifted closed.

"Five. You feel the rays…" "Four." The doctor's voice grew quieter. "Hear the rain patter on the pond. You're fully at peace. Repeat after me. I am at peace."

Cordy's eyes seemed glued shut, unable to open. Her legs and arms were dead weight on the gurney. "I am at peace."

"Two…You're on the ocean. Feel the waves."

The gurney seemed to sway.

"One…You are floating in space. It gets cold, so your body must adjust. Nothing you hear or say—"

Her floating body came to a stop with a bump.

"Cordy! Where are you taking her?" echoed in the background.

"Usher?" Cordy asked.

"We're going to special procedures. Perhaps you'd like to come along?" The doctor's voice seemed upset.

"Why are you taking her there?" Usher asked. "She signed discharge papers. I just drove up the car to take her home. Did her condition change?"

"See for yourself," the doctor said. "Cordy, tell Usher that we need to go."

"We need to go," Cordy repeated.

"Why?" Usher grabbed her hand. "Oh Geez, you're freezing." He rubbed her fingers and arm.

"Yes," the doctor said. "We think something is going on with her hypothalamus."

The cart started moving again. The doctor's voice seemed to float. "Come along."

Usher kept hold of her hand as they moved.

"We need to use the scanner," the doctor said. Something dinged. It sounded as if they were in an elevator. "It's in the basement."

Cordy heard another ding, and the door whooshed open. Voices faded. She tried to open her eyes and speak, but nothing happened. She squeezed Usher's hand. At least she tried to. He didn't squeeze back. Her heart slowed as she drifted toward a warm white light.

* * *

Agent Usher Hastings stepped from the elevator into a hallway cluttered with old equipment and boxes. "Where are we? The dungeon?"

The doctor laughed. "It feels that way sometimes, but the scanner is down this hall." He turned toward the nurse. "Prep her for the procedure. I want the results ASAP. We'll be in my office." He motioned for Usher to take the lead in the opposite direction.

Two men in white surrounded Cordy and the nurse. "Right this way. We're ready and waiting." They pushed Cordy's gurney down the hall with amazing speed and turned into a room a few doors down.

"You see. She's in good hands." The doctor reached into his pocket.

Usher's military-honed senses went on alert. He swung around with his elbow.

"Ah, ah, ah," the doctor jumped aside and held up a vial. "I have the antidote. If she doesn't get it in the next four hours, Cordy will die for real. Sorry, but I only have enough for one person." Like a cobra, the doc stuck the agent with a needle.

Doc pushed on the plunger, but Usher wrenched around, broke off the needle in his arm, and slashed the heel of his hand across the doc's neck.

The doc flew backward and dropped like a brick. Air rushed from his lungs when he hit the floor. It didn't stop him. He rolled and kicked Usher's leg behind the knee.

Usher dropped to the floor. A trace of blood and fluid dripped down his sleeve. "Hate to foil your plans." Usher spun around and kicked the doc in the ribs.

The vial flew into the air.

Usher caught the glint of reflected light. Frantic to get his hands on the bottle, he dove for it in midair. His fingers brushed against the glass container, but it spun out and away as the lights flicked off. Usher heard a clink and felt along the floor in total darkness. His hand bumped the object. He snatched the vial and pocketed it.

There was a shuffling noise behind him. Something struck the back of his head, and everything blanked out.

SECRET KEY

Fritz and Agent Kelly arrived at Andrew C. Baird Detention Facility during shift change. They wove their way through a crowd of angry protesters outside the fourteen-story high-rise and made it to the front door. "Let's see what Walt has to say today," Fritz said.

"Are you planning to work out a deal with this dirtbag?" Kelly asked.

"My gut says he's guilty of more serious crimes than kidnapping Inga." Fritz pushed through the front door and headed for the elevator.

Thirty minutes later, a guard escorted Walt into the interrogation room. The orange jumpsuit was too long, and the pant legs hung to the floor over his shoes, causing him to shuffle to the table. Cuffs circled his wrists. "Git outta here and leave me alone," Walt said. "I'm saying nothin' to you."

The guard moved around the table and nudged him into a chair. "You know the rules. Anything you say can be—"

"Yeah, my Miranda Rights." Walt sneered. "I know. I've been through this before. You won't leave me alone until I sign that waiver." He nodded to Fritz. "Prop a pen in my hands. I'll sign, but I ain't talkin'."

Fritz handed Walt a pen and placed a briefcase on the table. Scrolling the numbers to unlock the case, he popped it open and pulled out a large file.

Walt glanced at the folder, scribbled his name on the form, and attempted to stand.

Fritz opened the cover of the file and slid it toward the prisoner.

Walt tripped and fell back into the chair. "Like I said, I'm not talkin' to you."

Kelly sat across from him. "We're investigating a kidnapping. I think it would be in your best interest if you helped us find Risa."

Walt ignored the folder. "Don't know what you're yackin' about."

Fritz took a chair between the two. "Then maybe you can tell me what you know about a skeleton key we found on your brother, Mick."

"Oh, that old thing?" Walt chuckled. "He's carried it around for years. Loved to hide it in his shoe."

"Does it unlock something special?" Fritz asked.

"Nah, I don't know why he loved that key so much, but he even showered with it. He used to wear it around his neck on a chain, but on Mick's thirteenth birthday, Vinny grabbed it and nearly strangled him. The chain broke, and I never saw the key again until last week when I caught him shoving it into his shoe."

"It must open something special," Kelly said. "What would be your best guess?"

Walt shook his head. "Nothin' special. My best guess, it's from that old house by the cemetery where he used to hang out. Of course, it's been abandoned for years."

"Which cemetery?" Fritz asked.

"Don't reckon I remember," Walt said. "Old Uncle Benny was buried there years ago."

"Here in Ann Arbor?" Kelly asked.

"Nah," Walt said. "Some Podunk town."

"In Michigan?" she tried again.

"Can't remember." Walt stood up. "Guard, take me back to my cell."

"You know Mick died, right?" Fritz hoped Walt would cooperate.

"Yeah."

"Then help me find Vinny." Fritz's face brightened. "Maybe we can help each other."

"You givin' me a deal?"

Fritz shrugged. "I'll put in a good word to your lawyer."

"Why should I trust you?" Walt kept looking toward the door. "Vinny threw Mick to the wolves. Just like he'll do me, and *he's* my brother."

Kelly said, "Then trust me."

Walt's face cracked a smile. "I always did prefer women." He shifted his weight and hung his head. "How's the old lady?"

"She's in a coma," Kelly said.

"I hadn't planned to hit her so hard." Walt glanced up at Fritz. "Vinny's still looking for your wife. You know he'll find her. He has friends everywhere. Let my lawyer know I warned you. It will look good on my record."

Walt didn't hesitate when the guard opened the door. He marched out of the room and didn't look back.

Kelly turned to Fritz. "What do we do now?"

Fritz ran his thumb over the skeleton key. A raw fury tugged at his soul. "We stop Vinny." Ice raced through his veins. "Let's get out of here, and I need to pick up a rental car so we can split duties."

NIGHTMARES

Tuesday, June 18 – 0738 MDT,
Enroute to Fort Collins, Colorado

Usher had bad dreams before, but this one felt so real that he knew he would drown as the violent storm rolled overhead, followed by peals of thunder echoing across the valley. Lightning illuminated the forest, creating eerie shadows of twisted tree branches that looked like monsters in the dark. Furious torrents of rushing water exploded over the riverbank. Trapped, he treaded through the water to save himself, yet the river kept rising until he crashed into a rock.

A shrill ringing pierced his ears, and Usher awoke with a start. The water morphed into a tangle of sheets. A siren blared overhead. He bounced against a metal railing. Covered in sweat, he shivered with fever. The same old nightmare plagued him, but this was different. Confused, he forced his mind to sharpen.

Officer Cordelia. He needed to save the girl from something. They were in trouble. That much he remembered. His head throbbed, and his body ached with each jolt. Someone had hit him over the head. He wondered if he'd suffered any brain damage.

Usher tried to activate the GPS on his wristwatch, but his arms refused to move. His legs felt like lead. The antidote vial dug into his hip with every bump. It reminded him of his mission. He had to find a way to slip the drug to Cordy, but he kept losing consciousness.

Something cold touched his hand as the vehicle turned a corner. Cordy? He forced his arm to press against her body. A slight vibration of his watch told him he activated the GPS. Relief washed over him until he realized it was Cordy, who usually tracked his watch, and she lay dying next to him. A lot of good his watch would do now. He managed to slip his finger around her wrist to check her pulse. Slow, but she was alive.

Cordy didn't move.

Usher squinted in the light and saw they were on a gurney in the back of an ambulance. A leather strap wrapped around Cordy's waist held her in place. He lay next to her with his legs cuffed to the rail. Only he could save her, but he had to move fast before his strength left him again.

He surveyed the area and realized no one else rode in back with them.

A clear plastic cabinet bolted to the wall revealed medical supplies. Usher inched his shoulder forward and reached through the rails for a syringe. The cuffs on his ankles caught and cut into his skin as he stretched his full length, but he managed to inch open the first drawer. His fingers were stiff, so he palmed a syringe, pulled his hand back to the cot, and wedged the device into his left hand.

Pain shot through his hip as he tried to fish the vial from his pocket, and his vision blurred. His sense of touch was numb and tingly, making it hard to grasp the object. Sweat dripped from his forehead. He rubbed his face against the sheet and tried again.

The ambulance hit another bump, causing the vial to move between his index and middle fingers. A wave of nausea made him gag. Swallowing back bile, he took some deep breaths and teased out the antidote bottle between his fingers. His arms shook, causing him to drop the glass bottle. It clinked against the rail. With a desperate swipe of his hand, he managed to scoop it toward his body.

Pain attacked as every nerve ending fired into spasms that rocked his body against the railing. His eyes grew heavy, and with senses dulled, blackness overtook him.

When Usher rose from a drugged stupor, he didn't want to move, but the ambulance was slowing. *Gotta act fast,* but his mind was faster than his body. Gravel crunched under the vehicle. *How long have I been unconscious?*

Usher flexed his fingers and noticed the syringe in his left hand. *Where's the vial?* Relief flooded over him when he found it tucked under his right arm. *How long have we been in the ambulance? Am I in time?*

Cordy let out a faint moan and stiffened next to him.

"Can you hear me?" he whispered.

She didn't answer.

Panic surged through Usher when he noticed there was no needle on the syringe.

Cordy's pale face contorted.

"Are you in pain?" He moved closer.

She was cold, and her lips had a blue tint.

Move faster! Usher turned from side to side, then glanced up and noticed an oxygen tank next to the head of the bed. A mask hung from a green tube slung over the tank. He inched his hand up and pulled the mask toward Cordy, fumbled to get the elastic around her ears to hold the mask in place, and with another stretch, he reached for the dial. It was too far away, so he pulled the tubing to get closer.

The blasted tank tipped toward the cart and nearly toppled over before Usher turned the dial to ten and managed to balance it back onto its wheels. He hoped for the best.

She needs that antidote. Now. Usher pulled himself to the edge of the cot, forced his shoulder and arm through the railing, and reached for the cabinet. The ankle cuffs cut his flesh, but he had to find a needle. *You'd think they'd have the syringe and needles in the same place.* The top drawer had none. Usher tried the second drawer. *Intubation equipment.* His hand was a good 2 inches from the bottom drawer.

As the ambulance pulled to a stop, Usher scooted even further toward the edge of the cart, pulled his body up over the top of the railing, and dropped his chest over the side of the cart, forcing open the bottom drawer. Pain shot up his legs, but he kept stretching until he grabbed a needle. It was in a wrapper, which he tore open with his teeth.

He heard the cab door of the ambulance open and slam shut. "Unlock the rear doors. I'm going to contact Vinny." *It sounds like the doc, but why would he be driving?*

"I'll be right behind you," a raspy-voiced man called out.

Usher lifted himself back over the railing and onto the cart. With the needle in one hand and the syringe in the other, he worked to pop them together. It took three tries, but he finally managed. *How much of the vial should I inject?*

He yanked the cap off the needle and blinked to get his eyes to refocus. The memory of giving his mother insulin injections flashed through his mind, and he drew air into the syringe. Holding the vial in his left hand, his arms shook, so his aim was off, and the needle missed the stopper.

Keys jingled, and the back door of the ambulance rattled. "I can't get the door open."

Doc swore. "You need to open the right door first, but I need both doors open to remove the cart."

"Okay, I'll try the other one."

"Jeez, Ace, hurry up! Do I have to do everything? Get those doors open and unload the back. I'm texting Vinny, and I don't have time for this."

Usher aimed once more for the rubber stopper and bent the needle, but it punctured the top. He injected the air into the vial to prevent a vacuum from forming, withdrew all the solution he could, and pulled out the needle. He turned, jabbed the needle into Cordy's arm, and pushed the plunger. "I hope this works."

Cordy didn't make a sound.

Usher's mind felt fuzzy, but he slipped into military mode—ready for action. He whipped off the oxygen mask and shoved the vial and syringe into a used needle box next to the oxygen tank.

"Okay, I unlocked the doors," Ace said.

"Great! Now unload that gurney," Doc shouted. "Get them inside, and then get rid of this ambulance. I don't want to be connected to their disappearance. Vinny's calling."

"Yes, sir," Ace called out. Usher heard gravel crunch as footsteps receded.

"Why do I always get stuck with the grunt work," Ace whined, probably after Doc was out of earshot.

As the back door swung open, Usher gargled and made a choking sound. Saliva dripped down his chin, and his body convulsed against the railing.

"Hey, Doc, I think he's having a seizure," Ace called out. "Come quick!"

PACKAGE FOR THE TAKING

Tuesday, June 18 – 1045 CDT, Ann Arbor, Michigan

Agent Kelly fidgeted in the passenger seat of Fritz's rental while heading for the University of Michigan State Medical Center. She planned to check on the status of a patient who had a cardiopulmonary arrest on the night of Jim's disappearance. Hospital policy required neat attire and no hair on the shoulders. She flipped down the car's visor to check her makeup and noticed her shoulder-length hair wouldn't meet the code. After twisting her long hair into a loose knot, she clipped it with a silver barrette. With one more glance, she made last-minute adjustments, straightened the lapel of her nursing uniform, and wondered if she could still access medical records. She hadn't officially handed in her termination notice, but she hadn't returned to work since Risa had been kidnapped four days ago. "I hope IT hasn't deactivated my employee code."

"There's one way to find out." Fritz drove his rental car to the entrance. "Call me if you run into any problems."

Kelly's fingers grasped the handle, planning to open the car door, and gasped, "Oh my God! Look over there. See that guy in the white lab coat? Is he the one you're looking for? He fits your description."

Fritz glanced around. "Where?"

Kelly pointed toward the medical building. "Over there, by the trash can. That's the lab tech I told you about. His name is Dave."

"I'm not sure. He's the right height and weight but not wearing glasses. I can't be sure until I get a closer look."

Kelly shoved her seatbelt from her shoulder. "Maybe he wears contacts. Dave's the one who stole supplies from the OR the night Walt attacked Risa."

"Do you know the guy he's talking to?" Fritz asked.

"No," Kelly said. "Oh, look! Did you see that? Dave just handed something to that man. Drive closer. I want to see what he's up to."

Fritz made a U-turn and drove in front of the medical building.

"No. He's leaving." Kelly's voice raised a notch. "Drop me off and park. She sprang from the car before it came to a complete stop and dashed for the sidewalk. A slight trip and she brushed against the man Dave had been talking to a few moments earlier. "Oh, I'm sorry, sir." She held onto his arm and steadied herself. She felt a lump in the man's pocket and snagged her fingers around the small bag while staring straight at him with great concern. "Are you all right?"

The bleached blond with a slightly bruised nose glanced down. "Yeah." He pushed her aside, "Watch where you're going next time!" He darted around her and ducked into the building.

Kelly pocketed the bag and peered around, but the man was nowhere in sight. Dave had disappeared, too. With a sly smile, she headed toward the hospital entrance.

Fritz met her outside the door with one eyebrow raised as if surprised. "That was a slick move."

Kelly laughed. "Not good enough. You caught on, and he helped me by pushing me aside." She tugged on the edge of a brown paper package. "Do you have an evidence bag?"

"Always carry one just in case." He pulled a packet from his coat and held it while Kelly slid the envelope inside. Fritz zipped the bag shut, pocketed the item, and opened the front door to the hospital.

"Submit that as evidence while I go to medical records." Kelly led the way inside the hospital. "What room was the patient in again?"

"Room 207."

Kelly scanned the lobby.

Fritz shifted his body so his back faced the guard behind the information desk, talking on a phone. "Find out if the patient made it or if I witnessed a murder in the making."

Kelly held up her cell. "I'll take photos of the record if I find it."

Fritz checked his watch. "How long do you need?"

"An hour, maybe two. I'll call you if I need more time." Kelly moved to the information desk. "Excuse me, sir, which way to medical records?"

The officer hung up the phone and pointed to his right. "Turn left after the restrooms. It's at the end of the hall."

"Thanks, officer." Kelly followed his directions until she rounded the corner. It dawned on her that she did not know the patient's name. Medical records needed a name and date of birth to pull one file from thousands. She didn't even have a doctor's name.

Kelly passed the nurses' lounge. Wait. That's what I need—a computer terminal. I know the patient's room number. Now I need to find out who was in that bed. She tried the lounge door and found it locked, and she didn't have the access code.

At that moment, a woman exited the lounge and nearly collided with Kelly. "Sorry. I'm late for a meeting."

"No problem." Kelly caught the door and slipped inside. There was an accessible computer, so she sat down and typed in her employee ID. 'No access,' flashed up on the screen. She tried again, but the results stayed the same.

Three loud chimes sounded overhead. "Code Blue, ICU..." blared through the intercom. The lounge cleared within seconds.

Kelly rushed to another terminal. A medical record remained on the screen. *Good, he didn't log out. I better intercept the screen before his code automatically times out. It allowed her access.* She pulled up Monday's midnight census and scanned down to room 207. Mrs. Edith Weaver occupied the bed. Kelly printed the report and did the same for Tuesday's midnight census.

Mrs. Weaver no longer occupied that bed or any other in the hospital.

Kelly ran off a patient death report. According to the record, Edith Weaver died in the ICU at 4:12 a.m. Tuesday.

Kelly called Fritz.

Fritz didn't bother with a greeting. "What did you find?"

"I need a deposition subpoena for a chart on Edith Weaver. The date of birth is 5/4/1945. She was admitted on Friday, June 13, at 3:10 p.m. and died on Tuesday, June 17th, at 4:12 p.m. Her body was picked up at 6:15 a.m. by Peterson Mortuary, and there was no order for an autopsy. McCoy may want to get the Medical Examiner involved."

Fritz mumbled something, and then it sounded like a door closed.

"I want to check her lab results, get a list of meds, and interview some nurses in ICU," Kelly said. "I'll need another 30 minutes. Can you meet me in the cafeteria? Are you still there? I can hardly hear you."

"Listen, I… See you soon."

"Okay, we'll make it 12:30ish." Kelly hoped he got the message, but she had work to do. First stop—the lab.

SO CLOSE, SO FAR AWAY

Tuesday, June 18 – 1138 CDT, Ann Arbor, Michigan

Anxious to hear from Agent Kelly, Fritz grabbed his cell phone when he heard Kelly's ringtone. "What did you find?"

Kelly mentioned a name and birth date while Fritz reached across the desk for a pen and a memo pad.

Annoyed, the latent print examiner rolled her eyes and snapped, "Detective, I'm trying to work here. Chat somewhere else. Do you want the results ASAP or next week?"

"Sorry, I'll move into the hallway." Fritz tiptoed out the door and spoke to Kelly, "I'll talk to McCoy about the subpoena and inform him of a potential murder victim. What's your next step?"

He didn't catch everything, but it sounded like Agent Kelly had plenty to do.

"Listen, I can't make it until 12:30," Fritz said. "I dropped off the evidence. That envelope contained a medicine bottle. The tech is running tests on the liquid. In the meantime, I'm at the fingerprint lab. See you soon." He disconnected the call.

Fritz poked his head in the fingerprint lab. "Sorry to bother you again, but any idea where I can find Officer McCoy at this hour?"

"Lunch," the examiner said.

"No, thanks," Fritz said. "I already have a date with Agent Kelly."

"Very funny. I meant McCoy's at lunch, but I'll take a rain check if you're serious."

Fritz shook his head and asked, "Any clue whose prints are on the package? I mean, other than Agent Kelly's."

"You're not going to like it," the examiner said. "Two sets dominate. One I don't have on file. The other is a right thumb and index print of Vinny Corenelli."

Fritz's jaw dropped. "You mean Kelly had her hands on him?" Fritz tore out of the room. "Damn, disguises!"

"Hey, Fritz, I've been looking for you," Officer McCoy called from down the hall with a smirk on his face. "Why did you tie up my team without permission?"

"I tried your office first," Fritz said. "You weren't in, and you didn't answer your cell. Anyway, we have Vinny's prints—"

"Save your breath." McCoy waved a hand. "I already heard the news, and he's buying cocaine off some lab tech at the hospital."

"Coke? Did your team tell you that?" Fritz kept in step with McCoy and headed down the stairs. "I didn't get that message, but I think Kelly knows the lab tech."

"Great. It's high-grade stuff, too," McCoy said, "running over 85%."

"I'll get you the tech's name, but I need a favor," Fritz said. "Remember Jim's kidnapping at the hospital? There's more. I think we have a murder case on our hands."

"On our hands?" McCoy opened his office door. "Don't you mean my hands?"

"Whatever." Fritz followed McCoy to his desk. "Let's join Kelly at the hospital for lunch, and she'll fill you in."

"Okay, but you're buying." McCoy scooped a handful of memos from the desk. "Lead the way."

LOST IN A TUNNEL

The tunnel of white light that beckoned Cordy at the hospital didn't lead her to heaven. Instead, it swept her away to a personal hell. Not one filled with fire and brimstone but like a cave beneath the ice. Her body trembled, yet she couldn't move. Voices echoed around her, but she couldn't speak.

The nightmare continued until something sharp jabbed her arm, and she thought she heard a man whisper into her ear, "I hope this works." Her body roused from a deep sleep, but she couldn't open her eyes.

Someone jerked beside her. A door opened, letting in sunlight, and her heart jolted into overdrive.

A raspy voice yelled, "Hey, Doc, I think he's having a seizure. Come quick!"

Footsteps crunched on the gravel as another person approached. "Take him to the bunker. I'll treat him there." It sounds like the doc.

"Do you mean the cellar?"

"No, it's underground. You'll recognize it when you see it." Doc said.

Moments later, metal rattled, and someone whisked away the man lying next to Cordy.

"What about the woman?" raspy voice asked.

Someone tugged at the sleeve of her gown. "Leave her, but she can't be wearing this hospital gown, or the Corner will trace her back to the emergency department, and I don't want anything tying her body to me," Doc said. He lifted her other elbow, slid off her gown, and released his hold. Her arm flopped onto her head. "She's dead." He pulled the sheet over her head and tucked it tightly around her body. Her fingers and toes tingled with the added pressure.

"What did you give her?" the raspy voice asked.

"A paralyzing drug. It causes deep sleep, so she can't remember anything, but I lost the antidote. It needs to be given within four hours, or she'll die. It's been too long to save her." Doc said.

"Would that affect her lungs and heart?" a raspy voice asked.

"Not for four hours. After that…"

Raspy voice said something else, but it faded in the distance.

"Hearing is the last sense to go." A warm breath rushed against her ear. "If you're not dead yet, you will be soon," Doc said. "I didn't mean for it to go this far, but sometimes pawns must be sacrificed."

Look at me. I'm alive! screamed in her mind, but her vocal cords failed her.

Doc leaned closer. "What a shame."

Raspy voice returned. "Hey Doc, did you give that drug to Braun, too? He's still unconscious."

"No, that's your handy work, Ace," Doc said. "I just heard from Vinny. He ordered us to take this woman to the morgue. Don't screw it up."

"I know just the place," Ace said. "What's the cause of death?"

"Self-induced drug overdose." Doc moved away. "I'll send my report. They won't suspect anything."

"What about fingerprints or my DNA?" Ace asked.

"Don't worry about it," Doc said. "You're delivering her to the morgue. Anyone who investigates would question if they *didn't* find your prints."

Gravel crunched. Doors slammed. The ambulance engine turned over moments later, and Cordy drifted once more.

VINNY − 5, FRITZ − ZIP

Tuesday, June 18 − 1308 CDT,
Ann Arbor, Michigan/1208 MDT, Fort Collins, Colorado

With ever-growing confidence, Vinny made plans for his next steps to lure Fritz to him. It hadn't been easy, but he finally had Risa and Jim right where he wanted them. Earlier this morning, Risa videotaped an urgent message for her brother. Now, he needed to deliver that message without being spotted by the authorities.

Vinny focused, deep in concentration, and jumped when his phone rang again. It was the second time in ten minutes, and he hated being interrupted. This cell phone was the worst thing ever invented. Irritably, he swiped his finger over the screen. "Hello. Who's calling?"

There was no answer, so he pocketed it only to have it beep again. This time, he shouted, "Hello! Speak to me." When he got no reply, he slammed the phone on the table. "Someone keeps calling, then hangs up."

Jules rolled his eyes. "That's not a phone call. It's a text message."

"Don't sass me, boy!" Vinny scrolled his finger across the glass screen. "Better be from Ace. It's been seventy-two hours, and still no word on Fritz's family." In frustration, Vinny swore under his breath as he tried to find the message.

"Give it to me." Jules pulled the phone toward him and tapped on the text icon.

"What does it say?" Vinny asked and peered over Jules' shoulder.

"I can't make any sense of this." Jules squinted and held up the phone as if that would make the message clearer. "Why would anyone leave such a non-descript text?"

Vinny yanked back the cell. "It's in code. You don't know the system." Irritated, he reached for the candy bowl.

"A code?" Jules hunched forward. "Great. Teach it to me."

Vinny popped a chocolate cream into his mouth and scanned the text. "Yes! Doc's men took down Braun. Cordy's on death row, and we have a bonus."

"How did you get all that from a tri-colored triangle, an arrow, and a smiley face?" Jules asked.

Vinny pointed in glee—my plan worked. "See this green line on the right? The arrow struck here, pointing at Cordy's heart. Braun is the blue line on the left, and the red line is the chief, who is lying flat, so he's not in our clutches. The smiley face is a bonus."

"What does a bonus mean?" Jules asked.

"Someone we didn't count on." Vinny dialed Doc's disposable phone.

"That you, Vinny?" Doc asked.

"I gotta know." Vinny asked, "Falcon or Emu?"

"Definitely, Emu," Doc said. "No fly zone. I lost the antidote. Girl's a goner. I injected the drug over six hours ago—too late to revive. She'll never fly again."

"Shit happens. We don't need her anyway. Who's the bonus?" Vinny asked.

"Braun's brother, Usher," Doc said. "I injected him, too, but I don't know how much juice he got before he snapped off the needle. It's still in his arm."

"What's his condition?"

"He's out cold," Doc said. "And I mean freezing, so he must have absorbed some of the stuff—even had a seizure, so he probably won't make it either."

"Have you heard from Ace?"

"Yeah," Doc said. "He's the one who led us to the stakeout, but he can't find Fritz's family."

"Bribe Braun while his brother's still alive," Vinny said. "We need to find Fritz's wife."

"Braun's still unconscious."

Vinny swore again. A stabbing pain gripped his ailing heart. He dropped the phone, clutched his chest, and gasped for air.

Jules grabbed Vinny's arm. "You okay? No, you're not. What should I do? Chest pain, chest pain. What do I remember about that?" He closed his eyes and then asked, "Is it your heart? I've read about this. Does your arm or jaw hurt?"

Vinny moaned.

"Never mind. Take a seat and remain calm. Relax." Jules led his older brother to the arm of the couch and then grabbed the phone. "Doc, what do I do? Vinny's pale and sweating like a pig. I think it's his heart."

"I warned him about his heart. Get him his nitro," Doc said. "I gave him a supply while in prison and told him to keep them with him at all times.

"Nitro, right. I should have thought of that," Jules scanned the room. "Where's your nitro?"

Doc called out from the phone, "It should be in his shirt pocket. Pop a little pill under his tongue."

Jules patted Vinny's pockets and held up a bottle. "These the ones?"

Vinny nodded. "Hurry."

Jules' hands shook as he twisted off the cover. Pills spilled onto the floor. "Sorry."

"Just give it to me!" Vinny grabbed the bottle and slipped a tablet into his mouth. A few seconds later, Vinny took a deep breath. "Hand me the phone."

Jules shoved it into Vinny's hand and scooped up the dropped pills. "Chest pain. I won't miss that sign next time. Want some water?"

"Sure." Vinny waved him off. He knew the lad wanted to be a doc, but his nervous energy taxed Vinny even more.

"So what's the plan?" Doc asked.

"If Ace can't find Fritz's wife and kid, I'm sure Usher knows where they are. Get that antidote!"

"Okay," Doc said, "but it'll be close. I'm not sure if I can get the med in time. Max, anyone who has made it so far has been six hours. Cordy hit that limit ten minutes ago, and Usher's time is drawing near."

"I want Fritz to pay. Midget has it in for Braun, so you know what to do once you get the location."

Doc asked, "Aren't you flying to Colorado?"

"Nope," Vinny rasped. "We stay in Michigan until we nab Fritz or find his wife."

"What is Jim and Risa's condition?" Doc asked.

"Risa's fine." Vinny wiped his brow. "She made a ransom demand this morning for Big Brother. Jim has a raging fever. Infected wound, I suspect. We'll leave him here."

Jules returned with a glass of water and passed it to Vinny. "What do you mean Jim has an infected wound? He needs antibiotics."

"Hush!" Vinny grabbed the glass and waved Jules away.

"How will you send Risa's message to Fritz?" Doc asked.

"Jules will deliver it to St Anne's Catholic Church." The phone gave a warning signal. "Dispose of your cell."

"What do I do with Cordy?" Doc sounded distraught.

"Don't matter none to me."

"What? Why'd I go to all the trouble if you don't need her in the first place?"

"You did even better. You have Usher instead. Deliver her to the nearest morgue."

Jules grabbed Vinny's arm. "You can't let her die. Do something. Jim could be next."

Vinny shoved Jules' hand away. "Gotta go, and Doc, burn your phone." He disconnected and turned. "I'm sick and tired of you making demands and asking stupid questions. It's none of your business, and I didn't kill the girl." His threatening voice became a deep guttural sound like a mad dog.

Jules crossed his arms. "No, maybe not the girl, but if Jim dies, you will have killed him. You can get help—"

"Enough!" Vinny glared. "Now, deliver that thumb drive as we discussed, or else."

Jules' eyes darted from Vinny to Midget. "What do you mean, or else?"

Vinny's brow furrowed heavily over dark, beady eyes. "It means don't screw up. Your life depends on it, or this is the last time I'll ever see you alive." He turned to Midget. "If anything goes wrong with my plan, you know what to do."

"The lad won't screw up." Midget swallowed hard, "but if he doesn't follow through, I will."

RANSOM DEMAND DELIVERED

Tuesday, June 18 – 1454 CDT, Saint Anne's Catholic Church

Jules fidgeted in the priestly attire he once again adorned for this special trip to St. Anne's Catholic Church. The thumb drive of Risa's recording for Fritz brushed against his leg as it lay in his brown muslin gown pocket. He walked along the brick plaza cast in shadow from the massive gothic spire to the left of the great cathedral.

A flutter in his gut told him this was wrong. Even the gargoyles overhead accused him, warning against the massive sin he was about to undertake. He had to do something to change the outcome. *I need to save Jim.* Clasping his trembling hands behind his back, he bowed his head in repentance.

Midget tapped Jules' shoulder. "Still have that flash drive?"

Jules nodded. "Don't worry. I know what to do."

Midget nudged Jules. "Then move along, boy. We don't have all day."

"Wait for me out here on the bench. I'll be back in fifteen minutes."

"Make it ten," Midget said. "Call me at the prearranged number if you run into a snag."

Jules fought back the fear that threatened to swallow him alive. "I won't let you down." He took a deep breath, blew it out, and moved to the entrance. *What will Vinny do to me if I fail? Please help me, Lord.*

When he opened the heavy cathedral door, peace filled his soul as if God had heard his plea. Jules was awestruck by the white arches lining both sides of the aisle, rising to the high peaked ceiling covered by brightly colored frescos. Rainbows reflected from the stained-glass windows. He dipped his fingers into the holy water, crossed his body, and asked for forgiveness. His footsteps echoed on the ceramic tile floor.

A nun kneeling at the back pew glanced up. "May I help you?"

"I'm looking for Father Murdock," Jules whispered. "I must see him immediately."

"Psst. Over here." A shriveled man poked his gray head around the corner of the confessional door. "Hurry."

Jules peered around the church, but no one seemed to pay any attention. The nun had bowed her head again in prayer. He moved to the confessional. "Father?"

"Step inside," the bent man whispered. "I understand you have something for me."

Jules moved behind a black curtain. "Are you Father Murdock?"

"That's what they call me."

"Are you really my Uncle?" Jules asked.

Murdock whispered, "Yeah. Some days, that doesn't make me very happy. I never liked Vinny, and I'm sure the feeling is mutual. I told him that I refuse to break the law for him or anyone else, but this is bordering my limits. So why are you here?"

"I have a special message for Fritz. Are you familiar with that name?" Jules reached into his pocket but waited for a reply.

"I know of him, and I'm only the messenger," Murdock said. "Fritz will receive the information within twenty-four hours, but I can't promise any results once it's in his hands."

Jules pulled the thumb drive from his pocket and pushed it through a small slit in the wall between the two men. "His sister's life is in grave danger. You must tell him my boss will not negotiate with anyone else."

The old man's wrinkled hand grabbed the drive. "Do you know what's on this, boy?"

"No. Like you, I'm only the messenger. I must leave now."

"Anything else?" the priest asked.

"Yes. Risa says, 'The key is reincarnation.' Be sure to pass it along with the drive. I must go now."

Sirens echoed in the distance. Midget rushed into the church, ducked behind the curtain, grabbed Jules' arm, and pulled him into the sanctuary. "Hurry. Let's get out of here."

Father Murdock appeared from the confessional. His face paled. "What's happening? Why the sirens?"

Midget stepped behind the priest and nudged him. "I have a gun. Do you understand?"

The priest nodded, but he slumped a little more, and disappointment showed in his eyes.

"Get us out of here, and no one gets hurt," Midget whispered, moving toward the church's back wall.

Father Murdock bowed his head and folded his hands in prayer as he walked across the aisle and tottered down four steps to a side door of the nave.

Jules followed his behavior and stepped behind the priest and Midget.

Murdock unlocked the door and swung it open. "Take the catacombs to the rear garden." He rested a hand on Jules. "Bless you, my son. Go straight. You're too young for this. Call me if you need help."

"I will," Jules promised, barely entering the catacombs when someone yelled. "Police. Don't anyone leave the building." Jules turned back toward the priest.

Father Murdock pointed to the left. "Go to the end of the aisle and down the stairs. You'll find a locked door to the outside. The key code is 'heaven.' I'll go back inside the church, and God forgive me, I'll try to stall the police."

"Thanks, Uncle Ah, Father," Jules whispered.

Keys rattled in the lock as Midget grabbed Jules' arm and ducked into a dark tunnel. Jules paused briefly, turned on the flashlight app on his cell phone to light the way to the stairwell, and hustled away.

DARKNESS TO LIGHT

Tuesday, June 18 – 1512 MDT, Fort Collins, Colorado

Ace drove the ambulance to the county morgue. He worked as an EMT to earn extra money and knew the ropes. He unloaded the gurney, wheeled it inside, and stopped at the front desk.

"Forms are on the counter," a crisp voice came from the cloakroom. Keys jingled. A punch of the time clock and the receptionist appeared. "You know what to do. I'm late." She shoved a purse strap over her arm and left the building.

Ace filled out the paperwork and pushed the gurney down the hall to the morgue. A chill raced up his spine as he entered. Sheet-draped bodies lay on metal tables lined up for autopsies. *I hate coming here.*

The medical examiner glanced up from his work when he saw Ace. "Anything special, or can it wait until the morning?"

"No hurry. Just another vagrant wasting the city's money."

The ME sighed through his mask and wiped his brow with the sleeve of the yellow paper gown, protecting his clothes from blood and bone fragments. "What's the cause of death?"

"Self-induced drug overdose," Ace said. "No relatives."

"We have too many unclaimed bodies already."

"Where do you want her?" Ace asked.

"Find a gurney willing to share." The ME went back to his work. "Anyone ask for an autopsy?"

Ace shuddered. "State can't afford it." He peered into the small glass window of the cooler door. Dozens of bodies stacked like cordwood covered a lower shelf to the right. More bodies lay on carts parked along the left wall. Most already held a couple of corpses, but he found a single occupant near the back. "Where's the assistant?"

"He went home," the ME said. "It's late. Just tag the stiff and leave the gurney near the front door."

Ace rolled Officer Joshtine Cordelia onto the morgue cart, but her toe tag read Jane Doe. He closed the cooler door and gladly left the morgue.

BENNY THE PRUNER

Fritz studied every aspect of the case, searching for any hidden clue that would tell him where to find Risa. He talked to the ME, reviewed lab results, and reread witness interviews. Descriptions of crime scenes blended together, but he'd personally go over every file again today on the off chance he missed a connection. Besides, he didn't want to go back out in the rain where the media lay in wait under their umbrellas, cameras ready to pounce.

Officer McCoy wanted nothing to do with the press, so he'd thrown Fritz into the fray. The cop claimed he had enough trouble appeasing the governor, who demanded to know how a war veteran returned home safely from Afghanistan only to be shot in the good old USA. He was not only shot in his own backyard but was also whisked away from a local hospital. Plus, some brilliant journalists reported that Jim faked his escape to rescue his wife, causing more investigations. Could the rumors get any wilder?

Fritz compiled notes and scribbled them on a whiteboard propped against the wall at the back of his desk. Rubbing his aching forehead, his thoughts kept coming back to the skeleton key. *Why would Mick carry it everywhere he went?*

Kelly entered the office with two cups. "How are you doing?" she asked, setting a mug on his desk. "I hope you don't mind tea. I can't stomach any more coffee."

"Thanks. I need a break." Fritz stared at the key lying on his dented, gray metal desktop. "Wonder what it opens." He fingered the three ornate curved scrolls that came together to form a cloverleaf on top of the key. A flower blossomed in the center.

Kelly pulled a squeaky wooden chair next to Fritz. "Walt mentioned a cemetery where they buried his Uncle Benny."

"I know. I searched for Benny Corenelli," Fritz said. "No match. I even searched death records in Michigan, Wisconsin, Indiana, and Ohio—nothing."

"Maybe his uncle came from his mother's side," Kelly said. "What was her maiden name?"

"I thought of that, too, but Mick's mother was also a Corenelli. They keep close family ties." Fritz jotted another note on the board. "Knowing the mafia, they're all uncles, cousins, and kinfolk." He held the key up to the light. "It's so ornate. You would think it opened a mansion, not some shack near a cemetery."

Kelly shuffled through several papers.

"What are you looking for?" Fritz asked.

"Mick's autopsy report," Kelly said. "What's his birth date?"

"It's on the board." Fritz pointed to Mick, DOB-August 30, 1980. "What are you thinking?"

"Walt said that Vinny nearly choked Mick on his thirteenth birthday when he yanked the chain from his neck. That would have been in 1993. Benny had to have died sometime before then."

Fritz turned to his laptop and typed 'Benny, Michigan, obit 1980s-90s' into Google. "Too many hits." He tried a few more renditions, but nothing. "I have an idea." Fritz grabbed the phone.

When Walt's lawyer found out who was calling, he chuckled. "Ready to make a deal?"

Fritz shook his head but replied, "Maybe if we get some answers."

"What can I do for you?"

Fritz heard the skepticism in the lawyer's voice. "Do you know Walt's Uncle Benny?"

"Benny, the pruner?" the lawyer asked. I've heard of him, but I never had the pleasure of meeting him. Why do you ask?"

"Was he Mick's biological uncle?" Fritz asked.

"I suppose so. Benny's long gone. Walt and Mick are brothers. So, Benny was an uncle to both of them. What's this all about?"

"So his last name was Corenelli?" Fritz waited for several seconds without an answer. He cleared his throat and tried again. "When did Benny die?"

"We got a deal I can work out or not?"

Fritz hesitated. Unwilling to allow Walt to walk away with a lesser charge, he answered, "Or not."

The lawyer groaned. "Go back to school and figure it out. Don't call back until—"

Fritz hung up the phone. "Ever heard of Benny the pruner?"

Kelly shook her head. "I'll see what I can dig up." She sighed, rested an elbow on the desk, and propped her head on her hand.

Fritz took another look at his colleague. She'd changed from her uniform into gray sweats. Her puffy eyes let him know she'd been crying. "Any word on the chief's condition?"

Kelly rubbed her temple. "He's in ICU, but you must be out of your mind knowing Vinny's gang has Officer Cordelia and Usher."

Fritz bolted from his chair as panic ripped through him. "Usher? He's supposed to be watching Laura! Wait a minute." He stepped within inches of Kelly, trying to grasp the meaning of what she'd said. "How do you know? Did I miss something? Why the hell didn't anyone tell me?"

Kelly's jaw dropped. "I'm sure I told you."

Fritz slammed his fist against the desk. "What else has been hidden from me?" He grabbed his jacket. "Are Laura and Marta safe?"

"I don't know, but I told you that Chief Jackson and Braun met with Usher on the morning Braun disappeared."

"Maybe you did, but I didn't know they were meeting in person," Fritz headed for the door and paused. "Did you speak with the chief?"

Kelly shook her head. "No. I talked with his doctor, but the secretary sent a text message a while ago. You must have a copy on your phone."

Fritz rummaged through his pockets and grabbed his cell. "Who's in charge while the chief's in the hospital?"

"I don't know that either," Kelly said.

Fritz checked for text messages. "It doesn't say much." He speed-dialed the agency to get more information, but it went directly to voicemail. Glancing at his watch, he swore. "They're closed." He left a message to call first thing in the morning.

"It's even later here," Kelly said. "Maybe we should get a bite to eat."

"You go ahead," Fritz said. "Sorry, I yelled, and thanks for your help. I'll see you in the morning." He shoved several files into his briefcase and fisted his keys. "I need to know that Laura's safe."

GETTING THE TRUTH

A silhouetted shadow moved closer to Agent Usher Hastings as he lay on a gurney in a cold, dark dungeon. He felt a rush of adrenaline pump through his veins when he noticed a shimmer of light glint from a silver gun barrel aimed at his temple. His heart raced as if he'd run a marathon, and a jackhammer pounded in his ears, making it difficult to hear. He was paralyzed to voluntary movement, yet his thighs and knees shook uncontrollably.

"You're still alive," A menacing voice echoed. "Guess you didn't get enough of Doc's magic potion—all the better for me. Where's Fritz's wife?"

The taste of bile lingered. With every ounce of energy, Usher shook his head. He licked his lips. "Don't know." At least that's what his mind said, but he couldn't hear any words escape his mouth.

The figure shoved the gun tighter against Usher's temple. "Where's Fritz's wife and grandkid."

Usher couldn't let his life end without finding Braun, and he wouldn't tell this man anything about Fritz's wife. *No time. It can't end this way.* His head didn't even flinch when the figure pulled the trigger.

There was a click. "Dang, no bullets," the shadowy man dropped the gun. "Maybe your life is unimportant to you, but we have your brother."

Usher's heart ticked up a notch. They have Braun? This can't be good.

A bright hallway light revealed Braun sitting in a wooden chair by the door. His pant legs were rolled up to his knees, exposing his calves. His bare ankles were taped to the front chair legs, and his feet rested on a metal sheet.

Usher barely recognized his brother's bruised and bloodied face. The menacing shadow headed toward the hallway and morphed in the light—the nurse who kidnapped Cordy. It was the first time Usher took a good look at this guy, who was maybe in his thirties. He no longer wore scrubs or a white lab coat and looked more like a mad scientist than a nurse. Usher noted the man's skinny legs, gangly arms, and Coke-bottle-lensed glasses.

The string bean of a man tripped on the leg of Braun's chair and muttered a swear word. He shoved his glasses up his hooked nose and disappeared from view.

The man returned shortly, wheeling a bulky machine with large metal dials. A cable that sprouted wires dragged along the floor behind the machine as he parked it next to Braun.

Usher's muscles jerked, and a roar ripped from his lungs, "No!" He wanted to say more, but his mouth felt full of cotton. That didn't stop his brain from screaming inside his mind—*an electroshock machine. Stay away from Braun.* Usher recalled his brutal torture four years ago while on assignment in the Congo—poker-hot pain exploded throughout his system, ravaging his body repeatedly until he collapsed, leaving him a babbling idiot for months after his rescue. He couldn't let this man do the same to Braun, but he couldn't give in and tell Laura's location either.

"From your reaction, you know what this little machine can do." The string bean of a guy chuckled. He ripped open the front of Braun's shirt and placed electrodes on his chest. "Now, I'll ask once again, Where's Fritz's wife? This is your last chance, or your brother will pay the price."

"Don't tell him," Braun hissed between swollen lips.

Usher shook his head, dreading what would happen next. *How much current will this ogre use?* He opened his mouth.

Braun shouted, "No! You have nothing to say!"

Usher tried again. "I…I—"

"Don't tell," Braun spat. Gritting his teeth, he added, "I can take whatever this lab rat dishes out."

"Can you? Really?" The lab rat's eyes scanned the room as if afraid he'd be caught. His hand shook as he cranked up a dial. With one last check of the room, he pushed a button. A loud crack split the silence, followed by a scream." Braun's body convulsed and went limp.

Tears pooled in Usher's eyes. He wanted to launch for the rat's throat, but he couldn't move.

Doc appeared in the doorway. His eyes narrowed as he bolted toward the cruel nurse. "What's all the screaming about? What are you doing, Ace?"

"Getting results," Ace cranked the dial higher. "I have orders and will carry them out, just like in the service—you understand orders, right?

"Stop right now!" Doc ordered. "You don't know who you're dealing with. I have a better way."

"Where's Cordy?" Usher eked out.

"Dead," Doc said. "A real shame, too. You lost the antidote. How does her death make you feel?"

"Where…is…she?" Usher paused between each word.

"The morgue," Ace said.

"Shut up," Doc snapped.

Usher closed his eyes. He hoped he'd gotten the antidote to her in time. He jerked when something pricked his arm, but he had no will to fight. "What did you give him?" Ace's voice sounded distant.

"Truth serum," Doc said. "He'll talk soon."

Usher slipped into darkness.

RISING FROM THE DEAD

Wednesday, June 19 – 0138 MDT, Fort Collins, Colorado

Cordy dragged her eyelids open and struggled to think beyond the rush of sensations that attacked her body. Her chest balked with each shallow breath. A wild tattoo of flutters grew into a thundering hammer and then eased to a steady heartbeat. Cordy shivered and pulled the sheet around her. It's so cold. "C-c-close the w-window— it's fr-fr-freezing." The mattress was hard as metal, and pain shot through her with every movement. She managed to roll over and realized she wasn't alone. Whoever lay beside her didn't move, was freezing cold, and hadn't bathed in months.

Confused, her mind traveled through a dense fog, seeking clarity. Memories flooded back. She'd been in the emergency room. *When? Why? Where's Braun? Oh, right, he's missing. The chief was shot, and what happened to Usher?*

Cordy's eyes widened. A whisper floated in her head—if you're not dead yet, you will be soon. The fetid odor grew stronger. *Am I dying?*

"Help! Is anyone out there?" Her voice rasped. She called again. *No reply.*

She tried to sit up, rolled off the gurney, and landed on the floor. Her trembling legs refused to hold her weight. Except for underwear, her nude body lay tangled in a sheet on the frosty floor. Everything was dark except for a small blinking red light. Images of bodies piled along the wall flickered in the ominous glow. I think I'm in a morgue.

Her numb fingers fumbled to remove the cloth that bound her feet, then dragged herself toward the light until she reached the wall. A dim light reflected off something above her—*a window.* Cordy ran a hand along the wall and hit something metal, *a handle.* Her knees tingled as she pulled herself to a kneeling position and leaned against a door. It took a few bumps with her shoulder before the door opened with a hiss, and she fell into the doorway. Cordy poked her head around the corner. "Anyone here?" Holding her breath, she listened.

Nothing.

Warm air laced with an orange-scented disinfectant filled her lungs. The odor stung her nose and throat as she crawled out of the cooler and nudged the door closed behind her. That's when she noticed the toe tag. *Why does it read Jane Doe?* The tag came off with a tug and ended up in a nearby trashcan.

A yellow cast from a lone incandescent light radiated from down the hall. "Hello. Is anyone here? Can you hear me?"

Not even a shadow moved from the lit area, but she spotted a restroom on her way to investigate and knew that was her next stop.

Cordy crawled across the floor to a chair and managed to pull herself to her feet. She flipped on the lights and opened the bathroom door. To her surprise, it also had a shower. A stack of laundry lay on a bench beside the door. After pawing through the pile, she found a pair of scrubs, a towel, and a washcloth. A bottle of body gel was on the wall.

A long, hot shower and shampoo felt like heaven. Wiggling her toes, she felt the numbness grow into a tingling sensation that crept up her torso and disappeared. The water warmed her clear to her bones. It washed away the aches along with the dirt. She dried off, slipped on the scrubs, and continued to explore the morgue.

Several lockers lined the wall. Two were empty, but in the third, she found a pair of well-used sneakers—a little big for her narrow feet, but she laced them up as snugly as they would go and was glad to find them. Her stomach grumbled. *When was the last time I ate?*

Cordy wasn't sure which morgue she was in or where she should go. She wandered down the hall to a lit office. A clock on the wall read 1:52 a.m. On the counter was a pot of lukewarm coffee. She helped herself to a cup. A bag of peanuts sat next to the pot, and she downed those, too.

On the desk lay her paperwork. Anxious to read the information, she found the address on the letterhead. It answered the question of her location—*about twenty miles from the hospital where she had been treated in the emergency department.* Scanning down the page, her eye caught '*cause of death—suicide*'. The death certificate was signed by 'Doc…' She couldn't read the scribbled last name, but she remembered Doc—the man who tried to kill her. He nearly succeeded, too. Her heart leapt in her chest at the thought. She wondered if the ME could be trusted or if he conspired with Doc—*time to leave before anyone finds me.*

Her fingers shook as she flipped through the phone book and jotted down a number. She tried to call a taxi using the morgue phone, but it wouldn't allow access. She even tried dialing nine first. There was no way it would allow a long-distance call to Fritz. Desperate to get help for Braun and Usher, she dialed 911. Even that number was blocked. She'd have to hitch a ride.

Cordy shuffled to the exit, twisted, and pulled on the doorknob. It didn't budge. *Locked from the outside. Where will I find a key?* She trudged back to the office, rummaged through desk drawers, searched bookshelves, and even tried lab coat pockets, but no keys. *Is there an alarm?* Cordy felt under the desk for a secret button or something that might call for help.

Nothing.

There were no outside windows. Sweat dripped down her back. Cordy took a deep breath.

What would Braun do? He'd pick the lock. Braun showed her how a long time ago. I can do this—she hoped. She found a toolbox with a flashlight and a small flat-blade screwdriver in the bottom drawer. A paperclip lay in a tray of the top drawer. She gathered her tools and went to work on her escape plan. Using the clip, she unbent the metal, put a slight kink on the end, and inserted it into the lock. Then, she used the screwdriver for torque. Rapidly jamming the clip in and out, the pins tumbled into place. To her surprise, it didn't take long to unlock the door.

Free at last. She switched the flashlight on to check the hallway. No one lurked in the darkness, so she flipped off the morgue light and closed the door behind her. *What next? I need to see the chief. Is he still at the hospital? What day is it, anyway?*

Cordy hated being out of control, and her mind kept floating back to Braun. Is he still alive? It was then she realized she loved him even with all his faults and possessive innuendos…*I have to save him. First, I must find Chief Jackson, if he's still alive. I'll need his help to rescue Braun.*

WATCH AND WAIT

Laura awoke early after a fitful night's sleep. She wasn't surprised to see the bulging blue-gray underbellies of rain clouds instead of the wispy pink sunrise. The air felt heavy and foretold of the upcoming rain storm. For some reason, it frayed her nerves.

To calm herself, she brewed some tea, settled into a Lazy Boy recliner, and picked up her metal knitting needles to finish a warm, cozy cashmere sweater for Fritz. Her needles clicked almost like a ticking clock as her nimble fingers wove the maroon yarn, growing row by row, as she fell deeper into the routine.

She was so engrossed with her project that she didn't notice anyone walking up the front steps to the porch and jumped at the sound of the doorbell. Maggie was in the kitchen, and Marta was still upstairs in her studio.

Realizing she was nearest to the door, Laura called out, "I'll get it." She set down her knitting on an antique tea table and glanced toward the oval window of the hideout.

Maggie rushed from the kitchen. "Don't open the door. Jake didn't notify me of any visitors, and it might be a trap."

The man stood by the door momentarily, and heavy boots clumped along the patio. A loud rap on the window startled Laura a second time.

Maggie placed a finger over her lips, pulled a cell from her apron pocket, and motioned for Laura to follow her into the hallway. "Jake, someone's at the door," Maggie whispered into the phone.

"I know," Jake's voice echoed from outside the window. "I'm standing out here. Have you heard anything from Usher?"

"No." Maggie disconnected, darted across the living room, and peeked outside from the curtain's edge. "One moment. Oh, wait, what's the code?"

Jake gave a secret knock followed by, "Magpie."

Laura waited for Maggie's nod and opened the door.

"You surprised me," Maggie said. "You never come up here without calling ahead."

Jake stepped inside. "Sorry, but I have a bad feeling. Usher missed his check-in call. He's never late. I should have heard from him an hour ago."

Maggie bolted the door behind him.

Laura asked, "Who's manning the gate?"

"I called Gus. He came right over. I thought I'd check on you in person." Jake surveyed the room. "Where's the little girl?"

Marta called down the stairs from the landing. "Up here, Jake. I've been painting. Who's Gus? I don't know him."

Maggie nodded at Jake. "We can tell them. They should know."

Marta ran down the stairs. "We should know what?" Pepper followed her down the steps. His tongue hung from the side of his mouth as he panted.

Jake knelt beside her, absently petting the dog. "Gus works for the FBI. He's assigned to you while Usher's on a special ops mission."

"Usher's in trouble?" Marta asked. "Did he push the magic button?"

Jake frowned. "Magic button?"

"On his watch," Marta said. "He showed it to me last week."

Jake slapped his forehead. "Does it really work?"

"Thank you, Marta. That's a great idea. I'll check the GPS." Maggie moved to the living room and tapped her fingers across the keyboard of her laptop. Locating the radio frequency outside Fort Collins, Colorado, didn't take long. "Let's narrow it down."

"I don't see any movement," Jake said. "Maybe he's not wearing the watch."

"Contact the FBI and see what they know," Maggie said. "I don't want to take any chances, and I'm calling Chief Jackson."

CALLING IN RECRUITS

When Chief Jackson heard the news of Usher's disappearance and that he had activated his distress signal, Jackson didn't hesitate to call his long-time friend, Officer Russ Bracken, for help. The chief's one regret was he couldn't take part in the action while recovering in ICU. "We have a hostage situation. Two suspects, males, both armed and dangerous. They kidnapped three members of my team and left me for dead."

"Do we have an ID on the suspects?" Bracken asked.

"Still hazy on the facts, but my gut says they're tied to the Corenelli gang. Old Vinny's orchestrating two angles at the same time, here in Colorado and another in Michigan. He may even be working on a third."

"Hedging his bets?" Bracken asked.

"Yeah." The chief stifled a yawn and rubbed his throbbing brow. Knowing he needed a clear head, he fought off the blurred vision and refused any pain meds. His finger tapped the side rail near the PCA unit. Relief was only seconds away. All he needed to do was push the button, and the peace-giving narcotic would flow from the pump into his vein. He needed a respite, but not now. Not before, he galvanized his plan to save his team.

"Has there been a ransom demand?" Bracken asked.

"Not that I know of," the chief said.

"Other injuries?"

"Braun and I were hit two days ago, but I don't know his condition," the chief said. "Then yesterday, someone nabbed Cordy and Usher. I'm unclear about the details, but I spoke to Maggie a few minutes ago. She tracked down Usher's radio frequency. He's located outside of Fort Collins."

Bracken cleared his throat. "Do you think we can negotiate their release?"

"Do you know Vinny Corenelli?" Chief Jackson asked. "These are his men."

"I get it," Bracken said. "They'll promise anything but will deliver only on Vinny's orders. Do you think the target is Detective Fritz Von Schlegen? We covered that news station earlier this month."

"I'm sure of it," Chief said. "There's bad blood between them."

"Do you think Vinny will demand an exchange of Risa for Fritz?" Bracken asked.

"He may make that offer, but I wouldn't count on him following through with the exchange." The chief explained the history between the two men.

"Do you have a plan?" Bracken asked.

The chief laughed. "That's why I'm calling. The surgeon confined me to ICU. It's in your hands, and I hope the Fort Collins SWAT team can come to Braun's aid."

"Hang on," Bracken said. "I'll patch in the Larimer County sheriff. We'll need his help to formulate a plan."

MASTER MIND

Wednesday, June 19 – 0310-0640 MDT,
Fort Collins, Colorado

After escaping the locked morgue, Cordy had to find a way to the Medical Center of the Rockies to ask Chief Jackson, who was in the ICU, for help to find Braun. She had no money for a taxi or a phone to call one. The buses wouldn't start running again for another two hours. Traffic outside the morgue wasn't promising either, so she walked six blocks toward the main road.

The brisk air whipped her wet hair into her eyes and nipped at her cheeks. She wished there had been a jacket to borrow along with the scrubs and shoes, but at least she wasn't outside, in the nude, walking the back streets of Fort Collins.

Cordy reached the main road. Remembering horror stories about hitchhiking, she made a three-hundred-sixty-degree search for the safest place to stand. Two cars passed by before she dared put her thumb out. Several more passed by without a second glance. She didn't want to step onto the highway for fear of being hit, so she found a bus stop, huddled in a corner of a bench, and must have fallen asleep.

After what seemed like hours, she forced herself back onto the side of the road before she froze to death. Her little tap dance to keep warm must have saved her because some kind soul stopped his car and rolled down his window. "You look like you're freezing. Why don't you have a coat?"

"It's a long story," Cordy said.

"On your way to the hospital?" he asked.

Cordy's jaw dropped. "How'd you know?"

He chuckled. "The scrubs were a big clue. Get in. My wife works in the emergency department. I'm on my way to pick her up."

"Thanks." Cordy moved around to the passenger's side and climbed inside. "Heated seats. I think I'm in heaven."

"What department do you work in?" the man asked.

"Oh, I don't…I mean, wherever they assign me."

"Float pool, huh?" He pulled away from the curb.

Cordy tried to think like a nurse. "They're short-staffed most of the time."

"Especially on the night shift," he added. "Did your car stall out?"

"Ah, something like that. I'm no mechanic, so I don't know what exactly happened to it, but I appreciate the lift."

"No problem. We'll be there shortly."

Cordy made small talk, asked about his wife, and then leaned back in silence.

He delivered her to the emergency entrance. "Will you need a ride home later today?"

"No, I'll call my brother to pick me up." Although she had no brother, he'd never know the truth. "Thanks for the ride." She climbed out of the car and walked inside.

She knew visiting hours hadn't started yet, and no one was in the lobby. Her eye caught a gleaming set of elevators across the wall from the information desk. Cordy pressed the up button, rode to the second floor, and ducked inside the ICU. When no one questioned her, she guessed the scrubs gave her license to find the chief, not that anyone could stop her. Not after everything she'd been through the past two days.

Even in the dim lights of the ICU, she saw nurses bustle from room to room. Cordy moved toward the main desk.

A man said, "I'm sorry, but you must leave. The chief needs his rest."

Cordy's head jerked toward the sound, thinking the man spoke to her. Instead, a male nurse stood in the doorway to ICU 5. "Where'd you get that phone?" He darted into the room.

Cordy spied a thermometer on the counter, grabbed it, and headed for room 5. When she entered the room, the chief glared at the male nurse and clung tightly to the phone's receiver.

"Don't touch—" Chief Jackson said.

The male nurse leaned down and unplugged the cord from the wall.

"Hey, I was on an important call." Jackson glared at the nurse. An officer in a dark blue uniform stood beside the bed.

For a moment, Cordy was afraid her boss would clobber the nurse, but he snatched up the phone, wound the cord around it, and headed for the door.

The officer stepped in front of the nurse. "Someone swiped his cell phone, so how's he supposed to make phone calls?"

"Are you family?" the nurse asked. There was a pause. "I didn't think so. You'll have to leave. Visiting is for family only, and it's not visiting hours."

"I was talking to a Larimer County sheriff, and he doesn't care what time of day it is," Jackson said.

"Well, I do." The nurse turned and bumped into Cordy. "Oh, good. You're just in time to take his vitals. I'll be back in a few minutes." He stepped around her and left the room with the phone.

Jackson raised his eyebrows, opened his mouth as if to speak, then snapped it shut when she popped the thermometer probe into his ear and whispered, "That you, Cordy?"

She smiled and put a finger over her lips.

The visiting officer moved toward the door.

"Wait, Bracken. We may need to change plans." Jackson said, "I want you to meet Officer Cordelia."

Bracken's eyes traveled over her. "Why are you in scrubs?"

"Long story."

The chief asked, "How did you get here? Are the others free, too?"

The male nurse returned. "You still here?"

Cordy moved between Bracken and the nurse. "I'm talking to him at the moment."

"Oh, in that case, I'll give you five minutes, and then you have to leave. And no more phone calls." The nurse glared at Cordy. "I mean it, and don't you dare bring him a phone."

The chief cleared his throat.

"Did you want his vitals?" She didn't wait for an answer. "Temp. 98.4, pulse 84," Cordy shoved the thermometer into his hands and walked him outside the door. "I'm off duty. I just came up to check on the chief, so I'll take Officer Bracken with me when I leave."

"Make it snappy."

When Cordy returned, the chief whispered, "Give me a quick summary of what happened to you."

"Later, I have to escort this officer out of ICU." She nudged Bracken. "I want in on the action. We need to find Braun and Usher."

Jackson said, "Okay, but listen carefully. Bracken will have to fill you in on our plans."

"How about over breakfast?" Bracken flashed a bright smile.

ACE KNOWS THE PLACE

Wednesday, June 19 – 1903 CDT, Vinny's hideout

Tired and hungry, Vinny swore as he pulled into the cracked flagstone driveway of his hideaway shortly after seven. A brisk wind caught the car door and ripped it from his fingers as he fumbled to grab his hat before it blew away. His task had been simple: to get some pain medication for Midget, but the day went to hell after meeting Dave at the medical center. Someone pilfered his cocaine, and he was sure it happened when some broad plowed into him outside the medical center. He'd almost made it back home when he discovered the theft. It took all afternoon for Dave to replace the bottle.

In the meantime, Vinny closed three offshore accounts and opened a fourth in Ace's corporation. The account would automatically wire funds back to Vinny if Ace didn't deliver the location of Fritz's wife in the next 24 hours.

Vinny dashed up the steps and across the veranda through the pouring rain. He was soaked by the time he reached the house. All he wanted was a good stiff drink and, of course, Fritz.

For some reason, the house was dark. Vinny flipped on the light, dropped his coat on the back of a chair, and headed for the kitchen. A bright red light blinked from the phone. Someone had left a message. Vinny called out, "Jules, why didn't you answer the phone?"

Rapid footsteps ran up the basement steps. The door flew open, and Jules ran into the kitchen. "Vinny, I'm glad you're finally home."

"How long have you been in the basement?" Vinny yelled. "And what the hell were you doing down there?"

Jules put his hands on his hips. "Risa says Jim's gonna die if we don't get him some antibiotics."

Vinny took a glass from the cupboard. "You were supposed to deliver dinner and then wait here for the phone call."

"I know, but Jim's leg is on fire. There's pus everywhere." Jules made a face. "There's a red streak. Risa says it's blood poison."

"What do you mean? How does Risa know his condition?" Vinny grabbed Jules by the collar. "What did you do, boy?"

Jules pulled away. "Risa's a nurse. Her husband's dying."

"So what?" Vinny smirked.

"But you promised." Jules glared. "You said no one would get hurt, and Jim's nearly in a coma."

"I didn't shoot him. He'll die of natural causes." Vinny pointed to the phone. "So, who called?"

Jules stared at the phone's blinking light and then toward the living room. "I don't know. I didn't hear it ring. Why didn't you have calls sent to your cell phone? No one uses a landline anymore."

"I hate those things, so who called?" When Jules shrugged, Vinny launched at him and slapped him across the face. His hands wrapped around Jules' shirt collar.

Midget ran down the hall, grabbed Vinny by the arm, and pulled him off. "If you're so hell-bent on finding out who called, check the machine, but leave the boy alone. And where are my drugs? I'm seething here in pain."

Vinny bared his teeth, but Midget stood his ground.

"Fine." Vinny tossed the meds at Midget, then stomped off and hit the play button.

"This is Father Murdock. Remember Apollo 13? You know that famous line, 'Houston, we have a problem.' Call me." The recorder beeped.

When Ace's voice came on the line, Vinny was about to punch the off button. "Just wishing you a happy birthday. There's an investment I'd like you to look at in West Virginia. My partner will be in touch with you soon to discuss the details. And you better have come through with the funds."

Midget poured two whiskey sours and handed one to Vinny. "So you think Fritz's wife is in West Virginia?"

"Ace's life is on the line. He'll make damn sure he has the facts." Vinny took a swig. "Now, to find out what ails the priest."

MYSTERIOUS OPPORTUNITY

Wednesday, June 19 – 2012 CDT, A block from St. Anne's

The priest jolted upright when the phone rang downstairs in his office. The sound echoed through the floorboards of his bedroom. Laying his Bible aside, he leaned forward, slid his toes into a pair of moccasins, and then used his arms to push off the seat of his wooden chair. He twisted his head from side to side to work out a crick in his neck as he shuffled out the door.

At the top of the stairs, he listened. The phone stopped ringing. The priest blew out a deep breath and nearly turned around. *What if it's Vinny?* A surge of adrenaline flushed through him. *Should I tell him the truth?*

"Father Murdock?" A nun stood at the bottom of the stairs. "Are you all right? You look pale."

"I'm fine. Thank you for asking." The phone rang again, and he nearly fell. His hand flew out and caught the railing in time, and then he trotted as fast as his seventy-eight-year-old legs could carry him.

The nun stood outside the locked office door. "Who would be calling at this hour?"

"Good question." Father Murdock turned the key in the lock and pushed past her. "I'll get it." Realizing he was a bit brusque, he added, "Would you mind getting me some warm milk?" He patted his belly. "Upset stomach."

She nodded. The priest picked up the phone. Out of breath, he held the receiver briefly before answering. Thoughts of Vinny's old man raced through his head. He'd vowed to care for his nephews no matter how rotten they'd turned out.

"Father Murdock, is that you?" Vinny asked.

"Yes, my son," the priest whispered.

"You mentioned Apollo. What's the problem?"

"One moment." Father Murdock checked the hallway and locked the door. "How did the police know to come here?"

Vinny hesitated. "Police? What are you talking about?"

"The officer was very thorough. He checked everywhere and demanded to know what the boy gave me." He went on to explain what transpired at the church earlier in the day.

A loud rap on the door caused the priest to gasp. "I'll be right there." After fumbling with the lock, he opened the door a crack. The nun held out a mug of warm milk. "Thanks." The priest's shaky hand grabbed the mug. "You are most kind."

"Are you still upset over the police?" the nun asked.

"No, God will protect." He sipped from the mug and turned on his most dazzling smile. "That'll be all for tonight, Sister. May you sleep well. I'll see you in the morning."

"Thank you. Good night, Father." The nun turned and walked down the hallway.

* * *

Vinny grumbled on the other end of the phone. "You didn't give them the thumb drive, did you?" Vinny popped a milk chocolate cream into his mouth as he paced around the kitchen table. "Well, did you?"

"Um, I..." The priest cleared his throat.

Vinny shouted, "Midget, why didn't you tell me the police were at the church?"

"What's the big deal?" Midget asked. "We got away."

"How did they find out?" Vinny asked.

Midget shrugged his shoulders.

"So what did you do with the drive, Father Murdock?"

"Don't get upset." The priest's voice was barely a whisper. "I took care of everything. You'll see."

Vinny felt his blood pressure rising and knew he had to control his temper, or he'd have another angina attack. "Tell me."

"God works in mysterious ways. When the officer demanded to know what the boy gave me, I was standing by the organ. A thumb drive of Beethoven's music lay on the bench. I pocketed it. When the officer asked me again, I fumbled in my pocket and gave it to him. He thanked me for my cooperation and left the church."

Vinny breathed again. "Now tell me what happened to Risa's ransom demand."

"I have a plan," Father Murdock said. "I don't want Fritz to come to the church. It would be too risky, so I made my own recording." The old priest told him what he'd done. "I'll arrange to exchange the thumb drive at a brothel. The church won't be involved. What do you think?"

Vinny let out a rip-roaring belly laugh. "I don't believe it. That's a far better plan than I ever could cook up. You're right. He'll never tie it to the church. One problem. How do you plan to contact Fritz?"

"I have a friend in the phone business. He set up a Robo-dial to every hotel and motel in the city until he reaches Fritz."

"What if he's not staying at a hotel?" Vinny asked.

"Where else would he stay? We can Robo-dial any set of numbers. It works like the old campaign calls we get so tired of."

"Why didn't you say something earlier?" Vinny asked. "Fritz would be in our clutches by now."

"Son, go straight," Murdock said. "Here's your chance. Free Risa unharmed, and Fritz, well, that's up to you and your conscience. With my plan, no one can tie his demise to you, if that's your chosen route. May God guide you to make the right decisions."

Without another word, Vinny disconnected the call.

RUDE AWAKENING

Thursday, June 20 – 0410 CDT, Ann Arbor, Michigan

Ten days ago, Fritz sat in front of a Colorado TV camera. Before the whole world, he swore to Vinny, "I'm still your worst nightmare. Long story made short. Your days are numbered."

Since that time, Vinny swooped into Detroit and kidnapped Risa and her husband while Fritz headed to Michigan. Then Vinny's men captured Fritz's entire team back home in Colorado. Now, Fritz wondered if it was *his* days that were numbered. Vinny held all the aces.

After forty-five hours without sleep, Fritz used his last ounce of energy to drag himself to bed around 2 a.m. The coolness of the sheets felt like heaven.

It seemed his head barely hit the pillow when a low-pitched buzz annoyed him. It wouldn't quit. He ran a hand across his brow and opened his eyes. The phone ringing finally penetrated his stupor. Fumbling the receiver, he mumbled, "Hello."

"Is this Detective Fritz Von Schlegen?"

"Yes, who are you?"

There was a pause and then a click followed by, "Hurry," a panicked voice shouted in a hoarse voice. "We need you down here, now!"

Through the haze of sleep deprivation, Fritz muttered, "Can't it wait 'til morning?"

"We have a ransom demand. It's from your sister."

"From Risa?" He switched on the light. "I'm on my way." Fritz hung up the phone and bolted out of bed. While he slipped his feet into his shoes, he zipped his pants and threw on a shirt. Only after dashing to the car did it dawn on him that he had no idea who made the call or where he needed to go.

The police station was the most obvious place, but the caller hadn't identified himself as an officer. Now that he thought about it, he didn't even know if the caller was a man or a woman. Fritz dialed the station. "This is Detective Von Schlegen. I need to speak to an officer."

The dispatcher forwarded his request to the supervisor.

"Did you just call me?" Fritz summarized his dilemma.

"It wasn't me." The officer had no clue about the ransom demand. "Hang on. I'll check with…" His voice muffled, then came back a few moments later. "I doubt someone from our station phoned you."

"No one else knows where I'm staying," Fritz spoke into a dial tone. A few cuss words later, he climbed out of his car, slammed the door, and headed back to his room.

The hotel elevator was slower than maple syrup in the dead of winter, so he took the stairs two at a time to the second floor. When he reached his room, he grabbed the phone and hit redial.

The voicemail answered on the first ring. "If you want to see Risa alive, come alone. Do not call the police. Pay close attention and follow step-by-step directions. This message will be deleted at the end of the call."

Fritz ran a hand through his pockets frantically, searching for a pen. When his fingers brushed against his cell, he snatched it and pressed record.

"…turn right on…" *Where did he say to go first? Pay attention.*

TAKING A TOLL

Thursday, June 20 – 0415-0558 CDT, Ann Arbor, Michigan

In Fritz's frantic search for a taped message from his kidnapped sister, he raced back to his car, drove over a curb, and nearly sideswiped a parked truck before he realized he had no clue where he was headed. "Can't find anything on this damn rental. Where's Google Maps?"

To his surprise, the screen lit up, and a pleasant female voice with a British accent asked, "Where would you like to go?"

Fritz replayed his cell phone's recorded directions. "…turn left at the Old Fort Road," then paused the message. A map came up, and the voice, which he soon called the lady, directed him downtown." He followed the lady's suggestions, missed a turn, and was redirected.

"…turn right in 200 meters and take the next left on…"

Meters? Really? I knew she was a Brit. Fritz drove several miles, past a 7-11, then right, left, right again, and he found himself driving past that same 7-11.

The lady beeped and said, "Your final destination is on the right."

All Fritz could see was an empty parking lot on the right, the 7-11 on the left, and then he realized he was on Port Rd. He pulled into the lot and searched the navigation system again for "Old Fort Road." He emphasized the F on Fort, not Port, but Google Maps couldn't find any such road.

Wish I remembered the first part of this message. Maybe I can find the place if I go to the next set of directions. He pushed play on his phone. "Go four blocks until you reach the toll bridge, stop at the gate. The thumb drive is inside the booth waiting for you." Fritz replayed the last sentence. *Does he mean a toll bridge or toll booth? A desk inside a toll booth?* Resigned to take one step at a time, he searched for the bridge first. All were farther than four blocks, but he tried a railroad, a suspension bridge, and the two overpasses.

After trying the four bridges, his fear turned to anger. He faced east directly into a glaring apricot sunrise and could barely see. He pulled over and dug through the glove compartment for his sunglasses. Once again, he listened to the recorded phone message, but no enlightenment came.

He finally called Agent Kelly at home. "This is your stinking city. Where the hell do I find Old Fort Road?"

"Whoa, good morning to you, too," Kelly snapped. "What burr got under your saddle?"

"Sorry," Fritz explained his frustrating situation.

"Give me the directions," Kelly said. "One at a time."

He repeated what he'd recorded.

"Did you say Toll Bridge?" Kelly clarified.

"Yeah, why?"

"The Toll Bridge is a mansion now used as a brothel located by the old fort," Kelly said. "It's in one of the worst areas of town. Where are you now?"

"Hopelessly lost. Even Google can't find me."

"Calm down." Something jingled. *Kelly must have picked up her keys.* "Check your phone and tell me the nearest crossroads and a GPS if you can find it. I'll be there shortly."

"I'm out in the boonies." Fritz read off the street names. "Sorry, I don't know anything about GPS."

A hefty, black truck with raised suspension flew over the hill, pulled onto the shoulder, and headed straight for him.

"Holy shit! I have company. Hold on." Fritz yanked the gearshift into drive, gunned the gas, and swung back onto the road to avoid a crash. The truck followed and rammed into the rear end of his car. His sedan bounced off the truck's grill and fishtailed onto the gravel shoulder.

"What's happening," Kelly asked.

"Black tank rammed me," Fritz muttered as he fought to stay on the road while speeding away.

"Did you catch a license plate number?" Kelly asked.

"Not yet." He'd driven about 500 yards when the black cab of the hulking truck appeared again in his rear-view mirror. Out of the corner of his eye, he caught a glimpse of a license plate. "Plate letters start with JOY. Can't talk." Fritz cut into the inner lane, saw the tank speeding toward him, and braced for the crash.

The truck pulled alongside his car and eased closer. The darkened windows hid the driver's face.

Kelly shouted, "I'm calling 911 and heading your way. Stay on your phone."

Fritz steered his sedan away as far as he dared, only inches from the median dividing the two directions. The truck slowed to get behind his sedan once more, then the driver revved the engine and slammed the sedan over the center line.

An anguished scream of tires ripped through the air. Scenery spun wildly around Fritz as the vehicle flipped, bounced, and skidded across the oncoming lanes.

What just happened?" Kelly sounded frantic, but Fritz didn't reply.

He clung to the driver's wheel as his body jerked toward the door like a rag doll. The airbag imploded, forced him against the seat, and caused a nosebleed.

Twin horns blasted. Air brakes hissed, and tires shrieked, adding to the chaos around him.

Fritz fought to see around the airbag, then watched in horror as a massive semi swung to the left to avoid his car and jack-knifed.

Through blue smoke and thick rubber residue, the back end of the semi crashed against his sedan. With a tortured wail of metal on metal, the truck bounced his vehicle upright again. Fritz squeezed his eyes shut until the final jolt. The car rocked and then came to a halt with a low moan.

At first, all Fritz could hear was his heart thudding against his rib cage. When he dared to look, the front end of his sedan folded like an accordion and pinned him against the steering wheel. Sunlight glittered over the shards of glass that had once been a shatterproof windshield. The passenger door smashed so far inward that he could almost rest his elbow on the ragged metal.

With amazement, he noticed the driver's door was still intact, but the car's rear buckled around him. Boxed in like a coffin, he released his death grip on the wheel and inspected all ten fingers to be sure they could move. His chest and shoulders sent shooting pains with each breath.

"Fritz, can you hear me?" Kelly sounded light years away.

"Fritz! What's happening?" shouted a frantic Kelly over his cell. "Talk to me."

I must have hit the speaker during the crash. "I'm…here." His breath came out in shallow grunts. "Fractured…ribs."

"You must have passed out. I've been yelling at you for ten minutes, and you're hurt. I can hear it." She sounded relieved to hear Fritz's voice.

"Car's totaled… can't breathe…head hurts." Fritz fought to stay alert, but dark spots blinded him.

"I hear sirens in the distance. Emergency help is on the way," Kelly said. "I'll be there…"

Risa, I failed you again. The words floated with him into unconsciousness.

FUMES

Thursday, June 20 – 0622 CDT, Ann Arbor, Michigan

Trapped in his demolished car outside of Detroit, Fritz drowned in the inky black sea of his mind. *I can't die. Not here. I need to find Risa and see Laura and Marta again.* A faint hum grew into a distant drone of sirens. It usually made his vital juices spark to life, but it only annoyed him at the moment. Bracing for another painful breath, he caught a faint tap, tap, pause, tap, tap, tap.

"Hey, Mister, are you all right?"

"No," Fritz gasped. "Hard to breathe."

"Sorry, I couldn't stop my truck in time." The man cupped his hands around his eyes and peered through the driver's cracked window. Grease covered the beds of his fingernails. As he backed away, the cuff of his denim shirt caught on the snap of his stained bib overalls. "We have to get you out of there. My tanker split by the force of the impact. There's gas pooling along the median."

Fritz reached for the handle and bumped his shoulder against the frame. "Can't open door."

"I know. I tried earlier," the man said. "The hinges are bent. Even my old crowbar failed."

Sirens came to an abrupt halt, and voices grew louder. "Back away from that car," someone warned. "Todd, get the foam and coordinate the team. Blanket the surface. Everyone else, clear the area."

The man in overalls didn't budge. "Officer, the driver's pinned inside. He's still alive. We have to move him."

"We'll use the Jaws. It'll take time to get him out."

"I have some tools in my truck."

The officer clipped off several more orders, but Fritz faded into darkness.

* * *

Agent Kelly pulled behind a long line of slow-moving cars. Lights flashed ahead. She inched her vehicle to the side of the road and drove along the shoulder as close to the accident as she could. She parked and flicked on her hazard lights.

Cars moved bumper to bumper, so Kelly ran along the embankment and stopped behind an ambulance. A jack-knifed semi blocked all northbound traffic. The remains of Fritz's rental lay beneath the rear tire. Firefighters raced along the sides of the vehicle and sprayed foam. A guy in bib overhauls wielded an ax against the driver's door, and then he stepped aside when a fireman approached with a heavy machine.

Another officer rerouted the cars to a detoured path. He glanced up. "Whoa. Where do you think you're going?"

"That's my partner trapped in the car." She darted around the man.

"No, you don't." He grabbed her sleeve and spun her around. "Stay back! This whole place could blow any minute."

"But Fritz—"

"We'll let you know when we get him out of the wreck." The officer eased his grip. "Look, I know how hard it is when a partner is in danger. Wait over by the ambulance. You can ride with him to the hospital."

"How bad off is he?" Kelly asked, but the officer had gone back to work. The grinding sound of hydraulic cutters drowned out her next words.

Twenty minutes later, Fritz appeared strapped to a backboard balanced between two EMTs.

Kelly grabbed his hand. "Fritz?" Crusted blood caked his face. The oxygen mask muffled Fritz's reply. She asked the EMT, "Is he going to be okay?"

"He's lucky to be alive. Want to ride in back?"

"I have my car," Kelly said. "What hospital are you taking him to?"

"Michigan Medical," the EMT said.

Fritz squeezed her fingers. "I'm fine." He pulled aside his mask and motioned to the EMT. "Give her… my phone."

A beat-up silver phone was thrust into her free hand.

"Get Risa's message." Fritz tried to open his swollen eyes, then squinted. "Promise. Bring it to me."

Kelly returned the handgrip. "Okay. I promise."

The EMT readjusted the oxygen mask.

She watched them load Fritz into the back of the ambulance. "Take care of him."

"We will," the EMT said.

Kelly didn't wait around for the ambulance to leave. She darted for her car. Whom should she call first? *Fritz said no police. Do I dare go to the brothel alone?*

A DATE WITH A MADAM

Agent Kelly had heard about the Toll Bridge Mansion in the old downtown area outside of Fort Wayne while attending college. The reputation was never good, and police frequently raided the district. At different times, the mansion had been a jail, a church, and who knows what else—businesses just came and went. She'd never needed to go there—until today, but she had no choice. Risa's life hung on Kelly's successful retrieval of the ransom demand. The recent renovation had cleaned up part of the area, but several blocks of shady property remained. The brothel was among them.

Kelly locked her car doors as she drove along the river, crossed numerous railroad tracks, and became lost on dead-end roads and one-way streets. Finally, the tan, nondescript two-story building came into view. Kelly imagined how the place came alive at night with alcohol consumption, drug sales, and prostitution. Every night was another party. After driving around the block, she thought the place looked more like a trash heap than a brothel. Broken glass and rubbish cluttered the side and back alleyways.

A security guard escorted a man out of the front door. Unsteady on his feet, the man's wrinkled trousers and disheveled coat told a story of its own. He had one shirttail tucked inside, and the other hung loosely over an undone belt buckle. Probably too intoxicated or stoned to know the difference. The guard had words with the man and pointed down the street.

Kelly wondered what waited for her inside. Would the guard prevent her from entering the building? She'd have to go inside sometime. Better to get it over with. Fritz would be at the hospital by now, anxiously awaiting her return with the ransom demand.

An idea flashed through her mind. Kelly climbed from the car, opened her trunk, and took out a briefcase. She straightened her skirt and marched through the front door. Off to the left was a glassed-in room. It was small enough that one might call it a booth. She edged closer. A thumb drive lay on a chair. She glanced around and edged toward the door.

The guard approached her with a sly smile. His steely blue eyes raked over her as if he were thoroughly assessing her body. "May I help you?"

Feeling uneasy, Kelly wondered if the guard thought she was a potential prostitute candidate and straightened to her full height. "I'm here to see the person in charge."

"Who may I say is calling?"

"I'm a legal advisor sent by the state." Kelly reached inside a pocket for her badge, but the guard turned and walked down the hall.

"I'll check if she'll see you." He took out a cell phone and moved into the shadows.

Kelly tried the knob, but the door was locked. Running in and taking the thumb drive would have been too easy.

Voices came from down the hallway. "I don't have time for this," a woman said. "Government bullshit!"

The man agreed. "I'll be in the office if you need me."

A middle-aged, buxom woman entered the hall. Kelly thought her perfect make-up kept her face from cracking a frown, but the woman wasn't happy. "What do you want now? I've shown you all the files on my girls. They're clean, respectable ladies."

"I'm not here about the girls," Agent Kelly said. "I need a favor. Someone placed a thumb drive on that chair." Kelly pointed through the window. "It's a matter of life and death that I get it."

"Is that so?" Madam hesitated before approaching the door. Why didn't you ask the guard? He could have gotten it for you."

"I didn't know if I could trust him," Kelly said.

"Hinkens is harmless." The Madam slid a slim hand into the bodice of her red velvet gown. "The key's right here." She inserted the key into the lock and nudged open the door. "I'll be but a moment." She moved to a camera and entered a code into a tiny box along the frame. Then she snatched the drive from the chair. She reentered a code and locked the door on her way back out. "You can never be too cautious in this business."

"Thanks so much." Kelly put out her hand.

"Not so fast," Madam said. "How do I know you're telling the truth? I'm going to see for myself what's on this memory stick first."

Kelly wanted to get it to Fritz ASAP, but she didn't want to put up a fight. "Only if I can see it, too. Then you have to promise I can take it with me as soon as we finish. Do we have a deal?"

"Deal."

The guard came out into the hallway. "Oh, you're still here. Someone briefly shut off the camera inside the booth."

Madam nodded. "It's none of your concern."

He grunted and went back into the office.

"Come. We'll go to my room. It's more comfortable than this stuffy lounge. It stinks of whisky and…well, you know."

Kelly followed Madam down the hallway into a private lounge, past exquisite bronze statues, and up an elegant spiral staircase. A plush red carpet covered the floor. They walked past a mirror-lined salon to the end of the hall. Madam again fished out a key from her secret hiding place and opened a heavy white door.

"Home, sweet home." Madam walked across a thick, rich-looking Oriental rug to an AV cabinet. "Would you like something to drink?"

"No, I'm in a hurry," Kelly said. "A friend's life is in danger, and I'm hoping to find her before it's too late."

Madam popped the thumb drive into her computer's USB port and pressed play. Tears ran down a woman's bruised face. "Fritz, I'm sure you know by now who is holding me hostage. I'm not allowed to say his name on this…"

There was a loud smack, and a whimper followed. A male voice said, "Recognize the voice. It's your sister's. She's still alive…barely. That's more than I can say for Jim. I'm sure he'll be dead by the time you hear this. You have until midnight, June 22nd. By then, I'll also have your wife and kid. I'm willing to exchange your life for all the others. Maybe not Braun's, but that's not up to me. His life is already in jeopardy. Meet me at the Cave. You know which one I mean."

A faint voice muffled in the background, "Key…reincarnation."

"Get her out of here," the voice snapped, and there was only gray noise in the background.

"What does he mean by the Cave?" Kelly asked.

"I have no idea," Madam said. She ejected the thumb drive and handed it to Kelly. "I hope you find your friend."

Kelly grabbed the memory stick and ran down the stairs. A couple of voices came from the guard's office. "You're sure it's a woman and not Fritz?"

"Uh-huh," the guard said.

"Too bad. I just fixed her car."

Kelly paused. She had to pass by the office to get to the front lobby.

"I don't want to hear this," the guard said. "Leave."

Kelly went in the opposite direction and disappeared through the first open door. After a quick glance, she realized it was the kitchen. No one was cooking at this hour, so she moved to the back door. A large, dented black truck on raised wheel suspension sat in the alley with its motor running. No one seemed to be in the truck, so Kelly raced to the driver's door. She hopped inside and drove around the building.

A man ran outside. He raised his fist and dashed toward her while yelling, "Get out of my truck, bitch!" He cussed a blue streak, but Agent Kelly kept driving. Soon, he disappeared from the rear-view mirror.

She pulled out her phone and held down the button. "Siri, Google Maps. Give directions to Michigan Medical Hospital."

"Directions to Michigan Medical Hospital. Turn right in point five miles…"

SWAT ATTACK

Usher jerked with a start and realized he was lying on a cold, bare cement floor. A throbbing pain along his temple made his head too heavy to lift. Dizziness enveloped him. His dry tongue ran over cracked lips. Crusted blood left a salty metallic taste. Worried, he tried to recall what happened. *Did I tell Doc about Laura's location? I must get out of here to protect her. I've messed up this assignment beyond belief. At least I found Braun.*

Trapped in a dark cellar, only a faint yellow light came from a basement window. It was paler than a candle but bright enough to see a dark lump lying on the floor on the other side of the room. The lump didn't move. Usher whispered, "Braun. You awake?"

The lump snored.

With great effort, Usher rolled to his right side and groaned. Metal cuffs scraped against his wrists and ankles. His left arm felt on fire, and he remembered the broken needle still embedded there. "Braun, can you hear me?"

When there was no reply, Usher squinted into the dim light and searched for activity nearby, but he didn't see any. He brought his cuffed wrists toward his chin and noticed the blinking light on his watch. *Thank God someone got my message. Help is on the way.* He checked the time, 4:40 am. "Braun," he whispered with greater force.

When there was still no answer, Usher hunched his knees to his chest and snaked across the floor until he reached the end of a chain attached to his ankles. The effort taxed his body into a heavy sweat. He called out again, "Braun."

"Huh?" A groggy mutter followed.

"Wake up. Company is coming. Get ready to bail."

Braun twisted and tried to sit up. "How? I'm chained up like a wild dog."

"Me too. I don't suppose you have anything in your pocket to use as a pick?" Usher asked.

"No," Braun mumbled. "I'm surprised you don't have one hidden away on your fancy watch."

"I'll keep that in mind for the future. In the meantime, we need to move fast. See if you can reach me."

Braun inched as far forward as his chain allowed. "Can you get closer?"

Usher extended his body full length as Braun did the same. Even with outstretched hands, they were still two feet apart. "That's as far as I can go."

"Too bad Cordy isn't here," Braun said. "I could use one of her hairpins."

The mention of Cordy sent pain through Usher. "I'm sorry. I tried my best."

"What?" Braun said.

Usher choked out, "Doc gave her something—poison, I guess. I didn't get the antidote to her soon enough. She died."

"Who? Cordy? Braun gasped. "How do you know?"

"I was with her when it happened," Usher remembered. Doc had captured Braun a day earlier, so he wasn't aware that Officer Cordelia had ridden with him in the ambulance. "He tried to inject me, too, but I broke the needle before he got much into my system. Doc sent her to the morgue last night."

"Nooo!" Braun slammed his wrists against the floor and fumbled to open his belt buckle. "She can't be dead! She's my future. No, I won't believe it. I…Damn it, Cordy, I told you to be safe. You never listen to me. Are you sure?"

"I'm sorry," Usher knew Braun was no longer listening.

Using the prong of his buckle as a pick, Braun worked at the cuff locks. "Doc won't get away with this!" A few minutes later, he flung the wrist cuffs aside and pulled off his belt. He did the same with his ankle cuffs. They didn't release right away, but he managed to get them loose. "Cordy, I promise to avenge you." Clenching his fists, Braun marched to the stairs.

"Where are you going?" Usher shouted.

Footsteps ran across the floor above them.

"Oops, I think we alerted the enemy," Usher said. "Get me out of here."

Braun gave Usher his belt. "If anyone comes down, I'll clobber them." He darted back to the stairs.

Usher struggled to get free of his cuffs.

An alarm sounded above. The lights flickered briefly in the stairwell, then turned brighter.

"Doc, check the monitor." Ace's raspy shout grew louder once the alarm turned off. "Couple of cars at the gate."

A telephone rang. Doc said. "Time to leave! Set the explosives. Let's go."

* * *

It had taken Russ Bracken most of yesterday to round up his SWAT team, move Chief Jackson from the hospital to a safe haven, and make a plan of attack. It was now 0530, and two police cars ran silently ahead of an armored van. Bracken pointed to a shadow as a sprawling three-story farmhouse appeared. "That's the place. The radio frequency is coming from there. It looks like the signal originated underground."

His elite team was home-grown. Except for Desmond, the newest member of the bomb squad, the rest had all served under Bracken in Afghanistan. Some were former Navy Seals, others were explosive breach experts, and all were combat veterans. They maintained agility, strength, and endurance—ready to face any crisis.

Bracken owed his life to these men. Six years ago, Chico, the van's driver, had carried his wounded commander over his shoulder through rounds of open gunfire to get him safely to the medics. Poncho, his second in command, had quietly assumed Bracken's duties during his absence. Poncho was a taciturn man with a powerful glare, and nobody doubted his authority.

Now, back on home soil, they spent five years working together as a SWAT team out of Fort Collins. Every man knew their role, did their job, and covered each others' backs. The team melded as one and was already geared up for action.

The first police car approached the gate, but the booth was empty. The road traveled the length of a football field beyond the gate before turning into a circular drive by the garden. "All clear here," an officer radioed.

Bracken scanned the area through his binoculars. "Poncho, check the floor plans and locate Usher."

Poncho sat in the back, searching a 2-D house plan using 3-D technology displayed on a large screen. His undeniable energy seemed to suck the air out of the van as he moved his muscular right arm and torso to adjust the image. A blinking red dot moved slowly across the lower half of the screen as the van approached a fenced property. "Got it. If Usher's still wearing his watch, he's moving toward a staircase in the cellar."

Bracken came closer to study the screen. "There's a garden in front of the house, and something metallic is below it. Maybe a bunker."

Poncho zoomed in. "If that's a bunker, it must be attached to the cellar. According to the floor plans, the wrap-around porch leads to the rear of the building." A flat roof extended above the garage, and a large satellite dish was mounted to the building. The house was dark inside.

The first and second police cars didn't open the gate and parked alongside the fence.

Chico drove the SWAT van forward, lowered his window, and stuck his head out for a closer look at a post attached to the fence. "Bracken, there's a ten-digit box embedded on a post, but I don't know the code to open the gate."

"Okay, park, and we'll go on foot."

Chico pulled forward, turned off the engine, and the men piled out of their vehicles.

Officer Bracken gave orders to his team leaders. "Let's spread out. Poncho, take team one to the right. Chico, take team two and go left. I'll head around to the back with team three. You know what to do."

Bracken motioned for team one to lead the way. Poncho and two men climbed over the gate and ran down the road. As Bracken motioned for team two to follow, the booth at the gate exploded with such force that it knocked Chico to the ground. Shards of glass and metal rained over him before Bracken managed to drag him to safety and called for an ambulance.

Chico held his ribs and limped forward. "I'm okay. Let me go with the team. I can still fight."

"Stay here." Bracken shoved the loudspeaker into Chico's bloodied hands. "Keep me informed if anyone else enters the property, then get treatment when the ambulance arrives."

A second blast came from the front garden and sent a cloud of smoke and a column of fire toward the sky. Team one hit the ground, or had they been shot?

Stunned, Bracken snatched the radio from his ceramic-plated vest. Even a high-velocity, small-caliber bullet would have a hard time penetrating his body armor. Braun shouted and tried to hail his men, but his ears roared so loudly that he couldn't hear anything. Afghanistan raced through his mind. *Are there booby traps along the road? Must protect my men.*

Bracken grabbed his submachine gun, ran through the now jagged but open gate, and headed toward the house. Exactly what he trained his team not to do, but if the perps had rigged the house to explode, the hostages might die. It was his task to get them out alive, and his men would be at the door soon. He needed to reassess the situation. He spied Poncho lying by the garden but saw no blood. "You okay?"

"Stay down." Poncho motioned for Bracken to get behind him.

Gravel spit into Bracken's face as bullets pelted the area. His foot caught on a trip wire as he dove from the driveway into the dirt nearby. His hand missed the Punji stick jutting out of a flowerbed.

A local police officer wasn't as lucky. The stick had caught him in the neck. Blood soaked the right side of his face, ran down his torso, and pooled on the ground. The man's vacant eyes told Bracken he was dead. The lack of a pulse verified it.

Bracken gave a silent prayer for his colleague.

Poncho moved under the front patio steps. He poked his head out, pointed to the rest of the SWAT team following them, and mouthed something, but Bracken didn't catch what he said.

Bracken crouched close under the patio, gave orders over the radio, and watched the men take cover. The ringing in his ears seemed to change in pitch. A whine followed by a coughing roar came from above the farmhouse. Tandem rotors throttled up, blades turned, and a helicopter lifted from the flat roof above the garage. The chopper hovered briefly, then headed south.

Someone leaned out the side of the helicopter, firing a high-capacity magazine assault weapon.

Chico, propped up by the gate, seemed to be their main target.

Bracken shouted into his radio, "Chico, take cover." His words drowned out as Chico returned fire at the helicopter. The bird lifted unharmed.

Moments later, Chico shouted into the radio, "What are my orders?"

"Stay put and keep out any reporters," Bracken radioed. "Poncho, warn anyone in the house and wait two minutes. Then the SWAT team goes in."

The officers obeyed. Poncho yelled, "This is the police. We have a search warrant. Come out with your hands up."

Two minutes later, no one came out of the house. The team walked around the building, checking for heat signatures with infrared cameras.

Bracken waved his arms, gathering the troops. "We need a change of plans. Only two images were noted from underground. I think they're the hostages, but the entrances are well-fortified with bombs."

The men huddled to discuss options.

SECOND THOUGHTS

Thursday, June 20 – 0010-0120 MDT, Fort Collins, Colorado

Yesterday had flown by. While Bracken rounded up a SWAT team, Cordy returned to the hospital late last night, and under high security, she escorted the chief to a private care center. The place belonged to a retired physician and an old family friend, Dr. Peterson. It was the best she could do on such short notice, but at least the chief was safe. Best of all, no one would guess where he was, and the doctor's house could be conveniently kept under guard 24/7.

After the Chief's four-hour nap, Cordy filled him in on the details of the undercover raid at the floral warehouse. She informed Jackson that Braun had been attacked and whisked away. She went on to include her kidnapping ordeal and how Usher had come to her aid and was incapacitated. "This wouldn't have happened if Braun had been on the watch like you had ordered."

They argued briefly until Cordy realized the chief needed to rest. His words were slurring, and he kept losing his train of thought, but the chief's parting words stung.

"I don't believe your spite for Braun for one moment. It doesn't disguise your true feelings." The chief watched her. His smile was at odds with the comments he tossed into the air. It smacked her heart and struck a nerve. "Go home. You deserve a rest. You'll figure it out."

Bracken magically appeared at 1:20 a.m. to drive Cordy home and told her to stay there and rest.

Thursday, June 20 –0459-0620 MDT, Fort Collins, Colorado

It was a good plan but proved impossible. She couldn't sleep, so she picked up a book. Chief Jackson's words about Braun haunted her. *Spite? Do I despise him? No.* Meeting Braun, it was lust at first sight. Then they moved in together. She couldn't get him to commit, so she threw him out. Seeing him again, the feelings for him were still there—*a deeper feeling, maybe even love.* Cordy blew out a deep breath. *I have no time for love, especially not with someone unwilling to commit, like Braun.*

After rereading the same page four times, she still couldn't remember what it said. The book dropped to the floor, and she switched off the lamp. The skylight allowed shadows to lurk among corners in her room. *What if something happens to Braun?*

She stared at the wooden beam above her bed until she thought she'd go mad. *Usher risked everything to save my life. I can't let them get away with this. I have to do something.* Her only focus was to save her friends and arrest Doc. *He tried to murder me and nearly killed Chief Jackson. Let's see how he likes being on the other end of a gun.*

Bracken had used Usher's watch GPS to locate him, and the SWAT team was already on site. She couldn't tolerate just sitting here any longer. It was time to act. She wasn't sure if she could help, but she had to try.

Cordy was a mile from the hostage site when she heard a blast. *Oh no! Usher. Am I too late?* Fear caused her heart to race. Already going 80 mph, she increased her speed. A helicopter flew overhead. Two cars, a van, and an ambulance drove close behind her as she approached a damaged fence.

A man in SWAT gear limped toward her. "Lady, you have to leave."

"Not happening. I'm Officer Cordelia. She showed him her badge. "Who are you?"

"Chico. But you can't stay here. It's dangerous."

Cordy wasn't leaving. "Where's Bracken? I need to talk to him. I met with him and Chief Jackson to plan this raid. Did they find Usher?"

Chico hesitated. "I'm not sure."

"Are there active shooters on the grounds?" Cordy said when Chico didn't answer, "Look, I'm not leaving. Can I use your radio to talk to Bracken? He knows me, and we've worked together in the past."

"No, he's busy." Chico put a hand on her arm. "I have my orders." He moaned as a news van pulled up to the gate. Chico radioed Bracken. "We have company. I think it's the press."

"That's all we need," Bracken said. "Handle the situation. Whatever happens, keep them at the gate. Don't let anyone get any closer. There could be more explosives."

Chico said, "You can count on me. Oh, some woman. An Officer Cordelia is here."

Bracken groaned. "Great! Tell her to stay put. Better yet, have her handle the news crews. I hate distractions."

Chico called out to Cordy. "Bracken says he needs you to stay and help me corral the media."

Cordy got close to the radio and asked, "Have you found Usher? Have you heard from him?"

Bracken replied, "No, but there are two heat signatures. Underground. We believe it's two hostages."

Cordy grabbed the radio. "Who are they? Is one of them Usher?"

Bracken's voice sounded clipped. We think Usher and his brother, Braun Hastings."

"Are they alive?" Cordy asked.

"We're working on rescuing them," Bracken snapped. "I don't have time to talk. Help Chico confine the news crews. Over and out."

Braun? He's here? She wanted to know that Braun was safe and alive. "I'm going in."

Chico moved past Cordy. "No. You have your orders. Stay low. I need to string crime-scene tape and lock down the area."

Cordy saw the news teams piling out of their vehicles. *They could get pushy and disrupt the rescue.* "Quick! Let's form the barrier first to keep the people out of our way. It'll buy us some time and space to breathe."

"Tape's in the van." Chico motioned.

"I'll get it," Cordy called over her shoulder. "Maybe we can enlist some help from the ambulance team. They're looking for something to do. She noticed Chico guarding his ribcage as he moved and noticed blood on his shirt. "You've been injured. Has a paramedic seen you yet?"

"I'm fine." Within minutes, reporters clustered behind the gate, and yellow tape fluttered in the breeze, blocking off the area.

Channel 9 crews flew in from Denver. They hopped from the chopper and jostled for a better position closer to the action. Cordy clenched her fists. "They love to feed the public's appetite for tragedy and horror."

"Step away from the gate," Chico said. Blood on his pant leg and a swollen black eye made some impact." A medic tried to put ice on Chico's face, but he refused. "I'm on duty."

One reporter shoved a microphone in his face. "Roll the cameras. We have with us a distinguished member of the Fort Collins SWAT team. Can you tell us what's happening and how you got injured?"

Cordy moved beside Chico and spoke to the reporter. "I'm sorry, but you have to move."

The microphone swung in her direction. "And who are you?"

"This is not a movie." Cordy pushed the mic from her face. "Lives are in danger. Maybe even yours. So shut off the camera and move back."

As always, during a hostage situation, each reporter felt they deserved the right to 'tell the news as it unfolded.'

"It's nearly 7 a.m.," a woman reporter from Fort Collins Channel 21 said, "I need a scoop for our newsroom."

A journalist from the Denver Post added, "This is history in the making. Our senior editor is holding a spot, hoping for a great photo and a snappy story."

Cordy wondered where he came from. Then she saw another helicopter had landed behind her car. "Let's get to work."

TRAP TRIPPED

The hair on Bracken's arms stood on end. Each hair told him to get the SWAT team out before anyone else got hurt, but he had no more time to listen. He had to act. Braun and Usher's lives depended on him, and the team had only reached the house.

"All right, change of plans. Since Chico's at the front gate, the rest of us will split into three teams," Bracken ordered. "I'm sending one member of the bomb squad with two SWAT troopers. Foley, you're with the bomb squad, right?"

"Yes, sir."

"You'll team with Poncho." Bracken pointed to the other partners and gave an assignment. "I'll head up the second team, and we'll cover the rear of the main building. Desmond, you're also bomb squad, so you'll team with me. Kayman, you're in charge of team three. Search all other buildings on the grounds."

"Yes, sir," Kayman said.

"After the explosions at the front gate, I'm not sure what we'll find," Bracken said. "I suspect tripwires at any entrances and throughout the house. Don't take any chances. Our bomb squad members will take the lead, find traps, and disable them as we go. Any questions?"

"No, sir," his team said in unison.

He focused on his team. "There's no need to go in silent. They know we're here, but keep in touch by radio."

With a nod and a few hand signals, the SWAT team spread out.

"Careful, there's a trip wire across the second step," Foley radioed. "I expect you'll find one on the back stairs, too. It's a clear fish line stretched across the stairwell at ankle level. I almost missed it in this light."

Desmond on team two radioed back. "Yup, my flashlight beam tracked the strand. There's another one on the top step, too. It leads to a wastebasket filled with gas canisters under the porch. If detonated, it would make a great bonfire."

"Nothing noted near the barn," Kayman reported.

Foley waved his light up each step. "No second tripwire here."

Bracken radioed, "Any cellar doors on that side?"

"No sir, I don't see any," Foley responded. "We even looked under the porch."

"They probably triggered the door as well," Bracken warned.

"We'll go through the front door on your signal," Poncho said. "Then we'll clear the first floor and meet you halfway. Foley will check for more bombs. I'm right behind him."

Bracken radioed back. "Desmond and I will come through the back, and we'll clear the rear of the building."

Since the door opened outward, Bracken positioned himself on the doorknob side near the path of least resistance. Desmond took the knee position, pointing his weapon toward the door. Bracken backed up with his gun aimed high and ready. "Each of you has a photo of Braun and Usher. Our goal is to free them and get out. Spare the lives of any abductor who surrenders. If threatened, shoot to kill."

Poncho and his team made similar moves, crouched at the front door, and waited for the signal.

Bracken kept one foot beside the entrance and stood in a boxer's stance, his knees slightly bent, and his body crouched forward.

Desmond surveyed the entrance, sniffed the air for warning signs, and listened. "Ready?" he radioed.

Teams one and three reported, "Ready."

Desmond grabbed his Hooligan tool and placed the claw into the doorjamb.

Bracken gave the command, "Now."

In a split second, Desmond cracked the wood, broke open the lock, and inched the door open. He ran his hand along the frame. "Explosive trip wire." He grinned at his discovery. Fortunately, it had enough slack to shine a beam of light inside. "It's a grenade. Pin's still in place." He disabled the threat.

Bracken checked with the other teams.

"We're in," team one said. Team three was still checking the grounds.

Desmond raised his shield. "Let's move in."

Foley entered the front door and reported, "I smell gasoline."

"Same here at the rear," Bracken said. "Proceed with caution."

Bracken followed Desmond. The team moved as one. Each man knew where to point his weapon and how to assess for any potential threats. Desmond made a one-hundred-eighty-degree sweep and stepped inside the door to the right. Bracken did the same and took the left.

Desmond moved around furniture, checked for more traps, and then pointed to a closet door slightly ajar off to the left of the entrance. "Bracken…"

Bracken nodded and covered Desmond as he inched open the door.

Desmond moved swiftly. "Another wastebasket filled with gas." A mousetrap balanced on the edge of the can. Tied to the trap's spring, he found a filament fiber wrapped in tin foil. A cable ran to an outlet in the wall. "If the mousetrap trips, it'll send off one hell of a Molotov cocktail!" He disabled the threat and made an okay sign, followed by two fingers raised in success.

"Room clear," Bracken said. As team one entered, an echo came from the front of the building from team two. The teams advanced through each room in the same manner until they met in the middle.

"No hostages yet," Poncho said. "But there are traces of blood in the entry."

"We'll call CSI and get forensics." Bracken signaled to the team. "Let's move up to the next floor."

Desmond walked along the side of the stairs. He checked for traps and then planted his foot firmly before advancing to the next step. He scanned the area with his flashlight in one hand and gun in the other.

Poncho and Bracken followed with their guns. Poncho moved forward while Bracken walked up the stairs backward, covering the rear.

Foley reached the landing, checked the balcony, and then moved up the next steps to the second floor. The team scouted and snaked through the second floor and then the third.

The team removed five trashcans of gasoline from the house. "Explosives cleared," Foley said.

Bracken breathed a sigh of relief. "Thermal imaging shows movement below us. How do we get to the cellar?"

His words died when an explosive went off at the back of the property.

"Team three, what's your status?" Bracken yelled into the radio.

"Need ambulance," came across the radio. "One dead, two injured."

A second blast closer to the rear of the building shook the floorboards.

"Team three, answer me," Bracken said. "What's your new status?"

"Two dead" came across the radio. "Fading...Bracken?"

"I'm on my way." Bracken tapped Desmond on the shoulder. "Come with me. Poncho, you're in charge. Find the cellar."

CROWD CONTROL

Cordy's mind raced as she paced outside the gate to Doc's hideout. *Is Braun still alive? I can't just stand around waiting. I'm going in.* She took two steps past Chico and was knocked to the ground as a blast shook the earth. Her ears rang at the sound of an explosion. Dust filled the air. *Braun!* Panic shook her to her core. Not fear for herself but for Braun, Usher, and the SWAT team. The world blurred around her. Choked up, she could hardly breathe.

News teams had also hit the dirt and were now getting to their feet. They rapidly clamored toward Chico. "What's happening now?"

Chico shouted, "Get back!" as the crowd surged even tighter, trying to take photos. Chico tried to hold them back. "Stay away from the area. Who knows how many bombs may go off?"

The crowd backed off a little, but they were wild with curiosity and the need to gain access just to put out a story.

Chico pushed through the crowd and limped toward Cordy.

Cordy swiped tears from her eyes. "Are the hostages alive?" Soot stains streaked her face. At this rate, she'd look like a raccoon before the day was over.

"I don't know." Chico let out a low moan as he reached for his radio. Blood oozed through the bandage where he'd patched wounds on his arm and shoulder, but it didn't stop him from action. "Bracken, are you all right? What's your status?"

Cordy scanned the area where news teams were pulling their gear out of their vehicles and crowded toward the shattered gate.

"Don't go any closer," Chico warned them, but they kept shoving past him. Chico spoke into the radio again, "News crews are invading my space. I can't control them."

"Cameras running," a female reporter announced, "Today, we get a view of our SWAT team in action. Even at a distance, I see we'll be here for a while." The reporter held up a schematic of the house. "According to this diagram, they must clear two entrances, three floors, twenty-two windows…"

Cordy turned away. "I know Doc said there's a bunker on the property."

"How do you know Doc?" Chico kept an eye on the house as they talked.

Cordy studied the crowd. They seemed busy with tasks of their own. She turned her back to them. "Doc kidnapped an FBI agent, Usher Hastings, and me at the hospital. He declared that I was dead and sent me to the morgue."

"Can you describe him," Chico said. "I shot at a man escaping in a helicopter earlier this morning."

"Suspect is mid-fifties, white male with graying hair, steel gray eyes, and goes by the name Doc," Cordy said.

"Yep, one of the men fits that description. What about the younger man with the baseball cap?"

"I don't know him," Cordy said.

"How do you know Officer Bracken?"

"I told you, Chief Jackson and I met with him yesterday." Cordy moved closer to the tape. "I can't stay here. I need to find Braun. I believe he and Usher are in the bunker. The crowd is under control, so I'm—"

A second boom shook the ground. Cordy hit the dirt. The explosion sent billows of smoke into the air, creating a frenzy among the crowd. "No! Please, not the hostages."

One news anchor dashed toward the gate. "Catch that on film!"

Another reporter pushed toward Cordy as she got up and brushed dirt from her knees. "Any word on what's happening?" Cordy pushed the reporter away, so he shoved his mic toward Chico.

A paramedic approached. "Can we go in?"

Chico radioed Bracken, "Ambulance is here. Can they drive in?"

"Negative," Bracken said. "Explosives planted in the yard. Send in the tactical medic with our BATT."

"Bracken, I'm coming, too," Cordy said. "I heard Doc say to take Usher to the underground bunker." She grabbed a helmet, threw on her Kevlar vest, and dashed toward the medic. "I'm coming with you."

The medic's radio crackled another message from Bracken, "We'll check on team three."

Cordy heard a door slam as Bracken signed off.

DOC, OVER AND OUT

Vinny's cell phone rang. He yanked it to his ear, "I'm listening."

"We got out in the nick of time," Doc said. "They'll never save Braun and his brother. Ace set so many traps a mouse couldn't get in there without blowing themselves up. They won't underestimate me again."

"Good," Vinny said. "Where are you heading?"

"Ace told you he found the Mrs.?" Doc filled in the details. "When do you leave?"

"I just got word that Fritz had a serious car accident," Vinny said. "Tsk, tsk. I wonder how that happened."

"So you're not going after his wife and kid?"

"Not so fast. I need to find out if Fritz survived," Vinny said.

"What about Risa and her husband?"

"Poor old Jim is done for. He'll have gangrene before long. I'll probably set Risa free after Fritz dies."

"You're getting a little soft, aren't you?" Doc asked. "That's not like you."

"The kid is hounding me," Vinny said. "I should have left him at the orphanage."

"How's Midget holding up?" Doc asked.

"At the moment, he's my saving grace."

"Yeah, he may be nuts, but he's an all-right fellow," Doc said. "I'm heading south. You can't reach me for the next 72 hours. After that, who knows? Any last words?"

"Is Ace with you?" Vinny asked.

"Nah, he has other plans." Doc hung up.

Vinny smashed his burner phone, destroying the chip to ensure no one could trace the call.

Midget entered the room. "Who called?"

"Doc is done with us. He's gone to freedom, and it sounds like Braun's getting his just reward." Vinny poured a glass of bourbon. "I'm celebrating. Care to join me?"

"Why not?" Midget held out a glass.

A few hours later, Vinny asked, "Where's Jules? It's too quiet around here."

"Don't know," Midget set down his glass. "He told me he felt cooped up and needed a walk."

"And you let him go by himself?" Vinny asked.

"There's nowhere he can get into trouble." Midget got a cup of tea. "We're outside a cemetery, for Christ's sake. Who can he talk to? The dead?"

"Yeah, I guess you're right. He's been moping around here for a few days."

* * *

Jules wandered down the gravel road toward the cemetery gate. *I promised Father Murdock I'd go straight. I have to get Jim medical help, free him before he dies, and figure out a way to save Risa.*

An old man stood with his head bowed over a fresh gravesite. He knelt and laid a bouquet of red roses on the dirt in front of the headstone.

Jules approached the man. "Sorry for your loss."

Tears dribbled down the man's chin. "She was my wife for fifty-two years."

"I lost my grandma a few years back. Everything's different, and I still miss her." *It was a little white lie, but it was worth it if it helped save Jim.* Jules helped the man back to his feet. "May I get a ride into town? My car broke down, and I must get my dear mother her heart medicine."

The man smiled a toothless grin. "Sure, sonny." The word came out in a slight whistle. "You live near here?"

"Just down the road a piece," Jules said. He looked around to make sure Vinny hadn't followed. "Can we go now?"

The old man shuffled toward an outdated Chevy. The rear bumper was missing. Rust covered the hood and around the taillights.

Jules tried the passenger's door. It wouldn't open.

"One moment." The old man stumbled into the car, picked up a cane, and punched the passenger's door in the right place, leaving it ajar.

The bent hinges moaned when Jules opened the door and slid onto a torn cloth seat. His right foot nearly went through the floorboards. "I can see the grass."

"Move over a bit and put your feet next to the console. The carpet will keep them in the car. Just don't take off your shoe."

"You sure this car will get us to town?" Jules asked.

The old man rasped out a laugh. "It may not look like much, but it's taken me to places for years. I think it'll make another ten miles. Name's Willis, by the way. What's yours?"

"Jules." He grimaced when he realized he'd given the old man his real name. *Oh well, Vinny will probably kill me when he finds out what I'm up to. At least there's a witness. I never should have left the center.*

Willis ground the starter a few times before the engine kicked to life. "Which pharmacy?"

"The closest one," Jules said, hoping he wouldn't have to walk back very far. "Surely there's one closer than ten miles from here."

"You got a prescription?" Willis asked. "Otherwise, a doctor needs to call one in."

"I took care of everything." Jules lied again and swallowed, hoping God would forgive him. He didn't even have any money. "Thanks for the lift."

The car bounced along the road at the fast speed of twenty mph. Jules didn't want to rob the man and wouldn't steal this car to make his getaway. "How much longer?"

"Keep your shirt on, sonny. It can't be more than an hour."

"What?" Jules asked.

"I'm spoofin' you." Willis chuckled. Twenty minutes later, he pulled the car off the main road, drove a few blocks, and parked in front of an outdated Walgreens. "Will this do?"

"Thanks," Jules said. "I don't have any money to pay for the gas."

"No problem, kid. I hope your mother feels better soon."

Jules moved toward the passenger's door and bumped against it. "What's the secret to opening—"

Willis lifted his cane and punched the door. "There you go."

Jules scooted out of the car. "Thanks again." He entered the store, wondering how to get the antibiotics Risa had written on the paper. She'd also added a phone number to call to get physician approval. Of course, he couldn't tell anyone about Risa.

The pharmacist was helping another customer when Jules got to the back of the store. Should he call 911 and report Vinny? Would they kill Midget? He had become Jules' favorite brother. What would the police do to him? All these thoughts ran through his head when the pharmacist asked, "Well?"

"Huh?" Jules asked.

"Did you need something?" The pharmacist poised his fingers over a keyboard, ready to type.

"Oh, yes." Jules handed him the crumpled note from Risa. "Please, it's a matter of life and death. Her husband is dying."

"If it's an emergency, take him to the hospital. I'll call 911."

"No!" Jules grabbed the pharmacist's hand to prevent a call. "I don't mean he's dying like in dead. I mean, he needs help…here. This is what I need." Jules pushed the list closer.

The pharmacist squinted at the paper. "We don't carry IV meds at this pharmacy. Nor do we have IV tubing or catheters. Sorry." He pushed the note back through the window. "Next."

Jules hadn't expected this. Now, what should he do? He had no money, no car, and no way of calling for help. "Can I borrow your phone to make a local call?"

"Sure," the pharmacist said. "Use the one at the desk. Dial nine to get out."

Jules frowned. The phone was an old one with a touch-tone dial. It was nothing like a cell phone—no way to find a phone number. "How do I search on this thing?"

"Ever heard of a phone book?" The pharmacist dug under the counter and handed Jules a large, tattered book. "Anything else?"

"No. Thanks." Jules took the relic over to the desk, looked up St. Anne's Catholic Church, and dialed the number. "May I speak to Father Murdock?"

"Who? I don't think…" The receptionist seemed flustered. "I mean…Did you say, Murdock?" There was a commotion in the background. "We don't have anyone here by that name." There was another pause. "Wait a moment."

Someone else came on the line. "Hello. Father Murdock's retired."

"Are you sure?" Jules verified the number. "He was there. I met him. Is there another priest on duty?"

"Yes."

"I need to talk to him." Jules picked up a business card from the desk. When the priest answered, Jules explained what he needed. "I'm at Walgreens." He read off the address. "Please, can you come and get me?"

The priest hesitated. "I feel you're not telling me the whole truth."

"I'll confess when you get here, but I need help, Father. I don't want anyone to die. I need help now." Jules felt as if he'd pass out. He'd never disobeyed Vinny before, but Jules had seen Vinny's rage and knew this would set him off.

"I can't come for several hours," the priest said.

"Forget it then." Jules sighed. "I'll find another kind soul to help me." He hung up the phone.

The pharmacist walked over to him. "I'm sorry, but I overheard your conversation. You sounded desperate. Is this a loved one who needs these medications?"

Jules swiped at his damp eyes.

The pharmacist put a hand on Jules' shoulder. "I know a doctor who may help you get the medications and equipment you need, but you can't tell anyone. He'd be doing me a favor."

"Thanks, sir. I won't tell anyone. Where can I find him?"

"He's my brother," the pharmacist said. "I'll call him and see if he can help."

"I don't have any money," Jules admitted. "Maybe I can work off the bill. Restock shelves, wash vials, do lab work—whatever you need."

"I'm not sure why I'm doing this." The pharmacist dialed a number and explained what he needed. "When can you bring them?" After a pause, "I know I'm asking a huge favor. Maybe he is, but he seems…" his voice dropped to a whisper, and Jules couldn't understand what the pharmacist said. "Okay, half an hour should be fine." He looked to Jules for approval.

Jules nodded.

Thirty minutes later, a man walked down the aisle to the pharmacy. He wore a white lab coat. A stethoscope hung around his neck. "Here are the IV meds and supplies. Who needed them?" he asked the pharmacist.

Jules approached the two men. "I do."

"One drug needs to be mixed. It's a powder now. Do you know how to do that?" the doctor asked.

"My friend's a nurse," Jules said. "She knows what to do."

A siren sounded outside the building. It stopped abruptly.

Jules didn't wait. He grabbed the bag with the IV tubing, syringes, and catheters. "Thanks." Stuffing the medication vials into his pocket with one hand, he grabbed the IV bags with the other and dashed to the back. "I have to leave."

"See, I told you he's on the run," the doctor told the pharmacist.

Jules climbed through the pharmacy's drive-through window and ran down the street. He darted into a store and watched the police car creep slowly by the window. It stopped. An officer got out of the car and headed toward the building.

Jules didn't see any customers in the store, and no one paid any attention to him. He walked to the back, plucked a dark jacket from the rack, and entered the men's room. He slicked back his hair with water. Then he stuffed the equipment and IV bags under his tucked-in shirt and zipped up the jacket. It made him look fat. He emerged from the bathroom and milled around a clothes rack. No squad cars were in sight, so he went out a back door into the alley. An alarm sounded.

"Stop," a man in the store yelled.

Jules' heart tripped, and a lump formed in his throat. He sprinted down the street.

The man ran after Jules. After another block, the man stopped to catch his breath. "I'm calling the police."

Jules hid behind a trash bin. He spotted a dark blue and white motorcycle leaning against a nearby building. Keys hung from the ignition. He had qualms about stealing the bike, but he had no choice.

Jules watched the man plod back to his store. Studying each direction, Jules hopped on the cycle, turned the key, and drove along back alleys to the main highway. Sirens sounded in the distance, but Jules didn't stop.

His heart thudded in his chest, and his hands shook with nervous energy. Every car he met, he feared it was the police, but he managed to make it back to the cemetery.

Now, his greatest fear was how to sneak into the house without Vinny finding out what he had done. Sooner or later, Vinny would discover the truth. Jules hid the motorcycle in the woods behind the house.

Vinny stood outside the front door. "Jules! Where the hell are you?"

In a panic, Jules emptied his pockets, removed the IV bags, wrapped them in the jacket, and placed them under the cycle. He mussed his hair, stepped into view, and stretched. "What time is it, Vinny? I had the weirdest dream. Wandering in the fresh air sure makes me sleepy."

"Get in here, boy. I've been searching for you for nearly an hour."

"Sorry, I didn't hear you." Jules dashed past Vinny and into the house.

Midget shook his head. "You think you're fooling anyone? Father Murdock just called."

"Who?" Jules asked, although he knew perfectly well who Murdock was. "What did he want?"

"Don't know," Midget said, "but Vinny wants your head on a platter."

"I know you called the church." Vinny stood in the doorway, glaring at Jules. "Where'd you get a phone?"

Jules refused to buckle. He stood taller. "It must have been someone else."

Vinny slugged Jules in the gut.

He dropped to his knees. "Why did you do that?" Jules gasped and rolled away from another punch. "For sleeping in the woods?"

"Is that what you call it?" Vinny stepped closer and kicked out at Jules, but he curled into a ball. The foot missed its mark and got his shin.

Midget grabbed Jules by the waistband and pulled him aside. "Enough. The kid has a right to sleep."

"You know, and I know that he did more than sleep," Vinny said. "I just don't know what he's done yet, but when I find out, there'll be hell to pay."

Jules swallowed with a gulp and dashed to his room. Unable to bring the meds inside the house at this time, he would wait until after dark to sneak them to Risa. He hoped he wasn't too late.

FEELING DEFEATED

Thursday, June 20 – 0700 CDT, Ann Arbor, Michigan

Fritz had faced danger before, but nothing life-threatening like this, especially when his family's lives were at risk. He could hardly breathe. His rib cage turned a dark shade of purple. Stabbing pain prevented him from moving.

The ambulance brought him to the Michigan Medical Emergency Department, where doctors and nurses hovered over him. Fritz had an IV in one arm and an automatic blood pressure cuff on the other. He was at the mercy of others.

The nurse shaved patches of his hairy chest and pasted on electrodes snapped to monitor cables that draped over the side rail. Every time Fritz moved, something beeped. If not the monitor, it was an IV pump, the PCA for pain management, or the pulse oximeter clamped to his index finger. A green hose hung around his ears, and nasal prongs pricked his nose.

"Up the oxygen to four liters," a doctor said. "His pulse ox is 86%. I want it above 90."

A nurse increased a dial on the wall. "BP is 90 over 60. I upped the IV so he doesn't go into shock."

The medical staff talked over Fritz as if he wasn't there. "I need… out of here."

The doctor actually glanced toward Fritz. "Not happening. Your X-ray shows three broken ribs. You're lucky none of them punctured your lung or liver, but they're bruised. In another two minutes, you'll be floating. I just pressed the PCA pump button."

Fritz heard the voices fade into a distant drone. The pain eased. His vision blurred, and his eyelids drifted closed.

The next thing he remembered, Agent Kelly tugged on his sleeve. "Fritz, how are you?"

He squinted in the bright light. The room filled with a faint beeping sound. "What? Where am I?"

"Don't you remember? You were in a car accident." Kelly's blurred face cleared. Concerned eyes stared at him.

"Oh. That's right." Fritz tried to sit up and let out a loud groan. "My ribs." He panted a few short bursts, then exhaled a shaky breath. "They must have moved me to another room."

"The doctor says he's keeping you overnight. It'll take a few weeks to heal those broken ribs." Kelly held up a thumb drive. "Feel up to listening?"

Fritz squinted as she loaded it into her laptop. His mind tried to grasp what she meant when it hit him. "Is that the ransom demand?"

"Yes. I've already seen it once."

"I want to see it, too. Then catch me up with what happened after the accident."

"Okay." She clicked on the file. "It's not pretty."

He nodded.

Kelly turned the computer in his direction so he could see the screen. Risa came into view. "…You have until midnight, June 22nd. By then, I'll also have your wife and kid." Risa interrupted, but Vinny spoke over her. "I'm willing to exchange your life for all the others. Maybe not Braun's, but that's not up to me. His life is already in jeopardy. Meet me at the Cave. You know which one I mean." A dull hiss marked the file's ending.

"What cave?" Fritz asked.

"I thought you'd know." Kelly moved the laptop.

"Play it again." Fritz squinted at the screen. "Risa said something in the background."

Kelly replayed the message.

"I have two days." Fritz groaned. "How the hell am I going to save Risa? I don't know what cave he means, and I know Risa said something in the background, but I can't understand her message. You have to get me out of here."

Kelly shook her head. "Have you looked into a mirror lately?"

"Get my computer." Fritz eased himself to a more comfortable position. "Maybe I can figure out Risa's warning."

"I'll bring your laptop, but—"

"Does McCoy know about the ransom demand?"

"No." Kelly removed the thumb drive and shut down her computer. "You told me not to involve the police. However, he does know about your accident. I found the black truck that forced you off the road. It's impounded, and the driver is under investigation. He also cut my brake lines, so my Lexus is in the shop for repairs. I'll tell you about it later."

"That's the least of my worries. I wish Braun were here. What's happening in Colorado?"

"I heard on the news the SWAT team attempted a rescue mission earlier this morning. Two men got away in a helicopter, and I don't think they found any hostages yet. The raid is still in progress, but there was an explosion, and it killed some SWAT members. According to the reporter, the team is still looking for Braun and Usher."

"What about Cordy?" Fritz asked. "There should have been three hostages."

"That's all I know," Kelly said.

"How's the chief?"

Kelly put her hands together as if in prayer and held them to her lips. A small whimper escaped. "I made several phone calls and found out the agency moved him from ICU to an unknown location. I can't get through to him, but the office assures me the chief is safe."

Fritz nodded. "Who can we trust?"

"I trust McCoy," Kelly said. "With his help, we can analyze this. I dusted the thumb drive for fingerprints. Mine will show up, and prints from the woman in charge of Toll Bridge, but I've handled the stick only by the edges and placed it into a plastic evidence bag, so maybe we'll get lucky."

"I'm sure that's Vinny's voice," Fritz said. "We need to find out where he's hiding Risa."

"I'll do my best." Kelly stepped away from the bed.

"Wait." Fritz cautiously pulled himself to a sitting position. His breath came out in jagged pants. "I want to talk to McCoy and get me out of here."

"I'm an FBI agent, but my first profession was nursing." Kelly eased him back onto the pillow. "Maybe I can swing a few favors. Let me work on it, but in the meantime, you need to rest." She punched the button on the PCA pump to give Fritz another dose of pain medication.

"Thanks. Only for an hour or so, then I…" Fritz yawned. "Get my computer—and that key." He drifted off.

SET TO EXPLODE

Thursday, June 20 – 0702 MDT, Fort Collins, Colorado

Back inside Doc's hideout, Braun was halfway up the cellar steps heading for a massive metal door when the first explosion dimmed the lights. The bulb overhead swayed, and the ground shifted. The stairway toppled and knocked Braun to the floor. He rolled away from flying debris.

Usher darted under a raised steel workbench. Chunks of concrete flew from the ceiling. Grit and fine dust showered the floor.

"Not again!" Braun swore under his breath. "Busted ankle."

Usher poked his head from under the bench. "You all right?"

Braun groaned and braced himself before standing. He managed to get up on one leg, but the other refused to bear weight. "Wonder what exploded?"

"It almost sounded like an echo—one from outside the bunker and another popped from the stairwell. Bet there's more." Usher dug through the top drawer and pulled out a roll of duct tape. He grabbed a pipe from the workbench, wrapped one end of the pipe with several layers of tape, and handed it to Braun. "Use this to steady yourself."

Braun stared up at the now-dented door above him. A step swung at the end of a wire, then came loose and nearly hit him as they fell to the top of the collapsed stairway. "If that was a trip wire, I was lucky it didn't blow us to bits. Better go out the back way." He hobbled to the workbench and leaned against it.

"Are you sure there's another exit?" Usher picked at the end of the duct tape to loosen it from the roll.

"Ace brought me into a small room filled with computers," Braun said. "I remember the bright lights hurt my eyes. He hooked me up to electrodes. I don't remember much after that. When it was over, he dragged me through a heavy vaulted door. I ended up here."

"Take off your boot." Usher tore off a strip of tape. "I'll wrap your ankle for more support."

Braun dropped back to the floor. His head spun from the pain. "I can't do it."

Usher loosened the laces and pried his swollen ankle from the boot. "This is going to—"

"Just do it before the whole place blows!" Braun gritted his teeth. "Is there a pulse? Last time, I nearly lost my foot."

Usher slid two fingers under the sock. "Yeah, but I need to realign the bones." Usher pulled on Braun's foot. It gave a loud crack, and Usher rechecked the pulse. "Good circulation."

Waves of nausea flooded through Braun. He gagged.

"Puke over there." Usher pointed to a corner away from him and continued wrapping tape around the ankle. "This reminds me of your old football injury."

Braun couldn't answer. He kept swallowing back bile.

"Okay, now brace yourself." Usher loosened the laces of Braun's boot and slid it over his injured foot. He laced the boot tightly around the ankle.

Braun grabbed the offered arm in one hand and used the pipe in the other to pull himself upright again. "Thanks."

"Which way to the vaulted door?"

Braun wiped sweat from his brow and pointed into the darkness. "Over there." Black spots threatened to steal his vision, but he had to keep moving. Blinking a few times and gulping in some air, he refused to faint.

Usher turned his watch beam to high. "I saw a flashlight on the workbench. You'll need it if we're going into the abyss."

Braun grabbed the light. "I'm not sure what we'll find, but if I pass out, you keep going.""

"We're in this together. Just follow me. Go slow and keep your eyes open for booby traps." Usher waved his arm around the room and studied the floor, walls, ceilings, and any shelves lining the bunker.

The flashlight dimmed as Braun moved around several stacked chairs leaning against a wall. He hobbled over to a ledge above the chairs and moved a cardboard box tucked behind a few beer bottles. A wire extended from the box. "Wait. Shine your light over here." He gently folded back the box lid. "It's a mini bomb!"

"I'll defuse it. You're a bit wobbly on that leg, and I plan to live another day." Usher grabbed the flashlight for a closer look and quickly disarmed the device.

Braun still felt woozy but watched closely in case he needed to disarm one quickly. "It wasn't very sophisticated, but it would have blocked our way to the vaulted door."

"Bet there is more hidden down here," Usher said. "You take the right, and I'll take the left. Let's work our way to that door."

They located five more small explosive devices and disarmed them.

Another blast overhead shook items from shelves. Both men landed on the floor with a crash. The air around them crackled with tension. "That one was a lot closer." Usher glanced at his watch. "Three minutes apart. Bet there'll be another."

Braun slammed his dimming flashlight against the palm of his hand. It brightened. "Look. I think we found the exit."

Usher ducked into a narrow tunnel. A red light blinked over a door where they planned to escape.

"I wonder what that blinking light means," Braun said.

"Shh, I think I hear something," Usher leaned closer. "Listen. There's a faint humming sound." He moved to his right and realized it was a motion detector device. A screen slowly descended from the ceiling, and a shadowy image appeared on the screen with a message, "I have a secret about your future. You're about to die in our evil rat's trap."

Usher headed for the door.

"Stop! C4 explosives," Braun shouted. His flashlight revealed a thread of wire running along the bunker door. His light followed the wire to a network of plastic explosives tucked into the beam joists overhead in the tunnel. "The place is wired to collapse the whole bunker. It'll bury us alive."

"Is there another way out?" Braun asked.

Usher carefully backed out of the tunnel. "I entered the underground on a gurney. It was a straight path from outside, or maybe there was an elevator. I'm not sure." The speaker hissed. "Thirty minutes until detonation."

Usher set his alarm for twenty-nine minutes. "That doesn't give us much time. If it blows, we're dead. We have to find another way out."

THE SEARCH

SWAT commander Russ Bracken ran out of Doc's house only seconds after the ground-shaking explosions that shattered windows, ripped and snarled the earth, exposing a hidden concrete barracks. Bracken knelt beside team three's leader. "Kayman, can you talk to me?"

Kayman held a hand over his left eye. A twisted metal door pinned Kayman's chest. "No warning." Blood trickled down his face and wrist. His cracked helmet lay on the ground several feet away.

Bracken leaned closer to hear the garbled words. "Used motion detector." Kayman said something else, "…era."

Foley, team one's bomb squad leader, dashed to their side and sniffed the air. He studied the ground with his torch.

Bracken scanned the yard. "Where's Desmond? He's supposed to be on my team."

"Tied up, so we changed places." Foley ran a hand along the door. "White residue—probably plastic C4 explosive." His light caught a device in the ground, partially covered by a screen. "There's something down here."

Bracken moved to peer into the hole. "Let's move this door." He grabbed a corner and started to lift.

Kayman gasped, "Don't…touch!" Blood spewed from his mouth with every word. He swallowed and tried to say something else.

Bracken lowered the door and barked into his radio. "Where's the medic?"

Kayman pointed and mumbled, "Ca…me…ra."

Bracken ran his hand along Kayman's side and snagged an infrared camera wedged beneath the door.

Kayman held up two fingers. "…still alive?"

After studying the photos, Bracken handed the camera to Foley. "Check this out."

"You think it's the hostages?" Foley asked.

"Maybe," Bracken waved as a van pulled up and parked. Cordy and the medic dashed to Kayman's side. "What are you doing here?" Bracken asked Cordy.

* * *

"I took a trauma course when I entered the police force," Cordy said.

"Good, I'll need some help." The medic set down a combat trauma kit, dropped to his knees, and slid his fingers over Kayman's carotid artery. "Get me the oxygen, IV, and intubation equipment."

Cordy dug through the kit, snatched the oxygen mask, tubing, and attached them to a small O2 tank.

Bracken took out his radar scope and scanned the ground. "I only see one heat source." He studied it closer.

"Only one?" Cordy felt panic grip her. *Braun or Usher?* That can't be right. There must be two. Are you sure?" A lump in her throat grew so fast that she had to swallow.

"Maybe there's another if they're standing together," Bracken said. "It would be easier to determine if the bunker wasn't so far underground. Kayman, when did you take this photo?"

Kayman didn't answer. His chalk-white lips stilled.

As much as she worried about Braun, Cordy had to stay focused. She placed the O2 mask over Kayman's face. The elastic caught on bone protruding near his temple. "He's in shock."

The medic examined Kayman's pupils. "The right pupil is smaller than the left but reactive. Turn the oxygen flow rate to ten liters per minute, and recheck his blood pressure."

"Kayman, can you hear me?" Bracken nudged the man.

Cordy motioned for Bracken to move aside as she pumped up the BP cuff. "His blood pressure is dropping, and his breathing is more labored."

"He was talking a moment ago," Bracken said.

"I'm surprised he could talk at all. His jaw is fractured." The medic turned to Cordy, "Spike a bag of Ringer's lactate. Clear the tubing and hand it to me after I start an IV."

Cordy followed orders.

Kayman's breathing slowed, and his lips turned blue.

"Quick, hand me the intubation equipment. He has a head injury, shock, and more." The medic grabbed the scope and tube from Cordy. He carefully inserted an ET tube to prevent further jaw damage and taped it to Kayman's cheek. He opened another gauze pack and wrapped it around Kayman's crown and jaw. We need to get him to a trauma center."

"Call Flight for Life," Bracken radioed to Chico. "Kayman's critical. Let's get this door off him."

"Wait. That heavy piece of metal could be holding pressure on any bleeders." The medic dug through his trauma kit, rechecked Kayman's pupils, and wiped the sweat from his brow.

"Do you have pneumatic anti-shock garments?" Cordy asked.

The medic nodded at the pack next to the medic bag. "Yeah, we call them PASG, but I'll need your help applying them. We'll have to coordinate our efforts to do this quickly.

Cordy dug out the PASG from the pack and laid it alongside Kayman. "Okay, ready when you are."

The medic scanned the area. "Can the ambulance drive to the front of the house?"

Braun checked with the ambulance crew. "I think so. I'll have them pull around to the front drive."

The medic took a deep breath and ticked off orders, "Okay, Bracken and Foley, lift the door off Kayman and move it aside, then call for the ambulance."

When the heavy door lifted, Kayman's eyes flew open, and his fists clenched as he moaned. Blood pooled under his abdomen, and his misaligned left leg lay at a 90-degree angle.

"Knee's dislocated." The medic knelt beside Kayman, grabbed his left thigh, and twisted his calf back in place. He adjusted the kneecap and felt for a pulse.

If the ET tube wasn't in place, Cordy was sure Kayman would have screamed with pain.

The medic quickly wrapped an ace bandage around the leg. "His pressure's dropping. Get the PASG on now!"

Cordy followed directions and slid on one side while the medic slid up the other.

Once they applied the pants to Kayman's lower torso, the medic pumped them up to maintain steady pressure on the lower extremities.

In the meantime, Bracken had radioed Chico to make the necessary orders to send in the ambulance. "Follow the medic's tracks, and don't deviate. There may be more traps."

The medic told Cordy, "Let's strap Kayman to a backboard and get him to the ambulance. Then we'll drive to the gate and wait for the chopper."

When the ambulance arrived, the paramedics whisked Kayman away.

"You need to go back to the gate, too," Bracken told Cordy. "It's not safe here."

"I'm not leaving until I know Braun's free."

"Yes, you are." Bracken glared at her. "That's an order. The chief expects you to take over the investigation if we fail. I need you to stay outside the perimeter and make sure Flight for Life has no problem with the media."

Cordy's eyes filled with defiance, but she reluctantly joined the medic.

* * *

With the door moved aside, Foley lifted the screen and assessed the stairwell that lay beneath. He returned shortly to report, "There's an underground control room. I heard a beep and found a camera hidden in the light fixture above the entrance. At the back of the room is a sloping hallway. At the end, a bridge-like ladder leads to the bunker."

"Should I call the team?" Bracken asked.

"No. Get Desmond out here," Foley said. "One wrong move could trigger any remaining charges."

Poncho radioed Bracken, "Desmond says we can't enter the cellar from here—the staircase was blown to bits. We have to find another way to rescue the hostages."

"Okay, I think we found another access point. We need you both out here," Bracken said. "Flight for Life is flying Kayman to a trauma one center."

"Roger," Poncho signed off, and the men came out the back door a few minutes later.

Foley briefed Desmond and turned to Bracken. "Sit tight until we clear the control room. I'll let you know when we reach the bunker. Then the SWAT team can proceed."

Foley came up the cement steps twenty minutes later, wiping sweat from his brow. "I'm not sure, but a computer system could have activated the bombs in the command post."

"Are you ready for the SWAT team?" Bracken asked.

"Not yet, but we've reached the bunker. The place is wired, and the detonators are on smart timers. We have found six charges so far, five are deactivated, and one is strapped to the bridge leading to the bunker door."

"Can you defuse it?" Bracken asked.

"Desmond's working on it."

"Any word from the hostages?"

Bracken patted his pockets for a cigarette, then remembered he had crushed and thrown away the last packet. He fished deeper for a stick of gum—no luck there either. He had to quell his nervous energy. Glancing at Foley's distraught expression, Bracken asked, "So you think there're explosives on the other side of the door?" Foley's stare said it all. "Right. They're moving slow—probably clearing as they go."

"I'd bank on it," Foley said. "Anyone here know computers? I'm not an expert, but I know a little. We need someone who can do an IP scan to show each device on the network, what it's doing, and which port it uses in the outside router, if any."

"I'll ask." Bracken radioed a request for anyone at the front gate who knew computers.

"I do," Cordy said. "I'll be right there. I'm sure they have remote user capabilities. I can't shut it down."

"I'll call the telephone company to deny access to all leased lines to this address." Bracken got on the phone.

"What about cable?" Foley asked.

"I'll take care of it," Cordy said. "Be there shortly."

WITH SECONDS TO SPARE

Learning how to solve problems at a moment's notice was something Cordy's father had stressed ever since she could remember. He challenged her to be the best at everything she did. She pushed herself to be the strongest, fastest, and brightest student in her class. He taught her what he knew about technology, computers, and weapons. When he died, a piece of her went with him. Was what she knew enough to rescue Braun and Usher? It unnerved her, but she had to try.

Bracken met Cordy halfway down the first flight of stairs to the underground. "Foley thinks a computer system in the command post might trigger the bombs."

"Is there a clock already activated?" Cordy didn't wait for a reply. She darted past Bracken and headed for a room filled with bright lights. With one glance, she knew she needed every ounce of courage and wisdom to engage each of her brain cells to its fullest to accomplish this task at top speed. Braun and Usher's life hung in the wings. It was up to her to figure out how to abort Doc's complex automated bomb scheme to rescue them. The challenge was hard enough without knowing Braun's life was in her hands. She blew out a deep breath. "Wow, what a setup."

A rack filled with computer equipment and multiple server banks lined one wall. A printer/scanner and two mini-computers lined another. A long, narrow wooden desk with two open laptops sat in the middle of the room. Her eyes locked onto a large overhead screen playing in full Technicolor, but there was no sound except for the low hum of the machines.

Cordy stepped up to have a closer look. A man walked in the shadows. His mouth moved, but she couldn't make out what he said. "Where's the volume?"

"It must link to this desktop under the shelf," Bracken said, "because the light blinks as he speaks."

"Good eye. I missed that." Cordy dropped to her knees, found a remote control, and increased the volume.

"...you triggered my devices." A wheezing laugh escaped the shadow. "You're too late. My plan is already set in motion. I'd run if I were you." The screen turned blank.

How much time is left? "It's Doc. I recognize his voice." She had to focus. Her mind spun like a spider's web, taking in everything. Hoping she didn't miss anything, Cordy rescanned the room. "Did Foley mention the equipment is on a wide area network? I don't like having these computers connected to multiple sites and controlled by that fiend."

"Probably a WAN, but Foley didn't mention it." Bracken knelt beside her. "I talked with both the phone and cable companies. They disconnected the external links, but this is the hub."

Cordy studied the mini-computer. "I'll see what I can do without setting off any more explosives." She tapped the keyboard, knowing she had no silver bullet to cure the evil set before her.

Bracken stood and leaned over her shoulder. "How long do you need?"

"Depends. First, I have to download my IP scanning system. It'll tell me what's on the network." She glanced at her watch. "Give me fifteen minutes. I need time to explore."

Bracken set a radio at her elbow. "I'm going to check on Foley. Notify me if you need anything."

After a quick study of the equipment, she tracked cables, found the router, and then sat down to work. Cordy's fingers flew from one keyboard to the next, but intrusion detection refused her access to any programs or files. "Come on." Cordy turned toward a laptop on the middle desk, stumbled, and accidentally knocked over a chair.

She leaned over to pick up the chair and caught her finger on something. Upon closer examination, she found a yellow sticky pasted under the seat. The corners were well-worn, and a smeared dot was on the right edge of the paper. In the middle of the note, in faint pencil, read SecretSociety. Scribbled below were six letters and two numbers. Cordy's heart thumped wildly in anticipation.

She typed in the username and password. "I'm in." She found a map of the underground facility, printed two copies, and called Bracken. "I have a map of the bunker. Send someone to get it. I can't leave."

The big screen above relit. Doc's shadowy figure reappeared. He shook his head. "Someone didn't heed my warning. Need a hint about your future? You're about to die in our evil rat's trap."

How does he know anyone is still here? Are there motion detectors feeding him information? She didn't see any, so she worked faster and uploaded the IP scanning system. It would take at least ten minutes to run the full scan. She set up a guest access code and elevated it to administrative status to disable services and block others. Cordy also created a backdoor account so that she could get access in case Doc changed the password in the future. Maybe she'd find something of value, like bank account numbers, names of colleagues, and plane ticket info. Not likely, but who knew?

Bracken darted into the room. "Where's the map?"

"They're on the printer." Cordy didn't even look up. Her fingers kept typing. "I ran off two copies, so leave one for me."

"Fifteen minutes until detonation," came from somewhere. It echoed but didn't seem to come from the large screen.

"No!" Cordy glanced about the room. There wasn't enough time. Bracken was nowhere in sight. A printed map lay next to her elbow. She grabbed the radio. "Bracken, did you verify that the phone and cable companies have disconnected all outside lines?"

"Yes, all cables leased to this address."

"That can't be, right?" Cordy asked. "How'd the shadow know? Wait, what about any lines leased to the Secret Society? That's the user name. Check it out."

Something popped up on the mini-computer screen. She followed the monitor cords to a receiver on a shelf beside the machine. A dim green light blinked below a dial. She turned it.

Somewhere close, a speaker crackled. "…far away from the door as possible."

Cordy straightened and leaned closer to track where the voice came from. "Usher, can you hear me?"

He didn't respond to her. "If it blows, we're dead. We have to find another way." She radioed Bracken, "I think I found the hostages. I hear them. A bright red light is flashing above the door. There's a large cable running along the frame." She tried another dial. "Usher, Braun, can you hear me?"

"Cordy, is that you?" Braun asked. "Or am I speaking to a ghost?"

"No, it's me. Are both of you all right?"

"Glad you're alive. I fractured my ankle, but what happened to you? Usher told me—"

"It's a long story," Cordy said. "I'll fill you in later."

Usher interrupted. "The whole tunnel to the doorway is lined with C4 explosives. There's a cable leading out the door."

"I know. Hold on." Cordy updated Bracken. "I have open communication with the hostages."

"Ten minutes until detonation," echoed through the room.

Cordy's gut twisted, and she flinched when the laptop computer beeped again. The screen flickered, and words scrolled rapidly down the screen. A thread of relief followed. "My program's working." Cordy picked up the map to study the door in question. "Bracken, can you see the end of the cable that goes around the bunker's door?"

"Foley and Desmond are checking on that as we speak," Bracken said.

"Braun says the tunnel is lined with C4 packets," Cordy typed away on a keyboard.

"I'll get Foley and have him talk directly with Braun and Usher." A rapid discussion came across the radio, and then Foley entered the control room.

"Are you sure about the C4 packets?" Foley asked.

"Let's check with Braun and Usher." Cordy moved aside.

"Can you confirm the packets are C4?" Foley asked.

"Move closer to the speaker." Cordy pointed at a small round mesh-covered apparatus.

Foley bent closer and repeated the question.

"I think so, but it's dark down here, and they're above our heads," Usher replied. "I'm using my watch as a light, and Braun's torch is dimming."

"Okay, I'll see if I can find the power." Cordy glanced around the room. A low-cut metal door, about four feet high, caught her attention. The rack of computer equipment blocked the entrance. Foley helped her push it aside, and she opened the door to a power panel filled with circuit breakers. A detailed label was beside each. "The bunker's breaker is tripped off. Do I dare reset it, or will it cause an explosion?"

Foley checked the box. "I don't see any traps." He flipped the switch.

"That's much better," Braun said. "Now that I can see the ceiling, I'm sure they're C4 blocks."

The laptop computer beeped. Cordy moved to check on the progress of her program. The hourglass spun. *Still searching.* The gauge showed three minutes until completion. It would be close.

The large-screen overhead lit up. The shadowed man reappeared. "As I suspected, someone's tampering with the computer system. Don't get your hopes up. I'll let you in on a secret. We wired C4 explosives to the bunker door. Anyone going in will blow to bits. If you cut wires, the bomb will detonate. If you power off the computers, boom, everything turns to dust. I'm the only one who can disconnect the system. This is my seven-minute warning."

"I'm glad he told us about turning off the computers," Cordy said. "I thought about tripping off the circuit breaker to the control room."

"Wouldn't matter. Everything is on a backup battery system, Foley said. "By the way, how does he know you're tampering with the computers?"

"I've been wondering that myself." Her program beeped. Cordy scanned through the IP data and hit 'locate all.' The list popped up, and she printed it. "There are thirty-five devices connected to this network. I counted twenty-six in this room, but there's one more I can't find. Somewhere at ground level is a satellite router that's still working. There's one smart device inside the bunker and three in the hallway outside between here and the bunker door."

"That only makes thirty-two. Where are the other three?" Foley checked the map against the smart device locations. "We'll deactivate these three." He moved to the speaker. "Usher, you need to get the one in the bunker. I'll tell Bracken to check out the router."

"Where in the bunker?" Braun asked. "We've already deactivated three down here, so that makes thirty-five."

Cordy was on her knees, searching for the missing item.

"Five minutes to detonation," came across the speaker. A foul laugh followed.

"Foley, where's the smart device in the bunker," Braun repeated.

Cordy bolted upright and hit her head on the desk. She rubbed her crown and glanced around. Foley had left the room. She grabbed the map. "Usher, it's on the ceiling, not far from the door. Can you reach it to disarm it?"

"Just a minute," Braun's voice came over the speaker. "We have to find it first."

Cordy nodded and muttered, "Where's that router?" I know it's near the mini-computer." She ran her hand along the top shelf overhead and bumped against something metal. The object was no larger than a cell phone with a small antenna.

Foley dashed into the room and picked up the speaker. "Braun, can you reach the C4 packets? They're quite stable. If you pull the detonator cap from each explosive, it will disarm them."

"They're too high to reach," Braun said. "Even if I could climb onto Usher's shoulders, we couldn't get all of them disarmed in the next five minutes. I don't see a ladder anywhere."

Foley studied the map spread out on the middle desk. "Do you see another way out?"

Cordy's eyes traveled across the map. She wasn't sure what to look for. "Did you deactivate the others outside the bunker?"

"Yeah, Desmond helped. I'm glad you pointed them out. Not easy to find, but the bunker's still wired."

The speaker crackled. "Four minutes to detono—" Cordy disconnected the satellite router and grinned when the speaker turned off. The outside intruder no longer had access to the building, but the timer had been activated.

Focus! "What are our options? I mean, if they can't disarm the explosives in the bunker…" Cordy programmed her watch, punched three minutes thirty seconds on her timer, and then added a one-minute warning alarm.

"It's up to you to stop the system from triggering the detonator," Foley finished the sentence for her."

"I'm on it," *Doc said, 'evil rat's trap.'* Sweat dripped down her back. Recalling how she worked through the puzzle to track down the floral business, she replayed Doc's words in her head. *Evil. What else does that spell? Veil, vile, live.* Live was a word she liked.

Foley radioed Bracken and included him in the discussion with Braun and Usher. Talking about bombs didn't interest Cordy. Her mind continued to play with Doc's warning. "You're about to die in our evil rat's trap." *The wording is off. It has to be a code. Dad always said to start backward. Trap could be rapt, tarp, part, maybe only part of the word. Rap, par, apt, pat, no tap.* She jotted on a piece of paper, "to live tap." *Now decipher rats, tars, arts—*

"There's a rough patch in the ceiling." Braun's words penetrated Cordy's thoughts. "It looks like putty in the shape of a star. Two wires are protruding—"

"Star! That's it!" Cordy turned to the laptop running her program and asked Braun, "Can you remove the wires from the star?"

"No," Braun said. "It's too high."

She went back to her puzzle. *It's up to me.* Adrenaline surged. Her mind raced. *Think!*

Foley asked, "Is there a long pole or stick you can wrap around the wires to pull them from the putty? You have to remove both at the same time."

Braun and Usher were in the middle of a heated discussion. "Use your crutch," Usher said.

"No, it's a metal pole," Braun said. "It could set off an explosion. Besides, there are at least fifty other packets."

"Here, wrap the end with my sock," Usher said.

Cordy tuned the banter out of her mind, picked up a pen, and scribbled, "You're about to die in our evil rat's trap." *Okay, to live tap…star? What about to die?* She glanced at the message and wrote, "You're <u>about to die</u>" *about, out, bout, no use the leftover 'r' from you're, abort.* Her mind raced on. She crossed out letters, rearranged them, and then wrote, "You die, or U abort to live, tap in…" *What letters are left over? Star. There's an extra e', or 'E. Stare? Probably not.* She added a star to the end of the line, "E'star?" Then, reread it once again. *You die, or U abort to live, tap in E'star.*

She glanced at her watch. "Two minutes until detonation," she announced.

"We haven't given up yet." *Isn't that like Braun? He would never give up.*

"I'm close," Usher said. "If I jump, I might be able to snag the wires and pull them from the star."

Cordy typed 'abort routine' under search in the computer. A username and password screen popped up. Above it read, "Link to mini-computer." Glancing at the sticky she found under the chair,

Cordy doubted it was the same code as before. *What is that smeared dot on the right of the paper?*

A gasp left her lips as Usher swore over the speaker. "So close. Another inch or two, and I'll have it."

Or everything could explode. "Wait!" Cordy hit the link button, and the mini-computer fired up. "I think I figured out how to abort the system." She moved to the terminal and typed in SecretSociety under the user name.

Her watch beeped the one-minute warning. She could hardly breathe. *Not enough time! Hurry!*

Cordy typed E'Star under password.

"Access denied" popped on the screen. Cordy clenched her fist.

Bracken came into the control room. He marched to the speaker. "Did you disconnect the wires?"

"Not yet," Braun said.

Foley wiped the sweat from his brow. "It won't matter. The remaining packets will blow as soon as we open the door."

"Not if we shut down the computers." Cordy's mind spun. *"E' maybe East?"* She tried again and typed EastStar as the password.

Once again, "Access denied" flashed on the screen.

She cried out in frustration. "Last chance!" This time, she typed *EasternStar* as the password. Cordy held her breath as her trembling fingers hit enter. The overhead lights went out. The room became so silent she could hear the breath escape her lungs.

"It worked!" Bracken shouted. "Foley, Desmond, meet us outside at the tunnel entrance. Poncho, help get Braun to the ambulance when we reach them. "Let's go."

"Wait," Foley said as they raced out the door. "Once we're inside the bunker, Desmond and I will disarm the bombs, and Poncho, get the hostages out of here just in case."

Cordy grabbed her flashlight and ran after them. When she found the vault door, it was already wide open, and Usher was heading up the steps. Fear nearly paralyzed her. "Where's Braun? Is he alive?"

Usher nodded. "Thanks, Cordy. He'll be here soon—busted ankle."

Relieved, her heart leapt at the sight of Braun standing at the doorway. Bracken was on one side of him, Poncho on the other, as they eased the man she wanted by her side out of the bunker.

Braun's gaze locked onto her face. That familiar crooked smile crossed his lips.

"Great job," Bracken patted her on the back. All the congratulations in the world meant nothing compared to seeing Braun's smile.

Braun reached for her hand and pulled her so close she felt his breath on her cheek. "Thanks, Cordy." He linked her fingers to his.

She held her breath. Her eyes remained fixed on him. Words failed her. Yes, she could love this man. In fact, her soul finally felt at ease with the decision. *If only he would commit to being hers and still allow her to make her own choices in life. It could happen.*

Foley and Desmond stayed behind to disarm the C-4 packets along the tunnel.

Bracken nudged them forward. "Let's get out of here."

When Braun released her hand, Cordy felt her adrenaline drain away. She followed the men up the steps, walked in slow motion across the yard behind Braun's stretcher, and breathed in the fresh air.

By the time she reached the ambulance, her legs could hardly support her weight. Braun and Usher were loaded inside.

News crews, paramedics, and colleagues had broken through the gates and surrounded her, throwing questions at the team. There was only one thing on Cordy's mind—Braun. She climbed into the rear of an ambulance with the freed hostages.

"We're back to where we started from." Usher smiled and patted her hand. "I'm glad you're on our team."

Braun mumbled his gratitude but quickly drifted away when a paramedic gave him pain medication. His hand still rested in Cordy's.

Usher tapped her on the shoulder. "Have you heard from Fritz?"

"One moment. Agent Kelly left a message." Cordy checked her cell phone for an update. "Fritz was in a car accident and is in the hospital. She received a ransom message from Risa. Kelly says we have two days to find her, and Vinny knows where to find Fritz's family. That was early this morning, so that leaves us just over 24 hours. I'll get an update when we get to the hospital."

"I better warn Jake," Usher said.

Cordy rechecked her text message and then pocketed her cell. "Kelly also says Fritz is grounded. The doc won't let him leave the hospital."

"Grounded? Not if I know Fritz." Usher smiled at Cordy. "As soon as they remove this needle from my arm, I'll catch the next plane to West Virginia. My job is to keep Laura and Marta safe, and I know Braun will get whatever he needs while in your capable hands."

FBI LEAK

Cordy spent the whole afternoon at the Fort Collins hospital with Braun. When the Emergency doc saw his ankle, he exclaimed, "I won't touch that break! You need an orthopedic surgeon."

Braun was still under heavy sedation, but he agreed to surgery. Usher co-signed the consent, and after the doctor removed the broken-off needle from his arm, Usher left for the airport to return to his duties in West Virginia.

Like a caged tiger, Cordy paced the waiting room outside the OR. She downed a cup of coffee, glanced at the clock, and called her friend, Dr. Peterson, to check on the chief. He was asleep, so Cordy went back to pacing.

People of all ages crowded the waiting room. They chatted loudly, and a man tried to strike up a conversation. Cordy wasn't in the mood to talk and wanted peace and quiet. One woman sitting next to her only spoke Spanish, worried her rosary beads, and crossed herself while repeating prayers to the Virgin Mary. Cordy knew the woman was distressed and needed some privacy, so she moved into the hallway to grab a soda from the vending machine.

Cordy phoned Agent Kelly, "Braun's finally having surgery on his ankle and should be out soon, but I wanted to get an update on Fritz and fill you in on our latest mission."

"Fritz is still in the hospital and hates being grounded," Kelly said. "Vinny sent a ransom demand. He says he knows where to find

Laura, and Fritz is worried Vinny will kill Risa, Laura, and Marta. Fritz can't wait to get back on his feet and out of jail, as he puts it."

Cordy knew the feeling and the frustration of hurry and wait. "We were so busy rescuing Doc's hostages, that I haven't had time to help Fritz keep his family safe from Vinny."

"But you are keeping his family safe," Kelly insisted. "You freed Usher so he can return to the safe house to protect Laura and Marta."

Cordy sighed. "True, but the medical system works at a snail's pace. It took all afternoon to get that needle out of Usher's arm, and he had to fly on standby to West Virginia. I hope he gets there before Vinny. Should I head there, too?"

"No, I know you want to be with Braun, and Fritz is safe as long as he's in the hospital, but," Kelly hesitated. "Fritz won't rest until Vinny's locked up, and we need to track down Doc and Ace. Can you focus on that while Usher keeps Laura and Marta out of danger? Ace is still pulling strings. I don't know how he's getting his information."

"I'll do my best. Chief Jackson may have some answers." Cordy heard, 'Officer Cordelia, please return to the OR waiting room' over the intercom.

"Gotta go. I'm being paged. I'll talk to you later." She disconnected the call and returned to the madhouse.

Cordy went to the desk. "I'm Officer Cordelia. Do you have any news on Braun Hastings?" She held out her authorization card, knowing the clerk wouldn't give any confidential information without it.

"He's out of surgery. The doctor will be—"

"Officer Cordelia?" the orthopedic surgeon interrupted. "Surgery went well, but Mr. Hastings will need to spend the night. Labs show he's dehydrated, and he lost a lot of blood. We gave him two units of packed cells in the OR."

"Can he go home in the morning?" Cordy asked.

"We'll observe him for the night and see if his lab work improves. You can visit him briefly, but he'll be groggy for several hours."

Braun woke up a few times but drifted back to sleep, so Cordy decided to run home for a quick shower, picked up her computer, and stayed at her friend's home, which was closer to the hospital. Plus, it allowed her to check on the chief's condition and gave her a quiet place to track down Doc and Ace.

Chief Jackson sat in a chair next to the bed. "Do you feel up to investigating now?" Unlike Braun, the chief was eager to get to work.

Cordy filled him in on the day's events. She explained how she hacked into Doc's computer system and set up a backdoor link. "Doc got away, but I have access to his data and will track him down soon."

Chief Jackson adjusted a pillow and leaned back. "I've gone over the files and researched between catnaps. I'm curious. Can you log into Doc's computer tonight before he makes any changes?"

Cordy dug her laptop from her backpack, plugged it in, and booted it up. "Where do you want to start?"

The chief placed the computer on his lap. "Do you have a mouse?" "I hate using that finger pad. And maybe a TV tray so I don't have to hold this."

Dr. Peterson walked into the room. "It's time to go back to bed."

"Not yet. I need to look up a few things first. Give me another hour."

"An hour?" Peterson laughed. "Cordy, you're the best medicine around. Call me when Chief Jackson falls out of his chair. I'll help you drag him back to bed."

The chief waved him away. "Wait, can you roll the over-bed table next to me? It's perfect—"

"Sure," Dr. Peterson said. "Do you want some hot tea?"

"Sounds great. You know how I like it," the chief said. By the way, Cordy dismissed the two guards, so she's on duty until the next shift arrives at 6 a.m."

"Make mine coffee," Cordy said. "It's going to be a long night."

Peterson moved the over-bed table in front of the chief's chair. "I'll be back with refreshments."

Cordy lifted the computer from the chief's lap and set it on the table. "I'll log into Doc's system, and we'll go from there."

"I think Vinny has access to top-secret data," Chief Jackson said. "How else would he know where to find Fritz and Risa?"

"I don't think Vinny is computer savvy, but Ace could hack into a system if it weren't secure." Cordy typed in her code.

"Access denied" flashed on the screen.

She entered it again with the same result. "One more try, and I'm locked out."

"How did you enter the system earlier today?" the chief asked.

"Through my program on the Internet, but I was on their system at the time." Cordy closed her eyes and reviewed each step in her mind. "What am I missing?"

"You think on it," the chief said. "In the meantime, let's log into the Homeland Security system."

"I don't have access." Cordy raised an eyebrow. "Let me guess. You've pulled some strings while I was away."

The chief nodded. "I want to run a check on Agent Islet."

Cordy gasped, "The nominee for U.S. Secretary of Homeland Security? My dad had a file on him. He's FBI?"

"He took command after Homeland discovered someone hacked into their computer systems. They planted spyware and stole thousands of top-secret files."

"Did Agent Islet work with you?"

"No, I can't say he ever worked *with* anyone. He's indeed a top FBI agent, but he's moving up the ladder too fast, in my opinion."

"President Spendorf doesn't think so." Cordy watched the chief enter his access code. It opened on the first try.

"The president wouldn't even confirm the nature of the attack, but heads are rolling." The chief pulled up Agent Islet's FBI file. "Congress subpoenaed two leading officials, who promptly resigned their posts before nominating Islet."

"I know. It's been all over the news," Cordy said. "What does that have to do with Vinny?"

"Islet has access to the most classified information in the United States." The chief handed the mouse to Cordy. "Print this off. Then, get into Doc's system and find a link. I have a gut feeling."

Dr. Peterson walked into the room with refreshments. "Are you sure your gut feeling isn't because you're tired?"

"Maybe I could use a rest," the chief admitted, "after my tea."

Cordy took two cups from the tray, handed a teacup to the chief, and set her coffee on the table. "May I use your printer?"

"My castle is at your disposal. Use whatever you need." Dr. Peterson pointed down the hallway. "It's in my office. You can link to it through your WiFi." He told her the printer's make and model number. "Print drivers are online. Let me know if you need anything else."

"Thanks." Cordy turned the laptop in her direction, loaded the drivers, and printed the pages Chief Jackson had asked for while he sipped his tea. "I'll be right back."

Chief Jackson yawned. "No rush. I'll just close my eyes for a few minutes."

When Cordy returned with the printed copies, the chief was snoring—his empty teacup propped on his lap. She smiled and took the cup. He didn't stir.

Dr. Peterson poked his head into the room. "I see the tiger fell asleep. Let's get him to bed."

Once they tucked the chief in for the night, Cordy moved to Dr. Peterson's office so she wouldn't disturb the chief. *I wonder if I can link Doc's computer into the FBI system.* It worked.

Cordy sent Doc and Ace an email indicating it was from Vinny. She then sent an email to Vinny from Doc. Although she knew it wasn't kosher, she planted a virus in the emails. The virus would allow her access to the computer network if anyone logged on.

While waiting, Cordy researched a few other high-profile sources. Her laptop flashed an alert. Someone had opened Vinny's email that she had created. Her software took control of Doc's computers. She deleted her emails from the FBI computer, removed the virus, and wiped all her transactions so no one could trace any activity back to her, the chief, or Dr. Peterson.

It took several hours, but she backed up Doc's entire system. As each file copied to her external hard drive, it deleted itself from view on Doc's computer, but it didn't remove the data. By morning, Cordy had proof that Ace hacked into Homeland Security's files. Cordy found downloads of Witness Protection files, diversions of national treasury funds into overseas accounts, and other tampering with homeland security records.

Maybe I can find something in Dad's old files. A secret folder on organized crime, mafia bosses, and foreign terrorists caught her eye. Several records regarding the mob boss, Joey Abbatiellio, old Corenelli gang members, and other mafia connections were saved under one main folder titled, 'The enemy.' *Many links are tied back to Agent Islet, Ace, and Vinny, but Doc's name didn't come up.*

However, there was no doubt how Vinny found out about Fritz's name change and his location. Risa's entire Witness Protection file was in Doc's database. Not only that, but Ace had located Laura's secure hideaway.

Cordy didn't wait to print the data. She made an urgent call to Usher in West Virginia.

"Cordy, how's Braun," gushed from Usher without her even saying 'hello.'

"Braun's fine, the chief's asleep, and Vinny's heading your way! He may even be there by now. Put out the alert."

"How did he find this place?" Usher asked.

"You're not going to believe me." Cordy filled him in on the chief's theory about Agent Islet.

"Cordy, I'd love to chat longer, but we need to button down the hatches double time."

"I know. I'll keep the chief informed," Cordy said. "Call me with any new developments."

"You do the same." Usher disconnected.

Now, all Cordy needed was to present the proof to the authorities. There could be no holes in her data. The leaks might go as high as the Attorney General. She loaded the tray with paper and hit print. She aroused the chief to discuss the details.

TIRED OF GAMES

Friday, June 21 – 0210-0516 CDT, Ann Arbor, Michigan

A battle for survival warred in Fritz's mind. He heard Risa call out his name in the darkness, but he couldn't reach her. He fought the urge to slip back into a drug-induced sleep. _Move! Get out of here and find her._ Fog clouded his mind. His body broke out in a cold sweat. Pain arced through him with every movement, but he refused to let it beat him.

He lay there in bed and tried to connect all the dots. Vinny kidnapped Risa, Mick died with that skeleton key tucked into his shoe, and Walt told him about Benny the pruner and the ransom tape—claiming that Vinny would soon have his family. _Laura and Marta could be in danger. Then, Risa's hidden message appeared, and he had only one day left to save his sister. And something about meeting Vinny in a cave._ Nothing made any sense.

Fritz checked his glow-in-the-dark watch for the time: twelve after two. It was early morning. He turned on the overhead light. His computer and an envelope sat on the bedside stand. Kelly must have stopped by sometime in the evening. _Why didn't she wake me?_

He reached to pull the stand closer and realized someone had disconnected the monitor cables and IV. He could move freely without setting off an alarm. A sickly odor oozed from his sweaty pores. Fritz gritted his teeth, grabbed the side rail, and rolled to his side. He kicked one leg from under the starched white sheet, scooted down, and dropped over the end of the bed. His knobby knees poked out from the short blue hospital gown, and cold air attacked his bare butt.

Fritz ignored the fire shooting up his chest and supported his side as he breathed. He forced himself upright. His fingers reached around to pull the slit together at the back of his hospital gown, and he hobbled to the bathroom. Standing under the hot shower, he soaped up and rubbed his sore muscles. The pulsing spray cleared his head and washed away some of the pain along with the odor.

Twenty minutes later, Fritz pulled his wrinkled clothes from the closet, limped over to the padded wooden chair, and settled into it, taking the unwanted pressure off his ribs. He forced one leg into his trousers, paused, and then slipped on the other leg. Discomfort mounted into agony. Hissing through his teeth, he stood and pulled up his pants. The nurse had cut off his shirt in the emergency room, so he found a clean gown in a drawer, wrapped it backward so the slit opened in the front, and sat next to his open computer.

Inside the envelope, Fritz found a thumb drive and the skeleton key. He inserted the drive and found a digital recording of Risa's ransom demand. Unable to decipher her message the first time, he listened to the demand twice more before slowing the recording. He heard Risa say, "The key is reincarnation." *Reincarnation? What does that mean? I need to get out of the hospital.*

Fritz knew it was too early to call Kelly, but he dialed her phone number anyway. She didn't answer, so he left a message. Then he tried Officer McCoy.

A grumpy voice answered, "Who's calling at such an ungodly hour? I just got to bed!"

"Sorry to wake you. This is Fritz. I need to talk to you, and it can't wait."

McCoy yawned into the phone. "I wondered how long it would take for you to wake up. Kelly and I reviewed the tape several times. She filled me in on the skeleton key, too. So, any bright ideas?"

"I don't know how bright my ideas are, but Risa left a hint on the tape," Fritz said.

"Yeah, we heard it, too, but what does it mean?" McCoy asked. "The key has something to do with a carnation."

"Reincarnation," Fritz corrected the officer.

"Oh, right," McCoy said. "Did she mean the skeleton key?"

"No, she doesn't even know about that." Fritz rubbed the brass object between his thumb and index finger. "The hub has a floral design. Maybe she did say carnation. Then there was that logo I tracked down in Colorado. I get the feeling everything is linked."

"What about the cave?" McCoy asked. "Kelly and I have a couple of leads to discuss with you. After a thorough search within a twenty-mile radius of the city, we found green grottos, ice caves, Bear Caves, salt caves, and a bar called Detroit Lion's Man Cave."

"Bear cave?" Fritz rubbed a hand over his face. "I met Vinny outside Detroit before the sting operation, but we never went into a cave." His head hurt. He couldn't focus.

"Do any of those names sound familiar?"

"No. It could be any of them, or maybe it's not a cave at all. You have to get me out of here. The clock's ticking. I have less than twenty-two hours left to rescue my sister."

"You sound tired," McCoy said. "The doctor hasn't discharged you."

"I don't care," Fritz said. "I'll sign myself out against medical advice if I have to."

McCoy sighed. "I'll be there in one hour." He disconnected the call.

Fritz padded down the hall to the nurses' station. "I need to see the doctor on duty."

"We don't call the doctor unless it's an emergency," the nurse said. "Is there anything I can do for you?"

"Yes, I need to leave the hospital ASAP." Fritz squinted through his swollen eyes and stood as tall as his ribs allowed. "I know there's a doctor on call in the building. Get him on the phone."

"That's not how it's done," the nurse objected.

"Fine, I'm leaving. Do I make myself clear?" Fritz demanded. "Where's the paper? I'll sign it."

"If you don't pipe down, I'm going to call the guard," the nurse warned.

"Yes, do that. I already called the police." Fritz grinned. "Officer McCoy is on his way."

The nurse frowned, picked up the receiver, and reluctantly placed a call to the doctor on duty. She turned her back to Fritz and whispered into the phone. "I have a problem patient. Can I give him a sedative?"

"No meds!" Fritz marched around the counter and grabbed the phone. "This is Detective Fritz Von Schlegen. I'm sorry to bother you, but—"

"Let him go," came from down the hall. The doctor headed toward the desk. "Agent Kelly warned me that you could be a real bear. You don't look well enough to leave, but I can't stop you."

"A real bear, huh?" Fritz wondered why 'bear' hit a nerve.

"Are you allergic to Tylenol with codeine?"

"No," Fritz said.

The doctor pulled open a drawer and grabbed a prescription pad. After a few strokes of his pen, he tore off the top sheet and shoved it toward Fritz. "Kelly's on her way to pick you up. She's arranged for you to transfer to a friend's home. Now leave this poor nurse alone to do her work."

"That's a deal." Fritz braced himself and moved like an old man back to his room. The effort exhausted him. Lowering himself into the chair, he stifled a groan and panted a few times. *I'll just sit here a minute. Then I'll pack up my computer.*

An hour later, Fritz opened his eyes to McCoy poking his shoulder. "Sleeping on the job again?"

"Nice to see you, too," Fritz said. "I see you stopped by to get Agent Kelly."

"Sleep is overrated." Kelly laughed. She stuffed the thumb drive and skeleton key into the envelope and pocketed them. "Help him into the wheelchair, and let's go to work." She grabbed Fritz on one side. McCoy took the other, and they eased him into the chair. Kelly picked up the computer and placed it on Fritz's lap. The two whisked him down the hall, into the elevator, and out the front door.

Kelly opened the back door to the dark SUV parked beside the curb. "It's going to be a long day."

Fritz eased himself into the vehicle.

Kelly went to the other side, moved a stack of folders toward Fritz, and sat down. McCoy returned the wheelchair and climbed into the driver's seat.

Kelly settled into her seatbelt. "How'd you get the wheelchair to the third floor and back here so fast?"

"I met a friendly employee who offered to take the chair for me." McCoy started the engine and pulled away from the curb.

Fritz glanced at Kelly. "Did you see anyone in the hallway coming downstairs?"

"No."

Fritz looked back at the hospital door. Someone in a white lab coat stood outside, smoking a cigarette and talking on his cell phone. He had the wheelchair parked next to him.

Kelly whipped her head around. "It's Dave! Stop the car and turn around."

"Did you forget something?" McCoy slammed on the brakes and made a U-turn.

Fritz nodded. "I think that helpful employee is calling Vinny as we speak."

The lab tech was nowhere in sight when they reached the curb.

Kelly was out of the car before they pulled to a complete stop. "I'll find him. He couldn't have gone far."

"Wait, Kelly!" Fritz rolled down his window and shouted, "Don't go after Dave by yourself. He's dangerous."

McCoy climbed from the driver's seat. "Wait here, Fritz. You'll only be in the way." McCoy darted into the hospital after her.

BAD NEWS

Vinny awoke to a jarring noise and vibration from his nightstand. He fumbled for the light switch and whispered into his phone. "Did you arrange everything as I asked you to?" The digital clock read 5:16 a.m.

Expecting Ace to answer, he was surprised to hear, "Vinny, the cops just sprung Fritz from the hospital. They may be heading your way."

Vinny shook his head, trying to wrap his mind around the call. "Who is this?"

"Dave. You asked me to update you on Fritz's condition."

"Oh…right. So tell me again." Vinny moved his legs over the edge of the bed. "I'm listening." A door closed from outside in the hallway. Vinny grabbed his pistol.

Dave repeated, "Fritz just left the hospital. Oops, the car's turning around. Gotta go!"

"Okay, thanks." All Vinny heard was a dial tone, so he hung up and turned off the light. He slid off the bed and crept to the door.

"Shh," someone said from downstairs. At least, he thought it was from that direction. Something dragged across the floor.

Vinny opened his bedroom door a crack. A faint light glowed from the hallway, leaving shadows along the stairs. He led with his gun and swung his arm in an arc.

Midget poked his head out his door across the hall. "Geez!" He hit the floor with enough force to knock the wind from his lungs.

"Oof!" Midget rolled back onto his feet. "Vinny, what the hell are you doing? You scared the shit out of me."

"Hush," Vinny scolded.

Jules moved to the bottom of the steps. "What's going on up there?"

"I could ask you the same thing," Vinny bellowed.

"Sorry, did I wake you?" Jules asked.

Vinny lowered his gun and peered around Jules. "You alone down there?"

"Of course," Jules said. "Midget's up there with you."

"Vinny, did you have another nightmare? And I'm supposed to be the crazy bastard." Midget went back into his room. The door slammed behind him.

Vinny ran down the stairs toward Jules. "What's going on? I heard noises."

"I just wanted some juice." Jules went into the kitchen to fetch his glass from the table. "Can I get you something?"

"No. Why are you all dressed in black?"

"You told Doc to dress me this way." Jules scratched his scruffy neck. "This beard itches."

Vinny pushed past Jules. He opened the closet door, moved into the living room, and peeked behind the couch.

"Did you lose something?" Jules asked. "I'll help you look."

Vinny swore, went into the kitchen, and poured himself some whiskey. "I know you're up to no good. I'm going downstairs to check on Risa and her husband. They better be tied up and drugged into a stupor."

"I followed your orders and brought down dinner," Jules said. "By the way, Jim died last night. It really stinks down there. You'd better bury him before the whole place reeks of death."

Vinny opened the basement door, flipped on the light, and gagged at the odor.

"I'm going back to bed." Jules headed down the hall.

"The hell you are. You'll dig his grave, and I don't want another word about it."

"What? Now? At this hour?" Jules asked.

"Midget!" Vinny called up the stairs. "Get dressed and come down here. Help Jules bury that stinking body."

Jules moved into the kitchen, dug through a drawer to gather a few supplies, and brought back a box of heavy-duty trash bags. "Don't bother Midget at this hour. I'll take care of it." Jules held his nose and moved down two basement steps.

"Wrap him in a sheet so you don't spread the stink. I need to call Ace." Vinny slammed the basement door. "Keep the smell down there."

* * *

Jules set down his stash on a step halfway down the stairwell. Then he used tongs to lift the vile bandages he'd stashed under the top step that reeked of pus. The odor got stronger. He picked up the trash bags and continued to the basement.

Risa lay curled up in the locked wrought iron cage, wrapped in an old bedspread. Her sunken eyes remained closed. She breathed deep and unlabored as if in a drugged stupor.

"Risa," Jules whispered. "Can you hear me?"

"Jules?" She opened her eyes.

He glanced around the basement and unlocked the cage. "It's safe. I'm alone. I told Vinny that Jim died. I need a shovel to dig his grave. Be careful not to make any noise."

"Thanks for the spare key." Risa got up from the thin mattress lying on the cage's floor, "and for getting the meds. Jim's fever broke during the night. He moaned so much I had to sedate him. I don't think he'll wake up for another hour or two. How do you plan to get him out of the house?"

"Make sure it continues to smell rotten down here. Vinny hates to get his hands dirty." Jules grabbed a long-handled spade and set it by the steps. "Fritz's deadline is today. Vinny's calling Ace. He's flying to West Virginia and will track down Fritz's wife and granddaughter. I'm not sure what his plans are for you, so be ready to move at a moment's notice." Jules moved behind the furnace and checked on Jim. "He sure looks dead."

"I did my best." Risa followed him and knelt beside her husband. She pulled the jacket Jules had stolen while in town over Jim's exposed arm.

"What happened to the IVs?" Jules asked.

"He's lying on them to keep pressure on the bags. Once he's outside, you'll need to be sure they're tucked out of sight." Risa removed the dressing over the gunshot wound to Jim's leg, smeared on antibiotic ointment, and then applied a new bandage. "When will you be back?"

"How long does it take to dig a grave?" Jules asked.

"That depends on the soil," Risa said.

"I saw a gravesite that had been dug up recently," Jules said. "Maybe I can use it."

Where will you really take him?"

"I made up a bed in the gardener's shed out back. He'll be comfortable, but I'll have to lock him inside. I can't have him wandering around once he wakes up."

"Promise me that you'll keep him safe," Risa said.

"I'll do my best, but how do we fake your death?"

"Fritz will save me. You must hide Jim and get away from here so you're not caught in the crossfire."

"What makes you so sure that Fritz will find you?"

"I dropped a hint on the tape. He'll figure it out."

Footsteps sounded from upstairs. "Sorry, but I need to lock you back in the cage."

Risa returned to the mattress lying inside the six-foot square enclosure, felt the pocket of her robe, and clutched the key. "Hurry back."

Jules locked the cage, took the spade, and went upstairs.

The basement door flew open before Jules reached the top step. Midget's pug-nosed face scrunched at the odor. "I was afraid you passed out down there."

"Are you going to help me dig, or is it up to me?" Jules moved across the hallway, opened the front door, and then turned toward Midget. "The odor is getting worse. I can't wait to go outside."

"Disgusting!" Midget slammed the basement door.

"I need a jet to West Virginia," Vinny swore from the kitchen. "No. I'm not taking any chances. Fritz is still alive. I thought that car crash was supposed to kill him."

Jules held his breath. He wanted to know the plan for Risa, but Vinny didn't mention her name.

Midget pushed past Jules. "I'll supervise you." He scooted outside. "Let's get to digging before Vinny yells at us again."

GOTCHA

Friday, June 21 – 0558 CDT,

Ann Arbor, Michigan/0458 MDT, Fort Collins, Colorado

Fritz felt old, outdated, and useless. Sitting alone in the dark, he waited while his colleagues raced after Dave. It gave his gray matter time to wander at will. The events of the past few days surfaced. A plan was emerging. *Benny the pruner. He must have been a gardener. Walt said he had a shed in some cemetery. Which one?* Fritz dug the skeleton key from the envelope and palmed it. Lost in thought, he failed to notice a man moving toward the car until a shadow blocked the streetlight coming in through the window.

The shadow leaped closer. "Get out of the car."

Dave! Where did he come from? Fritz tried to peer around the shadow, hoping to see Kelly or McCoy. *They must still be inside.*

"I said get out of the car!" Dave threw open the back door and pulled Fritz from the SUV. "You're coming with me."

Fritz tried to protect his screaming ribs. "What do you want with me?"

Dave shoved Fritz against the car. "Why are you and that broad hounding me?"

"I'm not hounding you. We have a few questions, and you can return to work." Fritz turned sidewise and used the key to scratch a big D on the rear car door.

"Nope, I called this meeting. Let's go." Dave grabbed Fritz's sleeve and shoved him.

"Good. Are we going to see Vinny?"

"Depends."

Fritz dragged the key across the car doors, trying to make a "V," but it looked more like an arrow when he glanced back at the mark.

Dave didn't seem to notice. He yanked off his tie. "Hold out your wrists."

"Why should I make it easy for you?" Fritz placed the key between his knuckles, rammed his fist into Dave's face, and raked the key down his cheek.

Dave screamed and threw up his hands in defense. Blood dripped between Fritz's fingers.

"Kelly! McCoy," Fritz shouted and moved a few yards toward the hospital.

"Okay. We'll do this the hard way." Dave moved like lightning. Head lowered like a bull, he tackled Fritz to the ground. The key flew from his hand.

Air whooshed from Fritz's lungs. He gasped at the sharp pain that ripped through him. Black spots floated before his eyes.

Dave jabbed an elbow into Fritz's fractured ribs again for good measure.

Fritz gritted his teeth, choked, and fought the urge to faint. Short pants of air only stoked the fire burning in his chest. He tried to get up and stumbled back to the ground.

"Should I hit you again?" Dave curled his fist.

Fritz glared. Bile rose in his throat at the thought of seeing Vinny. The bastard had Risa. It was time for a showdown. His body had to tolerate Vinny's beating. It was the only way to save her, so he held out his hands.

Dave pulled Fritz's wrists together, bound them with one end of the tie, and then knotted the other end to Fritz's belt. He yanked Fritz onto his feet and glanced around.

No one raced from the hospital to rescue Fritz.

Dave tugged the tie to test the knot and pushed Fritz into the shadows of the parking lot. "We'll take my car."

Fritz tucked his elbows around his ribcage and hobbled forward until they reached Dave's silver Mazda.

"Vinny wants you alive." Dave thrust him into the passenger's side.

Fritz smacked his head against the roof. He swore. "Don't damage the merchandise."

"Oh, you won't mind the bruises. You'll join Jim in an unmarked grave when Vinny's done."

"Jim's dead? What about Risa?"

"Your sister's old news. Vinny's going after your wife and that cute little granddaughter."

How did Vinny find them? I don't even know where they are.

Dave brushed away blood from his cheek with the sleeve of his lab coat and closed the passenger door. He went around the car to the driver's side and got in. With a thud, his door closed, and the Mazda screeched away.

Black spots swam before Fritz's eyes. Nausea roiled in his gut, and his ribcage was on fire.

Dave took a corner at high speed. It threw Fritz off balance. He reached for his seatbelt. The twisting motion nearly made him pass out.

Dave was on his cell phone talking to Vinny. "I have Fritz. Where should I take him?"

Fritz braced his legs in a wider stance—*better watch where we're going.*

Dave's eyes shot up to search the rearview mirror. "No, I'm not being followed. Benny's torture cave? I know the place."

Oh God, that Benny! Fritz felt as if another fist had punched him in the gut. *Reign Carnation. The flower of love. How could he have missed that clue? It's not a bear cave. It's a bare cave where Benny reigned over his sex slaves. That's where Vinny has Risa?*

"Let me talk to Vinny." Fritz reached for the phone with his restrained hands, but Dave disconnected the call.

"You'll get your chance." Dave punched an address into the car's GPS. "Sit back and relax. We'll be there in half an hour."

DIGGING UP TROUBLE

Jules hoped his plan for Jim's escape would work, but claiming Jim died during the night had backfired. Now, Vinny ordered him to dig Jim's grave—something he hadn't expected—back-breaking work at the crack of dawn.

He dug through the loamy soil until his spade hit packed earth. The tough, dry clay refused to budge until he jumped on the metal blade, driving it into the dirt. He wiped sweat from his brow and glanced over at Midget, who supervised while sitting on a chaise lawn chair sipping lemonade. "How about sharing that ice-cold drink with your slave?"

"When you've earned a sip, I'll make sure you get one." Midget crossed his short legs and slurped. "Aaah," he exhaled with pleasure. "Dig deeper. A dog could easily find Jim's bones at that depth."

Jules slammed the blade into the ground several times and dumped another shovelful of dirt. A blister on his right hand broke open and oozed a sticky stream onto the handle. "I've had enough! It's your turn."

The front door slammed. Vinny ran down the porch steps and toward his car. "Quit bickering and get that body in the ground. Midget, come with me. Dave has Fritz, and they're heading this way. We'll meet them at the gate."

"How'd he manage to capture the detective?" Midget set his glass on the ground and headed for the car.

"Pure, dumb luck." Vinny pulled the keys from his pocket.

"I'm driving." Midget climbed into the car.

Vinny tossed the keys through the open car window. He turned toward Jules. "Take care of Jim while we're gone, and don't get any ideas. You've been skating on thin ice lately. Now's your chance to make up for it."

"You can count on me." Jules rammed the shovel into the hole and tossed a massive chunk of clay aside. He kept working as the car's engine roared to life.

As soon as the vehicle moved from sight, he threw down the spade. Jules picked up the abandoned glass and downed the lemonade. He hoped he didn't have to dig another grave for Fritz. *They're going to the cave in the back of the shed. I can't take Jim there now. We'll have to move fast.* After looking over his shoulder one more time, he headed for the house.

LATE DISCOVERY

Back at the hospital, Agent Kelly couldn't find Dave in the lab or in the unit he was assigned to. She talked to Dave's supervisor, but he hadn't seen his employee since sometime around two. Kelly remembered she met Dave in the main OR while working undercover with Risa. It wouldn't hurt to check there, so she punched in the code to open the door to the operating room.

Kelly went to the lounge, gowned, and put on a surgical cap and shoe covers. The main operating rooms bustled with activity. She asked everyone she met, but no one had seen Dave. Frustration mounted as she raced against the clock. Where is he?

Most employees worked the day shift, so Kelly went to the sleep lab, where the staff only worked evenings and nights. She spoke with the clerk. "Good morning. Have you seen Dave, the lab tech on duty last night?"

"No. We only had one patient. He had his labs drawn on admission." The phone rang. "Anything else?" The nurse didn't wait for an answer and picked up the phone.

Kelly waved and left the surgical area. She stopped by the lounge once more to remove her gown, mask, and foot coverings, then radioed McCoy, "I can't find Dave. What about you?"

"No luck so far. The security guard and I started on the top floor. We're now on second."

"I've searched the first floor," Kelly said as she stepped into the hallway. I'll check with the lab again, then let's get Fritz back to the office. Time is wasting."

"Okay," McCoy said something to the security guard, then added. "Meet me at the front door."

Dave hadn't returned to the lab, so Kelly went into the lobby. McCoy and the guard stood by the entrance, and they exchanged contact information.

Kelly noticed that Fritz hadn't moved the car. The headlights were still on, but no one was inside, and the rear door was open. "Where's Fritz?"

McCoy went outside. "He probably got tired of waiting—"

"Look!" Kelly ran to the car. "There's a large D scratched on the rear door, and someone ran a sharp object along the side." She stepped on something and knelt beside it. The piece of metal glinted in the light.

"What is it?" McCoy moved up behind her and leaned over to take a peek.

"The skeleton key. Fritz wouldn't let it out of his sight." Kelly picked it up with two fingers. "There's blood on the key. I'll bag it for DNA."

McCoy stared at his car. "How could he?"

"What?" Kelly asked.

"Scratch my car like that," McCoy snapped.

"McCoy! It's just a car. Fritz's life might be in danger." Kelly studied the long scrape across the back and front door. "It could be a sloppy 'V' for Vinny? A 'D' for Dave?"

McCoy pointed at a splotch of blood. "Looks like Fritz didn't go down without a fight."

They tracked drops of blood that ended abruptly at the parking lot.

Kelly dashed for McCoy's patrol car. "How much of a lead do you think they have?"

"We have no idea where they've taken Fritz. Besides, I have to call this in as a crime scene." McCoy made the call. "Bring an extra car and gear. We need to find Fritz."

Kelly went to the Administration Office to get Dave's license number from his parking permit. When she returned, she found McCoy dealing with the investigation team.

McCoy called in an all-points bulletin on Dave's vehicle and license number. "Hope someone spots the car and calls it in."

"I can't just stand around here." Kelly chewed on a thumbnail as she paced. "What were you going to do after we picked up Fritz?"

"Have breakfast and go through those folders," McCoy said. "We'll be here for another ten minutes, tops."

A chill raced up her spine. She'd lost Risa, let Dave slip through her fingers, and now, Fritz could die. Kelly went to the SUV and picked up the folders. "I'll be in the lobby reviewing these files. There has to be a clue we've missed. Come get me when you're ready to leave." Her cell phone vibrated in her pocket. Checking the ID, it was Cordy.

Kelly's words rushed out, "Fritz is missing, and we have less than 20 hours before Vinny plans to kill Risa."

Cordy asked, "Should I fly to Ann Arbor to help find Fritz?"

"Officer McCoy and I are doing our best to find him," Kelly said. Any updates on Ace?"

"He took a Delta Air flight to Canada." Cordy filled her in on the details about Doc and Agent Islet.

BRIDGE OF HOPE

Friday, June 21 – 0845 CDT,
Ann Arbor, Michigan/0745 MDT, Fort Collins, Colorado

Fritz couldn't believe he had allowed Dave to capture him. Heading for Vinny's, Fritz broke out in a cold sweat. His clothes clung to him, and nervous energy raced through his veins like a river running wild. According to the GPS, it was only three miles to the cave. This might be his only chance. The old road was filled with potholes, and no one seemed to travel on this deserted stretch.

Like a mirage, a bridge came into view. Fritz braced himself for impact. He threw his full weight over the car console and slammed into Dave. Fritz's restrained wrists reached for the steering wheel, latching on with both hands.

"What are you doing?" Dave shoved back and hit the brakes.

Tires spun, and the car skidded, but Fritz refused to let go of the steering wheel. He yanked harder.

"Let go!" Dave jabbed Fritz's chest a few times. The car swerved onto the gravel shoulder. The bridge got closer. The iron girders and trestles shimmered in the sunlight. "We're going to crash!" Dave slammed his elbow one more time into Fritz.

Fritz screamed and let go of the steering wheel.

Dave fought to control the car. His knuckles turned white as he formed a death grip on the wheel. The car jolted and then spun 90 degrees as it hit the edge of the bridge. A girder broke loose. Glass shattered around them. Metal screeched as the rear of the car careened against the truss.

Fritz slammed against the passenger's door. He spun around, lifted his feet, and kicked Dave in the head.

Dave moaned, so Fritz kicked him again.

Dave collapsed over the steering wheel. The horn blasted under the weight of his body.

Fritz shoved him aside, and the horn stopped. It took a few minutes to slide off the tie. He worked the knot open that bound his wrists. The car sprawled across the bridge. Fritz climbed out of the car and went to the driver's side. He pulled Dave from the vehicle and dropped him on the ground. Fritz turned the car around, drove over the bridge, and fished for Dave's phone. He drove down the road before placing a call.

"Hello." Kelly sounded hesitant.

Fritz took a jagged breath. "Are you still at the hospital?"

"Fritz. Where are you?" Kelly sounded nervous, which was unlike her. "What happened?"

"Dave found me. I'm three miles from meeting Vinny. I need backup. Where's McCoy?"

"I'll get him."

It took a few moments for McCoy to get on the phone. "Are you heading into a trap?"

"Vinny's waiting for Dave to drop me into his hands. That's not going to happen without you as a backup." Fritz checked the GPS and read off his coordinates. "Careful when you cross the bridge. Dave's lying on the shoulder. He might be conscious by now."

"We're on our way," McCoy said. "Don't do anything stupid until we get there."

He also heard Kelly's voice in the background, "And don't do anything stupid once we arrive." The two chuckled. A car door slammed, and an engine roared in the background.

SOMETHING FOUL

Friday, June 20 – 0910 CDT,
Ann Arbor, Michigan/0810 MDT, Fort Collins, Colorado

As soon as Jules walked into the house, he knew something was wrong. That powerful stench was much too pungent, nearly as foul as downstairs. The basement door was closed. A quick study of the living room indicated that Vinny had been up to something. Jules found blood smeared across the floor—a trail led from the basement door along the living room carpet and into the kitchen.

Ragged breathing came from the other room.

Jules hadn't heard the car return, but maybe his brothers had come in a back way. "Vinny?" Jules called out. He opened the closet door, pulled out a golf club, and hid it behind his back as he crept into the hallway. "Vinny! Are you okay?"

A low moan came from somewhere near the back door.

Jules stepped around the couch, raised the club, and ducked through the door.

"Don't hit me!" Jim lay curled up in the corner by the fridge. "Oh, it's you." He breathed a sigh of relief.

"What happened to your IVs?" Jules asked.

"Risa capped them." Jim held out his arm as proof. "You have to help her."

"Why? What happened?" Jules darted for the basement door.

"She's not down there," Jim called out. "I told her to run upstairs and put on some clothes. Vinny came downstairs a few minutes ago and told Risa that Fritz was on his way. He'll kill all of us."

"Did Vinny see you?" Jules asked.

Risa entered the kitchen. "I told him that Jim died during the night." She had on a pair of Midget's socks and shoes. His pants were the length of Capris on her. A belt gathered them around her waist. "As soon as I heard the door slam, I opened the cage and got Jim. We had a terrible time climbing the stairs. He had to sit and scoot himself up each step while I held his injured leg." She held out a clean T-shirt for Jim. "Put this on, and let's get out of here."

"My brothers aren't far from here," Jules said. "Vinny's waiting for Fritz at the gate."

Jim slipped into the shirt.

"Where should we hide?" Risa asked.

"I was going to take Jim to the shed. There's a cave at the back wall, but I'm sure that's where Vinny will take Fritz." Jules glanced out the window. "No sign of them yet. Do you think you can ride a motorcycle?"

Risa's mouth dropped. "I'm not leaving Jim, and there's no way he'll stay propped up on the bike."

"Yes, you are leaving," Jim demanded. "I'll be fine. Get help before they kill Fritz."

"Won't they hear the motorcycle?" Risa asked.

"Go through the woods," Jules said. "I'll show you the way, but first, let's hide Jim in the trees. As far as Vinny is concerned, Jim died. Vinny won't be looking for your husband. Besides, I'm supposed to have buried him by now."

"Do you have a spare gun?" Jim asked.

"Not me," Jules said. "Why did you come into the kitchen? You should have gone straight out the door."

"I thought maybe I'd find a phone, but I guess Vinny took it with him."

"Yeah, he's paranoid," Jules said. "He doesn't even trust me."

"We need something to defend ourselves." Risa went to the entry closet. She ran her hand along the shelves, rummaged through coat pockets, and pulled aside the hangers. Along the back wall, she found a holster hanging on a peg. Inside was an ivory-handled pistol. "Do you think it's loaded?"

Jim grabbed the gun and checked for bullets. "Only three. Is there another clip?"

Risa checked but came up empty. "This will have to do. We don't have any more ammo."

Jim managed to get to his feet. "Leave it with me. I just got out of the military and have more practice than either of you."

"You need a cane, and you're bleeding all over the place," Jules said. "Bandage his leg, and I'll find a walking stick. Then, no more delays, or I'll be on top of Vinny's hit list."

Sirens sounded in the distance. "Hurry!"

Jim buckled the belt and shoved the gun into the holster.

Gravel crunched outside the front door. Jules pulled aside the curtain. "It's Vinny." Jules grabbed an umbrella and threw it toward Jim. "Use that as a crutch. Risa, take him out the back way. I'll stall them."

"Be careful, Jules," Risa said as she helped Jim limp out the rear door.

AMBUSHED

Fritz had nodded off while he waited for McCoy in Dave's Mazda parked a mile from the old bridge. He jolted awake to the sound of a siren. A few minutes later, a patrol car approached with its lights flashing.

Officer McCoy parked in back of Fritz and got out of the car.

Fritz opened his door. "What's going on?" He stepped out of the Mazda. "I thought we'd go in silent. Vinny thinks I'm coming alone with Dave, not with guns blazing! He'll kill Risa first and ask questions later."

"Not my call," McCoy said. "My partner ran the siren and captured Dave by the bridge. Kelly found that lost narc key in Dave's pocket. It still had the lime-green wrist coil around it. I'm sure he's been stealing drugs from the hospital. Kelly went back for your gear. She'll be here soon. Dave is heading to the station with my partner."

"That wasn't wise," Fritz said. "We could have questioned Dave. Maybe he'd even cooperate and lead us straight to Vinny."

"You had your chance, and by the looks of you, he's not in a cooperating mood." McCoy snickered. "Have you seen your face?"

Fritz tapped his tender chin and cheek. "More bruises?"

"Dave has a few scrapes of his own. Guess you gave as much as you got."

Agent Kelly drove past the two men, stopped the car, and yelled out her window, "Get in, Fritz."

"So it's just the three of us?" Fritz asked.

McCoy nodded. "We'll go silent from here. I'll call for backup if needed."

Fritz headed for Kelly's car. "Don't expect me to sit back and let you do all the hard work, as you did at the hospital."

McCoy kicked at a rock in the road and mumbled under his breath, "That's gratitude for you." He returned to his patrol car and called over his shoulder, "We'll meet outside the cemetery gate."

Fritz checked his handgun, struggled into a Kevlar vest, and then scooted into the passenger's seat. His foot brushed against a helmet. "You came well-prepared."

"I knew you didn't have your equipment with you at the hospital." Kelly drove nearly two miles and slowed as she passed an antique marble gate.

Fritz tightened his grip on his .45 mm pistol. The lush grounds went as far as his eyes could see and ended at the edge of forestland. Giant trees lined both sides of the gravel paths, crisscrossing the luxurious lot. "Are we going to a cemetery or a castle?" Intricate headstones, statues of angels, tombs, and even mausoleums stood out in the distance. "Vinny could be hiding anywhere."

"I'm sure he's watching for us," Kelly said. "That's why I drove on. We need a different approach than the front gate."

McCoy flashed his lights, and Kelly pulled over. He got out of the car and climbed into the back seat of Kelly's cruiser. "You must have the same gut feeling that I do. Front gate's too easy to monitor."

"Let's get out and travel on foot," Fritz said. "I'll go around to the front gate as Vinny expects. You two go into the woods and cover me."

*　*　*

The morning air hung thick with ambivalence. Jules nearly choked when he dashed out the front door and met Vinny's glare. "Did you bury him yet?"

"Just finished, got a glass of water, and thought I'd see what you're up to." Jules' heart thudded a tattoo of irregular beats as Vinny's calloused paw reached for the front door. "I thought you were meeting Fritz at the gate."

Vinny shook his head. "Didn't you hear the sirens? Police are on their way. We're taking the chopper east to find the Mrs."

Jules stepped in front of the door. "What chopper?"

"Midget, you know what to do."

"This is what I live for." Midget tore across the lawn to the shed.

"What's the plan?" Jules swallowed the lump in his throat.

"Don't panic, boy. We'll load up Risa and get outta here." Vinny pulled on the handle.

Jules didn't move as the door slammed into his back.

"Get outta my way!" A crackling sound came from Vinny's pocket. "What the…oh, the radio." Vinny fished it from his pocket and hit a button.

Midget's gravelly voice said, "…spotted Fritz heading your way. Leave now!"

"If he's in range, shoot the bastard!" Vinny poked a finger into Jules' chest. "Get Risa and meet us at the edge of the cave. The chopper's waiting. You better be there in three minutes, or you're dead."

"Yes, sir!" Jules flung open the door and darted inside.

A shot rang out, but Jules was out the back door searching for Risa.

* * *

Fritz was halfway through the graveyard when he heard a pistol crack. *Risa!* Adrenaline pumped through him. *I'm too late.* Fear and anger merged somewhere in his gut and twisted it into knots.

Weapon drawn, he darted from one headstone to another, making his way across the cemetery. Another shot cracked. A chunk of granite spit into Fritz's cheek, and a bullet whizzed past his ear. He dove for the ground behind a statue. His ribs cried in agony, but the vest gave some support. *Where's Vinny?*

Fritz glanced up at the large winged sculpture hovering over him and felt blessed. Out of the corner of his eye, he sensed movement.

"Psst. Are you out here?" A young man crawled from one granite stone to the next. "Stay down."

Is that man looking for me? Confused, Fritz aimed his gun. *Why warn me to stay down if he means to kill me?* Fritz held his breath and watched.

The young man looked over his shoulder and must have caught a glint of the gun aimed at him. "Don't shoot! I'm Jules. Vinny's brother. I'm not hunting you."

"Why would I believe you?" Fritz motioned with his gun for Jules to get away from the stone. "Are you armed?"

"No. I freed Risa. Careful with that gun, she's out here somewhere, and I don't want anyone to hurt her." Jules moved nearer, using a crabwalk over the grass.

"That's close enough."

Jules leaned against the winged statue and raised his hands.

"Where's Vinny?" Fritz stayed close to the ground and kept Jules covered with his pistol.

"They're getting away. Something about a chopper."

"They? Who's with him?"

"Midget went to the cave behind the shed." Jules slowly lowered his arms and pointed. "I guess that's where you'll find them. It's at the rear of the lot."

Fritz motioned for Jules to move. He trained his gun on the man but kept his eyes alert for Vinny.

Action from the woods let Fritz know that Kelly and McCoy were on the move, too.

As they neared the shed, Midget screamed, "Run for your lives." A volley of popping sounds drowned out his maniacal laugh. Smoke blasted into the air, followed by a noxious odor.

Midget tore out of the building dressed in full body armor. A gas mask covered his face, and the little runt carried a machine gun strapped to his shoulder. He swept the muzzle back and forth, shooting in front of him as he ducked behind the mausoleum.

Kelly and McCoy opened fire.

Fritz and Jules dropped behind a cherub. Fritz held fire until he could clearly see his target.

Jules reached for Fritz. "Jim's alive—"

Warm blood splattered Fritz's face. The sickening metallic smell nauseated him. At first, he thought this was the end and waited for the pain to set in.

Jules' body jerked with a gasp. His bloody fingers slid from Fritz's arm as the young man slumped. Bright red blossomed across his shoulder, soaked his chest, and pooled beneath him.

"Jules? Can you hear me?" Fritz asked.

"I'm dying—leave me!" Blood spewed from Jules' lips. "Save Risa." His eyes darted toward the woods, rolled, and glazed over.

Fritz's gut wrenched over the loss of such a young lad who had given his life to save Risa. A bullet raised a clump of grass near Fritz's foot, jarring him into action. He crouched low, fired, and ran for the woods. Kelly covered him with return fire until they were together at the edge of the trees.

McCoy nursed a wound to his left arm, but he still could shoot. "I called for backup."

"Hope they get here in time," Fritz said.

Another smoke bomb, and Midget was on the move again. This repeated two more times.

"Is Vinny out there?" Fritz couldn't see him, but the rapid gunfire retreated toward the rear of the cemetery.

"I don't think so," Kelly said.

All firing paused for a moment. The roar of a turbo engine and a tandem rotor split the silence.

"Vinny's getting away. Jules said something about a chopper," Fritz said.

"Who's Jules?" Kelly asked.

"Vinny's brother," Fritz crossed himself. "I think he freed Risa. The poor lad was shot trying to tell me."

The helicopter lifted with its nose down. It briefly hovered above the tree line.

Three shots erupted in the distance. Neither McCoy nor Kelly had fired. The chopper rocked, spun like a kite, and someone fell from the open door before it disappeared. His scream echoed and died with an abrupt thump.

"He should have packed a parachute." Jim limped beside Risa, who nestled against a tombstone. "Sorry, I aimed for Vinny, but he got away."

Fritz moved to his sister. "Thank God you're alive!"

She wrapped her arms around him.

"Careful." Fritz flinched. "Broken ribs."

"I told Jules you'd save us." Fritz stiffened. Risa stepped back. "What's wrong?"

"It's Jules," Fritz said. "He's dead."

Sirens sounded in the distance.

Risa glanced around. "Where is he?"

When Fritz pointed toward the cherub statue, Risa rushed to Jules' side. Fritz followed close behind.

Risa dropped to her knees. "We need an ambulance. His lung is punctured. He's at death's door, but it hasn't closed behind him." She rolled the lad onto his wounded side. "Jules, hang on. Help is on the way."

Everything seemed to happen at once. Fritz grabbed Jim's shoulder when he heard a helicopter hover overhead. "Get down. Vinny's back."

Jim shook his head. "No. It's Angel Medflight." An ambulance, a police investigation team, and the medical examiner stopped a few yards from them and piled from their vehicles. An EMT took vital signs and triaged each wound. The ME verified that Midget was dead.

Risa only left Jules' side after the Medflight team started an IV, inserted a chest tube, and loaded him on the chopper. After they were airlifted, she returned to make sure Jim and McCoy were treated. Then she climbed into the back of the ambulance.

An EMT had bandaged Fritz's wounds. Risa asked, "Are you sure you don't need further medical attention?"

"No. I'll be fine. I've had enough clear liquids to last a lifetime. Take care of Jim."

"Will I see you at the hospital?" Risa asked.

Fritz shook his head. "I'm leaving. Vinny's going after Laura and Marta. The criminal investigation team will take over here and they will check out that skeleton key. It should open the gardener's shed. Agent Kelly will drop me off at the airport."

The paramedic closed the rear ambulance doors, and they drove away.

MISERABLE TRIP

Vinny sipped Champagne and peered out the window of a private jet heading into West Virginia. He sat in the co-pilot's chair, the best seat on the plane. "Got any pretzels? All I see are peanuts. Those can kill."

The pilot shook his head and manned the dials in deep concentration. Sweat beaded on his brow.

The majestic blue sky turned to pinnacles of clouds and turned to heavy fog as the plane descended. Vinny glanced at the dashboard. The rapid movement of the altimeter needle caught his attention. "What's going on?"

"Señor, the weather could be a problem." The pilot's thick Spanish accent annoyed Vinny.

"Then rise above it," Vinny snapped. "I'm paying first-class rates."

"Sí, but we has to land sometime. I'm no eagle to fly in circles."

Vinny checked his watch. It was past five in the afternoon. He blew out a breath in disgust. "Fine!"

"Put on your seatbelt."

"I'll do as I please," Vinny said.

The pilot crossed himself. His knuckles turned white as his fingers clutched the flight yoke. Bolts of lightning lit the sky. The plane jolted from turbulence as the aircraft fought through angry clouds.

Vinny's seatbelt closed with a click. "Satisfied?"

The pilot's lips curved, but he only cleared his throat.

Vinny's stomach lurched with every jerk of the jet. He didn't want to use that little vomit bag, but his insides threatened a revolt. Twenty miserable minutes later, a fissure opened, and Vinny watched structured plots of land turn into gray city blocks with grid-like avenues. "Where are we?"

"Just past Charleston. We land at the airport?"

"No! You know where I told you to land."

"Sí, señor, but my flight plan—"

Vinny pulled his pistol. "You will do as I say."

"Of course, señor. I always do." The pilot's eyes darted between Vinny and his controls. "Put away the pistol. Makes me nervioso."

Vinny didn't lower the gun until they flew beyond Yeager Airport and approached a grassy runway. The twin-engine King Air 250 turboprop kissed the grass and glided to a smooth stop.

The pilot peered over at Vinny. "We land, señor. When will you leave? I must refuel."

"I'll call when I'm through with business." Vinny holstered his pistol, climbed from his seat, and looked out the window. "Where's my car?"

The pilot peered out the side door and pointed. "Over there, under the eaves."

"No one's in the car."

"Wait here so you don't get wet," the pilot said. "I'll find your driver." He popped the door and jumped to the ground.

Vinny looked heavenward at a crack of lightning, followed seconds later by a clap of thunder. Hail pelted the ground. His joints agreed it was a miserable day. He couldn't wait to get a good night's sleep. Then, he'd set out for the safe house before dawn. According to his sources, Laura was only an hour away. Vinny was so upset with Fritz for killing Midget that he vowed to take no hostages. They would all die.

CONSPIRACY

Usher made it back in time to cover late-night security at the safe house where Laura and Marta hid. His cell phone rang. Checking the caller ID, he grinned. "Cordy, how's Braun."

"Braun's fine, the chief's asleep, and Vinny's heading your way! He may even be there by now."

"Hold for a moment, while I notify Jake." Usher grabbed his radio, "I just heard, Vinny will be here soon. Notify Maggie, and put out an alert."

Usher got back on the call with Cordy. "Anything else we should know?"

Cordy filled Usher in on a major leak she had discovered in the case. "Chief and I have set the FBI in motion to make arrests for Ace, Doc, and the nominee for Secretary of Homeland Security. It'll be all over the news by morning. We have enough information to hold Vinny for another twenty years, and maybe even life if we can catch him. I understand Jules came through surgery and is willing to testify against his brother. Risa and Jim are by his side, and Risa says Jules was so helpful in caring for Jim that they plan to help Jules enroll in medical school this fall. I know you're busy, and Fritz will be there soon. Keep them safe and stay in touch."

"Thanks for the warning. Later." Usher disconnected the call. He studied the multiple monitors sitting in front of him. The security system collected and processed data from cameras strategically hidden throughout the compound. Infrared devices also lined the rock walls surrounding the grounds. All is quiet so far.

At 4:16 a.m., a motion detector along the far south wall alarmed. A beacon of light rotated to give a wider view of the area. It could have been an animal, but Usher took no chances. "Jake, notify Maggie. We might have an intruder."

"Do you want her to wake Laura?"

"Not yet. Let's make sure we have a real threat." Usher tapped a few keys to widen the scan range.

Jake nodded and called Maggie.

"Put her on speaker phone," Usher said.

"Maggie, Usher wants to talk to you." Jake pressed the speaker button.

Usher leaned closer. "Let the dog out. I'm not sure what we're dealing with here, but it wouldn't hurt to have an extra nose on the job."

"I'm going downstairs to check the house surveillance tape and boot up the emergency link to your system," Maggie said. "Keep in contact over the link."

"Be careful. Fritz alerted us a couple of hours ago. He's on his way. Vinny is at least five hours ahead of him."

"How does Vinny know about this place?" Maggie heard a faint beep as she switched on her computer system. "Do you suspect a leak?"

"A major one. Cordy is investigating a high-ranking FBI agent. She'll need proof and plenty of it to get the man at the top, but if anyone can gather that data, Cordy can." Usher paused. "Jake, can you handle the tower?"

"It's locked up tight. I'll be fine."

"Okay, I'm heading for the house." Usher opened the tower door.

"I'll be waiting," Maggie said. "I just let Pepper out."

FRIEND OR FOE

Vinny woke at three in the morning, anxious to get his final revenge. It would be sweet. He'd dreamed of this day since Fritz's sting operation landed him in prison. Like tears from heaven, the rain poured as if grieving for Vinny's lost past—a past robbed by Fritz. *He'll soon get his just reward.*

The low-riding rental car hit every bump on the slick cracked pavement and gravel back roads. Lightning lit up the woods at times, but he had to crawl along to find his turnoff. He knew Fritz's grandkid and his wife, Laura, were well-protected, but where? There were no houses, run-down shacks, or high-walled gates. Trees everywhere he looked. Doubt ate at his gut, sure he had passed the place by now, but he drove on, hoping for a glimpse of the metal tower that Ace promised marked the hideaway.

A white beacon flashed up ahead and warned him of danger. Not wanting the beam to shine on him, he turned off his headlamps, pulled onto the shoulder, and parked under a cluster of trees. Vinny checked the GPS. This had to be the place. The rain seemed to let up, so he dug out a flashlight, got out of the car, and strapped on his backpack.

Scanning the ground as he walked, Vinny made his way through the forest. He ducked whenever the beam came his way. Slick grasses and sinkholes made the nighttime trek more dangerous. He darted around bushes and shrubs. The grade continued to go uphill. Vinny's stomach growled the more he exerted himself. *I should have eaten breakfast.* After stumbling over a fallen tree, he took off his backpack and sat on a log. He dug out a chocolate bar, peeled off the wrapper, and threw it on the ground. Moments later, he'd devoured the whole treat.

Clouds parted, and the moon made a brief debut. Ahead, about two hundred yards stood a rock wall that went straight up at least twelve feet high. *That must be it. Now to find the dugout that Ace promised went under the barrier. Which way? Right or left?*

He decided to go in the direction away from the road. Even in the damp weather, Vinny worked up a sweat. He slid off his backpack, took off his jacket, and tied it around his waist. Heaving the backpack over his shoulder, he gave a bone-weary sigh, crouched beneath the tree branches, and walked along the perimeter of the rocks.

He shone the flashlight and examined every crevice along the ground as he went. The light caught a patch of leaves that appeared packed tightly against the wall. Vinny knelt on the ground and used his hands to clear them away. Beneath the cluster was a three-foot piece of plywood that lay wedged against the rock wall. This had to be the place. He tugged at the plywood. It gave way.

A dog gave a low-pitched growl, snarled, and barked viciously.

Another low growl and a nose poked from under the rock. Ace never mentioned a dog. Vinny swatted the nose with his flashlight—*a big mistake.*

The plywood slid further away from the wall throwing a clump of dirt into Vinny's face. The dog's head poked through the opening. Snapping jaws leapt for Vinny's ankle, grabbed hold, and shook his leg with a mighty force. His pants tore along with a chunk of skin from his shin as Vinny yanked his leg free. Blood and saliva covered his trousers.

Vinny muffled a scream. A second glance showed the plywood moving even further from the rock. The dog's hips seemed stuck as he inched his way through the larger hole—*a German shepherd.*

Vinny slammed his good foot against the plywood's edge. He shoved the board back against the rock barrier, forcing the shepherd to retreat, and blocked the dog's escape. Fierce eyes glinted. The dog yipped as it pulled his head back. Vinny kept a wary eye on the opening and wedged a tree branch in front of the hole blocking the dog's exit.

The beacon's light swung in his direction. Vinny crouched behind a bush. His chest ached. He popped nitroglycerin under his tongue, and when he felt safe, he limped away. It seemed to take forever before he made it back to the car. He fished through his pockets but couldn't find the car keys. *I must have lost them in the woods.* Since this vehicle was a rental, he didn't have a spare set.

The damp ground made a path of crushed grass. He cursed. His ankle throbbed. Torn and slick with blood, the top of his stocking rubbed against his skin, forming a blister below the dog bite. He didn't want to retrace his steps, but how else would he find the keys? If he had an older car, he might have hotwired it, but not this model. Vinny took off his backpack and shoved it into the back seat. He shivered and then put his coat back on.

"Hey, Mister. You by the car." A guy in a rain slicker ran toward Vinny. "Can I have a lift? My car ran out of gas a mile back."

Great! He thinks I'm a good Samaritan. Thunder clapped overhead, and the heavens opened up with a torrent of rain. Vinny limped to the front of the car and collapsed into the driver's seat.

The stranger moved to the passenger's side without an invitation and climbed inside. "I'm grateful for a little shelter." He pulled back his hood.

Vinny slammed his door. "I'm no cabbie! You'll need to find another ride." He glared at the man. The eerie light from the storm hinted at the man's features. A jagged scar ran from his left cheek, down his chin, and puckered across his neck. His hair was the color of pale straw. Vinny's already stressed heart gave a jolt.

"Yeah, I see it in your eyes. You recognize me."

"Joey, I...I meant to call you." Bile stung the back of his throat. *How did my archrival find me? Ace warned me. Why didn't I listen?*

"You're two weeks behind," Joey said. "Mick never was late, but you fixed him, didn't you."

Vinny held steady to Joey's gaze and slowly slid his palm to rest on his holstered gun.

Joey's hand shot out. "I wouldn't if I were you."

Vinny stared at a snub-nosed pistol. "I have your money. All of it…in a separate account. I'll get it for you today."

"No need to panic. I have plenty of time to get what's mine." Joey held the gun steady in his right hand. With his left, he ran a pale finger along his collar. The man licked his lips. "This parting gift you gave me still burns."

Vinny swallowed the lump in his throat. "I paid my dues in the federal PEN."

"Let's not play any more games." Joey dropped his hand and the pistol disappeared.

Vinny knew money talked more than words when it came to his boss. "I'll pay double what I owe you, and we'll call it even."

Joey's eyes narrowed, but he didn't say anything.

Vinny had to think fast. He hated dealing with the devil. Nothing came to mind. It was as if his brain had dried up like a prune. *Keep him talking.*

"I didn't come for the money." A husky laugh rolled from Joey's sneering lips.

"If not the money, why are you here?"

"I could ask you the same thing, but I already know. You've let the business go while hunting Fritz. That ends tonight."

Vinny felt another pain clutch his chest. *Can't show fear.* "We'll work together. Like the old times."

"When you thought you were the boss?" Joey asked. "I don't think so. I've been shadowing you. The FBI is after you, and Fritz will be here within the hour."

"How much is he paying you?" Vinny asked. "I'll triple the amount."

Joey shook his head. "You're pathetic. Fritz isn't paying me one bloody cent."

"Huh?" Vinny's jaw dropped. "Then why are you here?"

"To collect, of course." Joey leaned closer. This time when he raised his hand, a switchblade appeared at Vinny's neck. "Scar for scar."

Vinny sucked in a breath.

"We won't leave a trace of blood in your car," Joey said. "Let's take a walk into the woods."

INTRUDER

Usher slipped out of the tower door, stayed in the shadows, and cut through the outer courtyard from tree to tree. Once he reached the arbor, Usher saw Maggie waiting on the veranda. Crouching low, she hid behind the banister, but the glint of her gun reflected off the porch light.

"Maggie, it's me," Usher whispered. "Go back inside. I'm going to check the grounds."

"Everything is locked up inside." Maggie darted down the steps. "I'll take the left, you take the right, and we'll meet at the back by the fountain." She didn't wait for an answer and headed around the building leading with her gun. Dressed in black sweats, she disappeared from sight seconds later.

As Usher approached the rear of the house, Pepper growled, gave a ferocious bark, and charged the back wall. The black German shepherd bounced backward and ran for the wall again, shaking his head and growling.

Maggie rushed for the dog. Someone screamed then cursed.

Usher caught Maggie by the arm and spun her around. "Shh. We have company." He spoke into his wristband. "Jake, brighten the searchlights to the south."

The dog sniffed at the back rock barrier. Ears flattened against his head, his tail stood erect, and his hackles rose, ready to pounce.

"I don't see anyone," Maggie whispered. Her gun pointed at the wall. "Must be on the other side."

"Get back to the house," Usher warned. "The dog's ready to attack anyone in sight."

"Pepper won't hurt me." Maggie inched forward.

"This might be a distraction," Usher said. "Get back to Laura and protect Marta. I'm going to the other side of the barrier. But first, I have to talk to Jake." Usher waited for Maggie to move.

"Yes, you're right," Maggie said. "I wonder if Marta heard anything from Bluebird."

Usher didn't wait for an answer. He dashed back to the tower. Maggie had her orders. She'd follow them.

FRITZ ARRIVES

Saturday, June 22 – 0400 MDT, Lewisburg, West Virginia

Rain pounded against the metal tower like a hundred drummers. Fritz stood outside the locked door, soaked to his skin. "Usher, let me in."

"Hold it right there," a man rushed behind Fritz. A gun poked him in the back.

Fritz threw his hands in the air. "Usher? It's me, Fritz." He turned to face a wind-blown man in soaked armor.

"Sorry." Usher lowered his gun and punched the secret key code. He pulled off his glove and laid his hand on the finger pad for ID. When the alarm dinged, Usher shoved open the door. "I'm glad you could join us."

Jake peered over the computer panels. "There're two men behind the south wall. One's Vinny, but I don't know who the other is. He's wearing a hooded coat."

Fritz wiped his soaked sleeve over his dripping face. "Vinny's here? Where's Laura?"

"Maggie has everything under control." Usher grabbed a sweatshirt from the back of a chair and handed it to Fritz. "I was just at the house."

"So you've seen Marta, too?" Fritz shrugged out of his coat.

Usher stepped around the council to get a closer look at the screen. "No, they're both in the house."

"You're sure about that?" Fritz groaned as he removed his soggy shirt, and struggled into the dry sweatshirt, all the while his ribs screamed.

"Let's handle Vinny first," Usher said.

"No, I want to see my wife first," Fritz insisted.

Jake hopped from his chair. "Look, the two men are fighting. One of them has a knife. I'm sure of it."

"Come on, Fritz," Usher punched the elevator button for the parking level. "Put on that Kevlar vest, and let's check out the action behind the south wall. Then, we can check on Laura. I'll drive."

Jake was already contacting Maggie. "Usher, take the wrist link. I'll keep you informed, and you can access the camera data. Fritz, take my raincoat."

"Thanks." Fritz slipped on Jake's coat and snagged the link on his way to the elevator. "Hey, he's right. I think the other guy is Joey A."

Usher grabbed the link and then handed it back to Fritz. "Strap it to your wrist. I'll drive. The elevator door opened. "Let's go."

MARTA'S INSIGHT

Saturday, June 22 – 0415 MDT, Lewisburg, West Virginia

Pepper barked louder than Marta had ever heard before. Rain pattered against the window. The outdoor lights flickered and went out. Her eyes adjusted to the darkness, but something was wrong.

She had to put on paper what her nightmare revealed. There was no way to put it into words. It was the man. The one in the cage that she'd painted back at the candy store. "Bluebird!" Marta whispered and waited in anticipation for the sound of fluttering wings.

"Momma!" she called a little louder. Marta climbed from the bed and peered out the window. The lawn lights were off, too. *They were never off. Something was definitely wrong.*

Bluebird gave her warning whistle from somewhere out in the hall.

Marta ran her hand along the bedside table and snagged her flashlight. She tiptoed to the door, leaned her ear against it, and listened. It was quiet, so she opened her door, turned on her flashlight, and headed for the stairs. When she got to her studio, a sheet was already waiting on the easel. Words were on the paper. She couldn't read the bright red letters, but she saw a picture of an open bookcase and a bowl of chocolate candies sitting inside the secret door to her hideaway.

Bluebird flew into the room, giving another high-pitched chirp warning Marta of danger.

Marta had heard from Usher earlier in the evening. Something terrible had happened to him while he was away, but Usher had refused to tell her what. *Did it follow him here?*

Marta dowsed the flashlight and crept downstairs.

"Marta, hide," came from the speaker. She recognized Jake's voice. "It's Vinny. Your gramps is on his way."

"Okay, Jake." Marta raced for the library. Bluebird flitted around the room, chirping loudly, and landed on the fireplace hearth. "Come with me, Momma." She opened the secret panel and went inside. The bird followed, and the panel slid shut. Marta used her flashlight to light the way and headed for the exit by the fountain.

Bluebird chirped again.

"I know," Marta said. "I'm not supposed to go outside. But you can, right?"

The bird's head bobbed up and down.

Marta whispered, "Okay. What's the plan?"

AVENGER

Vinny's ticker pumped so erratically that he felt light-headed. After all the effort to end Fritz, Vinny feared his life would ebb away at the hands of his boss. He bolted forward.

"There's nowhere for you to go, Vinny." The arrogant bastard rushed at him from behind. Vinny swung around in time for the blade to miss his neck. Instead, it sliced Vinny's upper arm.

Joey swung again, a knife in one hand, a gun in his other.

Vinny ducked, grabbed a fallen branch, and whipped it across Joey's face.

Joey fired, but he was knocked to the ground, and the shot went wild. Blood streamed down his scarred cheek where the branches had nicked him.

Vinny kicked at his boss when a dog snarled and leapt toward him. He yelled, "Shoot him, Joey!"

Joey fired. The dog howled and flew backward. Joey popped off another shot. This time, it hit Vinny's upper arm.

Vinny couldn't remember what happened next. All he knew was he went wild. He emptied his gun, and when he looked up, Joey lay in the grass like the snake he was. Blood pooled around his neck and shoulders. His eyes gave a vacant stare. Rain washed the blood from his chest.

Vinny didn't even check if his boss was dead. He stepped over the dog and headed for the rock wall. He had to get inside the compound.

He found the plywood already moved away from the hole, and the dog no longer blocked his way.

The sound of an engine approached. Gravel crunched as a car pulled to a stop. Vinny grabbed his injured arm and tucked it around him as he scooted into the muddy hole to get to the other side.

There was no reason to go in silent. That dog's ferocious barking had already warned them, and the backyard floodlights had popped onto full brights. As soon as his arm and head poked through to the hideout's side, Vinny shot out the lights. He was attacked by a small red bird that went straight for his eyes. He screamed, grabbed the barrel of his weapon, and tried to hit the bird with the butt. The gun went off in his hand.

Vinny gasped and realized the bullet had ripped through his collarbone.

The bird chirped and disappeared as Pepper recovered enough to attack Vinny's ankle once again.

Vinny squirmed and felt the muddy hole collapse around his body.

RUSH TO RESCUE

Fritz heard a shot and panicked. "Step on it! Laura! Marta! They're in danger."

"Maggie just called for help," Jake said over the radio. "Someone shot out the backyard lights. Bluebird gave her a warning, and Marta is safely hidden behind the shelf in the library, but Laura refused to hide and ran to the kitchen. There's no sign of her."

Fritz seethed. It felt like his heart jumped into his throat and choked him. "If Vinny touches one hair on Laura's head…"

Usher radioed back to Jake. "We're on our way."

"Where's Pepper? He's not in the yard," Jake said.

"He found an opening in the fence," Usher said. Joey shot him."

Fritz tuned into his wrist link, "Maggie, stand guard at the back door. Don't let Laura leave the house."

Usher barely pulled under the trees when Fritz shouted, "Stop the car!" Fritz was out of the SUV before it rolled to a stop. He bolted for the wall.

Usher ran after Fritz, gun drawn, rushing through the thick grass in the dark. He tripped over Joey's body. He slid a finger over the man's carotid. "He's dead.

Fritz kept running and followed a trail of blood to a muddy hole beneath the rock barrier. The yard lights were out, and an alarm still sounded.

Vinny had squirmed into the hole in the fence face-first. Pepper growled. His hackles rose as he limped on three legs and grabbed

Vinny's ankle. The dog snarled, and his jaws clamped around Vinny's foot, shaking his head from side to side.

"Let go!" Vinny screamed. His words were garbled, but he was squirming, still trying to get through the opening in the wall that had caved in around him, pinning him to the ground.

Maggie shouted from the other side of the wall. "Drop the gun, or I'll shoot."

"Pepper, release." Usher grabbed Vinny's other leg.

Pepper let go of the man's ankle and collapsed, whining and licking his shoulder.

Two shots were fired. "I warned you," Maggie shouted.

Vinny yelled, "Don't shoot. I give up."

"I could have hit you if I wanted to," Maggie said.

"I can't breathe," Vinny's voice cowered. "Don't let me die."

A few seconds later, Maggie called out, "I cuffed his hands. He's no longer a threat. Leave him until the police get here."

* * *

"Is Vinny subdued?" Laura called out as she ran from the house and stopped beside him. Turning toward Maggie, she asked, "Did you shoot him?"

"No," Vinny mumbled. "It was an accident—some bird flew at me, and I...gun went off." Sweat beaded Vinny's brow. "Thirsty. Need water? I'm so weak."

"Where's Marta?" Laura asked.

"She's safe," Maggie radioed to Jake, "I need a first aid kit."

Laura glanced down at Vinny and called over her shoulder, "I'll get it." She dashed inside the house, found the kit, poured a glass of water, and popped a straw into the glass.

Bluebird fluttered over a bowl of chocolates, and Laura remembered the Dream Creams. She snatched two candies from her hidden stash and darted back to Vinny, who was still trapped under the wall.

Laura knelt next to Vinny and held the straw for him to drink. "You're looking pale. Do you want a sweet to get your energy back?"

Vinny nodded, "Got any chocolate?"

Laura held up a Dream Cream. "I just made these. They're mint flavored."

Vinny gladly let her place it into his mouth. He moaned as Maggie cleaned his shoulder wound.

"That's a nasty cut on your face." Laura used an antiseptic gel to wash away the oozing blood from his cheek.

Vinny stared at her. "Got any more chocolate? That was good."

Laura dropped another candy into his mouth as he became more relaxed.

"Promise you won't let me die." Vinny's pupils dilated. He squinted. "Where am I?"

Fritz shouted over the radio, "Is he still alive?"

"He's calming down, but he has a large gash in his neck and shoulder," Maggie said. "Laura called for an ambulance, and she brought me the first aid kit. I'm doing what I can to stop the bleeding. Come around to the house."

Laura added, "Fritz, I gave Vinny a truth drug. It'll wear off in 10 hours, so now's the time for the police to ask their questions, while he'll tell the truth."

Fritz radioed. "Did he murder our daughter?"

"That was my brother, Mick," Vinny said. "He rigged the car, but it wasn't meant for your daughter. It was meant for Fritz. Mick's dead," Vinny yawned.

"The police are on their way," Fritz radioed, "I'll be right there."

* * *

Usher was loading Pepper into the backseat when Fritz reached the car. Usher radioed Jake, "Have Maggie call the vet. Pepper was shot. He's in the backseat but losing a lot of blood. The little fighter wouldn't give up."

"Maggie's busy. I'll call the vet," Jake said. "I'll meet you at the house."

The yard became silent as the alarm turned off.

A display on the wrist link lit up as Usher pulled to the gate. Jake swung open the door, but Usher didn't stop. He drove around a curve to the front of the house and slammed on the brakes.

"Let me out!" Fritz yanked open the door, flew through the arbor, and around to the back of the house. "Where's Laura and Marta?"

Usher followed. Sirens sounded in the distance.

Fritz stepped back behind the veranda railing when he saw Vinny's upper body trapped under the wall behind the fountain. Laura and Maggie were kneeling on the ground. Usher dashed up to the other side of the fountain and met Fritz.

Vinny's breathing came out in moaning pants. He was in no shape to fight.

Fritz gasped as he saw Marta's blonde head poke up from the rocks by the fountain. Bluebird was on her shoulder. "Momma saved us from the bad man. She says he won't hurt us anymore, and Gramma gave him the magic candy so he will tell us the truth."

"She did WHAT? How? Oh, we can talk about it later." Fritz knelt and hugged Marta, then wrapped Laura into his arms, "I've never been so afraid in all my life. I love you." He scooped them into a bear hug. He stepped back and noticed the little red bird fluttering overhead and waving her little purple wing. "Is Bluebird okay?"

Marta smiled and nodded. "Thanks, Momma. I know you have to leave now, but I'll see you soon. Give Daddy big hugs and kisses."

The bird flew into the air and disappeared.

Two paramedics came around the fountain, followed by two police officers. Maggie stood and motioned to Fritz. "Come inside and wait for the police to do their work before they interview you. Laura's made you plenty of chocolates while you were away, and they aren't the Dream Creams."

Laura smiled slyly, "Those are special, ONLY for Vinny. I hope I'll never have to make them again. Next time you 'go fishing,' I'm going with you. But for now, I made your favorite chocolates."

"Mmm, chocolates. Have a few extras for a friend?" Usher patted Fritz on the back. "It's over, Fritz. We'll take it from here. Vinny's singing like a songbird, answering questions, and we're recording his answers. You've been exonerated, and Vinny will be back in the PEN soon."

Jake's voice came over the wrist link. "The vet's here with Pepper. She says the dog will live to fight another day and is heading your way. Would one of you meet her at the arbor?"

Maggie said, "I'll go. I want to check on Pepper."

Fritz glanced at the wrist link where the latest news announced, "The FBI has arrested the nominee for Secretary of Homeland Security…" Fritz unstrapped the band. "Looks like Cordy took care of those FBI leaks. Kelly texted, and says Cordy also tracked down Doc and Ace, and they will soon be at Vinny's side." Fritz handed the link to Usher. "I hope never to use one of these again, but thanks. I owe you."

Usher grinned. "You can pay me in buttercream toffees."

"You, Braun, and Cordy can have a lifetime supply." Fritz headed for the house with one arm wrapped around Laura and the other around Marta. "I can't wait to take my family home."

The End

AUTHOR'S NOTE

Thank you for reading <u>Sweet Revenge</u>. I loved writing it and hope you enjoyed reading it. If you did, please tell a friend and consider leaving a review on Amazon. Your sincere feedback means everything to me. I hope to have another story to share soon.

PREVIEW OF RAPID RESPONSE
– CHAPTER 1 WARNING—BIO ATTACK

FBI Agent Dr. Joshtine Cordelia, known to most as Cordy, had enrolled in MIT at sixteen and earned dual PhDs in computer and forensic science. She had followed in her late father's career path and was now the FBI's lead analyst on cyber security. She knew risks hovered in plain sight. Most went undetected until disaster hit. It was 10 p.m. when she had placed several encrypted files and a dossier of military secrets into her translator and research program. It would take a few hours to run, so she headed for bed, hoping to catch some sleep.

As usual, that gnawing feeling grew with each passing hour until it roused Cordy out of bed and led her downstairs to brew a pot of java. *I know there's more in those files. What am I missing?* With a splash of cream added to her coffee, she took her favorite red Valentine mug to her office, opened her laptop, and logged into her darknet account. Two more files had been added to her search, which triggered alarm bells. "…a deadly agent worse than COVID-19, will strike the U.S. and sweep the globe…"

"What form will it take? Anthrax? Ebola? Or something worse?" Cordy muttered under her breath. "Who? When? Where? There must be some clues. I know it." Her mind jolted into overdrive as she thought of the millions of lives that could be lost. She dug deeper into the files.

For maximum security, Cordy worked all morning from her home. Her wrist alarm vibrated, reminding her that she was due in the office in one hour. *Already? Never enough time! I can't miss my meeting with Chief Jackson, and I can't stop my research.*

Being a control freak, she hated disorder and being uninformed. She clenched her fists as her mind spun, bouncing from one dilemma to another. *Can we stop this attack? I wonder what the chief wants that's so urgent. Why won't Jackson just tell me what's on his mind?*

Retired FBI Agent Chief Jackson had been mentored by her father Josh, and now she had become his mentee. Jackson was a private investigator and her ex-boss. He also shared his office building with Cordy and had called her asking for a huge favor—one that he couldn't divulge except in person. Cordy had already rescheduled their appointment once, but he wouldn't have asked if it wasn't urgent. She sent a quick text message, "Chief, I'll be there soon. Have you heard from Braun?"

Not waiting for a reply, Cordy compiled her latest findings and scanned the facts once more. Fear clutched her throat—*millions, it said millions.* She still didn't know the type of bio-attack—by whom, how, when, and where remained a mystery. *It's time to brief U.S. President Isaac Spendorf. We have to confront this head-on.*

Cordy took measures to ensure the security of her updates to her boss. She transferred data from her protected web files to her TOR account, which concealed users' identities and online activity from surveillance and traffic analysis. Two minutes after disconnecting, she sent the data to ping President Spendorf.

She texted a final message to her fiancé, Braun Hastings, who was a commander in the Joint Special Operations Command and was on a special assignment for the President. As she logged off the darknet, she noticed the sparkle of her diamond ring and couldn't help but smile as she thought back to the previous Friday night. *After four years, it happened right here, as I sat at my desk in disbelief, Braun finally committed, knelt on one knee, and looked up at me. 'Will you marry me?'*

Cordy hardly remembered what she had said, but she couldn't wait to become his wife. He leaned closer and kissed her. If it were any indication of their life together, she welcomed it. *That was three days ago, and I haven't heard from him since. Why hasn't he called?*

They hadn't set a wedding date yet, and now wasn't the time to plan, but Cordy hoped to tie the knot soon. She'd even picked up a Bride's Magazine on her last trip to the store. She had barely perused the journal yet. *No time. Maybe next week, but every wedding gown seemed too frilly, too lacy, or just not her style.*

She checked her watch and groaned. *Focus, Cordy. I need to be at the office in 30 minutes.* Shoving her thoughts of Braun out of her mind, Cordy hurried upstairs to take a hot shower. Running late, she didn't bother to dry her hair, quickly dressed, and headed to work. Her mind was still racing like a cat chasing a laser light, trying to get a grip on the elusive news.

Order <u>Rapid Response</u> **for the rest of the story.**

ABOUT AUTHOR - JILL S. FLATELAND

Jill S. Flateland,
RN, BSN, CCRN, MBA

There is nothing like a good mystery. Suspense novels get my juices flowing. <u>Sweet Revenge</u> is the first in a series of action-packed thrillers introducing Agent Dr. Joshtine Cordelia (Cordy) Crisis Series.

Her venture continues in <u>Rapid Response</u>, where Cordy fights a bioterrorist attack. An astronaut unknowingly transports a potent virus, created without gravity on the space station, back to Earth. This virus is more deadly than our recent Covid epidemic. Not only does it devastate the lungs, but it also attacks the brain. Risking exposure, Cordy rushes to find a cure when U.S. President Spendorf, his key advisors, and many members of Congress become infected.

Next in the series, <u>Crashing The Grid</u>, sends Cordy and her team to reverse a cyber attack on NYC that shut down the power grid, water treatment plants, and more. Cordy's adventures continue in

<u>Combating Chaos: All Systems Down</u>. Cordy and her new husband, JSOC Agent Braun Hastings, hunt down a Russian terrorist, General Okueva, who enlists student hackers to disrupt the New York Stock Exchange and major financial systems. Foreign forces have also attacked London and Rome. Cordy and her team risk their lives to stop the terrorists.

I'm currently writing *Caught Unaware*, where Cordy has been promoted to a new cabinet position at the Cyberspace Crisis Agency. A massive cyber attack on Washington, D.C. challenges the team to pull out all stops to defend the President, especially when drones attack the White House. I hope you enjoy these fast-paced novels.

Although my background is over 40 years in healthcare as a critical care nurse and the CEO of an Urgent Care Corporation, I've been a writer all my life. My husband, Byron, and I live in Colorado, and we travel extensively.

In 2006, I retired and ventured into the wider writing world. In 2011, I published <u>A Lightning Slinger's Tales of the Rails</u>, which tells of my aunt, Dr. Vera E. Williams' life as a female telegrapher during World War II. She worked for the railroad to make enough money to get her degree in teaching.

In 2014, we published <u>Ding Dong! The Rural Schools Are Gone,</u> a story of my two aunts, Vivian V. Lund (age 97 at the time, died at 104 in 2022) and Dr. Vera E. Williams (age 88 at that time, died at age 90 in 2016), who were both teachers during the early twentieth century.

I entered my fifth novel, <u>Until We Meet Again,</u> in the 2014 Colorado Gold Contest at the Rocky Mountain Fiction Writer's Contest. The novel became a finalist in the suspense category. *Tobias McFitzroy's old tombstone lay cracked in half and sinking under its weight in a cemetery outside a Colorado ghost town northeast of Fort Collins. The old stonemason had carved his own epitaph. It read, "Until we meet again. 1830 – 1899." Unlike most people, it didn't mean when he'd meet them in heaven. He couldn't. He hadn't made it that far.*

Sales Support a Worthy Cause

Byron and I are actively involved with two Non-Governmental Organizations (NGOs). The first is **Angel Covers**, who helped open Vill-Angel Medical Clinic in the center of a rural farming community in Katale, Kenya, allowing poor families to receive high-quality healthcare.

As Director of Healthcare Services, my goal is to help expand the clinic to offer maternal-child care. Many families have no car to travel to a hospital, the nearest being 17 kilometers from the clinic. Some have a motorcycle, others have a cart pulled by a donkey, but many walk on foot.

Most women deliver babies at home, but the infant mortality rate in Kenya is six times higher than in the U.S. (Kenya has 30 infant deaths/1000 births compared to the U.S., which has 5 infant deaths/1000 births.) Some women travel up to two hours on foot while in labor to receive care during high-risk pregnancies. Plus, children are at the highest risk for death within the first 28 days. Most die of pneumonia, diarrhea, and sepsis. Our clinic can treat these ailments, and provide follow-up care as needed.

The second is Seeds of South Sudan, where donations help rescue refugees from Kakuma Refugee Camp in Kenya, allowing orphans to attend boarding school in Kenya. Once these students graduate, they plan to return to South Sudan to help rebuild its economy, infrastructure, and create a stabilized country.

You, too, can help. Part of the proceeds from the sales of these books help support these causes, and I thank you from the bottom of my heart. We know you have many choices for purchasing mystery novels and methods of donating to worthy causes, so I'm grateful that you chose to help support these charities.

OTHER BOOKS WRITTEN BY JILL S. FLATELAND

Thriller Series:

Sweet Revenge
Rapid Response
Crashing The Grid
Combating Chaos: All Systems Down

Suspense Series:

Until We Meet Again

Secret Series:

Secrets & Chandeliers
Family Secrets & Betrayals
Secrets Lost Among Forget-Me-Nots
Secrets of Grayson Mansion

Family Memoirs:

A Lightning Slinger's Tales of the Rails
Ding Dong! The Rural Schools Are Gone
Chugs & Hugs: Growing Up In A Train Station Vol 1
Chugs & Hugs: Growing Up In A Train Station Vol 2
Chugs & Hugs: Growing Up In A Train Station Vol 3